MASTER

of

SHADOWS

JAYNE THORNE, CIA LIBRARIAN BOOK TWO

TWO TALES PRESS

NEW YORK TIMES BESTSELLING AUTHOR

JOSS WALKER

AND R.L. PEREZ

ALSO BY JOSS WALKER

Urban Fantasy

The Eighth Road (with R.L. Perez)

Tomb of the Queen (with Alisha Klapheke)

Master of Shadows (with R.L. Perez)

Writing as J.T. Ellison

Standalone Suspense

It's One of Us (February 28, 2023)

Her Dark Lies

Good Girls Lie

Tear Me Apart

Lie to Me

No One Knows

The Lt. Taylor Jackson Series

All the Pretty Girls

14

Judas Kiss

The Cold Room

The Immortals

So Close to the Hand of Death

Where All the Dead Lie

Field of Graves

The Wolves Come at Night (Coming Fall 2022)

ALSO BY R.L. PEREZ

For all of the librarians who've influenced us,
and those they will show the path.

And for Randy and Alex:
our permanent franchise love interests.

1

A VERY BAD PREDICAMENT

Tick.
Tick.
Tick.
Tick.

The simple white-faced clock hung on the wall over the door, its second hand stuck in place at the number thirty, the slim metal shaking, trying to move forward, but never able to break free. The repetition was hypnotic, annoying, jarring, insistent. At times, it lulled CIA Librarian Ruger Stern into a semblance of rest. In other moments, as right now, it grated on his nerves and set his teeth on edge. He was exhausted, drained. Torture was expected; he'd known the moment the fight was lost and he was taken that things were going to get bad, fast. He didn't realize it was going to be death by the relentless, monotonous irritation of a ticking clock. He felt like he was living inside a metronome.

In actuality, he suspected he was stuck inside a Time Catch.

Handy things, Time Catches. A kind of parallel realm in which time stood still. While the rest of the world moved on at normal speed, not even realizing he was missing, weeks, months, years could pass in a Time Catch.

People went mad in Time Catches. Got lost in time and never came out.

Tick.

Tick.

Tick.

With great effort, Ruger forced his body upright, mentally cursing himself for slacking on his training. He'd been so focused on working with his new recruit, Jayne Thorne, bringing her up to speed, that he'd sacrificed his own very necessary magical homework. It had been far too long since he'd done the Time Catch simulation. If he'd practiced more often, he would've been better prepared. But now, his big body struggled to adapt, and each breath felt like it was saturated with water. And the ticking clock was causing him borderline panic—the TCO used that sound to indicate the simulation was about to self-destruct. With every tick, his brain was telling him that he could go up in smoke at any moment. Their enemies knew this, and were using it against him.

He had no idea how long he'd been trapped here. They could leave him here to rot, and when his team found him, he'd be nothing more than a skeleton.

Don't think like that, he told himself. *Remember your training. You are a powerful officer and magician. You've got this.*

He surveyed his surroundings for the hundredth time. The tiny room resembled a classroom, empty except for the one desk he was chained to. The door was locked from the outside. He'd already made it as far as the doorknob before some kind of magical trip wire was activated, alerting his captors to his movement. He'd lost that fight, and they'd taken no more chances after that; he'd woken handcuffed and bound to the desk. A large mirror took up the space of an entire wall. He knew enough about interrogation techniques to know it was a one-way window.

They were watching him.

He couldn't access the Torrent. He'd already tried dozens of times. Judging by his sluggishness and the drained feeling tugging at his body, the room had to be lined with some kind of dampener. Maybe they'd hit him with a Suppression spell? It would explain how he couldn't use magic.

He was locked in this room at their mercy—whoever *they* were.

"Can we get on with it?" he called.

Hours passed, or maybe minutes—he'd stopped trying to keep track of the ticking—when the door finally opened.

A tall, thin figure strode toward him. Recognition jolted through his body, giving him a spark of energy he desperately needed. He knew that face—the sharp cheekbones and dark, stormy eyes. Her inky black hair was tied in a knot at the top of her head.

Gina Labelle. The Head of La Liberté, a terror organization as fanatical, if not more so, as the Kingdom.

Not dead, as they'd heard. Very, very much alive.

He'd suspected as much. These malicious leaders tended to disappear into the fabric of the Torrent when things got tough. He'd been investigating a sighting of her when he was ambushed.

He'd never seen Labelle in person before—only knew her from photographs and surreptitiously obtained video. She was a dangerous magical terrorist, one of the most wanted in their systems.

So he'd been taken by La Liberté. This could work in his favor.

She stood before him and crossed her arms, her thin eyebrows lifting expectantly.

"Madame Labelle."

"Ruger Stern. We meet at last." A French accent laced her surprisingly vibrant voice.

"You could do me the courtesy of uncuffing my hands from this desk. I'm hardly a threat to you in this place."

A brittle laugh. "Diminished you may be, but dangerous still, I believe. Do you have anything to offer me, Ruger Stern?"

"Offer *you*? I was minding my own business when your thugs jumped me."

Labelle clicked her tongue and dropped her arms. "What do you expect? You were hunting me, and they can be very protective."

"Then let me go, and we'll call it even."

"Oh, I think not. Your people are riding to your rescue as we speak. We've just received intel on the team sent to extract you."

Ruger made sure his face was blank, giving away nothing. *Which team?* he wondered. But he already knew.

Jayne.

Amanda wouldn't have sent anyone else. Not when this sort of dark magic was involved.

His heart twisted. Jayne was good, but she was still so new at this. And he wasn't there to warn her. To protect her.

Labelle bent over so they were at eye level. "Tell me where the grimoire is…and I'll let them live."

Ruger met her gaze evenly. Though his insides roiled uncontrollably, every ounce of him taut with fear and worry, years of training kept it buried deep. His face remained impassive. Apathetic. "Grimoire? You need to narrow that down a bit, Madame Labelle. There are a lot of grimoires out there." The bravado was costing him; his hoarse voice tore at his throat.

Gina's eyes tightened, but her mouth spread into a smile. "Excellent. I was hoping you'd say that. Now I get to face this infamous Jayne Thorne I've heard so much about."

Ruger resisted the urge to flinch. Confirmation Jayne was coming for him.

But how did Labelle know?

It doesn't matter. The mission comes first. This had been drilled into him since he joined the TCO. If even one of their agents divulged information, all their enemies would know they could be broken.

Ruger would *not* be broken.

"What, no threats?" Gina asked, sounding disappointed. "What about *When I get out of here, I'll slit your throat,* or *You're no match for the powerful Jayne Thorne.*" She cocked her head, her skeletal form making her appear raptor-like.

Ruger raised an eyebrow. "If you give me a script, then I'll know what I should say. I'd be happy to play the part. Whatever strokes your pathetic ego."

"Do not test me, Ruger," she seethed, sounding more French than before—as if her anger brought out more of her native tongue. "Your darling protégé will fail. We know there are five grimoires, and we know one has already been found."

"Then you know it was destroyed, and is of no use to you."

"Magic can't be destroyed. Controlled, perhaps. Throttled. But with the grimoires together, no matter how tattered, we will open the Torrent again. And you'll have no one to blame but yourself. Now. Tell me where the grimoire you're hunting is located."

"No."

The fury in her eyes almost made him wince. She had her magic, but he was bespelled, couldn't fight back, couldn't think, couldn't do anything but try not to utter the word, the location he suspected. Pain rippled through his body as she danced around him, throwing spells, trying to force out an answer. He was bruised and hurting when she finished with him, but hadn't broken.

"Fine," she panted. "*D'accord.* We will try something different."

A snarl echoed through the chamber, and pain exploded in his cheek. Bright light seared his eyes, momentarily blinding him. He sucked in ragged breaths, but he couldn't get enough oxygen. His vision darkened before clearing once more. In front of him, Gina stood stiffly, her arm outstretched. Ruger's dizziness gave her the appearance of a distorted reflection in a mirror.

No…that wasn't his dizziness. She *was* distorted. Her image rippled and shifted. Growing wider as if she'd put on fifty pounds, shrinking back down, then getting portly again, fully obscuring the lithe, lethal figure she'd been before.

Alarm pressed in on Ruger. *It can't be.*

In an instant, Gina returned to normal, breathing heavily, her face splotchy and her eyes full of rage, flashing an almost unearthly red. Pressure built inside him, and the word formed unbidden on his tongue. He couldn't help it, he couldn't stop himself, she was pulling it out of his very being…he'd never felt magic like this before, it was terrible, awful, too much to bear…

"*Maintenant*, Ruger. Tell me, now! Where is the grimoire?"

"Fon. Taine. Bleau."

The pain stopped, so suddenly he nearly fainted in relief.

Labelle stormed from the room, leaving Ruger gasping for breath, his head reeling from what he'd just experienced.

It couldn't be…

But despite his injuries, despite his weakened state, he knew what this meant. He had endured years of training against hallucinogens to ensure his mind remained intact. He hadn't been drugged. He hadn't been seeing things.

Gina Labelle had shifted. She was a Rogue.

And because he had failed, she now knew where the grimoire she sought was located.

2

TO BEGIN AGAIN...

Jayne Thorne steeled herself with a deep breath and stepped into her sister's kitchen, mouth watering at the incredible smells emanating from the oven. "Blueberry pie? Nom!"

Sofia looked up from the cutting board, where she was chopping tomatoes. There was a smudge of flour on her cheek. "Yep. Your favorite. And lasagna, and salad, and meatballs, and spanakopita, too. I have some frozen phyllo, and I know how much you love your desserts." She took in Jayne, and dismay crossed her delicate features. "Wait. Why do you have your purse? You can't leave. You just got here. We haven't even had a proper chat yet, and I made all this food... Where are you going?"

Jayne ran her hand up Sofia's arm. "I'm sorry, Sofia. I don't have a choice. My boss has summoned me. There's a problem, and they need me."

Sofia's eyes narrowed. "What problem?"

Jayne wrestled with the answer. *Can I tell her? Is this a secret?* Finally, she said, "It's Ruger. He's gone missing."

Cillian came through the door at that moment, hair still damp from the shower, carrying both their bags. "I'm sure he's okay," he reassured her.

"They wouldn't be asking me to come in if there wasn't something really wrong. I'll be back as soon as I can, Sofia."

But Sofia was already dusting off her hands and grabbing her purse and keys.

"You are not leaving my sight again, Agnes Jayne Thorne. I'm going with you, like it or not."

"I like," Jayne said, smiling warmly at her sister. Overbearing, protective, and downright bossy, Sofia was still the only family Jayne had left. Jayne didn't count their mother.

If Jayne brought Sofia to the CIA, her sister would hover, but Jayne could do with a little hovering right now. The past week had been a challenge. Her first undercover mission for the CIA's magical branch, the Torrent Control Organization, had ended in a blaze of fire, literally. She'd been gifted an Earth totem by Queen Medb and had some seriously magical powers she had no idea how to access. And now her mentor Ruger was missing? It was a lot. "But don't you dare call me Agnes in front of my boss, or I shall be forced to turn you into a toad forever."

"Agreed."

"Good. But you might want to get that pie out of the oven and bring it along."

Sofia drove them back into downtown Nashville while Cillian marveled aloud at the strangeness of the car on the right side of the road. They carried all the food Sofia had made to Jayne's small apartment, noshed on the still warm lasagna and pie, and opened a tub of Jeni's honey vanilla bean ice cream to sustain themselves until the portal could be arranged. They were all tense, though, and Jayne couldn't help but worry. If Ruger needed *her* help, the wheels really had come off the bus.

Finally, at the appointed hour, Jayne opened the door to her small apartment and recognized the long, harshly lit corridor that signaled the portal was dumping them right into the bowels of the CIA's headquarters.

Jayne led them through the hallways, past curious glances of women and men in suits, feeling a tiny thrill at the sense of belonging. She was a CIA officer tasked to the Torrent Control Organization's Library Division, a magical Master, a top-notch librarian, and damn it, she belonged here.

Amanda Newport, Jayne's boss—or rather, her boss's boss—was stiff and no-nonsense as always, lips tight, spine rigid, a very tidy bun atop her head. When Jayne, Cillian, and Sofia stepped into her office, Amanda's face registered surprise. "Jayne," Amanda began, the familiar tone of disapproval stark in her voice.

Jayne shrugged apologetically. "Sofia was there when I got your message and insisted on coming. After everything we've been through, I couldn't say no."

Amanda's lips went, if possible, even thinner. "The information in this briefing is highly classified."

Of course she would drop the C word. "It's okay. Sofia is my sister, and she can be trusted with whatever information you need to share."

Amanda and Jayne stared each other down, tension rippling between them.

"Jayne, really, it's fine, I can—" Sofia said, but Jayne cut her off with a hand.

"Seriously, Amanda, I want her here."

Finally, Amanda blinked and gave a curt nod. "Fine. You're saving me a trip, Sofia. I'd like to debrief you again, personally. We'll simply do that sooner than I'd planned."

Before the trumpets of victory could sound in Jayne's brain, immediate unease spread through her. "Debrief her again? Why?"

"I like to hear about things firsthand," Amanda said with finality.

When Jayne thought of Sofia, trapped and imprisoned and tortured by the people working for her own mother, she felt sick. And Sofia probably felt ten times worse.

"She's already been debriefed. There's no need to put her through all of it again."

Jayne was more than prepared to fight Amanda with another staring contest if need be, but Sofia touched her arm.

"It's okay," Sofia said gently. "I mean, it's the CIA, right? Can't exactly say no."

"I do it all the time," Jayne muttered, and she could have sworn Amanda's eye twitched in response.

Cillian cleared his throat from behind Jayne and arched a single eyebrow. "Why don't we get back to the mission?"

"Right. Ruger." Jayne straightened in her chair. "Lay it on us, Amanda."

Amanda slid a file folder across her desk to them.

"We've sent several teams to find Ruger, obviously, but they haven't had any luck. He's simply disappeared," Amanda said, curtly tapping an orange file folder covered in a slew of letters Jayne could barely read upside down. She squinted at them: TS//SI//TCO//HUMINT. Her training told her that was Top Secret//Special Intelligence//Torrent Control Office//Human Intelligence. The CIA's acronym system was pretty easy once you knew what things stood for; otherwise, it looked like alphabet soup. "This is everything Ruger collected on his assignment before he stopped checking in."

Amanda's eyes drifted from Jayne to Cillian and then landed on Sofia. She frowned, and Jayne knew her boss was deciding how much to reveal. While she and Cillian were trained TCO officers, Sofia was, for lack of a better word, *not*.

"He was on the trail of La Liberté," Amanda said finally, handing Jayne the folder.

"La who?" Jayne opened it and started flipping through the reports, including pages of notes in Ruger's untidy scrawl as well as a few photos of a tall, skeletal woman with steely eyes and a fearsome scowl that could put Amanda's to shame. She read the first page quickly, absorbing the meager information.

Cillian peered over Jayne's shoulder at the file. "What is La Liberté?"

"According to Ruger's notes, a magical terror organization. Sheesh, another one? I thought the Kingdom..." Jayne trailed off. That was silly of her. Of course there would be other groups who would want control of the magical world. The Kingdom was simply the one Jayne was closest to.

"Yes, Jayne. Another one. La Liberté adherents are local to France and have a propensity for dramatics and violence. Similar to the Kingdom, they believe in forcing magic back into the world, casualties be damned. But unlike the Kingdom, they don't believe in plunging us into the Dark Ages to do so. Their methods are more...incendiary."

"Just what we need. More terrorist baddies," Jayne said under her breath. "Do you have any evidence they abducted Ruger?"

"No evidence, but he was in France on their trail, and if he crossed paths with La Liberté, I can't imagine their not trying to take him. But that doesn't rule out other theories. One is that Ruth is involved. She certainly has reason to want Ruger dead."

Sofia stiffened, and Jayne took her hand, squeezing it in comfort while Amanda continued the briefing. Unlike Jayne, Sofia wasn't accustomed to the directness with which Amanda conducted her meetings.

"Ruger was investigating Alarik's contacts in Paris and discovered Ruth had been inquiring about grimoires, but the trail went cold after that. While it's possible La Liberté was unnerved by his presence and sought to thwart him, it's also possible he stumbled on some important information about the Kingdom, and Ruth retaliated. He went off-grid before he could share what he discovered. That was three days ago."

Jayne suppressed a shiver. *Retaliated* could mean abducted, tortured, or even killed. She didn't want to think about Ruger's mangled body, and pinpricks of worry dotted all over her skin. "What can we do? You want me to go in after him? I'm ready. Get me a portal to Paris, and let's do this." She shifted forward in her seat, ready to spring into action Rambo-style.

"You can train with your Rogue."

Jayne blinked. "Come again?"

Amanda lifted her phone and said into the mouthpiece, "Pierce, send him in."

A few seconds later, the door opened, and a broad-shouldered man with graying hair and light brown skin stepped in. He looked like the perfectly polished CIA agent he was, complete with elegant suit, shiny shoes, and short, slicked-back hair. He even wore the signature stern expression of pretty much everyone in this building.

"Jayne, meet your new mentor, Hector Ortolan," Amanda said, waving her hand at the newcomer. "He'll be training you and Cillian for this mission."

Jayne eyed Hector uncertainly. "I don't want a new mentor."

"Most officers feel this way when they're just starting out. It's completely normal." Hector smiled kindly, and it made Jayne want to smack him.

"I mean," she said, struggling to reel it in, "I already have a mentor. Remember, his name's Ruger? Big guy? Goatee? Saved my bacon a few times in Dublin? Taught me everything I know?"

Amanda sighed. "Don't get lost in the semantics, Jayne. Though Ruger will be pleased to hear your defense of his place in your world." She gave Jayne a rare smile. "This is exactly why we need you in order to find him. Your connection to Ruger is strong enough that the Locator spells you'll be taught could work where the rest of the TCO teams have failed."

"Cool," Jayne said.

"Yes. So, mentor, trainer, whatever you want to call Hector, feel free. He'll provide the specialized training for this particular mission. And you and Cillian have only recently bonded. You need supervision in order to establish a secure magical connection between you two. Hector's right—you *are* still new to the

TCO, and to your powers. We just need to hone the knife a bit more."

Jayne drummed her fingers against the arm of her chair. The idea that Amanda thought she could succeed where the powerful TCO officers had failed was both nerve-wracking and exciting. "Okay...so where will we be training? Quantico again?"

"There isn't time for that. You'll use the training facility here at the TCO."

"And then what?" Jayne prompted, eyebrows raised.

"When Hector agrees you're ready, then we'll send you to Paris to track down Ruger."

Jayne resisted the urge to pump her fist in the air and shout, *Hell yes!* She was ready to dive in, to kick some La Liberté ass and get Ruger back. Assuming they had taken him. If Ruth was behind it, well, all the more reason to kick some ass. She and Jayne had some unfinished business.

To Jayne's surprise, Sofia blurted out, "No!" Her blue eyes were blazing, her crimson-stained lips tugged in a fearsome scowl. Jayne recognized the fierceness of her expression. There were three modes to Sofia: the Lioness, the Flirt, and the Paranoiac. Right now, she had activated Lioness Mode.

"Sofia, it's all good," Jayne started, but Sofia's venomous gaze was fixed on Amanda.

"She is not going to Paris."

"The heck, Sofia? This is my job."

Sofia finally turned to look at her. "You want to go after some random homicidal maniac who abducted Ruger? Are you trying to get yourself killed?"

"I find your lack of faith disturbing," Jayne said, but she could tell Sofia wasn't in the mood for *Star Wars* jokes. "Look, this is what I'm meant to do. You have nothing to worry about."

"Right, like I had nothing to worry about when our mother raised Queen Medb from the dead and almost killed you?"

"Point taken. But I don't have a choice here, Sofia. I've been marked. Chosen. Whatever the hell you want to call it. I didn't ask for this, for any of it. But I won't just sit around and do nothing while Ruth tries to destroy the world. And you wouldn't want me to."

"Yes!" Sofia's arms flailed like a lunatic. "Yes, that's exactly what I want you to do. Do nothing—and stay alive."

The old Jayne might have liked that option. But now? Jayne couldn't believe Sofia was saying this. It was patently unfair. "Hiding from trouble might have been your mantra, but it's certainly not mine. Have you *seen* my magic? I can help. I know what I'm doing."

"Or you can watch yourself become just as twisted as Ruth is."

Shock jolted through Jayne. "Do you really think I'm capable of becoming like her? Seriously, Sofia?"

Sofia closed her eyes and rubbed her forehead. "Yes—no. It's just...I've seen what powerful magic does to people, Jayne. Once upon a time, Mom used to be good. But her thirst for power changed her. I don't want the same thing to happen to you."

"Nothing is going to happen to me. And I do not have a thirst for power."

"Oh really? You are not the same person you were a month ago. My fun-loving, silly, all-I-think-about-is-books-and-pie sister is gone, and I don't even recognize you anymore. You're different, and that terrifies me."

Jayne tried to stow away the hurt at that remark. She hadn't gone searching for ways to become a Master magician, would have been quite content with her life before. But to be rare and unique and brilliant at something? To acknowledge that the freaking CIA had hired her to protect the world? To have magic, formidable magic, with powers as yet untapped? Yes, Jayne had changed. She'd killed in battle. She'd gone undercover in a terror organization and survived. She'd fought their mother head to head, and healed the mortal wound Ruth had inflicted on Cillian.

She'd been chosen by the Earth goddess herself, carried the Earth totem in her body.

There was no going back. And perhaps the strangest part? She didn't really want to.

But the idea that Sofia thought she would turn into the same sort of monster as Ruth Thorne? That ticked her off.

"So what, I quit the TCO, and we run for the rest of our lives, constantly shoving our heads in the sand? We did that for long enough, Sofia. It's not living."

"It's the only way to stay safe."

"I don't want to stay safe anymore. I'm done hiding. This is worth the risk."

"Maybe to *you*."

"Yes, because I'm not a coward like you are!"

Jayne wasn't sure when she'd risen from her chair, but she towered over Sofia, her hands balled into tight fists. Sofia was standing, too, mouth quivering. They were shouting now, nose to nose, spitting and hissing like a couple of alley cats.

"You don't understand anything, Jayne. You were too young."

"Then enlighten me! I'm not too young anymore. Or will you just keep hiding the truth from me like you always did?"

"That's not fair. It was for your own protection!"

"How is ignorance protecting me? You should have been honest with me so I would know how to take care of myself."

"And look where that's gotten you." Sofia waved a hand to Amanda, who was looking deeply uncomfortable. "You're diving headfirst into danger that will get you killed."

"Come on, like your plan was any better? Forcing me to live a life of lies? Controlling me? Manipulating me?" Jayne huffed a bitter laugh. "Which one of us is more like Mom now, huh, sis?"

Sofia was seething, her expression so full of anger it made her unrecognizable. No...it made her look more like Ruth. And the sight terrified Jayne more than she cared to admit. Anger roiled inside her like a monstrous beast, lashing out. Her magic rose to the surface, and she felt her forehead glow with heat. White sparks ignited between them, but Jayne couldn't tell who summoned them, and that set her off all over again. *That's right. Sofia has magic. She's known about the Torrent this whole time.*

And she never told me.

Though Jayne would never admit it in a million years, a teeny tiny part of her felt like Sofia was a stranger to her now. It was ridiculous, of course. Jayne hadn't even known magic existed outside of books until a few weeks ago, much less that she was a powerful magician in her own right.

But this was different. Sofia had known about *everything*— their mother, Ruth, and her magic, which was the same power that flowed through both sisters' veins.

Jayne and Sofia had always shared everything, laid bare every secret. Or so Jayne had thought. She was sick of being lied to. She was sick of the secrets and betrayal. She was sick of it all. And if Sofia thought that Jayne would just sit back and do nothing, she was sorely mistaken.

She started to tell Sofia exactly what she was thinking, but Cillian was there, stepping between them, arms raised, blue eyes firm and unyielding. "All right, you two, settle down," he said, his Irish accent broadening in his distress. "We need no more of this fighting."

They ignored him. More white sparks danced in the air, and Jayne felt Cillian tense beside her. The sparks grew brighter, one flickering onto Amanda's desk, where it quickly burned a hole in the mission file and made the room smell of brimstone.

"Enough!" Amanda shouted, shocking them both into silence. She slapped her hand onto the tiny spire of flame shooting up from her desk. "Stop this, both of you."

"Fine, Jayne," Sofia said. "You want to fight for this? Die for this? Go ahead. But I won't be around to watch." She stormed out of Amanda's office, slamming the door behind her.

Jayne blinked fiercely to ward off the heat stinging her eyes, letting what just happened sink in. Sofia wasn't going to stand by her as she fought for the magical world. She had chosen to walk away instead of help.

The realization hurt more than she wanted to admit. But Jayne didn't need her sister for this mission. She could take care of herself. She learned that in Dublin when she'd embraced her magic *without* Sofia's help.

Jayne turned to a clearly annoyed Amanda, who was busy putting the contents of the file in a new, unburned folder. She was embarrassed, and hurt, but she tried to hide it. She was not going to fall apart in front of her sharp-as-a-razor boss, of all people.

"Glad we got that squared away," she said. "We good here, Amanda? We need to train. I want to get on Ruger's trail as quickly as possible."

Amanda fingered the charm on her necklace, a tiny muscle in her jaw leaping. Oh no. Was she going to take Jayne off the case? No, no, no. Not now. Not when she knew she could help.

"It was just a stupid fight, Amanda. It has no bearing on my ability to do my job. My sister has always been overprotective of me. I apologize for losing my cool like that. I swear it won't happen again." She was babbling. Damn it, why did Sofia have to pick a fight in front of the one person Jayne actually wanted to impress?

Amanda set the file down and nodded. "Yes, Jayne. I understand. You and your sister have been through a lot these past few weeks. You're dismissed. Hector? You know what to do."

Hector's dark gaze hadn't changed at all, as if he witnessed sisterly drama on a regular basis. Heck, Jayne didn't know— maybe he did. Maybe he had a huge family and they were all screamers.

"Follow me. I'll show you to the training center." He strode out the door without bothering to see if Jayne listened.

Before Amanda could change her mind, Jayne grabbed Cillian's elbow and guided him from the room, barely pausing at the sight of Sofia standing in the antechamber, her back to them, shoulders shaking with silent sobs.

3

A FORCE FROM WITHIN

The moment Cillian stepped between the two arguing Thorne sisters, a sizzle of energy crackled along his skin as if the hairs on his arms had been set on fire.

White sparks ignited in the air, and something otherworldly called to the Rogue magic within Cillian, summoning it to life. A shifting, quivering sensation rippled outward, spreading to the tips of his fingers and toes. The powerful urge to change forms made his very bones rattle.

What the bloody hell is wrong with me? The last time he'd felt magic this powerful had been at Medb's tomb. But here in Amanda's office? Why the hell would he get the urge to shift right here?

No one seemed to notice. The girls were still arguing. Hector and Amanda still watched in uncomfortable silence. No one seemed to realize that Cillian was fighting a very primal need to shift into a different form—whether that be a wolf or a goddamn tarantula, he had no idea. He clenched his teeth, his hands curling into tight fists as he suppressed the call, shoving it so deeply inside himself that his vision almost blackened completely. His mind shut down, and for a second, he forgot who he was and why he was here.

Only seconds had passed, but it felt like an eternity. When Cillian could finally breathe, when his vision cleared and the insane magical presence had left him, Jayne was practically dragging him after Hector, while Sofia kept her back to them. A murky haze clouded his mind, as if he'd spent all afternoon in the pub and was hammered.

"Hey," Jayne said, elbowing him gently. "You all right? You seemed like you were on another planet just now."

Cillian's brain finally came back into focus, his attention returning to the hallway in front of them as they followed Hector's brisk pace. "Yeah, it's just—are *you* all right? That wasn't pretty back there."

"Oh, you ain't seen nothing. We Thorne women can be cutthroat, let me tell you."

Although Jayne was trying to laugh it off, Cillian could read the unease in her tense posture, the anger and sorrow mingling in her eyes. Cillian wasn't one to push, though, so he played along. "I've seen you angry before, love. I know how the sparks fly. Though maybe you can avoid setting our boss's desk on fire next briefing."

"Aye, aye, Captain." Jayne winked at him, and he grinned. "I did think Amanda was going to explode for a minute there."

Hector led them up a winding flight of stairs to a set of double doors. Without preamble, he pushed open the doors, revealing a large gymnasium, complete with padded mats, weights and dumbbells, and a punching bag that Cillian yearned to get acquainted with immediately.

"I've reserved the training facilities for our specific purposes," Hector said, whirling to face them. "I suggest you use the most of your time while you have access to this place. It isn't Quantico, but it still provides a safe, contained environment to practice spells."

"Great." Jayne clapped her hands and jogged in place. "Let's get started."

"Very well," said Hector. "I'd like to get a sense of your range, Miss Thorne. Show me a basic Block spell."

Jayne's eagerness visibly dimmed. "Dude. A Block spell? That's child's play. Ruger and I were doing way more complex stuff."

"Then a Block spell should be no problem for you."

Cillian's eyebrows shot up. This guy had balls, or no brains, to be pushing Jayne when she was still on simmer. Cillian estimated it would take less than half a minute before Jayne knocked him on his ass. He wished he had popcorn for the show.

"All right." Jayne lifted her chin, her eyes alight with a fire Cillian knew all too well. He found himself backing up a few paces.

Magic rippled in the air, tickling Cillian's skin. The spell spiraled toward Hector, knocking him off his feet so he spun backward, landing hard on the mat across the gymnasium.

Cillian snorted loudly, then covered it with a cough. Yep. Fifteen seconds to downed trainer.

"How was that?" Jayne shouted across the room as Hector stumbled to his feet, his hair askew and his suit a bit wrinkled from the hard landing.

"That was no ordinary Block spell, Jayne," Hector chided, striding toward them as he adjusted his necktie. "What did you do?"

"Oh, I just layered a Block spell with an Attack spell. Super easy." Jayne grinned broadly, the picture of innocence.

Cillian gestured to the man's suit. "You might want to change, mate. Before she rips into you again."

Hector ignored Cillian's advice.

"Block again."

"I already showed you a Block spell!"

"Do it again."

"Damn it, Hector, how is this going to help me find Ruger?"

"Your magic is no different from any muscle. You need to

stretch it first before you move on to the more difficult training. Now, Block."

Hector flew across the room again, crashing hard against the wall.

"Um, sorry?" Jayne said, fighting back a laugh. Cillian loved seeing her like this. Saucy and sarcastic. Much better than being crushed by Sofia's concern and worry.

"Again," Hector said, this time putting up his hands.

But Jayne didn't comply. "Amanda said I needed specialized training for this mission. Let's get to that. Pretty please?" she added when Hector scowled.

"You don't want to push yourself, Jayne. Trust me. It's my job to make sure you don't burn out."

Jayne stopped moving, and her face shifted. "Oh. I see what you're saying. The Adepts who try higher magic have a tendency to light themselves on fire. I'm not like that. I have a lot more control. I won't spontaneously combust. Promise."

Hector scratched his chin. "You need to build up your magic over time to avoid catastrophe. That's what Amanda wants me to do for you, fine-tune your magic so it's at the ready."

"But Ruger's life is at stake," Jayne said, softer this time. "If he's been captured, you know what he might be going through. I'll practice like mad all day, cross my heart and hope to die. But let's get to the spells I'll need to rescue him. The spells we'll need."

Cillian stepped to her side. "I agree with Officer Thorne, mate. I've seen her in action, and she's not going to burn out."

Hector shot a look at Cillian. "Very well. We'll bring in the Rogue."

"The *Rogue* has a name," Jayne said. "It's Cillian Pine. And he's way more Cillian than Rogue, so you might remember that as we train."

Cillian again felt the spark of happiness he was becoming accustomed to when she spoke of him to others. Their connection must be enhancing his emotions today, he thought. He was feeling loose and ready, and very protective. He'd enjoyed watching her kick this guy's ass. Now they could do it together.

Hector looked mildly amused by Jayne's scolding. "Pardon me, Officer Pine."

"No worries, mate. All good. Crack on."

"You probably already know that the TCO has little information about Rogues," Hector said, hands clasped in front of him as if he were a distinguished professor giving a lecture at Oxford. "But many of us were trained in the basics just in case we encountered one. Rogues are drawn in by powerful magic. Not just the presence of someone's magic, like yours, Jayne, but powerful spells, too. It's a siren's call to them."

Cillian nodded. This explained how he was able to shift so easily at Medb's tomb. The necromancy spell had been the most powerful feeling he'd ever experienced.

"A Rogue's magic is like the tide," Hector went on. "It has highs and lows. During the highs, the Rogue cannot resist the transformation. The call is too strong."

"The call?" At the words, Cillian's body went taut, the veins in his arms and neck standing out. Something about that term unsettled him. Hell, all of this unsettled him. It wasn't easy to find out you had some sort of weird magical monster living inside you, ready to be brought to life at a moment's notice. He had to force himself to ask politely, "What does that mean?"

"The call of magic," Hector said. "Whether that be your Master's magic or someone else's. A Rogue's power is always meant to be malleable. Transformed by someone else. You are a tool to be utilized. Don't ever forget that."

"Hey," Jayne said, jabbing a finger at Hector. "Cillian isn't a tool. He just sometimes becomes a really big wolf."

"Which is exactly what we need to work on. Cillian, can you shift on your own?"

"What, like now?"

"By all means."

Cillian went deep inside, imagining himself growing, the fur tickling his legs and belly, the sense of power and strength.

Nothing. His eyes shot open to find both Jayne and Hector watching him.

"Now you understand," Hector said, not unkindly. "Rogues don't perform their own magic. You are dependent on Miss Thorne. You must feed off her power to access your own."

Hector smacked his hands together and bounced on his toes, obviously excited to be getting to the good stuff. "Training you two together will be quite different from training you alone. You need to adjust your mindsets. Instead of simply pulling from the Torrent, Jayne will also need to feed that magic to you, Cillian. And, in turn, you need to learn to draw on your entwined magic, to identify the way it looks and sounds, the way it smells. Because in a high-stakes battle with other Adepts, there won't be time for you to figure out which magic belongs to you and which belongs to the enemy. You wouldn't want to bond with the wrong Adept."

Cillian blanched, glancing over at Jayne, whose mouth was open in a small O of surprise. "Can that happen?"

"There are no documented instances of it. But my job is to think about the possibilities no one else has considered. We also thought Rogues extinct, but Mr. Pine has shown us the folly of our ways. Anything is possible."

"But I thought Rogues could only bond with Masters. That's what Ruger told us."

"Again, we simply don't know, because no one here has seen this in action except for you two. You're the first Master we've seen in a long time, Jayne. And your magic accelerated far quicker than anything we've come across in the history of Adepts. Magic is changing. It is unleashed, in many ways. I wouldn't be surprised if more Masters pop up in the future. And because of that, more Rogues. We need to be prepared for anything."

Jayne touched Cillian's hand. "Okay. No pressure, right? Easy peasy."

Hector nodded. "To begin, I will be on the attack, and Jayne, I want you to cast the Block spell and call on Cillian to shift at the same time."

Jayne shifted into a fighting stance, then froze, her mouth twisting in a confused grimace. "Uh, how exactly do we do that?"

"Just as Cillian needs to focus on your particular brand of magic, you need to focus on his. You've seen him shift before, right? Remember everything you can about that moment, and seek out his magic within the Torrent. As if it's a spell you're summoning. Cillian, you need to focus on it, too. Channel the same energy you felt when you've shifted before."

Cillian was feeling more nervous by the minute. Jayne's cocky attitude had vanished, and she was turning inward, getting that look she did before she blew up in frustration.

"We can do this," he said, giving her a smile. "We've done it loads of times."

"Whenever you're ready." Hector raised his arms, glancing between them expectantly. When Jayne and Cillian both nodded, Hector pulled a sphere of blue energy and twisted it between his fingers before launching it at Jayne.

Cillian jumped to her side only to get hit smack in the face with the trainer's magic and go down onto the mat in a heap.

Jayne was cursing up a storm, and he was decidedly not a wolf. He hadn't felt her pull on him at all.

"Damn it," she hissed. "Sorry. Okay. Let's try again."

They set up side by side again. Cillian focused on what he remembered about his first shift. The bright white light. The intoxicatingly sensual feel of Jayne's magic. The smell of the cool night air. The way his body rippled and stretched, elongating as it changed forms. Nothing.

Hector's magic crashed into Jayne this time, sending her flying backward. She collided with a padded wall and crumpled, hitting her shoulder hard. Though every ounce of instinct in him said *rush to her side, pick her up, protect her,* he stayed in place. Jayne was not the kind of woman who wanted to be rescued, especially in front of a superior.

With a groan, she sat up, weaving a bit before hauling herself to her feet. Her eyes were blazing. "You okay to go again? I think I almost had it that time."

He grinned, stepping closer to wipe a little blood from the corner of her mouth. "I am if you are."

This time, when Jayne shut her eyes, he felt it. The call. He could smell her magic intensely, the heady scent of fresh roses, the comfort of woodsmoke. She drew on his power and he felt her access the Torrent, felt his body tighten in response, so similar to when they were together...

Jayne threw up a Block spell just in time. Hector's blue magic fizzled, and Cillian felt himself pop as he transformed into a large silver wolf, blinking slowly at the scene as if bored.

"By the goddess," Hector breathed. "You're magnificent."

Jayne whooped, pumping her fist in the air. "Skadoosh!" she said triumphantly. When Hector and Cillian only stared at her, her smile faded. "*Kung Fu Panda?* Really? Oh, come on, you two are no fun."

Hector was circling Cillian like he was a mint-condition used car. "How do you feel?" Hector asked. To his credit, he didn't look the least bit uncomfortable being in the presence of a massive wolf. More like entranced.

"I feel weird, to be honest," Cillian said.

"Can you hear him?" Jayne asked Hector. When Hector shook his head, Jayne ruffled Cillian's neck, making shivers go down his spine. He felt things more in this form; his senses were on high alert.

"I'm going to have to translate for him."

"No problem. I hope you won't mind, but this is the first time

I've seen a Rogue shift." Hector whipped out a notebook and started peppering them with questions.

"Is this how he always transforms?"

Yes.

"Is he bigger or smaller than the last time?"

Same.

"Did it hurt to shift?"

No.

"Did you feel the call?"

Yes.

"Can you feel Jayne's magic now?" Hector asked.

Could he ever. *Yes. It's surrounding me, like I'm inside some sort of bubble of energy. It smells like roses. And...something earthy.*

"Woodsmoke," Jayne added with a small, private smile.

Yeah, that's there, too, but there's something else. Something like... the woods on a wet day—

"Moss?" Jayne suggested.

That's it.

"I think that's *your* magic, Cillian. To me, your magic smells like moss and sage."

"It could be a combination of both of you," Hector suggested, clearly able to piece together their conversation even without hearing Cillian's side. "A Rogue-Master relationship would produce its own particular kind of magic. It would make sense that your connection would be merging the two scents. That's good, Cillian. You should focus on those smells. It will help to ground your abilities. Well."

Hector put away his notebook, loosened his tie, and rolled up his sleeves. Gone was the skeptical Adept, replaced by a man who finally understood Jayne's power.

"This is simply wonderful. What an experience. Okay, Jayne. Shift Cillian back to his human form, and we can go again. It is vital, for you both, that this shift is seamless every single time."

4

ICE, ICE, BABY

Jayne concentrated on Cillian, mentally willing him to shift back to himself, but nothing happened. *Okay. This isn't just wiggling my nose. I need the Torrent.*

To explain the Torrent to a nonmagical creature was challenging, even to someone with as broad a vocabulary as Jayne's. The first time she'd accessed it, by total accident, she'd thought she was losing her mind. She'd touched a minor grimoire in the Vanderbilt archives vault and a bioluminescent river of stars had flowed around her, glowing green and undulating as if driven by a breeze. Now, only a few weeks later, she was marked as a Master magician and had control over the fate of the magical world, along with the lives of too many to count, because of her ability to access this starry otherworld.

At least accessing the Torrent wasn't hard anymore. She reached for the river of stars and sought out Cillian's familiar mossy scent.

It wasn't there. All she found was the flowing Torrent, open and welcoming. Myriad spells floated past her, but nothing resembling Cillian or his magic.

"Shit." Jayne searched and searched but found nothing familiar. She didn't like this. It felt like her magic was misbehaving. She'd had such easy control throughout the training session, but the second she and Cillian started to work on his shifting, it had all fallen apart.

She searched deeper, looking for anything that felt Cillian-like. *You can do this, Jayne. He's in here, with you. You know it.*

Nothing.

Maybe it's because Hector is making me force him to change. Maybe that's unnatural. Maybe we are supposed to work in concert. A spike of triumph. *See? Cillian's not a tool after all. Your history books are all wrong, pal.*

As if attracted by the defiance in her mind, a new presence swelled inside her, icy and cold and not at all like the warm familiar buzz of her own magic.

Jayne tried to push it down, but it roiled within her, rising like an ice-cold tide threatening to swallow her whole. The river of stars flickered as if about to die out, and Jayne clung to it in desperation. *Please stay,* she begged. *Don't leave me!* She needed the Torrent. She couldn't do magic without it.

As if responding to her plea, the river gleamed to life once more, and the strange cold feeling began to recede. Gritting her teeth, Jayne tried a different approach, focusing on the smell of Cillian the Man instead of Cillian the Rogue. Soap, clean cotton, the light musk of sweat from a good workout...

"Okay...I feel your power." Cillian's disembodied voice rang in her ears.

"Good." Jayne resisted the urge to bounce on her feet again. It was a process for him, just like it was for her.

"I can feel our...our connection."

As soon as he said it, a ripple of white and gold magic flickered across his hands, twining up his arms like spiderwebs. Jayne's heart lifted. It was working. This was exactly what it had looked like the first time he'd shifted.

Something tugged within her as Cillian pulled on her magic.

She held perfectly still, waiting. Not reacting. *Come on,* she urged. *You can do this.* She wasn't sure if she was directing her thoughts toward Cillian, or their magic.

Cillian's form began to shift. He rose in height, then shrank again. His body morphed like they were in a fun house with all those weird twisty mirrors. Though, knowing this was *real* made it look almost disturbing. His body was suddenly silly putty, being stretched and molded in different directions.

So close. We're almost there. She waited for that moment when their magic snapped together like two Legos, when their bond solidified and he could shift at will...

But instead of snapping, something *cracked.* A bolt of white-hot flame seared through Jayne's chest, making her stagger backward. A fierce churning shuddered violently inside her, making her magic spin out of control. Alarmed, Jayne released her grip on the Torrent. The sudden break from her powers zapped her down to her bones as if she'd been electrocuted. Her limbs tensed, and pain radiated from every inch of her before she collapsed on the mat.

Cillian groaned, his voice muffled by the chaos raging in Jayne's mind. Her vision blurred, the ceiling of the training center fading in and out of focus. After a moment, Cillian shouted, "Jayne!" The fact that he'd taken this long to notice her wipeout indicated he'd experienced the same disorientation as she had.

When she resurfaced, Cillian was in his human form again, panting and wiping sweat from his brow. His face had taken on a greenish tint.

"That...was not at all fun," he said. "What happened? Did you feel lost like I did?"

Remembering the strange icy feeling, Jayne nodded. "Lost and alone. And cold. The ice... It was terrible. And then I was pretty much electrocuted. Did you get zapped too?" He nodded. "Oh, Cillian, I am so sorry. I won't let that happen again." She turned to Hector. "Do you know what happened? Did you feel it too?"

But Hector was frowning at her, his gaze focused on Jayne's forehead.

"By the Goddess," he breathed, rubbing his chin, his eyes full of awe. The hard-ass teacher was gone again, replaced by someone almost...reverent. "They mentioned a marking from the totem, but I never imagined..." He blinked and drew closer, all ire fading from his expression. "Tell me how this works for you. Do you feel any different when you perform spells?"

Oh. She must be glowing again. Medb's Earth totem gift at work. Jayne shifted her weight. "A little. Stronger, usually. Some of the more powerful spells draw out a strange presence inside me. Something I've never felt before." When Hector's face turned unreadable, Jayne added, "Is that normal? Or should I be worried?"

Hector took out a small handkerchief and wiped his forehead before folding it into a tight square and replacing it in his pocket. He was trying to decide how much to share, Jayne realized.

Cillian took her hand. "Come on, mate. Give it up. We need to know these things."

Hector's lips pursed. "There are limits to what I can share, and not only because some of the material is classified, but also because we simply don't know. No one has raised a Master magician before, let alone been gifted a totem from one. This is unprecedented. As such, I urge you to exercise caution. We have no idea who—or what—this 'strange presence' is. If you unleash it, it may try to take over your magic completely. It could take over your mind. We've had documented possessions before. It's possible this puts you at risk, Jayne. You should do all in your power not to use this strange magic until it can be studied and understood."

Jayne wanted to argue, but Cillian jumped in before she got anything out.

"I disagree," he said. "If Medb bestowed some of her power on Jayne, she should use it. Cultivate it. If we're going to keep the grimoires out of the hands of the bad guys, we're going to need every advantage we can get over the Kingdom, or La Liberté, or whoever else we come across. If they try to hurt us, she needs to know how to fight back. I need to know how to fight back with her."

Hector's demeanor had shifted, his face granite in the harsh unnatural light the gym. Gone was the reverent trainer. The hard-ass was back.

He's scared, Jayne realized. *Scared of my power, scared of Cillian's.*

"I applaud your courage and the sentiment," Hector said. "We can work on these higher magicks later, once we've done some more research. For now, while you're in this room, while you're training with me, we will stick to the known world. I will teach you how to find Ruger, how to execute your mission. Nothing more. Am I clear?"

Cillian clearly expected her to fight back, but Jayne wasn't at all eager to revisit that awful icy feeling again. It reminded her too much of her mother.

"Okay, Hector. We'll do it your way. What's next?"

5

A TEAM FOR THE AGES

It had taken three walks around the CIA campus, four cups of chamomile, and one good old-fashioned crying jag before Sofia had calmed down enough to submit to Amanda's debriefing. While she'd been tempted several times to simply scamper back to Nashville and say to hell with all of them—the CIA and the TCO and magic in general, including her stubborn little sister—Sofia was also scared. Scared of what was coming, of what might happen. She'd operated from that place far too long. And that's why she was so ticked off. Jayne had been right when she said Sofia was holding her back.

Amanda had looked incredibly relieved when Sofia returned to her office and said, "Okay. Let's do this."

Now, Amanda attached one final lead to Sofia's temple and handed her a thin vial of liquid. "This won't hurt a bit, I promise. Now, drink this. It will alter your brain waves to allow us in."

"Is this what you do for every debriefing?" Sofia took a sip of the thin, purple liquid, gasping at the bitter aftertaste. "Ugh. Bottoms up." She drained the glass.

Amanda took it from her, then adjusted the wires at Sofia's temples.

"Not necessarily. You've hidden your magic for so long that I think you've overwritten your memories to keep yourself safe. Like a trauma victim creates a safe place for themselves to retreat when things get hard. This drug relaxes your inhibitions so I can access the memories accurately, without any sort of filters you may have put in place to protect yourself or protect those you're recalling. The parental relationship is strong, and even though your mother isn't your favorite person, there is still a tie that binds you, and we need to be sure your memories are accurate."

"Are you saying my mind has been lying to me this whole time? That my memories are wrong, somehow?"

"I'm saying it's possible your memories have been tampered with to keep you safe. We need to give your mind a bit of a boost to make sure you're experiencing the real deal."

"Well, *that's* not creepy." She was feeling warm, too warm. "Is this going to be like that thing from Harry Potter? The Pensieve?"

"You Thorne girls and your books. You do know those are stories, not reality, yes? No, this is a scientifically proven method that will give us a movie of your memories. You will be able to guide me to what I need."

"So I can pick which memories you see?" She didn't like the idea of the CIA poking around in her private thoughts. She wasn't even ready to share all of those with Jayne just yet, let alone these complete strangers.

"As long as you direct your thoughts appropriately, I'll only see what you want me to."

That was a relief. Sort of.

Amanda lifted her phone and said into the mouthpiece, "Pierce? We're ready."

Sofia frowned at the tall, skinny man with glasses who stepped in and waved awkwardly at her. She'd been too upset to speak to him before. He looked no older than nineteen, his face smooth like a baby's. He clutched a notepad and pen and positioned himself behind Amanda as if practicing to be her shadow.

"Are you going to watch, too?" Sofia asked uncertainly.

"Pierce is only here to record minutes on the debriefing."

Sofia swallowed around a knot in her throat, feeling uncomfortable with the presence of another witness to her experiences. But it made sense. They needed to record this all somehow, right?

She felt very warm now. Languorous. Like she was on a chaise longue beside a sparkling pool on a hot summer day.

"Good," Amanda said, looking at the screen. "You're ready. Show me what happened when the Kingdom kidnapped you."

Sofia focused on that horrible moment. Her vision twisted and spun like the shapes inside a kaleidoscope, and then, she no longer sat in Amanda's office. She was marching purposefully through Boston's Logan airport, her hand sweaty as she clutched her duffel bag. The back of her neck prickled with every step, and she kept shooting glances over her shoulder.

"Did you feel like you were being followed?" a disembodied voice in her ear asked.

Sofia yelped in surprise, the sound echoing as if she were in a tunnel. And yet, she continued walking past souvenir shops and restaurants as if completely unaffected by Amanda's voice or her own cry of surprise.

"What—what's happening?" she asked. She heard her own voice as if it were in her head, but her lips weren't moving. Curiously, she tried lifting her right hand, but nothing happened. She was stuck inside this version of herself, right after she'd left Jayne in Dublin.

"You are repeating a scene of your memory," Amanda explained. "But don't be afraid—we are still sitting together in my office. I'm seeing what you see, and we can still speak to each other. But your body is trapped in the loop of the memory. You can disconnect it at any time. It's important that you know that."

"Right." Sofia felt dazed. "So, there's, like, two versions of me right now?"

"No. It's more like you and I are watching from afar, unable to interfere. We are merely observing."

"Well, you, me, and Pierce, right? Are you here, too, Pierce?"

"Here!" said a thin, chipper voice.

Amanda cleared her throat. "Now, back to the scene at hand. Did you feel like you were being followed?"

Sofia focused on the sensations of the memory—the sweat gathering on her brow and neck, the shallow breaths, the incessant prickling along her back...

"Yes," she said. "Definitely."

"How did you know?"

"I can't explain it. It's like a sixth sense. A feverish, panicked feeling. Prickles on my skin."

Other Sofia was nearing the exit, and she quickened her pace. When she stepped through the automatic doors and strode toward the terminal bus stop, something in the air shifted. Sofia felt it and went stiff, inhaling deeply.

"What is it?" Amanda asked.

"You think I know?" Sofia snapped.

"You clearly sensed something. Walk me through it."

Sofia sighed, concentrating. This was too bizarro, sifting through her memories, looking for that thing she couldn't put her finger on at the time—what was wrong about the moment. Then it hit her, and she gasped.

"I smelled the magic."

"What did it smell like?"

Sofia paused. "It smelled like Ruth's magic." She remembered it clearly, the hint of iron and rotting violets. It was subtle, mingled with other smells she didn't recognize—as if whoever cast the spell had merely been close to Ruth moments before. But it still sent a curl of dread coiling in her stomach.

It happened in a flash. One second, Sofia stood there, pale and afraid, and the next, several masked figures appeared and grabbed her, shoving a sack over her head. Everything went dark.

"Did they knock you out?" Amanda asked.

"Not right away." Sofia shuddered as she remembered the panicky feeling of being bound and gagged and shoved in the back of a van. It was the stuff of nightmares.

"Describe it to me. Smells, voices…"

"All male. A few Irish accents. I smelled…alcohol and woodsmoke and an earthy scent I knew was dark magic but I'd never experienced before."

"Did they speak to you?"

"No. I tried to fight my way out of my restraints, and then they knocked me out."

Amanda made a noise that sounded like a grunt of approval. "Got all that, Pierce?"

"Got it," he said.

"All right. Sofia, can you take us to your next memory, please?"

Sofia really didn't want to, but once the suggestion was planted in her mind, she couldn't stop it from rippling into existence. Her surroundings shifted and warped as if she'd just jumped into a wormhole on *Star Trek*.

She sat, bound and gagged at a round table, her brain sluggish and sore from the effects of the Time Catch and whatever drug Alarik had given her. The gag in Sofia's mouth cut into her cheeks, making her head throb. It tasted vile, like rubbing alcohol and old socks. The ropes around her wrists dug into her skin, but the sting was the only thing keeping her awake.

"This was when Alarik taunted me about Jayne," Sofia said in a hollow voice, eager to get past this memory.

"Did you know about her assignment with us at the time?" Amanda asked.

"No, I didn't. He told me about it, and I thought he was lying."

Alarik himself showed up, menacing, cruel, and just as disturbing as Sofia remembered. His eyes gleamed with a creepy hunger that made her shiver. But she lunged in his direction, all fire and fury, quelling her own unease as she tried to attack him. She was embarrassed by his laugh. As if she was nothing. Not a threat at all.

"Did you know about Ruth then?" Amanda asked.

Sofia huffed a sigh. "*No.* I thought the Head, whoever that was, had killed my parents. I didn't know she was alive."

She had tried tuning out Alarik's words. Hearing his slick voice made her feel ill. Her skin turned cold when he mentioned Jayne. Icy dread twisted in her gut, but it mingled with resignation. She was tired of running. She told Alarik as much.

"You wanted it to end." Amanda's voice was soft and thoughtful. There was something unreadable in her voice. Something that made Sofia's raging thoughts go still.

"Yes. I thought if he killed me, Jayne would be safe." The words sounded distant. Like someone else was speaking.

The gag returned to Sofia's mouth, foul and soggy. Alarik left. Teresa pressed a gemstone to Sofia's forehead, and she managed to stay silent as agony racked through her brain.

"We don't have to go through this," Amanda said. "Just tell me what information you gave up."

"I didn't give up anything."

Amanda paused. "But they tortured you—"

"Yes, and I told them nothing." Sofia's tone was biting. "I went through years of cancer and chemotherapy. I know how to endure pain." She remained stoic as Teresa sent waves of powerful magic into her skull, drilling into her again and again.

"Show me the questions they asked." Amanda prodded.

Sofia complied, allowing Amanda and Pierce to relive the interrogation with her. Jayne's job, her magic, their history. Their parents, what she remembered about their deaths. Fresh pain sliced into her, and her body jolted.

"Move on," Amanda urged, her voice coming out in a rush. "There's no need to relive this part. Skip forward, please."

It sounded almost as if Amanda couldn't stomach watching

Sofia getting tortured, but Sofia had no objections. She let the moment go and focused on what happened after—after Teresa had tortured her, after Alarik had returned and worked his twisted magic against her himself, after she'd passed out from the pain. The numb throbbing in her head was a welcome relief compared to the magical shock therapy from earlier.

Amanda scribbled something on her notepad. "Did you see anyone else? Did Alarik speak to anyone on the phone or out of view that you could tell?"

Sofia knew what Amanda was asking: Were there any other players in the game they should know about? But she shook her head. "Only Alarik, Teresa, Max, and…and Ruth." *My mother.* Sofia had long since dropped the affectionate term of *Mom.* Years ago, when Ruth threatened Jayne's life for her own magical gain, Sofia had severed that emotional tie. Ruth wasn't her mom any longer. She was the enemy.

Even so, she would never forget the moment she faced her presumed-dead mother. The woman she both loved and hated. The woman who forced Sofia to live a life on the run, constantly looking over her shoulder, worried that Jayne would fall prey to the same magic Ruth had…

Sofia's shoulders tensed. She didn't want to do this. She didn't want to let them see her soul. But the drug made her weak, susceptible to suggestion. She couldn't stop her mind from bringing up her past.

Amanda's voice came from far away, almost gentle. Almost. "Relax, Sofia. Let the memories come."

So, reluctantly, Sofia did.

"Is this her?" a soft voice asked.

Something familiar pricked Sofia's memory, but her brain felt like sludge. Though something dark covered her face, her vision still spun. She felt like she was on a boat, swaying back and forth, back and forth.

"Yes, ma'am," another woman said. Sofia recognized her voice

—it had to be the woman with the dark hair who tied her up. Teresa. But that first woman... it couldn't be...

"Show me," the first voice ordered.

Ice pooled in Sofia's stomach. The authoritative command in that voice. The accompanying flash of hunger in the woman's eyes.

It was a hallucination. It had to be. Ruth Thorne was dead.

A searing light burned against Sofia's eyes, and she winced, her head pounding with agony. As her eyes adjusted, she made out a tall figure in front of her. Blond hair streaked with gray. Cold eyes the eerie color of tornado clouds. Thin lips curved into a cruel, triumphant smile.

Sofia's mouth fell open as she stared blatantly at her mother. She couldn't breathe. Her brain had completely frozen.

Ruth stared down at her, a small gasp of surprise escaping her lips.

Sofia wasn't sure what Ruth had expected, but it wasn't this. It wasn't her.

For one tense moment, Ruth and Sofia stared at each other with equal shock and horror. Sofia's body was numb with disbelief. Though she distantly registered the peril she was in, all she could think about was: Why? How? Was her father alive, too?

Then Ruth spoke, and all the revulsion and anguish Sofia had buried for years sprang forward in a sickening wave of torment.

"Hello, Sofia."

"She wasn't expecting you, was she?" Amanda asked, her voice jolting Sofia from the memory. Amanda's office slowly returned to view, but Sofia couldn't shake the harrowing feeling of looking into her mother's eyes for the first time in years.

"No. I don't know who she thought I was. Not Jayne, certainly."

Amanda was silent for a moment. Pierce scribbled something on the notepad. Then, Amanda said, "Tell me about Maximus."

Sofia's tongue felt heavy in her mouth, so she only nodded. Gradually, another memory came into being, swallowing up Amanda's office.

"You awake, lass?" whispered a voice.

Sofia flinched away instinctively, expecting another blow to her face. Her face still burned from Alarik's surprisingly forceful punches.

"It's all right," the soft voice said, drawing nearer. "I won't hurt you."

Alarik had said the same thing. But when Sofia hadn't answered his questions, he'd changed his tune.

Something cut through the restraints on her wrists, and the ropes fell away. Sofia stiffened, looking up to find a bulky redheaded man now working at the knots tying her feet together. When he finished, he tugged her gag free. Sofia spat and coughed, trying to clear the foul taste from her mouth.

"Who—who are you?" she rasped. Suspicion prickled along her skin. Was this a trap? A ruse to get her to trust her liberator and spill her secrets? Because it wouldn't work. Sofia trusted no one.

"The name's Maximus," the man said, and Sofia detected a Scottish accent. "I saw what they did to you. It—it's not right. None of this is right. I see that now." His gaze grew distant for a moment, then he shook his head. "I'm getting you out of here."

But Sofia didn't move. She stared at Maximus through narrowed eyes. "How can I trust you?"

"I just freed you, lass!"

Sofia took a ragged breath. Worst-case scenario, this was a trap and she would just face another beating later. As long as she kept her secrets to herself, everything would be fine. Jayne would be safe.

Sofia stood, her legs wobbly from being tied down for so long. Maximus caught her by the arm and helped her hobble toward the exit. Her body still felt sluggish from whatever drug they'd given her, but she shook her head violently to clear it. She had to get out. She had to—

"What are you doing, Maximus?" asked a cold voice. A voice that was all too familiar. A voice that made the hair on Sofia's arms stand up as a chill raced down her spine.

"Did you actually *see* Ruth kill Maximus?" Amanda asked, her sharp tone cutting through the vivid memory.

Sofia inhaled shakily. "No. Her men dragged him away. And I suspect she would've had someone else, like Alarik, take care of... of the task. Ruth never liked getting her hands dirty."

Sofia's head pounded with a dull ache, and she yanked at the wires attached to her head until they pulled free. She was done with this. Her muddled brain couldn't take any more of it.

To her surprise, Amanda didn't object. Instead, she drew out a plastic bag from a drawer in her desk and placed it in front of Sofia.

"Tell me about this."

Sofia sat forward to stare at the bag. Inside, she could barely make out the bracelet she had worn on her wrist for years. The chain was tarnished, and one of the beads had chipped. She found herself subconsciously rubbing at her wrist where it had rested. The Suppression spell had subdued her magic for so long. But when she'd been diagnosed with cancer a second time, she knew it had gone too far. That was when she'd removed it. It wasn't worth the risk if it killed her, and she couldn't protect Jayne if she was dead. But even with it away from her skin, the effects had lingered, so she'd put it in the bag, worried the spell could still impact the air around her somehow.

"A witch made it for me," Sofia said. "It blocked my magic." She remembered dragging Jayne to Miami under the guise of spending a relaxing spring break on the beach when in truth she was trying to track down an old contact of their father's.

"How?" Amanda asked, her thin brows knitting together.

Sofia shrugged. "I don't know. The woman uttered a spell in Spanish. I couldn't understand it."

Amanda lifted the bag to scrutinize the bracelet, her gaze intense. "The TCO will need to run tests on this."

Sofia nodded. "Of course." Given that the bracelet and its Suppression spell had almost taken her life—had almost ripped her away from Jayne—Sofia would be happy if she never saw it again.

Amanda set the bag down, clasped her hands together, and leveled a hard look at Sofia. "Why did you want your magic blocked?"

"I worried it would consume me like it had my mother. That it would endanger Jayne somehow. I wanted to give her a life away from that."

Amanda nodded. Behind her, Pierce wrote something else down on the notepad. "And...now?"

"Now what?"

Amanda looked up, eyebrows raised. "Now that Jayne is with the TCO, what do you intend to do about it? About your magic?"

A knot formed in Sofia's throat, and she swallowed hard. When she'd found out Jayne had joined the CIA, that her sister had magic after all...Sofia's world had shattered. Everything she'd feared had come true. Jayne was powerful—more powerful than Sofia had ever been. Possibly more powerful than Ruth, though Sofia had no idea if Ruth's powers had grown over the years. Everything Sofia had done to shield Jayne from the world of magic had been for nothing. She felt purposeless. She felt like a failure.

To be honest, she didn't know what the hell she wanted anymore.

Her eyes burned with unshed tears. "I want to keep my sister safe. I—I want to keep her away from all this. Away from magic and from Ruth."

Amanda's lips thinned. "It's a little late for that, don't you think?"

"She'll be killed if she stays with you!" Sofia snapped.

"And what do you think will happen if you pull her out? You think Ruth will just leave her alone? Jayne is a Master, Sofia. The Kingdom will want her no matter what, and she is safer with us than with you."

Sofia flinched, the words striking her like a blow. But Amanda was right. Sofia hadn't been able to protect Jayne.

Amanda's gaze softened. "You know your sister can take care of herself, right?"

Sofia inhaled a shuddering breath as tears stung her eyes. "I can't help it. I've watched over her our entire lives."

"Then maybe you need a new way of looking at things."

Sofia frowned as Amanda pulled out a stack of papers and slid them across the desk to Sofia. "This is an application to become a consultant for the TCO."

"What? But I—you can't—" Sofia sputtered.

Amanda leaned forward, her eyes earnest. "No one knows Ruth Thorne like you do. You can help us take her down. You want to keep Jayne safe? This is the best way to do it. Join our team. Put your skills and your memories to good use."

Sofia felt frozen in place, immobilized by shock and terror. Another tear fell, dripping onto the desk. Her gaze flicked from Amanda to the papers in front of her.

"The only way to defeat Ruth is with magic," Amanda said. "We're going to bring her down, Sofia. The question is: Will you help us?"

Sofia wrung her hands together on her lap, her pulse skittering. This went against everything she had fought for—a life without magic, a life free from conflict and fear.

But she was past that now. There was no turning back. Amanda was right: Sofia needed a new way of looking at things.

"You'll help me stop her?"

Amanda nodded. "If it's the last thing I do."

Before she could change her mind, Sofia snatched the papers and started filling them out.

6

A BROKEN PATH

Jayne and Cillian practiced bonding their magic for another hour before Cillian seriously started to look ill, and they called it quits.

But she was just getting started. While Cillian left to shower and change, Jayne grabbed a granola bar, downed a bottle of the special vitamin-and-mineral-infused water the TCO kept on hand for magical training, and, feeling refreshed, returned to the mats, ready for more. A bubble of relief filled her when Hector didn't refuse.

"You've used the Tracking spell before, yes?" he asked. When Jayne nodded, he continued, "There are many different variations of a Tracking spell—Find spells, Carry spells, Follow spells…"

Jayne's brow furrowed. "You know, I've always wondered… What's with all the simplified spell names? What are we, in kindergarten? When can we start working on some *Alohomora* or *Wingardium Leviosa?*"

Hector gave her a deadpan look.

Jayne shrugged. "I'm just saying it sounds kind of juvenile."

"If you must know, we used to use Latin names for spells, but nobody speaks Latin anymore. And we realized that overcomplicating spell names was getting officers killed. It's best to keep it simple. In the heat of battle, you don't want to struggle to remember the right spell. Straightforward plainspeak, like many other law enforcement organizations have moved to, works best."

Jayne sighed wistfully. It made sense, but she really wanted to use some bona fide fantasy spells. Maybe in Elvish. Only then would she feel legit.

"It's a bit trickier to use a Tracking spell on living things, since they are constantly moving and changing," Hector went on. "Once the magic latches onto the target, it can sometimes get lost amidst the chaos of human nature."

"Very profound," Jayne complimented.

Hector ignored her. "It helps if you know the person well. Similar to how you call on Cillian to shift, you will be trying to locate Ruger's particular magical signature as well. The clearer you can imagine it, the stronger the link will be. Now, it's important to note that you can't use a Tracking spell on something that is cloaked by magic. The trail will go cold. But it should lead you to the last location before the cloaking, wherever his scent is strongest."

"Sounds more like a bloodhound than a spell."

"In a sense."

"Should we get Cillian back here? I mean, he's the *real* bloodhound."

"Let him rest. The spell is accurate and can span large distances. But yes, in the future, using your Rogue's sense of smell will assist you in your search as well."

"Please stop calling him 'my' Rogue. It's depersonalizing. This is hard for him. A few weeks ago, he thought he was part of an organization to save the Earth. Then the poor guy meets me, finds out his friends are terrorists, magic is real, and oh, by the way, a very large wolf resides inside him, just waiting to be called out to kick some magical ass. It's been a lot."

Hector frowned. "But he *is* your Rogue, Jayne."

"He's not mine or anyone else's. He's his own wolf. Now, what if I layer the Tracking spell?" Jayne asked, eager to change the subject. The idea of Cillian belonging to her in some way made her deeply uncomfortable. Not only did that feel claustrophobically like forever, she didn't like the idea of taking away his free will. That's what Ruth and Alarik were all about, and Jayne would never, ever be like them.

"I wouldn't recommend it. Layering it with something else might taint the quality of the spell."

"But if I layer it, maybe I could get through a Cloaking barrier."

Hector cocked his head at her. "I've never heard of something like that."

"Let's give it a whirl. Cloak yourself."

"Jayne, I really don't think—"

"Humor me! Come on, I just want to try it."

Hector's expression remained stern and unamused, but the whisper of magic in the air told Jayne he had just Cloaked himself. Excellent. Game on.

Magic, she'd come to understand, was purely logical, limited only by the level of creativity specific to each magician. What she imagined to find in the Torrent might not be the same as another magician would, but the end results were the same. Envision what you need, and it will appear.

Jayne reached into the Torrent, easily finding the triangular shape of the Tracking spell she'd used so many times in Dublin. Then, she pictured herself drawing open a set of sheer curtains. A spell appeared, rippling like fabric. Jayne pulled on it, layering it with the Tracking spell. When she opened her eyes, Hector had vanished, but she knew he was still there. She breathed in deeply, trying to remember the specifics of Hector—his facial expressions, the tone of his voice, the scent of his magic. It was one of those weird things where she could remember what he looked like, but not specific details. She didn't know him well enough just yet.

A faint tendril of his magic lingered in the air, a hint of citrus mingled with sandalwood. Jayne focused on it, bringing the spell forward. A force slammed into her, and something popped in the air. In an instant, Hector stood before her, eyes wide and face a mask of utter shock. It quickly turned to glee.

"It worked," Jayne said.

"It did."

"Let's do it again."

Once she could successfully toss the spell at Hector without a second thought, he pointed at the clock. "I think that's enough for the moment, Miss Thorne. Hit the showers. And I must say, well done."

"Can we try looking for Ruger with this spell now?"

Hector's eyebrows furrowed. "Well..."

"Come on. Just let me try. Just in case. I mean, if I can find him right now..."

"All right. Clear your mind. Relax. Let the Torrent open for you."

Hector's voice was hypnotic. The river of stars embraced her.

"Envision Ruger."

She brought the big man into her mind's eye. He was dressed as he had been the first time they met, in the Vandy vault, in a well-cut gray suit. His eyes were closed, though, as if he was asleep. It was eerie, seeing him like this.

"Now the spell," she heard Hector say.

She pulled the spell to her, then cast it toward the sleeping giant. It spun like a boomerang, slicing right through Ruger, landing back in her hand. He hadn't even twitched. And she had no sense of him.

"It didn't work."

She opened her eyes, and Hector squeezed her shoulder. "It's okay, Jayne. Locator and Tracking spells are much easier when you're within proximity of the target. And you're just starting to work this magic. Cut yourself some slack."

"I don't know that Ruger has that luxury, Hector."

After they'd cleaned up, Hector treated Jayne and Cillian to dinner at Rocco's, an Italian restaurant a few miles from Langley in the Virginia town called McLean. Jayne enjoyed a delightful feast of New York–style brick oven pizza—the best pizza she'd ever had in her life—alongside an extremely dirty martini and a huge slice of key lime pie for dessert. Hector, much more relaxed out in the real world, cast a Silencing spell to make sure none of the other diners overheard, then regaled them with stories about the training mishaps of less powerful Adepts. It felt downright gossipy, and Jayne might have enjoyed herself if she wasn't worried sick about Ruger.

Once they were stuffed full and a teensy bit tipsy, Hector drove them back to Langley and offered to do some more spell practice before they turned in for the night. Jayne liked that idea; the martini had made her feel looser. Maybe she was too tense, and that's why she couldn't change Cillian easily.

As if Hector read her mind, he said, "Sometimes, being relaxed helps Adepts access their magic."

"I'm game if you are. But I'm so full I may throw up on you," Jayne warned.

They returned to the training facility, and Hector pointed her to a chair.

"You can stay seated. No physical movement required. Just practice what you showed me before—the layered Tracking spell. It's best if Cillian is here when you do it so he knows what it feels and smells like."

She took a seat. Hector and Cillian also drew up chairs so they formed a creepy little circle right there in the gymnasium, ready for Jayne to work her magic mumbo jumbo. All they needed was some white chalk, candles, salt, and an Ouija board, and the whole summoning circle would be complete.

It took a few tries, Jayne's brain sluggish from so much pizza and gin, but she was finally able to replicate the layered spell she'd performed earlier, de-Cloaking Hector as before. When Hector instructed her to do it and call Cillian to shift at the same time, Cillian blanched.

She patted him on the knee. "It's all good. I'm all warmed up. It won't be weird like before."

Jayne straightened in her chair before reaching the Torrent again. Her layered spell awaited her, shimmering and ready. Before she grabbed it, she imagined Cillian's Rogue scent, sage and moss, and called on it.

The same heavy force slammed into her, kicking her out of the Torrent so violently her head throbbed.

"Ouch!" she cried out, wincing from the intensity of it. She'd never been thrust out of the Torrent before today. She felt like a performer yanked off the stage with a hook because the audience had booed her. Shaking her head, she turned to look at Cillian, who also rubbed his forehead as if he, too, had been mercilessly shut out.

"What happened?" Hector asked.

"Something blocked us again," Jayne said. "I reached for Cillian, and…it was like something broke. I couldn't reach the Torrent after that."

"Was it that strange presence you told me about earlier?"

Jayne shook her head. "No, I didn't feel that at all. This was different. Something new."

Hector frowned. "Try again, let's see if it repeats itself."

Jayne tried again, and the same thing happened. This time a searing ache pulsed in her brain, reminiscent of the nauseating ocular migraines she used to get before she'd known about her magic.

"Good God, that's awful." She massaged her temples, eyes scrunched shut as she tried to ward off the incoming headache.

"For an Adept of your power, that's quite unusual." Hector stroked his chin, eyeing Jayne like she was some kind of test subject. "What if you tried again, but just with the Tracking spell? Leave Cillian out of it."

"I think she's done for the night, mate," Cillian said, his expression hard. He sat upright in his chair, arms flexed and muscles taut. "I'm done, too. Let's call it, aye?"

Hector faltered. "Ah…all right. I expect you both back here at eight o'clock sharp."

Hector showed them to their rooms upstairs, though Jayne remembered the path from the last time she'd been in Langley. Inside, portals ran to their respective apartments in Nashville and Dublin. "They're temporary, so don't overuse them; it weakens their link. Get some rest. I'll see you in the morning."

Without a word, Hector turned and strode down the hall. Jayne didn't see him enter another room, and she wondered if he was reporting to Amanda first before heading home. Her stomach tightened with unease. A lot of strange things had happened during their training sessions. She didn't think the report would be all A-pluses.

It didn't matter. Just like the portals, this was all temporary. Though she and Cillian hadn't fully mastered her calling him to shift, she felt strong enough to go after Ruger. Tomorrow, she hoped. She was worried about him.

"Good night, Jayne." Cillian was standing by the door that led to Dublin and his flat there.

"Hey. Want to come in for a nightcap?" Jayne asked Cillian. Truth be told, she didn't want to be alone just yet. She worried that thoughts of Ruger being tortured and dismembered would come floating back to her mind, and she couldn't handle that right now.

Cillian seemed relieved by the invitation. "I'll never say no to a drink with you, lass. Lead on."

Jayne threw open the door and stepped through. A happy sigh escaped her lips as the comforting presence of her home surrounded her—the shelves of books, the spicy garlic scent of last night's lasagna, the greenery visible just outside the windows. She didn't realize how much she needed home until this moment.

Being here made her think of Sofia. She couldn't be in Nashville without reminders of her sister. The ache in her stomach was so potent that the relaxed smile slipped right off her face. God, they'd left things in such a bad place. She whipped out her phone, checking for texts or calls, but—nothing.

Jayne shouldn't have been surprised. This had been a really nasty fight. It normally took Sofia a few days to cool off, at least. And even then, there was no telling if Sofia would be waiting for an apology from Jayne first. Jayne still wasn't sure if she would offer it. She wasn't sorry for living her life *or* for working with the TCO. She would never apologize for that.

Cillian's handsome blue eyes lingered on every feature of Jayne's home as if he were trying to memorize it all, and Jayne felt a sense of shared intimacy in this moment. Maybe one day he'd like to come here on a more permanent basis.

After pouring them some red wine, Jayne clinked her glass with Cillian's and took a sip. They were silent for a moment, sitting at the table in quiet contemplation. Then, Cillian said, "Are we going to talk about it?"

"Too much talking, not enough doing," she said, wiggling her eyebrows suggestively.

He laughed but grew serious again. "I mean are we going to talk about that weird icy…presence that gripped you earlier? It was pretty strange, Jayne."

"Oh. That." Jayne drummed her fingers on the table. She could do without the reminder. If that thing was living inside her? She shrugged. "I mean, we didn't exactly think Medb's totem would come without side effects, did we?"

"Aren't you a little worried about it?"

"No. I mean, I *am*, but not right now. We have bigger things to worry about." She gnawed on her lower lip as her thoughts turned again to Ruger.

"Ruger's fine, Jayne. He's a tough bloke. He can take care of himself."

"I know," Jayne said quickly. "I just—once we get him back, then I'll be able to breathe."

Cillian ran a hand down his face. "I'm sorry, I swear I'll get the hang of it soon. This bloody magic thing is still new for me."

Jayne frowned. "It isn't your fault, Cillian."

"Isn't it? Your magic is bang on, Jayne. But every time I'm thrown into the mix, everything is banjaxed."

Jayne's brow furrowed. Generally, she could keep up with his Irish-isms—well, sort of—but *banjaxed* was a bit of a head-scratcher. Before she could ask, Cillian went on, "It doesn't help that I'm shit-scared of all this."

"All what?"

"Being your Rogue?"

Jayne huffed. "You aren't *my Rogue*."

"Yes, I am. You heard Hector! I'm just a tool to be utilized by a Master magician. To be wielded like some kind of weapon."

"Oh my God, Cillian!" Jayne set down her wine and took his large hand in hers. "You are not just a weapon. You are a kind, courageous kickboxer with a heart of gold and a dazzling personality. I liked you before I even knew you were a Rogue. You"—she tapped his broad chest—"are more important than all of this. You know that, right?"

Cillian snorted and took another drink. "Easy for you to say. You're the one who can make me do whatever you want."

Jayne arched an eyebrow. "Oh, really?" She rose from her chair and plopped down on his lap. He jolted in surprise, his hands easily finding her waist as if it were the most natural position for them to be in. She wrapped her arms around his neck and leaned close, her nose brushing against his cheek. "Shall we test that theory?"

Cillian nipped her earlobe, and shivers of pleasure rippled down her body. "Point made. I'm at your mercy."

"Want me to conjure up the castle keep?" she asked, laughing.

"I just want you, witch."

7

ROGUE MAGIC

Jayne stared up at the ceiling of her bedroom, wrapped comfortably in Cillian's strong arms. She couldn't sleep. Her mind kept shifting from thoughts of Ruger to Sofia to that strange, icy presence inside her.

Though she was otherwise perfectly content nestled in the cocoon of Irish bliss, she couldn't just lie there. With a huff, she wriggled out of Cillian's grip, who muttered something about "the black stuff" before turning over and going back to sleep.

After tugging on a T-shirt and a pair of sweatpants, Jayne slipped into the kitchen to grab a slice of blueberry pie. She thought about curling up with her latest read, Robert Jordan's *The Eye of the World*, but even diving into the magical society of the Aes Sedai and the epic search for the Dragon Reborn couldn't take her mind off her worries. She downed her slice of pie in record time, cleaned the dish, swept up all the crumbs, and scowled at her front door as if it had insulted her mother.

On second thought, please insult my mother. It would probably make her laugh, and if anyone deserved to be insulted, it was Ruth Thorne.

Finally, Jayne threw open her door, blinking against the harsh lights that assaulted her eyes.

Yep. The portal was still intact. Good.

Without hesitating, Jayne put on her sneakers and disappeared into the hallway of the TCO. There had to be a library here somewhere. She was, after all, an officer in the Library Division, which made her a bona fide CIA Librarian. It would be an embarrassing misstep for them *not* to have a library. And it was weird she'd never seen it, to boot. Jayne strode down the hallway and descended the stairs, feeling an odd sense of familiarity mingled with unease because it was the middle of the night.

Be cool, Jayne. You belong here. You're not doing anything wrong. She lifted her chin in case anyone watching on their ubiquitous cameras thought she might look suspicious. But so far, there was no one here but her.

After a few minutes of idle wandering, she found a door labeled *TCO Library*. Bingo. There was a biometric fingerprint reader on the wall. *Here goes nothing,* she thought, mashing her hand against the black screen. It glowed green and something *thunked*. She yanked open the door, taking in a breath, eager for the scent of cracked leather and ancient manuscripts.

Instead, all she got was dust. Piles and piles of it. The stuffy room looked like it hadn't been touched in years. There were about ten metal shelves with books tipped here and there, some spine out, some pages out, some stacked—*dear God, stacked*—in piles as if they were manuscripts. A saggy armchair had been shoved in the corner as if someone had thought, *Oh, right, you need a place to sit* and had thrown it in last-minute.

Jayne's mouth fell open in horror and anger. How could the Library Division of the TCO be so careless and disrespectful of books?

She strode inside, intent on setting things right—starting with reorganizing and dusting the shelves—when a shimmering light sparkled in front of her as if she'd stepped through a misty, transparent veil. With each step she took, the room expanded, like a filing cabinet that kept sliding out farther and farther. The dust vanished, and the dilapidated books shifted into a cleaner, more organized array of spines. The shelves stretched on and on, the books multiplying to fill them, until Jayne found herself in a massive two-story hallway filled with gleaming bookshelves from floor to ceiling, with comfortable sofas, long wood tables, and sconces to light the way, ending in a large, mullioned window. A perfect, glorious library, all hidden inside the walls of CIA Headquarters.

Okay. Bonus points for cool, TCO.

"First time?" said a small voice.

Jayne glanced around in bewilderment. For one wild minute, she thought one of the books was talking to her. At this point, she wouldn't have been surprised. Anything was possible, right? It would save on audiobook production, for sure, if the books could narrate themselves...

Focus, Jayne.

"Hello?" Jayne replied.

"Over here." The voice came from across the hall, and as she turned, a reference desk appeared, blending in so well with the shelves that Jayne had glanced right over it before. Behind the desk was a plump older woman with gray hair and glasses, waving at her cheerily. She wore a neon-green hand-knit Christmas sweater, even though Christmas was months away, and Jayne realized she'd seen this woman before. She worked for Joshua, the CIA director's direct report. He was one of the few nonmagical people in the CIA who knew about the TCO.

"Oh, hi." Jayne waved and approached the desk, feeling completely in her element in this miraculous hidden library. "Yeah, this is my first time. I keep expecting Doctor Who to pop up or the Tardis to start making those whooshing sounds."

The woman's brows furrowed.

Jayne cleared her throat. "Never mind. I'm Jayne Thorne." She stuck out her hand.

"I know who you are, dearie." But the woman shook her hand anyway. "My name is Katie Bell."

"Oh my God, seriously?" A surprised chuckle burst from Jayne's lips. "That—that's amazing."

Now Katie was looking at her like she had escaped from an insane asylum. She shifted slightly, and Jayne wondered if she was about to push the button to call security.

"Katie Bell was a character in the Harry Potter series. Got cursed by a necklace. Um, anyway," Jayne plowed on before Katie had her thrown out, "can you help me with some research? I'm looking for anything you have on Rogues."

Katie's eyebrows shot up. "Are you now? In the middle of the night?"

Jayne forced a laugh. "Yep. Can't sleep. Thought I'd make myself useful."

"I thoroughly understand that sentiment. Both not being able to sleep and wanting to be useful. Terrible insomniac, that's me. Let's see what we can find for you." She scooted to the side where a small laptop sat. Squinting, she typed in a few things, then scrolled, chewing on her lower lip in concentration. "I'm afraid we don't have very much, and what we do have is quite basic. It's been...well, wait just a minute. What's this?" Katie typed away for a moment, her face glowing green in the reflection of the screen.

"Do you want me to guess?"

She looked up at Jayne, a bit befuddled. "There are two books on Rogues here."

"Great. Give me the call numbers and I'll go fetch them."

"You don't understand. They weren't here until you asked for them. That's quite strange, don't you think?" Katie tapped a pencil against her lips. "Then again, you are our first true Master in centuries. It stands to reason there are certain magicks that will only be revealed to you instead of the rest of us mere Adepts. Follow me. Let's go find your tomes."

The explanation was so practical Jayne found herself nodding, but part of her wanted to dance. There was so much she didn't know about the magical world, yes, but there was a great deal her bosses didn't know, either. If Jayne's magic could summon books on various topics that no one else had access to? Yeah. This might all just be worth it.

Katie slid out from behind the desk, making it rattle slightly, and led Jayne halfway down the hall. Jayne spied a volume on interracial magical species, which made her think of Cillian, and her curiosity burned within her. She made a mental note to come back here and scour everything she could find.

"Here we are." Katie stopped in front of a set of shelves that crawled up the wall almost all the way to the ceiling of the second floor.

"Oookay. Want me to summon them, or something?"

Katie shook her head. "Don't be daft." She snapped her fingers, and a large oak ladder detached itself from the end of the row and rolled along the track from the corner, stopping right in front of them.

She climbed up with surprising agility for someone her age and hoisted two thick texts from the fifteenth shelf. She brought them carefully down the ladder, handing them to Jayne one at a time. Jayne clutched the heavy tomes to her chest, inhaling the familiar and soothing scent of old parchment and vellum. It smelled like paradise.

Katie snapped her fingers again and the ladder scooted away, replacing itself between the bookshelves.

"You're going to have to show me how to do that," Jayne said, impressed.

Katie placed her hands on her hips. "Bosh. I'm sure you can figure out how to make a ladder behave, Jayne Thorne. Now, that's all we have, dearie. If you can't find what you're looking for in there, let me know. There might be some other texts that mention Rogues. Maybe with your magic combined with mine, we can dig a little deeper and see what we find."

Jayne smiled warmly. This woman seemed like a kindred spirit—someone unafraid of getting sucked into the black hole of research. Jayne rather enjoyed it, actually, and judging by the glint in Katie's eye, she felt the same way.

"Thanks so much," Jayne said. She looked around the library for the best place to sit. She wanted a little privacy while she discovered more about her boyfriend's true nature.

"Oh! Just a second." Katie snapped her fingers again and a pair of shelves on opposite walls parted, opening to reveal a sitting area with two cozy armchairs and a few laptop tables. There was even a tea caddy in the corner, fragrant and steaming, and a plate stacked with crustless sandwiches, scones, and clotted cream.

Jayne beamed. "A secret bookshelf compartment? And snacks? This is the best library ever."

After piling the sweet cream on a raspberry scone and pouring a perfectly made cup of tea, Jayne set up her own little study nook and got to work. There was nothing she loved more than a good research project, especially in the quiet hours of the night when no one would disturb her.

The first book she dived into was an extensive history on Rogues, which provided a fascinating insight into their magic and how, exactly, it worked. Thanks to a nice Moleskine notebook and fine-point gel pen that appeared at her elbow, she took copious notes as she read.

Thousands of years ago, Adepts tried accessing spells to control and manipulate animals. Their hope was to simplify their lives by communicating more easily with their burden animals such as horses and cattle, but the spell went awry. Instead, the magic was infused directly into the animals, making them sentient. Horrified, Jayne read how this magic mutated over the centuries—how Adepts tried warping it to create their own kind of monsters to do their bidding, how these creatures rebelled and destroyed cities, how the beasts waged war on all Adepts to seek retribution for the enslavement of their kind...

Eventually, the wars got so out of hand that the Council of Mages, the governing body of power at the time, harnessed the Rogue magic and distributed it to the twelve Master magicians around the world, housing it inside them for safekeeping. Their magic was powerful enough to keep the volatile Rogue magic at bay, protecting it from being unleashed on the world.

Over time, this Rogue magic was passed on through generations. If the gene presented itself, an Adept could shift forms at will, but only if bonded properly to a Master magician.

"Fascinating," Jayne murmured, running her finger along the page of the book. "So, Rogue magic originally came from mutated animals, then merged with the magic of Master magicians? Neat-o!" Her thoughts turned to Cillian. Technically, he was a descendant of a Master magician! How cool was that?

She continued reading, her brain practically going haywire from the information she was taking in—or maybe from the caffeine.

Depending on the amount of Rogue magic passed down through the bloodline, the text read, *Rogues will possess different traits. Some reside in packs and live in the wild. Others live in a more civilized manner alongside nonmagic cultures. If the Rogue magic is more potent than the Adept magic, the pull to the animal within will be stronger. This will also vary depending on the bond to the Master magician. A connection between Rogue and Master is not always sure. Some Rogues and Masters can perform together with an insecure bond. In the past, some Rogue communities even formed harems to supply multiple Rogues to a powerful Master to ensure the magic could work properly. But if the bond between Rogue and Master is not solidified, then eventually, over time, the bond will deteriorate and collapse.*

Stunned by what she'd read, Jayne looked up from the text, her jaw slack as she processed this. She sifted through a dozen emotions at once—shock and confusion at the thought of multiple Rogues bonded to the same Master, followed by bewilderment at the notion of a bond not being solidified and then deteriorating. The idea that a Rogue and Master could function together even if their bond wasn't secure was strange to Jayne. If the bond wasn't exact, then wouldn't the magic not work at all? Wouldn't there be red flags right off the bat?

But perhaps there already *were* red flags...

A tendril of dread worked its way through Jayne's chest. She tried to shove it down, but she couldn't ignore it any longer.

Was it possible that Cillian wasn't meant to be her Rogue after all?

8

THE END OF THE WORLD AS WE KNOW IT

Gina Labelle clutched the amulet dangling from her neck, focusing on the power emanating from it, the soothing warmth it offered.

Goddess willing, it would provide the power they needed tonight.

The full moon shone high in the sky, reflected in the Seine below. The twinkling lights of Fontainebleau gleamed, illuminating the magnificent architecture of the château like a beacon calling them home.

This would work. It had to.

"Is everything in place?" Gina asked.

Her lieutenant, who had been gazing up at the moon, his dark eyes glassy as if he were transported elsewhere, looked down on her. His face shifted as it always did when he met her eyes. He probably wasn't even aware that he did it, but the subtle wariness in the murky depths of his brown eyes, the tightening of his lips, the slight flare of his nostrils all gave him away.

Gina knew him too well. She saw right through his façade.

"All set." His deep voice was low, too quiet for the others to hear. He dropped his gaze before murmuring, "We do not have to do it this way."

"The time is now," Gina said firmly. "We've waited long enough."

A muscle twitched in the man's jaw, and for a moment, fire scorched in his gaze, reminding Gina so much of another, so very like him, that she faltered—but only for a moment. She matched the intensity of his stare, refusing to back down. The call of the beast within her rumbled, eager to lash out at him for challenging her, but she silenced the creature.

At long last, her lieutenant dipped his head in submission. As Gina knew he would.

"Brothers and sisters," Gina called, summoning her comrades to her side. "The time is now. Join me. Make sure your amulets are at the ready."

Soft footsteps pattered around her as the dark figures formed an enormous circle in the courtyard. Together, they joined hands, and already, Gina could feel the energy humming between them and their shared magic.

This would work. Yes, it would.

Gina focused on each face she knew so well, her keen eyesight able to see so much better than they could. Her nose sifted through each unique scent of magic, each one powerful and singular and *hers*. Every single brand of magic here belonged to her. She'd trained them all. She could almost taste the spell they had concocted together.

So close now.

Around her, the Adepts started to chant, their low voices blending together, the smooth French a whisper against Gina's ears. She drew on the power from the amulet around her neck, which grew hot, pressing against her skin like a brand. But she welcomed the heat—it meant the spell was working.

Pulling on the magic swelling around her, she accessed the Torrent and found the spell waiting for her, layer upon layer of what they had constructed hours earlier. It was a beautiful creation, crafted specifically for this purpose.

It would not fail. Gina was certain of this.

She extracted the spell carefully, her pulse thrumming with anticipation, her blood hot and eager. *Yes. We have waited so long for this. Our freedom arrives today. We will access the grimoire, release the Master within, open the Torrent for good, and assume our rightful place at its head.*

Gina unleashed the spell, sending it skyward, flinging it wide so it could be freed just like her people. Just like magic should be everywhere. Her eyes remained fixed on the spiraling ball of light as it flew toward the moon as if drawn to the illumination, a shooting star of magic. It crackled, splitting through the night air like fireworks. The ground rumbled, and a wide smile spread across Gina's face. Triumph soared through her. It was working.

But the rumbling continued, escalating until Gina found herself swaying, caught off-balance. An explosion echoed in the distance as if a nuclear bomb had detonated. Several people cried out in terror, and Gina's elation iced over into dread.

The ground split, and a host of voices screamed in the night.

Panicked, Gina created a portal and called to her people. Holding it open was nearly impossible, but most of them made it through to safety before the whole area collapsed.

Most of them.

She had no idea why, but the spell had gone horribly, horribly wrong.

9

IT'S GO TIME

Jayne woke alone after copious wacky dreams, including one with her and Cillian flying on some sort of carpet in the sky à la Jasmine and Aladdin, but Cillian was in his wolf form and deathly afraid of heights. It took her a minute to put things together in her sleep-deprived brain. Nashville. Ruger. Sofia. Rogues.

Cillian.

She rolled over to find the bed empty, and an apple on top of a note on his pillow.

See you in the gym.

She yawned, stretched, dressed in yoga pants and a T-shirt, and munched on the apple while some oatmeal cooked. She was disturbed by the night's adventure in the library, that was for sure. She checked her phone, but there was nothing from Sofia.

Jayne scarfed her breakfast, then brushed her teeth, swiped on some ChapStick, tamed her hair into a fluffy ponytail, and took off through the portal for the TCO training center, nodding greetings at the people she passed in the halls.

Hector and Cillian were sparring, and she watched Cillian's moves in admiration. After a particularly enthusiastic roundhouse kick that left Hector sprawled on the mat, she started clapping slowly and advanced.

"Morning, sleepyhead," Cillian called. He held out a hand for Hector, hauling the older man to his feet. Hector raised a brow, and Jayne knew she must look disheveled but didn't care.

"Morning. Let me warm up and we can get to work."

She did some arm and leg swings, lunges, back rotation and leg curls, stretched her neck and arms, then did some air punching and kicking. She winked at Cillian and said, "Bring it, wolf."

"Hold on," Hector said. "You can spar later. I want you to work on shifting Cillian. It's very important that you master this. Your Rogue—

"Cillian," she enunciated.

"*Cillian*," Hector said with a sigh, "is the catalyst for your magic. When you're tracking Ruger, you need to work in concert. I want you to be able to shift him as quickly as snapping your fingers."

"Isn't that going to hurt?"

"I can take it, Jayne," Cillian said. "Let's go."

She danced in place for a moment, then shut her eyes and threw herself in the Torrent. She called Cillian's magic. Nothing happened.

"Damn it." She tried again. This time Cillian's nose grew dark and long and whiskers sprouted, but nothing more. He looked ridiculous.

"Grrrr. Why is this so hard? It's always been so seamless before."

"You're very tense, love," Cillian said, whiskers flickering. "Breathe. Relax. We can do this."

The Torrent greeted her again, swirling around her head, making her feel light and floaty. This time she made Cillian's left hand into a paw, and he yelped in surprise, but nothing else.

Hector was cheerleading from the sidelines. "It's all right, Jayne. Try once more. You can do this, I saw it happen yesterday."

"Argh. We're wasting time and Ruger could be dying! I'm done training, Hector. It will work in the field when I need it to, I know it."

Hector was unfazed by her outburst. He merely crossed his arms, eyebrows raised. "You think you're ready? Prove it. Make your Rogue shift."

"His name. Is. Cillian," Jayne bit out through clenched teeth. Hot blood pulsed through her, a combination of anger and the power of what felt like a million spells she'd practiced over the past twenty-four hours. The exhaustion of the night before wore at her, making her temples throb.

"Make *Cillian* shift. Now."

Still rankled at the thought of making Cillian do *anything*, Jayne straightened and met the Irishman's glance across the training mat. "Ready?" she asked him.

"I was born ready." He flashed her that crooked smile she loved so much.

Slightly softened by his dogged determination—pun intended —Jayne exhaled a soothing breath and accessed the Torrent. She tried to relax, and in response, the river of stars slowed, flowing through her and around her, warm and comforting. There. That was better. She imagined the scent of Cillian's magic, moss and sage, and man, then called on it, drawing it forward like a spell...

A heavy force slammed into her, knocking her backward. Pain exploded in her head, radiating down her body in rivulets of agony. Jayne cried out, her body jerking as if it were on fire.

"Jayne!" Cillian was at her side in an instant.

"I'm all right." As suddenly as it began, the pain vanished, and Jayne heaved a deep breath. The pulsing in her brain lingered, and she squinted through the dark haze clouding her mind. Even if the strange injuries hadn't disappeared right away, she had the ability to heal herself, thank God. Though she wasn't sure if Hector knew that, and for some reason, she wasn't quite ready to reveal this mind-blowing ability of hers to him just yet.

Cillian extended a hand and helped her to her feet. She met Hector's gaze, seething at the smugness in his face. Not a lick of concern in his eyes, oh no. Nothing but *I told you so.*

What a bastard.

"Let's go again," Jayne said, her tone hard.

"Jayne—" Cillian protested.

"It's why we're here, right? The longer it takes for us to figure this out, the worse things get for Ruger. Let's try again."

Before they could take their positions, the doors burst open, and Amanda strode inside, her face paler than usual and her eyes steely. Hector immediately straightened, and Jayne's heart tumbled. She knew from the fierce look in Amanda's eye that something was wrong.

"Training's over," Amanda said tersely. "There's been a terror attack in France. We need you in the field. Now."

She jerked her head, and Jayne, Cillian, and Hector hurried to follow after her. Amanda led them swiftly out of the training room, down the long, bright hall, and into a conference room. A woman with strawberry blond hair awaited them. She bounced on the balls of her feet and flashed a wide grin when she caught Jayne's eye.

"Oh my God, Jayne Thorne!" she gushed, pushing up her glasses before they slid off her nose. "I know all about you! I mean, not like I've been stalking you, or anything, it's just that, like, it's my job to read up on all the TCO officers, and—"

"Cillian, Jayne, this is Quimby Cain, our tech expert," Amanda said. "She's developed some technology that will assist you on your mission." She shut the door and handed them thick file folders. "We received intelligence about a massive earthquake that occurred just outside Paris overnight. The local authorities tried to keep it quiet, but something of that magnitude is hard to cover up. Especially from the TCO, which looks specifically for these kinds of anomalies."

Jayne leafed through the contents in her folder, glancing over various pictures of Paris architecture, headshots of strange men, and detailed notes about local Parisian magic. "What do you mean, 'these kinds of anomalies'?" she asked, but the sinking feeling in her stomach told her she already knew.

"The earthquake wasn't natural," Amanda said. "It was magical —unlike anything we've ever seen. This was much bigger than your standard spell gone wrong."

Jayne's brows crinkled. What could be worse than an Adept spontaneously combusting and bursting into flames? Well, that was a stupid question. Spontaneously combusting and causing a natural disaster would be way worse.

"Do we know who or what caused it?" Cillian asked, leaning forward, jaw taut and eyes fierce. He looked like he could shift into the predator that lived inside him at any moment.

"Our agents found traces of powerful magic nearby," Amanda said. "Their notes are in the file." Her eyes cut to Jayne. "And, to our knowledge, the only thing powerful enough to cause something like this is a Master's grimoire. From our intel, we suspect La Liberté is responsible for this tragedy. We believe they were after a grimoire, and the earthquake was the result of a necromantic spell gone wrong."

Jayne sucked in a sharp breath. Of course, it made sense. That was why she, the CIA Librarian, was here.

"With Ruger going off-grid, and his last known location being so close, we're convinced the events are connected," Amanda said.

Oh God. A hard lump of terror worked its way up Jayne's throat. "You don't think he was there, do you?"

"It's possible. I don't believe in coincidences."

Jayne suddenly felt ill. Ruger was dead. She knew it. That's why he'd been floating so weirdly in the Torrent with his eyes closed, and the spell hadn't latched onto him. These psycho-terrorists used a crazy magical earthquake to kill him, and she was too late because she couldn't get her damn magic under control and save him in time.

"Would they really do something so public?" Hector asked, crossing his arms.

"If La Liberté is behind it, absolutely. This attack sounds like the kind of thing they would do. It sends a message."

Attack. The words rang in Jayne's ears, numbing her whole body. "Were—were there any casualties?" she asked.

Amanda's eyes filled with regret. "The earthquake leveled the commune of Fontainebleau. The French authorities are still searching for survivors, but as of right now...it looks like the body count is near a thousand."

"My God," Jayne breathed. *A thousand casualties.* And she'd thought the Kingdom was bad...

A stunned silence fell. A muscle tensed in Hector's jaw. Cillian jerked a hand through his hair and muttered something that sounded like "pile of shite."

"Why would La Liberté be willing to hurt so many people? That feels...beyond careless. It's provocative. They must realize we'd come for them. That we won't stand by and let terrorists hurt civilians."

"Perhaps that is exactly why they've done this, Jayne. So we will come after them. Which means you and Cillian must be extremely careful. This could be a trap, this could be a spell gone wrong, this could be a new threat entirely. You must ascertain what, exactly, has happened."

Jayne couldn't handle the tension anymore. With a weak smile, she said, "Guess it's time to assemble the Avengers, huh?"

Cillian rolled his eyes, the corners of his mouth twitching. To Jayne's surprise, Quimby let out a high-pitched giggle.

Amanda, however, remained as stoic as ever. "The BMC is doing their best to cover it up," she said. "But there's only so much they can do. As far as the public is concerned, there was an earthquake, nothing more than a natural disaster. The fact that magic was involved has been kept a secret, of course."

"BMC?" Cillian repeated.

Before Amanda could respond, Jayne said, "The Bureau of Magical Control—a division of the General Directorate for External Security. It's the French version of the TCO." Her eidetic memory was coming in handy as she continued her officer training. Reading the known history of the world's magical origins and the various international organizations that governed them was almost fun. Almost.

"Correct. The BMC doesn't want to cause panic among their people," Amanda said. "They've cast a powerful spell on the area to block it from the public while they investigate and eliminate any traces of magic, but it won't last forever."

Jayne clicked her tongue and shook her head. Almost a thousand people had been killed, and the BMC was worried about inciting panic? Too late for that...

Amanda turned to Hector. "How has training been going? Do you think they're ready?"

Hector grimaced, and a swell of fury and indignation rose in Jayne. She answered for him. "We're fine. We can handle this, Amanda."

"I'm asking Hector," Amanda said, her tone steely.

After a pause, Hector said, "We've had some setbacks. But she's mastered the Tracking spell. In fact, she's far surpassed my expectations for it. Shifting her Rogue—Cillian—has proved more difficult. But she is ready for the mission."

Jayne was surprised. Mixed praise, certainly, but she hadn't expected Hector to agree to send them off already. What a damn relief. Training was great, but things were getting real.

Amanda huffed a quick sigh and nodded. "Very well. That'll have to do. Quimby? Perhaps your accouterments will help Jayne and Cillian on their path. Go on."

Quimby beamed, wiggling her shoulders excitedly. "Yay, my turn! Okay, so, Ms. Newport told me we might have to put you in before you guys were totally and completely ready, I mean, fully trained, because, you know, you're like new to all of this, but I know you're a total badass, an actual legend in the TCO, I mean, they should write comic books about everything you've done so far, and—"

"Quimby," Amanda warned, but Jayne was totally charmed. Finally, someone in the CIA who was as big a socially anxious nerd as she was. But to have someone fangirling over her? It was weird.

"Right. Sorry." Quimby dug into her bag and pulled out an elegant gold-and-pearl broach in the shape of a red rose. She grinned at the look of befuddlement on Jayne's face. "There's a camera in the center." She pointed to the apex of the curling petals. "Press this button here." She gestured to an almost invisible button on the side. "It'll send video images straight to us. Totally encrypted and untraceable."

She handed the broach to Jayne, who immediately pinned it to her sweater. "Handy! I feel like a real spy now."

Quimby snickered and dug into her bag again, withdrawing something that resembled a bottle of Sofia's perfume from Victoria's Secret. Just thinking of her sister made Jayne's stomach ache.

"And how is a tiny bottle supposed to help us?" Cillian asked, cocking his head as he scrutinized the glass in Quimby's hand.

"I call it *Magic in a Bottle*," Quimby said, gesturing in the air dramatically like she was pitching the idea for a venture capital investor. Jayne grinned, deciding she liked this girl. "I was able to harness the essence of several basic spells and capture it in this bottle. If you need an extra boost, kind of like jump starting your car, just smash this bottle, and *boom!* You're good to go."

She passed the bottle to Jayne, who ran her thumb along the cool glass. Though it seemed like the tiny bottle held nothing but air, the magic inside thrummed against her skin. She thought of how she and Cillian had struggled to connect. Perhaps this would give them that final push they needed.

"So, it's kind of like…a Poké Ball, but with magic inside instead of a Pokémon?" Cillian asked.

Quimby blinked and offered him a surprised and elated laugh. "Uh, yeah. Exactly!"

"You know Pokémon?" Jayne asked with a raised eyebrow.

"You aren't the only one who knows things." Cillian was blushing, which made him ridiculously adorable.

"I have three more in here." Quimby passed her small satchel to Jayne. The glass bottles within clinked from the movement. "And please tell me how it works for you! I'm eager to develop more projects, so I'd love your feedback. You know, if you absolutely hate it, you can be all, 'Quimby! That was the worst idea ever! Please make something more useful, like a…laser beam that can defeat enemies in one shot, or a storm that creates darkness over a desert for miles.'"

Jayne snorted. "If only those were real."

"Right? Thank you, fantasy writers, for giving me unrealistic expectations about magic."

"Seriously! A Room of Requirement would be great right about now."

They both laughed. Cillian ran a hand down his face and muttered, "What dangers have we unleashed, putting these two in a room together?"

In a clipped tone, Amanda said, "Back to the point, ladies, please? Jayne, your mission is to find Ruger, obviously, but also to discover what La Liberté is after, and stop them before they take any more innocent lives. But tread carefully. We already know they aren't afraid to make a scene or get their hands dirty. Fontainebleau is proof of that."

Jayne immediately sobered, remembering the seriousness of her mission. *Ruger captured. A thousand dead in Fontainebleau. Focus, Jayne.*

"This mission isn't for the faint of heart. So, if you can't handle this, you should leave now." Amanda straightened in her chair. "This is your only opportunity to turn down the assignment."

No one said a word. Hector held Amanda's gaze, his eyes grim, and Cillian stared, stone-faced, at the floor. Even Quimby remained silent, her mouth small as she gazed around the room.

Amanda nodded stiffly. "Good. You will be staging out of Paris, and we've arranged a safe house for you in the city. Fontainebleau is forty miles southeast of Paris. We've set up a one-way portal to the forest outside of the Château. La Liberté and the French government are on high alert right now, so you must be very cautious how you move about the area. We don't want to draw attention to you. There is plenty of public transit between Fontainebleau and Paris. Assess the situation, make your way to the safe house, and await more instructions." She clasped her hands together and glanced over each of them. "Any questions?"

Um, yes, Jayne wanted to say. *I have about a million and a half questions.* But as she watched Amanda, she saw the depths of the older woman's concern. Her vulnerabilities. The slight tightening of her eyes. The thinness of her lips. The clench of her jaw.

Amanda was extremely worried about Ruger. She was putting on an impressive front, all-business and no-nonsense. But Jayne could see through it. She knew, because she was doing the same thing.

Taking the lead, Jayne stepped forward, trying to ignore how much her mind spun from what she'd learned today. "We'll get him back, Amanda."

Surprise and hope glinted in Amanda's eyes for a moment before the impassive mask took over once more. Her voice shook slightly as she said, "I know you will."

10

EN FRANÇAIS, S'IL VOUS PLAIT

While Amanda finalized the portal to Fontainebleau, Hector led Jayne down the hall for some last-minute training. Which made her all the more confused when he took her to the TCO Library.

"Training?" Cillian asked as he trailed behind them. "In a library?"

"Hey, I like to break a mental sweat, too," Jayne said, quoting *Dodgeball*.

Hector ignored them both and strode inside. Like before, the room shimmered and stretched as they passed through the magical barrier. Jayne, who had already experienced this, still grinned broadly at the sight of the shelves elongating. But Cillian stumbled back, snatching a bookshelf to catch himself before he fell over in shock.

"Watch the books!" snapped a curt voice.

Cillian immediately straightened as Katie Bell approached, several jolly knitted reindeer stitched to the front of her lime-green sweater. She swooped in and swatted Cillian's arm, ever the strict librarian tasked with protecting the sacred books of the library.

"If you're going to be roughhousing like some toddler, then you can get out now, boy!" She swatted him again for good measure.

Jayne snorted, and Cillian shot her a dark look.

Katie's expression softened as she looked at Hector. "Lovely to see you again, dear. What can I help you with?"

"You as well, Katie. We're here for the French-to-English dictionary," Hector said.

She scratched her chin. "Larousse? Or Collins Robert?"

"Collins Robert. Unabridged."

"Very well. The newest edition was released only a month ago. Excuse me while I retrieve it for you."

"My French actually isn't that bad," Jayne said as Katie bustled off. "I can probably make do."

"One of the benefits to being a CIA officer, Miss Thorne, is an accelerated immersion in languages. Your high school French will not be adequate for your mission. And this isn't just any dictionary," Hector said, and Jayne could have sworn his eyes gleamed.

When Katie returned with a hefty book that looked as old as the librarian herself, Jayne understood why. Thrums of magical energy wafted from the book, rippling in waves that caressed Jayne's skin.

Jayne shot an accusatory look at Hector. "Oh my God. Is this a grimoire?"

Without preamble, Katie deposited the book into Jayne's arms. "Go ahead, dearie. I think you know just what to do with a book like this."

Jayne caught the book, glancing from Katie to Hector in utter bewilderment. "But I—how—what kind of spells are in it?"

"Just one," Hector said, shoving his hands in his pockets. "A Linguistics spell. It'll make you fluent in French."

A hysterical laugh bubbled up Jayne's throat at the absurdity of it all. "You're kidding, right? This French-to-English dictionary will make me *fluent*? That's a bit obvious, even for you guys."

Hector gave her a deadpan look that would put Amanda's darkest expressions to shame.

Katie, however, offered a light-hearted chuckle. "Oh, dearie, you don't even know the half of it. Years ago, the TCO was like a chicken with its head cut off, losing track of all kinds of spells, putting them in the wrong books and all that. That's when they brought me on board. I set them straight, made them understand it was best to keep things simple. This was the easiest way to remember where all the languages are! German spells in the German books, Spanish in the Spanish, and so on and so forth."

Cillian raised his eyebrows. "That...makes a lot of sense, actually."

"Any day now, Jayne." Hector's voice was laced with irritation, and Jayne realized with smug satisfaction that he didn't like Katie airing out the TCO's dirty laundry like that. She suddenly liked the woman a great deal more, if possible.

Jayne cracked open the book, cradling it in the crook of one arm as she enjoyed the musty, ancient smell of old leather and worn parchment. That must be the scent of the spell, as the book itself was crisp and new. She lifted her free hand and pressed her palm against the page.

Warmth spread through her fingertips as the spell washed over her like a hot spray of water. Energy swelled within her, and myriad shapes and words appeared in her mind. A blast of light burned in her mind, and she jerked her hand back suddenly.

"How do you feel?" Hector asked, his voice sounding strange.

Jayne didn't hesitate. The words came smoothly. Easily. "How would you feel if you were about to be thrown through a magical portal into a strange forest halfway across the world?"

Hector smirked, and Cillian's head reared back. Katie tittered slightly, covering her mouth with her hand like a schoolgirl.

Only then did Jayne realize Hector had asked the question in French...and she had responded in kind.

~

A few minutes later, Cillian, Jayne, and Hector stood in front of a heavy metal door—the portal that would take them to Fontainebleau. Jayne bounced on the balls of her feet, torn between anxious and excited. Yes, she was excited. She was ready to unleash her magic and kick some serious ass.

Lord, who am I? she thought in bewilderment. She had never imagined herself to be the violent type, though she'd been known to take out a heavy bag or two during kickboxing training. But here she was, in the real world, itching to pummel something. Maybe it was her restless magic talking.

"Remember to be wary of that strange presence you told me about," Hector said quietly. "And if you can't call Cillian to shift, then it isn't the end of the world. You're still a powerful Adept, and Cillian can hold his own in a fistfight if need be."

"Thanks, mate," Cillian said, and Jayne couldn't tell if it was sarcasm.

"Good luck, both of you. We're all counting on you." Hector stepped aside.

"No pressure or anything. Thanks for the training, Hector." With a deep breath, Jayne shifted her bag across her shoulder and threw open the door. It was heavy, but her arms hefted the weight easily.

The forest was quiet, and once through the portal, Jayne could feel the disturbance in the air. There were no sounds outside of the two-tone call of sirens. Cillian stepped through after her, on high alert, muscles tensed in case he'd need to spring into action.

The forest was empty. They were alone.

"This isn't creepy," Cillian said.

"You aren't kidding. I feel like we should try to communicate silently or something is going to rise up out of the forest floor and eat us."

"I shouldn't let you watch those horror films anymore, should I?"

"Nope. Let's move out," she replied.

They moved carefully toward the sirens, clambering over large jags in the ground and uprooted trees.

Even though Amanda had prepared them for the devastation, Jayne's breath still caught in her throat, her blood turning to ice in her veins.

Heaps of rubble and cracked concrete surrounded them, unrecognizable compared to the pictures Jayne had studied in the file. The once magnificent château—a castle home to the kings of France, an Italianate beauty whose immaculate grounds spanned more than three hundred acres—was now a mass of fragmented stone. It looked like someone had taken a giant wrecking ball to the entire area. Dust, pebbles, jagged boulders, debris both big and small... And, to Jayne's horror, her eyes were drawn to what looked like severed limbs and burned corpses. The dead who hadn't been accounted for yet.

This was no longer a city. It was a burial ground.

Jayne didn't realize how much the sight affected her until a tear rolled down her cheek. She felt her heart splintering in as many pieces as the château had. Her chest ached and twisted as they moved closer, her shoes crunching against the shattered ruins of Fontainebleau. She tried her best to avoid stepping on human remains, though they were hard to distinguish. Everything looked like ash.

But no matter where she looked, her heart dragged with the heavy weight of what had been lost here. Avoiding looking at corpses only drew her focus to the magnificent architecture that had been completely demolished. She had never been here before, had never experienced the town's beauty in all its glory, but she could still appreciate—and mourn for—what it had once been. As a librarian, she marveled at artifacts that preserved the world's history. Each book, each relic, told its own story, the beauty contained within just waiting to be experienced.

Surveying this broken town felt like she was looking at an ancient text—the Book of Leinster, even—after someone had burned it to a crisp. She wanted to scream.

"What kind of messed-up fecker would do this?" Cillian growled, sounding more like a wolf than a man.

"The kind we're going to curse into oblivion," Jayne said, a solemn vow that she would end the monsters who'd caused this.

The two of them stepped over the remains of the château as they made their way to what they presumed to be the center of town. Beneath the wreckage, Jayne could barely make out the pavement that marked where roads had once been. Now, they were riddled with cracks and fissures as if Hell itself had been prepared to swallow this place whole.

The closer they got, the more apprehension filled Jayne's chest. What had appeared to be a small valley was actually a massive crater in the center of the extensive gardens. And a crowd of well-dressed official-looking people surrounded it. Amanda had mentioned the BMC would be investigating.

"Time to make some new friends," Jayne muttered as they strode toward the officials.

A few men and women were on their cell phones, muttering in hasty undertones. One woman with glasses and a notepad was furiously taking notes while she circled the crater. A pair of men in polos wielded an odd machine that looked like a cross between a camera and a telescope. They aimed the device at the crater and peered through the eyehole, then exchanged a few hurried remarks before repeating the process.

"What're they saying?" Cillian asked, leaning closer to Jayne.

"Oh! Right." She squinted at the officials, focusing on their conversation. Though her ears strained, she couldn't make out any words. "Damn. Wish the Linguistics spell came with amplified hearing. I'd pull one from the Torrent, but I don't want to draw attention to ourselves yet." She nudged Cillian, and they inched closer, trying to appear as if they were inspecting the crater just like the others.

Gradually, Jayne could sift out phrases from the conversations, like *magic signature* and *source of the spell* and *damage to the Torrent.* The last phrase made her blood chill.

She conveyed all this to Cillian in a whisper. "Do you think they were trying to attack the Torrent? I thought they were after a grimoire."

"I don't know. But if that's what they were after, it would make sense that they would interrogate Ruger. He works for the Torrent Control Organization, for God's sake. It's his *job* to know all things Torrent-related."

Jayne bit down on her lip as she considered her options. Everything here felt wrong, and she couldn't place her finger on why. Darn it, she didn't have a choice. She couldn't tell what was going on without her magic. If Ruger had been here during the attack, she needed to know. It was time to use the Tracking spell.

"Cover me. I'm going in."

"You said—"

"I know. But I feel something, and I need to check it out." With a deep breath, Jayne closed her eyes to access the Torrent. Before the river of stars could consume her, a warm hand gripped her forearm. Her eyes flew open as she found herself face-to-face with a dark-haired Frenchman, his brown eyes flashing with a warning.

"I wouldn't do that if I were you," he said.

11

MISSION IMPOSSIBLE

When Sofia agreed to become a consultant for the TCO, her blood was thrumming, her heart pounding with anticipation. Agitation and anxiety flowed through her so potently she thought she might explode.

But a day later, after an exhausting amount of paperwork and questioning—including a comprehensive lie detector test—Sofia was ready for a drink. Or a nap. Maybe both.

Pierce had remained throughout the entire ordeal, and Sofia had to admit the kid had stamina. He never once sat down, his hand flying across the notepad as he took notes. Sofia wondered what in the world was so fascinating about her personal life that he could be jotting down. The thought made her squirm in her seat.

When Sofia stifled her third yawn, Amanda suggested they break for lunch. Within minutes, she had a platter of sliced baguettes brought in, along with fruits and cheeses. Sofia tore into the bread, delighted to find it fresh and warm, as if it had come out of the oven moments ago.

"How are you feeling, Sofia?" Amanda asked, spreading butter on her bread.

Sofia swallowed before answering. "Overwhelmed."

"That's understandable. This is a lot to take in."

"It's not just that. It's...returning to all this. I thought I'd left it behind forever."

"Working with the TCO won't be like practicing magic with your mother." Amanda's voice was steely. Her rigid expression left no room for argument. "I can promise you that."

Sofia nodded. Already, she could tell that much. But she was more worried about what might awaken inside herself.

Amanda's phone rang. She set her bread down and picked it up. "Newport here... Yes." She paused. "Are you certain?" Her gaze shifted to Sofia, who straightened at the look Amanda was now giving. Like a hunter who has just spotted a very large stag. "Very well. Thank you." Amanda hung up, clasping her hands together on her desk. Already, she was back in CIA mode, and Sofia had a sneaking suspicion their short lunch was over. "My team has raided an old Kingdom hideout. They found your father's journal. You probably aren't aware, but the Kingdom stole it from your sister's flat in Dublin. Cillian, actually. Before we turned him."

Sofia sucked in a breath, her heart hammering a warning rhythm. *Wrong wrong wrong,* her pulse seemed to say.

"They're sweeping the area for traps," Amanda went on. "But, assuming it's all clean, we'll need you to investigate and tell us what you find."

It took Sofia a moment to process what Amanda was saying. "I'm sorry, you want me to *what*?"

"It's time for your first field exercise, Sofia." She rose from her seat and turned to Pierce. All she had to do was nod at him and he sprang into action, disappearing from the room in a flash.

Sofia jumped up, too, but in indignation. "If Ruth left that journal there, you can bet your ass it's a trap."

Amanda arched an eyebrow. "We aren't amateurs. If there are any surprises waiting for us, we'll find it."

"If I go to that hideout, I'll be caught or killed," Sofia said through clenched teeth. "You will, too."

"And if we don't, we're no closer to finding Ruth," Amanda snapped. "There are risks to this job, Sofia. I thought you understood that. No more burying your head in the sand. Remember?"

Sofia ground her teeth together so hard her head throbbed. The impulse to run, to grab Jayne and flee far from this place, burned through her like a wildfire.

But thoughts of Jayne reminded her of their heated argument —and how everything had changed. She had no idea where Jayne was. And Sofia had agreed to help.

Fighting her instincts, Sofia nodded stiffly. "Fine. But if we die today, I'll be very upset with you."

Amanda's lips twitched as she led Sofia out the door.

Sofia felt all kinds of uncomfortable when Amanda's driver took them to an airstrip where a private jet awaited them. Amanda had said they couldn't risk portaling to the location in case it alerted any lingering Kingdom Adepts to their arrival. While this made sense, Sofia had never dreamed she'd get to experience such luxurious travel. The spacious cabin had soft, supportive leather seats with plenty of room to stretch her legs or recline as far back as she wished. Food and drinks were only a simple request away, as well as a large television screen, multiple laptops, encrypted Wi-Fi, and even a sofa that converted to a bed.

If Jayne were here, she would crack some joke about how it felt to be a mafia boss flying in style, and where were the gold-plated toilets? The thought made Sofia want to laugh and cry all at once.

Amanda insisted Sofia make herself comfortable, since she had to take a meeting, so Sofia had a pot of chamomile tea brewed and half watched *Dirty Dancing* on the screen in front of her. It was one of her favorites, but she couldn't pay attention. She was scared, and she was worried. She found herself wishing Jayne were there to comment on Patrick Swayze's smoldering looks, but then remembered she was still angry with her sister for those hurtful things she said—and her blatant carelessness in the face of so much danger. Perhaps Sofia *had* done her a disservice all those years in shielding her from the threats of the world. If Jayne had been more aware, maybe she'd exert more caution.

Knowing Jayne, probably not.

The flight to Cleveland wasn't long. Sofia had barely gotten through cataloging all the things that could go wrong, both on this mission and in France, when she and Amanda had to disembark the aircraft. A mild chill whispered against Sofia's skin as she blinked up at the skyscrapers winking in the distance, their lights twinkling against the darkening sky. Sofia had only been to Cleveland in passing during one of their many moves across the country over the years. She inhaled deeply, trying to discern if the air here felt different.

Not really. It felt the same as all the other places she'd been to.

A black Town Car awaited them on the airstrip, and Amanda slid inside without preamble. Steeling herself, Sofia climbed into the backseat next to her.

"My team just finished sweeping the area," Amanda said, her eyes on her phone. "It's clear. We can enter as soon as we get there."

Sofia nodded automatically, though she was not reassured in the least. Knowing Ruth, she had something else up her sleeve. Something the TCO wouldn't anticipate.

Then again, that was why Sofia was here, wasn't it? She straightened in her seat, trying to quell her nerves. In the face of danger, she often warred between fight and flight. Flight almost always won over, but there was still a bit of fight left in her. She tried to conjure that now, but it had been buried so deep she wasn't sure it would awaken.

The driver weaved downtown, past busy intersections and buildings so high they seemed to pierce the sky. At long last, he pulled to a stop in front of an abandoned warehouse, its steel doors locked with chains and spray painted with graffiti.

Sofia was accustomed to grit and grime. She spent years working as a bartender, after all. As she stepped out of the car and surveyed the area, she couldn't deny this was the perfect spot for a hideout. Supposedly abandoned. Easily overlooked. A hideous scrap of forgotten real estate that passersby would be eager to walk right past.

A shiver skated down Sofia's spine as she thought of Ruth and several other members of the Kingdom holed up in this place. How much dark magic had this warehouse seen?

Upon their arrival, a man and a woman wearing bulletproof vests emerged from the warehouse. Amanda waved them over.

"Sofia, this is Tamara and Seo-joon," Amanda said, gesturing to each of them. "They lead our tactical team."

Tamara, all kind eyes and full lips, nodded politely. Seo-joon was intensely handsome and broad-shouldered. He looked vaguely familiar, like she'd seen him on television or something.

Before Sofia could ask, Seo-joon said, "I was there at Medb's tomb." He offered a friendly smile, as if he hadn't just referenced a deadly necromantic event that had nearly ended the world.

"Right." Sofia tried to smile back, but it felt more like a grimace.

"Go ahead and walk us through," Amanda said, adopting her usual authoritative no-room-for-negotiation tone.

Seo-joon led them into the warehouse. The heavy metal door creaked loudly, and Sofia took in an expanse of rusted metal walls and storage nets hanging from the sturdy beams supporting the ceiling. Several cots lined the room, and heaps of trash sat in clumps as if the members of the Kingdom had left in a hurry. Some belongings had been left behind: clothing, knapsacks, books, and various papers. Several TCO officers dressed in black were tagging items and scanning them with strange devices Sofia had never seen before. The air smelled pungent, ripe with a mixture of aromas that tickled her nostrils. The most potent of them all was hot iron and rotting violets, so intense it almost made her eyes water.

Ruth Thorne. It was impossible to ignore, as much as she wanted to shove the horrifyingly familiar sensation from her mind. A flood of memories returned to her, memories of Ruth submitting her to all manner of cruel and barbaric experiments to test her magic in the name of "the greater good." And Sofia, too young to know any better, had allowed it because she had loved her mother and wanted nothing more than to please her.

Until Ruth had gone too far and tried to sacrifice Jayne's life for the sake of a spell.

Sofia pushed the memories down deep. She would unpack them later. But for now, she needed a clear head. She took a steadying breath and reminded herself that while Ruth was a sick and twisted creature, she wasn't here right now.

The thought, while small and feeble, still gave her some semblance of comfort.

"We've swept the area for all sorts of spells," Seo-joon said as he gestured to the room at large. "Nothing has given off any kind of magical frequency…except for the journal."

Sofia's spine went rigid as she recognized her father's journal lying on a metal desk in the far corner of the warehouse.

"What kind of frequency can you detect from it?" Amanda asked.

"Nothing we've encountered before," Tamara said. "It's cloaked somehow. Whatever is blocking it, it's powerful."

"It's Ruth," Sofia said at once. "It has to be. She wouldn't leave something like that just lying around. If she wanted it that badly, she wouldn't leave it without it a reason."

"We've found no trace of Ruth Thorne's magic," Seo-joon said.

Seeing Sofia's brows furrowed with confusion Tamara clarified, "What he means to say is each Adept's magic leaves a certain signature, almost like a heat signature. Our tech logs each signature and stores it in case we need to reference it later. And the magic we've found within that journal doesn't match anything we got off Medb's tomb."

Sofia frowned. Ruth's magic would've been all over Medb's tomb. It was possible she had gotten another Adept to inspect Henry Thorne's journal, but that was unlikely. Ruth didn't like sharing secrets with others. And God knew she was powerful enough to take care of this task herself.

"Do you mind if I take a look at it?" Sofia asked, glancing from Amanda to Tamara.

Amanda's eyes sparkled as if she'd been waiting for Sofia to ask. She waved a hand to the desk in invitation, and Sofia approached it slowly, every ounce of her tingling in anticipation. Her skin prickled, her instincts still screaming at her that this was a trap, that Ruth was waiting around the corner for her to slip up. But upon hearing that Ruth's magic wasn't on the journal, Sofia's curiosity overwhelmed her fear. She cocked her head at the journal as if it were a puzzle to be solved instead of an enemy to be feared.

She'd known as soon as Henry Thorne asked her to give the journal to Jayne that there was more to it than she suspected. But Henry had never been included in Sofia's magic lessons with Ruth—whether by his request or Ruth's insistence, she didn't know. Sofia had always assumed Henry hadn't possessed magic. To her, the journal had been a sentimental gift.

Now, she wasn't so sure.

She reached the desk, which seemed to thrum with energy. A swell of power curled from the leather cover, and Sofia reached out a hand to catch it.

"Careful—" Seo-joon said in warning, but it was too late.

Warmth tickled Sofia's fingertips, and she closed her eyes, suppressing the urge to recoil from the magic rising within her.

Her mother's voice rang in her ears: "To begin again, the world reborn."

Cold pinpricks of dread danced along Sofia's arm, but she sensed a second presence within the magic. Another voice layered behind Ruth's. A deeper, gentler voice.

"The magic of the earth unlocked."

Sofia inhaled sharply, withdrawing her hand. She hadn't heard that voice in years, and the sound of her father's warm tone made her eyes sting and her heart twist with agony. God, she missed him. His tight bear hugs and his gentle smile, the scrunched-up focused look he got when figuring out a puzzle.

"What is it?" Amanda asked tentatively.

"My father," Sofia said in a tight voice. "I can sense him here."

"You have his blood in you," Amanda said. "Ruth doesn't. Perhaps that connection allows you to tap into whatever power this journal holds."

Blood. Sofia remembered Ruth teaching her that blood was one of the conduits to the Torrent, back when it had been harder to access. There had been many lines Ruth was willing to cross to get more power, and cutting open her daughter was one of them. Sofia had the scars to prove it.

Before she could overthink it, Sofia tugged out one of her hoop earrings and used the point to prick her forefinger. When a bead of blood welled up, she let it drop on top of the journal. Someone gasped behind her, but she couldn't tell who it was. The crimson droplet splashed on the leather cover.

Magic snapped in the air like sparks from a fire. A shimmering curtain whispered against Sofia's skin, causing goose bumps to rise on her arms and neck. Heart racing, she leaned forward, squinting as the journal seemed to shift on the desk. The embossed title, which read *Entreaties and Proverbs*, rearranged itself to read: *Henry Thorne's Guidebook to Magick and the Torrent.*

"Oh my God," Sofia murmured. She snatched up the journal,

her hands shaking, and flipped through it, her breaths coming in short spurts. Instead of the usual vague and confusing adages she remembered, the pages now consisted of complex formulas and mathematical equations along with disjointed phrases and notes, all in her father's slanted handwriting. It looked nothing like the journal she'd held on to for all these years.

Sofia's head was spinning, her heart hammering. Her blood had unlocked the journal. Ruth hadn't left it behind as a trap—she'd left it behind because it had been useless to her.

For once in her life, Sofia had achieved what Ruth Thorne hadn't.

12

STRANGERS IN THE NIGHT

Jayne struggled to process what had happened. Not only had this guy snuck up on her—and Cillian—but he had just ordered her not to access the Torrent. She scrutinized the man, debating whether to dropkick him or shout colloquial French invectives in his ear. He was so. Very. French. The long curling dark hair, the perfect lips, the eyes the color of a caramel latte. He needed a shave. He was tall and lean and wore a clean-pressed suit that looked like it cost more than Jayne's monthly rent. All that was missing was a white linen jacket thrown over one shoulder and a cigarette clamped between his fingers. He had a badge on a lanyard around his neck that read *Agent Lowell, BMC.*

"Mademoiselle. Monsieur. This is a closed scene. I must ask you to leave immediately," the man said, dropping Jayne's arm. His English was flawless, with a slight French accent.

Recalling what Amanda had drilled into her, Jayne straightened and said, "We're government officials from the United States—"

"I know who you are," Agent Lowell said. "You have no business here. Please leave."

Her mouth clamped shut. He knew who they were? How? This mission had been as tight-lipped as a deadly state secret.

Jayne was determined not to be put off by this strange man who seemed to know more than she was prepared for. And who possibly had prettier hair than she did.

"We've come a very long way"—she gestured to the giant crater—"to examine this disaster and report back to our superiors. Much like you, I presume."

The man's eyes narrowed. "This isn't your jurisdiction, nor have we requested your help."

"This directly relates to a case of ours."

"That is not my problem. It's time for you to leave." He reached again for Jayne's arm as if to escort her physically from the scene, but Cillian stepped forward, his bulky arms crossed, highlighting his impressive biceps.

"Who *is* this arse?" he asked Jayne, though his steely gaze was fixed on Agent Lowell.

Lowell's chin lifted. He wasn't as muscular as Cillian, but he was slightly taller. He lifted the lanyard away from his chest. "Agent Tristan Lowell of the BMC. That stands for—"

"We know what it stands for," Jayne said, mimicking his patronizing tone from earlier.

Lowell flashed a grin, revealing teeth that were just a little too white. "Good. Then you'll know we have the situation well in hand."

Jayne let her arms fall against her thighs. "Look, we're not here to get in your way. We just want to make some observations. I need to know what's going on. I will stay out of your way, I promise."

Lowell's thick eyebrows lowered. "Forgive me if I don't just take your word for it. The people behind this attack made similar promises, and look what happened."

Her blood ran cold. "You know the people who did this?"

Lowell said nothing. His cold gaze shifted to the crater, and something hardened in his expression.

Jayne tried again. "We're on assignment, just as you are. If you force us to leave, we'll just keep coming back. You wouldn't want us drawing unnecessary attention because you're too stubborn to read us in, would you?"

Lowell's stare drilled into Jayne, and within her, her magic swelled to life, an automatic defense, as if it detected the threat. White sparks flew. This was new, this physical manifestation of her magic. She hoped she wasn't glowing. But she wasn't about to let this man know she was unsettled. *Knock it off,* she told her magic, and the sparks fizzled out.

"We can work together on this," she said quietly. "Let us help you."

Lowell shook his head. "We are not a team. And you need to keep that magic under control. You're drawing enough attention showing up unannounced as it is."

Quoting Aragorn, Jayne said sagely, "This day does not belong to one man but to every man. Let us together rebuild this world that we may live our days in peace."

She expected an Amanda-esque glare, but to her surprise, Lowell rolled his eyes. "You are misquoting. It's 'This day does not belong to one man but to *all*. Let us together rebuild this world that we may *share* in the days of peace.'"

Jayne's jaw dropped. Did he just one-up her *Lord of the Rings* reference? She ran the quote through her mind again, seeing it on the page as if she was reading it, and damn if he wasn't right. Nerves, probably, messing with her head. Or this idiot. Lowell was smirking again, and it made her blood boil. She was already on edge, this guy was in her way, and *no one* out-quoted her.

Get it together, Jayne. Don't let this guy get under your skin. You have a mission.

Clearly sensing her indignation, Cillian touched her shoulder and stepped forward. In a low voice, he murmured, "We want the same thing as you, mate: to bring whoever did this to justice. We saw similar acts of violence in Ireland only a week ago."

Lowell's gaze shifted to Cillian, his brows furrowing. "Ireland? You mean what happened at Rosses Point?"

Jayne's magic swarmed inside her like a hive of bees, making chills go up and down her spine. *Wrong, wrong, wrong.* What the heck was happening?

Cillian stiffened. "What happened at Rosses Point?" Fear laced his tone, and Jayne wondered if he had friends there.

"A massive tidal wave hit the village." Lowell frowned. "You claim to have been in Ireland, yet you haven't heard about it. How is that possible?"

How indeed? Jayne's mouth felt dry. Why had Amanda not told them about this? Her brain worked furiously, trying to put the pieces together...

Icy dread filled her as everything suddenly made sense. Necromantic magic was performed. Natural disasters followed.

Rosses Point was mere miles away from Medb's tomb. Something from that night must have caused the tidal wave. Maybe some kind of residual magic...or the Kingdom had retaliated after their defeat.

Ruth had retaliated. From what Jayne knew of her mother, she didn't accept failure. And Jayne wouldn't put it past her to destroy a village in a fit of rage. The woman was a monster.

This was not good.

Though her tongue felt heavy in her mouth, Jayne forced herself to say, "Yes. Yes, we knew about it, and we know who was behind it. We think they may be behind this, too." It was a stretch —Amanda had told them La Liberté had caused the earthquake, not the Kingdom. But if this natural disaster was the result of powerful magic, Jayne would bet her left arm that Ruth was nearby. That must be why she felt so odd, so off-balance.

She felt Cillian staring at her, but she forced herself to level a stern look at Lowell. His caramel eyes assessed hers as if he could see right through her fibbing.

"The Kingdom, you mean?" Lowell asked.

"Yes. Is that your assessment as well?"

In a very French manner, he idly waved his hand in the air. "Perhaps. *D'accord.* Do what you must. But don't touch anything, and whatever you do—" He grabbed Jayne's arm again, drawing near enough for her to get a whiff of his scent, an infuriatingly appealing combination of vanilla and soap. "Do *not* cast any spells." His voice was barely above a whisper. "This area has seen enough magic, and there are…complications when you try to access the Torrent."

What kind of complications? Jayne wanted to ask, but anger took over her thoughts. Lowell's grip on her arm made her want to flip him onto his back. She clenched her teeth and shot him her best *fight me* look.

"Get your hands off me," she enunciated. "Or I will break your arm. I don't need magic to do that."

Infuriatingly, his eyes danced with amusement at her threat. "I very much doubt that, mademoiselle."

He released her arm and took a step back, inclining his head. "I'm sure we'll be seeing each other again soon." Without another glance, he sauntered off, leaving Jayne fuming and Cillian on alert beside her, growling lightly under his breath.

When Lowell was a safe distance away, Cillian said, "What the hell was that?"

"A total douchebag, that's what," Jayne grumbled.

"No, I mean, what happened at Rosses Point? You didn't tell me."

Jayne blinked, remembering there were more important things than the French asshole. "Right. Um, that was a lie. I didn't know about the tidal wave. But…it must have been the Kingdom. After what happened at Medb's tomb."

Cillian ran a hand down his face. "God, that's effing brutal. How—how could we not know? We were just there!"

"It must have happened after we left. I'm particularly annoyed with Amanda for not bothering to mention it." Jayne remembered something Amanda had said: *The TCO looks specifically for these kinds of anomalies.*

Oh yeah. They totally knew. And they hadn't mentioned it at all.

Irritation mingled with confusion and helplessness, forming a chaotic spiral in Jayne's mind. High dark magic equaling some sort of natural disaster was terrifying. It was almost as if the Torrent was fighting back—but innocents were dying. All the magic she knew was in concert with the world, not antithetical. She was so far behind…

"Okay. One thing at a time." Jayne rubbed the spot where Tristan Lowell had gripped her, counting her breaths to clear her head. "Let's see what info we can get from here, and we can ask Amanda about Rosses Point later." She didn't want to believe what Lowell said about using spells in the area, but if there was even a chance he was right, she couldn't risk it.

Cillian's gaze was distant, his jaw hardened in that look that said he wanted to punch something.

Jayne touched his shoulder. "You good?"

Cillian nodded, though she could feel how distraught he was. "It's just…all of this is a bit much sometimes, you know? The Kingdom, some of them were my friends, at least until I found out what they were up to. And if they did this, I don't—" He broke off, shaking his head. "I feel like I never knew them at all."

She rubbed his arm. "I get it. Really, I do." If anyone understood the gravity of realizing someone you thought you knew was completely different, it was Jayne. Sofia had magic. Ruth had magic. Everything in her life had been a lie. The reminders twisted inside her like the fatal slice of a knife. "All we can do is keep calm and carry on, right? Or is it keep calm and crack on, as the Irish would say?"

He smiled, but it didn't quite reach his eyes.

Jayne leaned in and pressed a tantalizing kiss to his lips. His cheeks turned pink, and he offered a lopsided grin that made her insides turn to mush.

"I know." She smiled impishly at him. With a wink, she whispered, "Later."

Cillian's eyes crinkled as that mischievous gleam Jayne loved so much lifted his features. "Minx."

Jayne bumped his hip with hers, unable to contain her giggle as she stepped back. Suddenly feeling hot, she peeled her long hair away from her neck and resisted the urge to fan herself.

She froze when she caught sight of a figure standing across the crater, staring at her. It was Lowell. His gaze was solemn and unreadable, but his eyes bore into Jayne as if he could set her on fire with just a look.

Trying to ignore the feeling of unease that rippled through her, Jayne turned away, forcing herself to focus on her assignment and not on the strange and insufferable man still watching her.

13

LET THEM EAT CAKE!

Being unable to access the Torrent certainly put a damper on things. But if Jayne was good at one thing, it was research. She figuratively put her librarian cap on and set to work. She activated Quimby's tiny camera, eager to document everything and send it to the TCO. Her magic burned within her, impatient and demanding, and the longer she pushed it down, the more itchy and agitated she felt.

She hadn't realized how much she fell back on her powers until she couldn't use them.

Not that she fully believed that Lowell fellow when he claimed she shouldn't cast a spell. But she was too nervous to try, especially in front of all these witnesses.

The warm presence inside her was a comfort. Even if she couldn't reach the Torrent, she still had her magical instincts, and she trusted them.

For instance, something inside her moved when she stepped inside the crater. A burst of blinding white light filled her vision, and the river of stars rippled in her mind, distorted and abnormal from what she was accustomed to. When she hopped out of the crater, the vision vanished, and Jayne teetered on her feet. Her head throbbed, a sickening reminder of the ocular migraines she used to endure. Seeing the Torrent like that disoriented her. It was like she'd been looking at it through a kaleidoscope.

Something was very wrong here.

Cillian, who had been inspecting the edges of the crater, approached her, his brows furrowed in concern. "You all right?"

"You know how we thought someone was trying to attack the Torrent? I think they might have succeeded."

"What do you mean?"

"It feels...off. Broken. I can't explain it."

Cillian pressed his lips together as he surveyed the crater. "Do you think someone cracked it open again? Like you did in Nashville?"

Jayne chewed on her lower lip. She highly doubted it. Ruger had implied that every magical creature on the planet had felt it when Jayne opened the Torrent the first time.

But...was it possible for someone to *rip* into the Torrent? A smaller, more controlled occurrence? Something that could stay under the radar?

That's stupid, Jayne chided herself as she glared at the massive crater in front of her. *This is anything but under the radar.*

"I told you not to do that," said a voice.

Jayne whirled and found Tristan Lowell standing casually a few feet away from her. How the hell did he keep appearing unnoticed?

Jayne clenched her fingers into fists. "Do what? Breathe? Exist?"

"No. Use magic."

"I didn't."

"Do not lie to me. You did. I felt it."

Jayne stilled. He'd felt her magic? But it had been an accident. She hadn't intentionally accessed the Torrent. The defense sounded weak in her mind, so instead she said, "How am I supposed to investigate what happened to the Torrent if I can't even inspect it?"

Lowell stepped closer to her, and the sudden movement made her take a fighting stance.

"Back off, buddy."

"Stand down," he snapped. "How do you know something happened to the Torrent?"

Jayne arched an eyebrow. "I *felt* it. Why, didn't you?"

Cillian snorted from behind her. To her surprise, Lowell smiled. As if he enjoyed arguing with her. The bastard.

"I know you don't trust me," Lowell said. "And you don't like me." Humor danced in his eyes. "That much is obvious. But believe me when I say that casting spells here is unwise, Jayne Thorne."

Jayne opened her mouth, then shut it. He knew her name? He had said he knew who they were, but she had never introduced herself. His belittling nature had eliminated all desire for pleasantries.

Unease prickled along her skin. Something was wrong.

Instinctively, she reached for the Torrent to summon a Block spell, hoping to shield herself and Cillian from whatever danger lurked nearby…

As soon as Jayne touched the Torrent, a heavy force slammed into her, knocking her off her feet. With an ungraceful "oof," she fell on her ass, her chest burning and her breath coming in sharp wheezes as if she'd run a marathon.

What the hell?

As she climbed to her feet, still winded, shouts erupted from those surrounding the crater. Explosions of light filled the air.

"Jayne!" Cillian was at her side in an instant, helping her to her feet. "What—"

The ground rumbled. Jayne yelped and clung to Cillian for balance. What was happening? Another earthquake? If this was an aftershock, it was damn strong.

"Holy hell," Cillian whispered.

Jayne followed his gaze and found an eerie green light surrounding the crater like a luminescent dome. Her heart stopped for a full beat, and in other circumstances, she might have made a joke about extraterrestrial beings coming to join the investigation.

But judging by the shouts still echoing around her, the quaking under her feet, and the magic sparking in the air, she knew exactly what this was: an attack by La Liberté.

Her muscles tensed, and she raised her fists. She might not be able to use her magic, but she sure as hell could do some damage. *Let them try,* she thought angrily. *Let them try to take me on.*

Her gaze snagged on a figure moving nearby. Tristan Lowell was taking off his suit jacket. He discarded it on the ground like it was worthless, and swiftly removed his cuff links and rolled up his sleeves as if he were about to get his hands dirty. Was he planning on fighting, too?

"Don't do it, mademoiselle," Lowell admonished. "You will regret it." The look he gave her wasn't quite sympathy... It was pity. And something more.

It pissed her off, the way he met Jayne's gaze with solemn, apologetic eyes. "I did warn you," he said, his hands lifting into the air as he closed his eyes.

Jayne's rage was momentarily quieted by utter shock. No. No way. He wouldn't dare...

The ground exploded. Dust and dirt swirled, creating an eerie haze over the crater. White lights danced in the air, making Jayne's head throb. People appeared from nowhere, shouting. Fighting broke out around her.

Lowell moved toward her just as she lunged at him, ignoring a sharp pain in her arm, right where he had been gripping her bicep earlier. She whipped her body in a spinning round kick, which should have taken him under the jaw and splashed him onto his ass into the crater, but Lowell easily sidestepped her blow as if he knew where she was going to move before she did it. She stumbled, and dizziness overtook her. The white flashes from the crater grew stronger.

It was as if the Torrent itself had altered her magic, throwing off her center of balance.

"Son of a bitch," Jayne growled, her head spinning. She feinted to her right, threw a roundhouse kick toward his thigh, but Lowell wasn't buying it. He grinned once, feral and mean, then saluted before bolting. He was gone before her spin finished, leaving her in her guard stance, alone.

Cillian lurched to a stop by her, blood dripping from his nose. It was clear he wanted to chase after the traitor—considering his behavior, Jayne hardly thought he was truly a BMC agent—but when Jayne swayed, he grabbed her shoulders instead.

"Are you okay? Give me a second, I'll hunt his ass down."

"Don't," she rasped. Her stomach churned, and she closed her eyes against the swell of nausea rising within her. All she knew was if Cillian chased after Tristan, the fake agent's crazy terrorist friends would kill him. And she couldn't protect him from that. Not when she felt like a truck had run her over.

Lowell had joined a crowd of jubilant figures that stood in the distance. One of them held a massive French flag. He hoisted it in the air and shouted in a powerful voice, *"Nous serons libres!"*

Jayne's blood chilled at the words: *We will be free.*

Lowell glanced over at her, too far away for her to read his expression. But she had no doubt he looked on smugly. He'd fooled her—impersonated an agent, made her think he was on their side.

But he was the enemy. He was a member of La Liberté. He'd only been investigating the devastation *he* had caused. Or waiting for her to show up, knowing that the TCO would send representatives to examine the destruction.

Jayne's anger coursed through her like a brutal current. She wasn't sure it was possible, but she hated Tristan Lowell even more. If that was even his real name.

But this was a good thing. He was an enemy now. Which meant she had permission to thoroughly kick his ass without feeling guilty about it.

And she vowed to do just that. Once she could see clearly. The dizziness had been joined by a raging fire in her arm, and she honestly just wanted to sit down with a cup of tea and an ice pack.

"Jayne, we need to get you help." Cillian's arms were around her.

Jayne shook her head. "No, I just need to cast a Healing spell and I'll be fine." Her eyes crammed shut, and a brief green glow enveloped her hands...before it flickered and died.

She grunted, exhaling sharply. Her body tensed as she tried again.

Nothing happened.

"Oh my God," Jayne panted, trying to keep her wits about her as the pain increased. "Cillian, the magic, the Torrent...it's *gone.*"

14

CIPHERS AND CODES

Sofia spent a quiet night alone in her Nashville apartment, eating chicken salad and trying not to dwell on the pressing emptiness around her. Sure, a few days ago, she'd thought Jayne and Cillian would be staying with her and they'd be having a grand old time together. Never in her wildest dreams would she have pictured herself estranged from her sister and best friend, having just signed on to join the TCO, and spending her evening poring over the magical journal of her previously assumed dead but actually alive father.

Several hours and a few glasses of wine later, Sofia had only managed to scribble notes about various mathematical equations that made her head spin in conjunction with the alcohol in her system. It was obvious Henry Thorne had written his journal in code—and for good reason, given that Ruth might have tried accessing it.

But it made the information contained within all the more valuable.

As requested, Sofia reported to Amanda's office the following morning, still impressed by this portaling process that allowed her to walk out her front door as if it were a hotel room linking her to the TCO. In Langley. Six hundred miles away. She took a few wrong turns but finally found the door to the office. Pierce sat at the desk with a cup of coffee and his ever-present clipboard.

"Nice to see you again," Sofia said politely. "Is she—" She gestured to the closed door.

"She's ready for you." Pierce offered a gentle smile that rattled Sofia's nerves. God, did she really look that feeble right now? She straightened, trying to appear more confident.

"Thanks." She strode forward, then hesitated. "Um...just out of curiosity, is Pierce your first name or last name?"

He opened his mouth to respond, but Amanda's door swung open.

"Good, you're here." Amanda jerked her head. "Come in."

Sofia hurried inside, and Amanda shut the door behind her. She waved to the chair opposite her desk before sliding into her seat, steepling her fingers together and looking very much like a stern principal. "Please tell me you've found something in the journal."

Only then did Sofia notice the harrowed edge to her voice, the subtle dark tint to her gaze. Something was wrong—something that made her sharper than usual, if that was possible.

Sofia sank onto her chair. "Unfortunately, no. He's coded the information in the journal somehow, and I'm definitely no cipher expert."

"Talk to Pierce. He can get you set up with our cryptanalysts." Amanda's dark eyes seemed to probe her for further information.

"Right. Okay. And there was one other thing that kept popping up." She pulled out her father's journal from her purse and slid it across the desk. She opened it to the page she'd bookmarked. "This symbol appeared on several pages. Does it mean anything to you?"

Amanda stared at the symbol, which looked like three triangles alongside each other. She blinked once. Twice. Three times.

Her face remained completely impassive. After a long moment, she said softly, "What do you know about the Guardians?"

"Of the Galaxy?"

"Of the Torrent."

Right. Of course they weren't talking about space super-heroes. At least Jayne would've been proud of her reference. If they were speaking.

"I've never heard of them," Sofia said honestly.

Amanda tugged on the chain around her neck, pulling it from underneath the layers of her button-up shirt and jacket. On the end of her necklace was a smaller version of the exact same symbol.

Something jolted within Sofia as if the trinket called to her, whispering in her ear. Her mouth felt dry as she asked, "What does it mean?"

"It's a symbol of the Guardians."

"And...are you one of them?"

"No. But my husband was."

Sofia bit her lip. She didn't know much about Amanda's husband. Just that he had died long ago, and it still haunted her.

"Before we continue this conversation, I need you to see something." Amanda tapped the keyboard, and the screen filled with photos. Some were satellite views; some were from the ground.

Each one sent a coil of ice traveling up Sofia's spine. A city submerged in water. Buildings shredded. Homes destroyed. "Dear God," she whispered. "What *is* this?"

"Rosses Point in Ireland," Amanda said. "Right after we left Medb's tomb."

Sofia's gaze snapped to Amanda's. "You think it's related to the necromantic spell?"

Amanda nodded. "That's not all." She pressed a few more buttons, and the views changed. "Look at this."

Sofia's stomach knotted with dread even before she looked at the photos. A different city, but the same kind of devastation. A leveled city, nothing more than hunks of concrete and debris. "Where is this one?" She was almost afraid of the answer.

"Fontainebleau, France."

Panic and terror welled up in Sofia's throat. "You mean where Jayne is?"

"That's why she's there, Sofia. To investigate. Some of those pictures are from her."

Relief loosened the tension she felt, but only a fraction. "Why are you showing me this?"

"We think the incidents are related. I've seen something like this before. Years ago. Before the Torrent had fully opened, there were various pockets spread around the world."

Sofia had heard this term before. In Miami, the witch she'd met with had referenced the same thing. "I've heard of those. Access points to the Torrent, right?"

"Yes. There were factions of magicians around the world who were trying to find a way to siphon the pocket's magical energies and use it as their own sort of mini-Torrent. There were others who sought to protect the portals. We call them Guardians."

"Did they succeed?" Sofia asked in a hushed voice.

"For the most part, yes," Amanda said. "We had a few incidents over the years, but the portals have remained protected. But now I'm beginning to wonder if La Liberté has indeed found a way to open a pocket, drain the Torrent's energy, and use it for themselves."

"So, what, like bottling up a jar of magic?" Sofia asked.

Amanda nodded. "It won't last long, depending on what they're using it for. But this presents dangerous opportunities for our enemies. If they can siphon that much magic and use it at the right moment, they could potentially tap into Master level power. They might burn from it, but these people have shown themselves more than willing to die to achieve their goals."

"What about the Kingdom? They are responsible for what

happened in Rosses Point, right? Does this mean they have access to these pockets of magic?" Urgency laced her tone. "Does Ruth have this knowledge?"

Amanda frowned. "Does Ruth know about the existence of the pockets, and of the Guardians? Most certainly. Does she know where they are? As far as we are aware, no. Only the Guardians themselves know the locations of the pockets."

"That's not what I meant."

"You're asking if Ruth Thorne has the magical ability to break open her own pocket into the Torrent? Unknown. I do know that La Liberté and the Kingdom are not allies. They hate each other. They are not working together. Which could help our cause."

Not working together yet, Sofia thought. If they were seeking the same thing, it was only a matter of time before their allegiances were aligned.

Sofia's gaze fell to the pictures on Amanda's phone. "I've been to one of those pockets, Amanda. And it didn't look anything like this. All this destruction...that's not normal, is it?"

Amanda's eyes gleamed, her mouth curling into the faintest of smiles. "I was wondering if you'd put the pieces together. No. Not normal. And you're right, they are different. The pockets are natural entrances, almost like caves that lead to the Torrent. What La Liberté is trying to do is *force* an opening. Like drilling into the Torrent. It creates a disruption in the magic of the Earth, hence the natural disasters. The energies are rebelling against it. They are sensing an attack against the Torrent."

A chill skittered down Sofia's spine. "You speak of it as if it's a living thing."

"The magic? Or the Torrent?"

"Both."

Amanda's smile widened. "Maybe they are." She stood from her desk. "At any rate, if Henry Thorne knows something about the Guardians, this makes it even more imperative that we unlock whatever is in his journal. If anyone knows how to protect the Torrent from these attacks, it's the Guardians." She picked up her phone and pushed a button. "Come on in, Pierce."

In seconds, Pierce, eager as ever, opened the door and stood at the threshold.

"Pierce, take Sofia to see Jameson." Amanda gestured to the journal on the table. "Cracking that code just became our number one priority."

15

HELLO, PARIS

"This is bad, Cillian. They broke the Torrent."

"Or they broke you. You look awful. Let's get you out of here."

Away from the center of the destruction, Jayne started feeling steadier. The pain in her arm receded, and the dizziness fled. While she sat on a fallen tree and caught her breath, Cillian worked his own magic and ferreted out the real BMC officials, who'd set up their field operations by the river.

It was a moot point. The BMC officials in Fontainebleau either didn't know anything or didn't want to share, and after La Liberté's little stunt, they refused to talk entirely. They weren't even impressed by Jayne's flawless French, which was very off-putting. But she couldn't blame them for being so tight-lipped, especially after that debacle with La Liberté. No wonder the officials were so shaken. They probably thought she was one of them because she'd spoken with Lowell. And he'd probably done that on purpose, the bastard.

Jayne used her cell to send an encrypted, coded message to Amanda, letting her know what had happened, that La Liberté had made a move, and asked for instructions.

The response came immediately.

We're on it. Get to the safe house. Report in from there.

Jayne still felt groggy, but it had now dulled to the manageable post-migraine hangover instead of the pulsing, throbbing, *I'm-going-to-die* agony. Her arm ached, though. Whatever had happened to her and her magic, she only hoped it was isolated to this singular incident.

She didn't dare consider what she would do if it wasn't.

But when she wasn't thinking of the incident with her magic, all she could think of was: *Ruger is imprisoned by these monsters.* What kind of horrors were they inflicting on him? They clearly had no respect for human life. Or the Torrent. Or magic itself.

Disposing of Ruger would be nothing to them.

A cold tendril of dread had taken up residence in Jayne's gut, twisting and wrenching until she felt almost as sick as when her magic had been sucked out.

Cillian came to her side in an instant, as if he sensed her weakness. "What's wrong?"

"We need to get to Paris. Do you think the trains are still running?"

He lifted his head and sniffed as if the breeze would give him the answer.

"I think so, but we're going to have to hoof it to the station. They have this whole area shut down to all private vehicle traffic."

They walked past the ghostly ruins of a once breathtaking city. Jayne had seen pictures. The château, specifically, had been a sight to behold. The thought of never again being able to marvel at such an architectural beauty made Jayne want to weep.

All that history. Gone in one selfish, destructive act.

Cillian took her hand, his calloused palm rubbing against hers. He seemed to read the fury in her face, because he said in an undertone, "We'll make them pay. I swear it."

Jayne nodded stiffly. "Damn right we will."

They got lucky; the devastation hadn't reached the train station, and the next departure was only ten minutes away. The pearly white train station looked more like an old-fashioned city hall than a bustling hub of public transportation. She and Cillian purchased their tickets and sat down to wait. Jayne bent over, her head in her hands as she circled through one agonizing thought after another—Ruger, tortured and bleeding, his magic completely drained, his body dismembered and broken just like the crumbled remains of Fontainebleau...

"Jayne." Cillian nudged her, and she realized the other passengers were boarding.

"Thank God," she whispered, unable to take the restless tension any longer.

Which made the sluggish process of boarding the train, listening to the conductor's soothing message in French, and waiting for the vehicle to move forward all the more agonizing.

She found Cillian checking his phone every five seconds, his thick brows knitting together. Jayne elbowed him gently, grateful for something to take her mind off her crippling fears.

"What's up? Texting your other girlfriends?"

Cillian managed only a half smile. "You remember Aldie and Ned? From the pub in Dublin?" When Jayne nodded, Cillian went on, "They keep texting me, asking me when I'll be back. Amanda gave me a story to feed them about getting some fancy job that requires me to travel a lot, but they know that's utter shite. Dublin is my home, and I worked all kinds of shitty jobs to stay where I was." He rubbed his forehead, suddenly looking years older. "When we were together, we were always acting the maggot, you know? But still...they're my mates. And they know me. They were there for me when—" He broke off and clamped his lips shut.

"When what?" Jayne prodded, placing a hand on his arm, which had gone tense.

Cillian exhaled, deflating slightly. "When Aaron—I mean,

Aaró—died. I know he was trouble, but he was like family to me, and I didn't know all that he was up to. So, the loss hit me hard. And Aldie and Ned, they were there when I needed them." A muscle pulsed along his jaw as he clutched his phone tighter in his hand. "I just don't know what to say to them, is all. They'd see right through any lie I gave them. And I don't want to lie."

Jayne looped her arm through his and put her head on his shoulder. She pressed into his bicep, trying to massage away some of the tension rippling across his body. "I'm so sorry. I can't say I can fully relate. Sofia and I moved all the time, so we were never in one place long enough to make friends like that. But it was still hard leaving behind the ones we did make." She brushed a kiss against his shoulder, enjoying the way his soapy linen smell mingled with the scent of fresh, sexy man and filled her nose. "You've had a rough time of it, my wolfish Irishman. Tossed around by the Kingdom, then switching sides, and leaving your home." Her hand worked its way up his back and she fiddled with the ends of his hair. "Is there anything I can do?"

Something deep rumbled inside him, making her toes curl in her flats. "I'm sure I can think of something." His hand found her thigh and slid up. And up.

Jayne yipped lightly as he found a less-than-appropriate area to explore. Even through the denim of her jeans, a delicious explosion of heat traveled up her legs and settled low in her stomach. Her cheeks flamed, but she couldn't deny the longing that swept over her. She missed having the hard muscles of his body pressed so perfectly against her. And Lord knew she needed to get out of her head for a minute.

Before things got too out of hand, though, Jayne snatched his arm and gave him her sternest expression. "We're undercover, remember? I'm pretty sure getting it on in public on a moving train—"

"Would be fun, yes?" Cillian leaned in and nipped on her lower lip.

"—would draw a bit too much attention." Jayne's voice went a bit strangled as he kissed her again, his tongue exploring hers. God, he was too sexy for his own good. And hers, for that matter.

Cillian laughed, his blue eyes gleaming wickedly, but he withdrew. Jayne wasn't sure if she was grateful or disappointed. "Fine. But as soon as we get to the safe house, I'll be all over you."

"Deal." Jayne winked at him before diving into her purse to pull out *Ella Enchanted*. Normally, she liked a denser read, but right now, she was in the mood for something light and fluffy. Something to take her back to childhood. To simpler times. Besides, Ella's voice was so carefree and amusing, even in light of troubles like ogres and curses. And she was a rebel. Jayne could really use some of that optimism right now.

She hadn't realized how quiet Fontainebleau was until she and Cillian stepped off the train and emerged in the bustling train station of Paris. Hordes of people surrounded them, arms and limbs bumping in a way that made Jayne deeply uncomfortable. She couldn't help but wonder who might be lurking, waiting to hurt them.

Great. Now she was getting as paranoid as Sofia.

A tiny piece of her anger toward her sister melted. If that's what Sofia had been feeling all these years, Jayne understood her frantic nature a bit more.

They followed the signs to exit Gare de Lyon. Jayne was eager for a breath of fresh air. And food. Lots of food.

When they made it aboveground, Jayne's mouth fell open.

"Well, helloo, you sexy beast."

Cillian tweaked her chin. "You talking to me or the city?"

"No offense, beast, but Paris has got you beat for the moment."

She couldn't help herself, she spun in a circle like a romance heroine, taking it all in. The magnificent buildings and architecture. The narrow roads and cobblestone walkways. The throngs of pedestrians expertly weaving through traffic. Shops were crammed next to each other, so close together Jayne could hardly tell where one stopped and another began. On top of them were rows and rows of apartments with iron balcony railings that made Jayne want to perch herself atop them and gaze over the city like a morose Jane Austen heroine.

Gare de Lyon looked more like a palace than anything else, with ornate pillars and breathtaking sculptures that towered over the courtyard below. And the great sweeping buildings overlooked the streets that split in several directions like the never-ending branches of a tree. It wasn't just a left turn or a right turn like in the States. It was like five left turns in one, or three sections of a right turn here, each one lined with buildings. The many avenues looked like the spokes of a wheel, endless and devastatingly confusing. As overwhelming as it looked to Jayne, the pedestrians and vehicles seemed to navigate it just fine.

A steady thrum of chatter and footsteps surrounded them. Though most of the passersby spoke French, Jayne caught a lot of English and other world languages as well. She itched to step through a portal into the TCO's magical library and grab some more of the dictionaries so she could eavesdrop properly. Her eyes flitted around as she struggled to take it all in. Tourists snapping photos. Vendors selling food and souvenirs. Children laughing. The smell of hot bread wafted in the air, mingling with the scent of cigarette smoke. Bodies pressed against her, so close they were almost suffocating.

Jayne felt dizzy for a moment from the sensory overload. She grabbed Cillian's arm, her eyes closing as she took several deep breaths. The itch to access the Torrent, just to give herself some breathing room, was so severe that she almost reached for the Torrent to cast a Block spell...against pedestrians.

Yeah. Not a good idea, Jayne.

What was wrong with her? She wasn't usually claustrophobic. Just severely introverted. She'd never liked large crowds, but they'd also never made her feel so lightheaded before, either.

The aftereffects of what happened in the Torrent. That was all it was. Surely, Jayne would feel like her perky self again soon.

The dizziness didn't abate when she stood still. Oookay. Maybe this was a more basic problem.

"Food," she announced. "Before we go any farther, I require sustenance, preferably in the form of pie, or I'm going to drop right in the middle of this adorable street."

"We're in Paris, love. How about crêpes instead?" Cillian pointed to a small crêpe shop across the street.

"Crêpes are perfection." Her stomach growled in response, making him smile. "After a quick bite, we'll settle into the safe house. Then, we can call Amanda and see what our next move is. I want to find him, Cillian. I want to finish this and go home." She was dying to send out the Tracking spell and finally locate Ruger, but after their run in with La Liberté, her magic still wasn't feeling right. The kind of weirdness she felt after drinking some barely expired milk or spending too much time in the sun. Dazed and a little unsettled.

Cillian touched her elbow. "He's fine, Jayne. He's valuable to them. I'm sure he's alive."

"I know," she said quickly. "It's not just that. I'm worried about my magic, too. Something just feels off. It's better—not as bad as in Fontainebleau—but I can't shake that wrongness I felt by the crater."

"You just need some sugary pastry goodness to set you right." Cillian guided her to the crosswalk, where they waited alongside dozens of other pedestrians to cross.

Jayne peered up and down the road, amazed at how much foot traffic there was. Downtown Nashville was always crowded with tourists and students on foot, though most people in the city relied on a car. But in Paris, in addition to the vehicles, there were tons of walkers, joggers, bicyclists, plus a handful of those buzzing about on their Vespas, which was the most European thing Jayne could think of. If she were to live in Europe, she'd want to own a Vespa. She'd have to add a storage compartment on the back for her books, of course.

When they entered the crêpe shop, warmth and the smell of hot fruit swelled around Jayne like a comforting embrace. The tension in her mind eased almost immediately, and as they took their seats, she relaxed slightly.

"I can't believe we're in Paris," she muttered, removing her jacket and draping it over her chair. "It hasn't really set in yet. In other circumstances, this would be the most romantic vacation ever."

"Well, maybe we'll have to come back then. Just you and me. No mission." Cillian's eyes warmed. "You can visit all the libraries you like."

Jayne pressed a hand to her chest. "A man after my heart."

She helped Cillian decipher the menu, which was in French, and ordered two crêpes with Nutella and banana while he ordered one with eggs and chitterling sausage.

After the attendant took their order and menus, Jayne asked, "Do you even know what chitterling sausage is?"

Cillian shrugged. "It's sausage, isn't it? What's not to like?"

Jayne bit back a laugh. Even though this was her first time in Paris, she knew from the cautionary tales of others that you had to be careful with French food. They certainly had weird delicacies here. Then again, Cillian was from Ireland. They had strange food there, too.

Jayne devoured her crêpes as soon as they were in front of her, moaning with delight and not even caring if she had Nutella all over her mouth. But Cillian took a bite of his and went as still as death.

"Something wrong, chitterling? I mean, darling?" she asked between mouthfuls.

"Not gonna lie," Cillian choked, taking a big gulp of his water. "This tastes like pig shit. Like, straight from the farm."

Jayne sniffed. "Smells like it, too. Stands to reason, considering…"

He glared at her, his face full of suspicion. "Do I want to know what I just ate?"

This time, she couldn't help herself. A laugh bubbled from her throat, and she nearly choked on her food. "Probably not. The look on your face…" She broke into another fit of giggles.

Cillian groaned and dropped his fork with a loud clatter. "God, woman."

Still chortling, Jayne slid her second crêpe onto his plate. "Because I'm feeling generous."

Cillian was laughing now, too, his eyes crinkling in a way that made Jayne's heart flutter. "I'm never trusting a thing you say. Ever."

"Probably a wise move. I don't trust myself most days."

16

OPEN DOORS

After finishing their food and consulting several maps, Jayne and Cillian made their way to the metro station that would take them to the arrondissement that housed the flat. Jayne found herself grateful for the giant "M" signs that led them in the right direction, charmed by the scrolling wrought iron with the stylized *M* on the white background. They descended the stairs, and the air chilled slightly from being underground.

"Hang on," Jayne muttered, pausing to inspect a complicated diagram of the metro lines. After consulting the map on her phone to remind herself where the safe house was located, she nodded once. "Right. This one." She pointed to the green line. "Green is line 12, to gold, line 10. We're heading to Le Motte-Picquet–Grenelle. We'll switch at Sevres–Babylone."

"How can you tell? It looks like gibberish to me."

"Just add it to my never-ending list of mysterious witchy skills."

Cillian muttered a few choice swear words as they tried to follow the signs to the right line. Thankfully, Jayne's ability to read French kept them from getting lost in the endless tunnels and winding turns, but even she had to admit it was a rather complicated system. Some signs indicated they should go upstairs, but once they did, there was no indication of where the green line was.

At long last, they found the right platform—only after Jayne checked the map about a dozen more times. Cillian muttered something that sounded a lot like "fecking Paris" as they sat on the bench to wait for the metro to arrive.

The beastly engine echoed from the depths of the tunnel before the roar intensified and the vehicle screeched to a halt before them. Jayne and Cillian joined the mass of people waiting to step on as the doors slid open. Shoulders and elbows bumped against Jayne, who clung to Cillian's arm as if it were a lifeline. Good God, there were so many people. And they really didn't care who they elbowed in their haste to climb onto the metro.

The seats were taken, so Cillian and Jayne stood, holding on to the poles for balance instead. The metro shuddered and lurched forward with such speed that Jayne yelped, clinging tightly to the silver pole beside her. She wasn't experienced in riding metros or subways. In Nashville, she'd either walked or taken the bus. Beside her, Cillian stared out the window as the murky gray tunnel whooshed past.

Less than half an hour later, they reached their stop and bustled off the metro with the other pedestrians. They followed the exit signs—which were much easier to follow than the signs directing them to the metro line—and they each breathed a sigh of relief once they were finally aboveground again.

After a brisk five-minute walk, they stood outside an elegant, towering building with marble pillars and iron balconies lining windows that reflected the setting sun. The road was narrow, crammed with cars on either side, but the area was definitely upscale. This certainly wasn't the slums.

"You sure this is the right place?" Cillian asked, arching an eyebrow.

"It's the address Amanda gave me. Come on, let's check it out."

They strode through the carpeted lobby, which smelled strongly of coffee, past the chaise sofa and soft armchairs surrounding a fireplace, until they reached the elevator. Or rather, the lift. Jayne's key was labeled 204, so they took the tiny lift up and located their flat.

She unlocked the door and stepped inside, her curiosity nearly overwhelming her. She stood in a vast, open living room with a gray sofa and matching chaise lounge. Directly in front of her were floor-to-ceiling windows with delicate white drapes, framing a balcony with a stunning view of the Eiffel Tower. Silently vowing to spend hours on that balcony reading, Jayne turned her gaze to the bookshelves and bit back a grin. Whatever mystic voodoo Ruger had done on her Dublin flat had been mimicked here as well, and her entire personal book collection filled the shelves. She spotted a breakfast nook with a small table and chairs and a small kitchen next to it. Everything was beautiful and...*excessive*, from the plush rugs on the floor to the awe-inspiring art hanging on the walls.

Swallowing down a bubble of incredulous laughter, Jayne strode down the hallway, counting just one bedroom. Either the TCO knew—and didn't care—that Jayne and Cillian were sleeping together, or they had a doghouse somewhere just for him. Jayne entered the expansive bedroom, finding a large four-poster bed with white drapes matching those in the living room, and a stunning gold bureau that looked like it belonged in Versailles. She registered no surprise when she pulled open the drawers and found clothes in her size.

She took a very quick shower, changed into yoga pants and a silky top, then joined Cillian in the living room and pulled up the program on her phone that allowed her a secure face-to-face with her boss. There was only one problem. When she reached into the Torrent, she couldn't access the spell to make the line secure.

"What took so long? And why are we not encrypted?"

Amanda asked immediately, avoiding pleasantries entirely. She looked even more tired than when Jayne had left her only hours before.

"I need you to do it, if you can," Jayne said. "Something is happening to my magic."

"What?"

"I'll tell you in a sec. Can you do the spell?"

Something warbled slightly on the screen as Amanda cast the spell to mask their call. "Done. What happened?"

Jayne filled Amanda in on everything they'd seen in Fontainebleau, including descriptions of the La Liberté members, specifically, the fake officer Tristan Lowell.

"Quimby's cameras worked perfectly. We were able to pull stills from your shots and have facial recognition running on everyone there. Now. Can you perform *any* magic?" Amanda asked when she was finished.

"I haven't tried anything significant yet. I wanted to wait until there weren't any witnesses, just in case something went haywire. But the Torrent is misbehaving. It's like the damn Tesseract."

At Amanda's blank look, Jayne shook her head. "No. Haven't tried anything more complicated than the Encryption spell."

"Try again. Something simple. Something physical. If you can do the basics, I wouldn't worry about what happened in Fontainebleau. It could have been a stress response."

"And if I can't do the basics?"

"Try."

Jayne shut her eyes and envisioned the Torrent. It appeared to her, but seemed to be flowing sluggishly instead of its usual pleasant swirling movement. She pulled a simple Shield spell from the river of stars and layered it over Cillian's body. At his suddenly confused expression, Jayne released the spell. "Well, I can do some magic, but it's very weak. Weird. Nothing feels right, Amanda."

Amanda hesitated. "All right. You've done a lot of new magic in the past few days. We don't have any more news on Ruger's location, but we're getting closer. Let's give you a bit of down-time while we plan our next steps. Rest. Recharge. And stay in touch. If you absolutely need to leave the flat and defend yourself before we find a solution, use the bottles Quimby gave you. Even if your magic is drained, those should provide you the boost you need for more complex spells."

"Right." Jayne would've used them earlier in the fight at Fontainebleau, but again: witnesses. Smashing a bottle wasn't exactly covert.

"I'm worried about Ruger," she said. "These La Liberté people are pretty scary."

"Ruger has trained for this. He can withstand a lot, Jayne. He's a fighter."

"So you think they *are* trying to attack the Torrent? Why?"

"Not attack, but force their way in. They want to tap directly into the Torrent's source of magic."

"Is that even possible?"

"We don't know. It's never been done before. But Sofia and I are working on another solution. We're trying to find other allies to help us protect the Torrent."

Jayne's fingers clenched more tightly on her cell phone, and she felt Cillian tense next to her. "Did you say Sofia?"

"Yes. She's working with us as a consultant."

Shock and rage mingled in Jayne, a cyclone of fire and ice. "Oh, she is, is she?" Her tone was biting, and she knew the rage had won out. All that bullshit Sofia had spouted about Jayne risking her life working for the TCO, and now she was doing the same thing? The nerve...

"Get some rest, Jayne," Amanda said. "I expect another report from you tomorrow."

Jayne said goodbye and hung up, her hands shaking. "God, it never stops, does it? As if worrying about Ruger isn't stressful enough. I've been fretting over Sofia ever since our fight, and she's going behind my back and doing the same thing she's pissed at me for!" Her hands curled into fists on her knees.

"Maybe it means she understands why you're doing it," Cillian offered.

"Then why hasn't she called me? Why hasn't she apologized? She's still radio silent, as if *I've* done something wrong. She's giving me the silent treatment, trying to guilt me into apologizing first. Not even a text." She made a gagging noise, part groan and part scoff.

"Jayne." Cillian took her hand, threading her fingers through his. With one swift movement, he slid her onto his lap, her legs dangling over the side of the sofa. "I think you need to shut off that big brain of yours for a moment or two."

"Easier said than done. It's been going haywire since we got here."

Cillian gathered her chestnut hair and gently swept it over one shoulder, then leaned in to press his lips against the side of her neck.

"Okay, that's...*oh*." She tensed when his tongue met her skin, all thoughts of Ruger and Sofia and Amanda vanishing from her mind. A slow smile spread across her face. "I like the way you think, you handsome devil." She wrapped her arms around him as he reclined her backward onto the sofa, poised above her with his arms braced on either side of her. As they shed their clothes and their bodies tangled together, Jayne found the sweet release she'd been longing for.

～

Later, she felt Cillian shift against her.

"Do you love me?" she asked.

"What?"

"You call me 'love' a lot. I was just curious."

He sat up, rubbing his eyes. "Bloody jet lag. What do you want me to call you? 'Mate'?"

"Well, that's sort of loaded, isn't it?"

The flush on his cheeks was quite becoming. "Mate as in friend. Not like you're my wolfish destiny person. Ah, bollocks. This is weird."

"I know. It's just...we haven't known each other very long, and there's a lot of strange stuff happening. We haven't exactly talked about things, and there's all this friction with you being my boyfriend and my 'Rogue' and stepping in to save me like my knight in shining armor, which I don't need, by the way, though it is cute, and...I don't know. Ignore me. I'm babbling. Yes, jet lag is mean."

He drew her close. "I certainly don't want to be anywhere but here, with you, right now. Is that enough?"

"I'm not asking for anything here, wolf. But I need to know that you aren't going to be leaping in front of any spells to save me, okay? I can handle myself."

"Like you did earlier? When you fell down in front of a terrorist? What, I'm supposed to walk away and leave you prone on the ground, twitching like a centipede?"

"Ha ha. I'm serious. This is real, Cillian. Life or death. Your whole world has been upended. Your friends are worried about you, you've pledged loyalty to the spy organization of another country, I'm—"

"You're Jayne. You're magical, you're funny, you're cute. You like books, you like pie. You like me, as far as I can tell. Your sister can be a bit difficult, and our boss is a right soith, but I'm having a good time here. Are you?"

"I am," she said solemnly. "That's why I don't want you to get hurt. If we're in a situation, and I can't shift you, and things go south, I would never forgive myself if something happened to you."

"You let me worry about that. You just focus on getting as strong as you can. We're good, Jayne."

He snuggled her into his arms and put his head back on the pillow.

Neither of them slept.

17

SPIES, SPIES, AND MORE SPIES

Lars watched the lights go out in the flat on the second floor where Jayne Thorne was staying. He tightened his coat more firmly around himself against the chilled autumn air. He despised surveillance. But it was what he was good at.

Retreating to the far end of the street corner, he pulled out his phone and called the Head. He strongly disliked talking to the formidable woman directly, but with Aaró and Alarik dead, there wasn't much of a choice.

"To begin again," said the cold female voice.

"The world reborn," Lars recited dutifully.

"What information do you have?"

"You were right. The TCO is here. The witch, and the Rogue. No sign of Ruger Stern. It's possible the rumors we've heard are true, and he's been taken. If La Liberté have him, it means they are a step ahead of us. Our enemies are closer to the grimoire than we feared."

"And Fontainebleau?"

"I couldn't get a proper reading. Whatever they extracted, they didn't leave any residue behind. They could have the grimoire."

The Head was silent for several moments. Lars waited patiently, his eyes still fixed on Jayne Thorne's window.

"We cannot fail this time," she finally said. "No matter the cost, we must retrieve the totem first. Far too much hangs in the balance."

"I agree."

"What do you propose?"

Lars faltered. "Me?"

"After the disaster in Ireland, I am in need of another lieutenant, Lars. Impress me."

Lars thought quickly. "Desperate times call for desperate measures. We have a powerful ally under our thumb. I say we use him."

More silence. Lars's pulse raced with the terror that he'd said the wrong thing, that he'd possibly given himself a death sentence.

At long last, the Head said quietly, "Send Blaine to run interference. Slow them down as best you can. In the meantime, I'm a step ahead of you. Our ally is already here."

The last thing Lars heard was an ear-splitting roar before the call disconnected.

18

GOTCHA!

When Jayne woke up, she checked to see if Amanda had messaged her with more news on Ruger, and, finding nothing, decided to take advantage of the lull to explore the glorious balcony. She brewed some green tea with mint from her emergency stash, pulled her familiar tattered copy of *The Hobbit* from her shelves, and slipped onto the balcony to immerse herself in Middle Earth. Cillian joined her an hour later, blowing a bit on a cup of steaming coffee.

"You look awfully comfortable," he said.

It took her a moment to transform him from Gandalf into Cillian. She closed the book. "Needed a distraction. No word from Amanda yet?"

"No. You need some activity. That will keep your mind off the mission for a few."

She grinned at him. "Oh yeah? What did you have in mind?"

He leaned close to her and whispered against her lips, "Spar with me."

She whooped with laughter and jumped to her feet. "Bring it, wolf."

They pushed the fancy furniture off to the side of the living room and warmed up with some stretches. It definitely wouldn't be comfortable getting smacked on her ass without the cushioned floor mats of the training center, but she needed the workout. Conveniently, her gym bag had magically appeared in the flat along with her books, so she had all the gear she needed. Jayne tightened her ponytail before donning her gloves. Hopping in place to get her blood going, she cocked a brow. "Don't hold back, Pine."

He gave her a feral smile. "I never do."

He swung first, but she was ready for it, ducking low and aiming a blow to his shins. He stumbled for a moment before righting himself and coming at her with unrestrained intensity. After a moment, they settled into a rhythm. Strike, dodge, parry. The sound of their gloves thudding and the force of Jayne's fists and legs connecting with his shoulders, chest, and thighs provided an oddly cathartic release. Her blows came harder and faster. Sweat dripped down her face and neck. Loose strands of her brown hair clung to her face. Heat rushed in her cheeks, and she knew she was a blotchy mess.

But she didn't care. The release was soothing, despite the aches in her body every time she took a hit.

When they were both covered in sweat, they switched gears. "Sending a Block spell your way," Jayne warned him. "Brace yourself."

"Do your worst."

Jayne laughed and tentatively reached for the Torrent. To her immense relief, the river of stars gleamed into view, though it seemed fainter than usual. She found the Block spell and threw it toward Cillian. He merely staggered back a step, as opposed to getting flung across the room like she'd done with Hector.

Cillian beamed. "Your magic is still there."

"Barely." Jayne rubbed her arm, where a dark bruise had formed from Tristan Lowell's nasty grip. "At least it's not volatile like those crazy Adepts who burst into flames. Let me try a few more." She summoned another Block spell, a Shield spell, and then a basic Attack spell. All of them shot forward with slightly less fervor than normal.

"Damn." Jayne rubbed her forehead. "I'll need a lot more power than that for the layered Tracking spell." She bit her lip, her gaze falling to the bag Quimby had given her.

"It's why we have them," Cillian pointed out. "I say we use it. If it leads us to Ruger, it'll be worth it."

"And if it doesn't, we have two more to use." Jayne nodded, her mind made up. "All right. First things first." She strode forward and grabbed Cillian by the collar, dragging him toward the bathroom.

He stumbled, laughing. "Where to, my lady?"

"You stink. We both need a shower. Might as well conserve water, right?"

After a hot shower and more than a few naughty moments that left Jayne feeling more breathless than her workout had, she dressed herself in a tan sweater and navy leggings along with matching tan ankle boots. She tied her hair back into a loose ponytail, not wanting it to get in her face should they come across a baddie or two, and returned to the living room to grab Quimby's bag.

Cillian shortly joined her, wearing a white T-shirt with a striped blue button-up shirt over it, along with jeans that hugged his hips ever so nicely. Jayne smacked his ass as he walked by, and he chuckled.

A discreet beeping came from the table in the dining room where her laptop was waiting.

"That must be Amanda."

She hurried over and accepted the call, happy to see Amanda looking downright excited.

"We've confirmed Ruger is in France, within a hundred miles of your location. It's time for you to try tracking him. Are you ready? Has your magic returned to full strength?"

"The body is willing, but the mind… Unfortunately, my magic is still weak. It's very strange, Amanda. Do you think the spell La Liberté cast at Fontainebleau rubbed off on me?"

"I don't know. Without testing, there's no way to be certain. All right. We should bring you home and—"

"No, no, please. Why don't I try the spell, and if it isn't strong enough, use one of Quimby's bottles? It's meant to enhance my abilities, right?"

Amanda's lips thinned. "Those are for emergencies."

"This qualifies. Finding Ruger is an emergency. I'll let you know how it goes. Jayne Thorne, over and out." She slammed the lid of the laptop closed, glanced up at Cillian. "In case she says no… Okay, I'm going in."

She stood and shook her arms to loosen them, ignoring the pain in her bicep. She closed her eyes and envisioned the Torrent. Still sluggish, like it was thick with magical mud, but flowing well enough. She looked for the Tracking spell, and it was nowhere to be found.

"Damn."

"Any luck?" Cillian asked.

"Nope. Plan B. The spell might not last long, so we'll need to act quickly," Jayne said, opening her eyes and withdrawing one of the glass bottles from the bag. It hummed inside her palm, seeming eager to be unleashed. Before she could second-guess herself, she chucked the bottle to the floor, and it smashed, sending shards all over the linoleum. Jayne's neat-freak brain immediately screamed, *Glass! Clean it up now!* But before she could act on the urge to sweep up the shards, they rattled and lifted in the air, sweeping into a wide circle as if a funnel cloud had emerged from the bottle. The pieces of glass withered into dust that gathered into a red ball of magic, and a burst of power filled Jayne's body, overwhelming her senses. She felt it spreading through her nose, her ears, her eyes, her entire body, tingling in every inch of her.

Jayne drew in a breath, and her lungs seemed to expand, filling her more than usual. She felt open. Unrestrained. Powerful.

"Oooh. Me likey."

She closed her eyes, and there was the Torrent, vibrant and green as ever. In a flash, she found the layered Tracking spell and grabbed it, focusing on everything she knew about Ruger. His mighty form, his deep, soothing voice, the trimmed goatee, the scar on the side of his crooked nose, the scent of his magic, earthy and warm like rich soil in the summer...

Then, he was there in front of her, but...*not*. His image was distorted, and he was smaller than normal. Squinting against the bright lights of the Torrent, Jayne realized he was in a chair. No, he was *tied* to a chair. The features of his face shimmered like bad reception on an old television.

Show me, Jayne urged, quelling the rising panic inside her at the sight of Ruger so helpless. *Show me where you are.*

Obeying her command, the Tracking spell shifted, revealing a wide bridge that crossed over a familiar river. The Seine sparkled in the light. On the other side of the river, impossible to miss, was the Louvre Palace, stretching wide across the expanse of the city. Nothing there, but a spot halfway down the bridge glowed...

Something smacked into Jayne, sending her sprawling on the living room floor. She groaned, shaking her head from the faint throbbing of being so violently shut out of the Torrent. Just like what had happened in Langley, training with Hector.

"You all right?" Cillian put out a hand to help her up.

"I'm fine. That was super weird. I got booted from the Torrent again." She closed her eyes, trying again, but the river of stars was gone. Not even a flicker of light. Inside, she felt cold and empty. No warm familiar presence. No spark of energy or power. But as she searched within herself, that same odd, icy feeling slithered to life, climbing to the surface.

Not now. She forced it down and offered a nervous laugh. "Probably just pushed myself into too much, too soon. But it doesn't matter. I know where he is, but he's cloaked. If my magic is still weak, we'll need the rest of these." Jayne grabbed Quimby's bag and swung it over her shoulder. The remaining two bottles clinked from within. Excitement thrummed in her veins as she used her phone to send a coded message to Amanda.

"We're coming for you, Ruger."

Jayne and Cillian took the metro, navigating through two lines before they reached their stop. After climbing several sets of stairs, they emerged aboveground, warmed by the rising sun and the usual crowd of chattering pedestrians. The towering marble buildings and iron balconies served as a constant reminder that Jayne was very far from home. Vendors and restaurants lined the streets. The air was filled with exhaust fumes and cigarette smoke and the delicious lingering scent of hot baguettes from a nearby cafe.

On the way to the bridge, Jayne bought a few chocolate croissants from a small pastry shop, claiming she couldn't kick anyone's ass on an empty stomach. She offered one to Cillian, and they munched on the buttery flaky goodness as they marched down sidewalks, crossing the street occasionally as they used Jayne's phone for navigation.

Several minutes later, Jayne was licking the chocolate off her fingers when she spotted the domed building that housed the Mazarine Library. She gazed up at it, awestruck by the sheer magnificence. Massive pillars supported the sculptures surrounding a small clock face, and the building stretched out, elongated on either side with grand windows reminiscent of those from a palace. God, what she wouldn't give to explore a library like that…

Later, Jayne, she chided herself, forcing her attention away from the library and toward the bridge. Vehicles whizzed by along the busy road lining the river Seine, and hordes of people used the crosswalk to access the bridge. The Pont des Arts was so wide that ten people could fit comfortably side by side without bumping shoulders.

Jayne's eyes skated over the benches, lampposts, bicyclists, and pedestrians atop the bridge. "Whatever is cloaking him is on the Pont des Arts. I'm not sure what exactly it is—could be a portal or a Time Catch, so prepare yourself."

"Never been in a Time Catch, but can't say I'm eager to experience it."

"It's definitely no picnic, but we're in this together, okay? We've got this."

As they stepped onto the bridge, Jayne's breath caught as she gazed upon the Louvre Palace, the magnificent structure along the Voie Georges-Pompidou on the opposite end of the river. It obscured the entire north side of the city. Somewhere inside that castle-like grandeur was the Musée du Louvre, its glass pyramid ceiling above a labyrinth of underground rooms containing thousands of art pieces that would make Jayne's heart grow three sizes.

She took a moment to close her eyes and clear her head. *Focus, Jayne. We're here to find Ruger.* Resolve filled her chest. She took a step forward, intent on searching every square inch of the bridge for clues.

"Jayne." Cillian flung out an arm to stop her, his body going taut.

Alarm prickled along her skin as she looked at him. His nostrils flared as he inhaled deeply.

Right. Wolf nose. Jayne wasn't sure she'd ever get used to that.

"Do you smell that?" he asked, his eyes closing as he got another whiff.

Jayne's mouth twitched. "Doubtful, Wolfy. You've got a better sense of smell than I do."

Cillian's eyes opened as he smirked at her. "It smells like magic."

Bingo. "What kind of magic?"

He sniffed again, then shook his head. "Nothing like I've smelled before. Not the Kingdom. But not the TCO, either. It's... a new kind of magic."

"What does that mean?"

Cillian lifted his shoulders in a helpless gesture, and Jayne knew this was strange for him, too. Besides, how would one describe a smell they'd never come across before? It would be like describing the color blue to someone who had been born blind.

"Can you tell if it's dark magic or not?" Jayne asked instead.

Cillian closed his eyes again, his brows knitting together as he focused on the scent. "It smells...similar to the magic at the crater. But with a hint of...feline."

Jayne's eyebrows lifted. "Feline? Really? Well, too bad I left my stash of catnip at home."

Cillian opened his eyes, his face paling. When he met Jayne's gaze, he said softly, "It smells like—like me, right before I...before I shift."

Jayne's stomach dropped. Now it made sense. *Feline.* Of course all Rogues weren't wolves like Cillian. Ruger had told her Rogues could shift into multiple forms.

"You smell a Rogue," Jayne whispered, her body tense with anticipation as she glanced around. "And if you can smell one, that means they can smell you, too."

But Cillian shook his head. "No, the scent is old. Whoever it is, they aren't here anymore."

Jayne grabbed his arm and urged him forward. "Lead the way, Wolfy."

"Don't call me that."

"Until you come up with a more suitable nickname, that's what I'll use."

Jayne followed Cillian, whose broad shoulders were stiff, the muscles in his back flexing as if he were preparing for battle. Jayne dragged her eyes from his alluring backside, scanning the surroundings for sign of trouble...or magic. Or both.

Cillian led them along the Pont des Arts, its wooden panels creaking under their footsteps. Jayne nearly smacked into him when he stopped short halfway down the bridge. On either side of them, passersby strolled onward without a care in the world. Jayne envied them.

"This is it," Cillian said, turning to face her. "The scent stops here."

"It's the right spot from the Tracking spell, too," Jayne murmured, crouching on the ground to see if she could find some sort of magical residue. When her fingertips brushed the slightly moistened old wood, a searing ringing blared in her ears. She winced, clutching at her head as the pain intensified as if someone had taken a drill to her skull.

She clutched at her head, gritting her teeth as she struggled to rise. Her vision blurred, but she made out dozens of figures approaching them from the other side of the bridge. Cillian tensed next to her, and magic crackled in the air.

La Liberté.

Jayne withdrew another glass vial from her bag and smashed it on the bridge. Wispy red smoke unfurled, and power surged in her veins.

"What're you doing?" Cillian asked.

"We can't fight them," Jayne said. "My magic is gone." And she had a sinking feeling that La Liberté had something to do with it. She focused on the burst of energy from Quimby's vial and tugged on the Torrent. It flickered to life faintly before her, and without preamble, she grabbed the de-Cloaking spell she'd used to layer her Tracking spell. She threw it forward, and a portal shimmered to life at their feet.

"*Allons-y!*" Jayne shouted, a tribute to both France and *Doctor Who*, before she jumped in. She heard Cillian's strangled shout as he followed suit.

19

THROUGH THE LOOKING GLASS

Diving through the portal felt like riding those damn spinning teacups at an amusement park. And, just like the last time Cillian was on that ride, he felt like puking. The world shifted and swayed, rocking like a boat amid a fierce hurricane.

Then, just as suddenly as it began, it stopped. Cillian fell head-first, tumbling onto the ground like the portal had literally spit him out. He choked, trying to breathe, but the air felt thinner here, colder and more brittle than atop a mountain. Beside him, Jayne groaned as she staggered to her feet.

"We have to go," she huffed. "They'll probably follow us in."

Cillian blinked, struggling to orient himself from the nauseating combination of dizziness and shortness of breath. He felt like absolute hell.

Slowly, he stood, realizing they were in some kind of wide marble foyer with an ornate display of octagonal shapes along the floor. Beside them was a winding staircase that led up to several floors.

"Nice place," he muttered. "Which way do we go?"

Jayne stretched her arms, no doubt trying to reach the Torrent, but either her magic was still broken, or it wouldn't work in this strange place. Cillian still couldn't tell if the portal had taken them somewhere or if this was a Time Catch.

The ground shifted, and seconds later a figure glimmered into view, rising from the floor. He lunged for them, sending a shower of green sparks that sizzled in the air. Cillian ducked, but Jayne aimed a high front push kick, connecting with the man's chest. He went flying, sprawling on the floor.

"I can't reach the Torrent, and we're out of time." Jayne pulled the last bottle from her bag and smashed it. The air quivered and thickened with power, but it felt sluggish, like frozen syrup. It didn't ignite in the air like the usual fireworks Cillian felt when she cast a spell. Something was definitely off here.

Jayne gritted her teeth, weaving her hands together as she summoned magic. "Come on," she growled. "We're so close."

Remembering how the Torrent had ejected her last time, Cillian had his hands out when her body suddenly jerked. He caught her before she went flying like the other guy. Her arms were trembling, and her skin was cold to the touch.

"Jayne—"

"I know where he is." She straightened, her face devoid of its usual healthy glow, and gestured up the staircase. "This way."

Cillian swore as she darted upstairs. Another figure appeared through the portal as Cillian tore after her, narrowly dodging a strike of magic that cracked against the marble banister. The staircase led to a corridor lined by a bloodred carpet and rows of dark mahogany doors. Vases and paintings of various European scenery decorated the hall. The corridor seemed endless, and every door appeared identical. None of them were numbered.

Cillian clenched his fingers into fists as footsteps thundered behind them. His blood roared in his ears, ready for a fight. He hadn't had a proper match in a while, and he was itching to pummel some Liberté scumbags into oblivion.

Jayne hurried down the corridor, passing by several doors with nothing more than a glance. When she reached a door next to a particularly ugly vase shaped like a curled-up noodle, Jayne stopped, her hair whipping over her shoulder as she glanced from the assailants rushing toward them to the door in front of her.

"No time like the present, eh?" She kicked at the door, but it didn't budge. She bit her lip, issuing a string of curses that would've made Cillian laugh under different circumstances.

"Here." Cillian slammed his shoulder against the door. It groaned but remained firm. Pain reverberated through his arm, shooting through his bones, but he hit it again, and this time, the frame split, and the door flew open. They scrambled inside to find a small room facing a window that spanned the entire wall. On the other side of the window was—

"Ruger!" Jayne screamed.

He didn't react. He was tied to a desk, slumped in a chair with his face so beaten and bruised he was almost unrecognizable. Stains of blood and sweat covered his clothes, and he looked like he hadn't showered or shaved in weeks. Nothing like the way she'd seen him in the Tracking spell.

"Good God," Cillian hissed.

Jayne raced across the room and flung open the door leading to what Cillian realized was an interrogation room. This was a two-way mirror so La Liberté could spy on Ruger while he was being tortured.

The sick bastards.

Jayne appeared on the other side of the window as she hurried to Ruger's side, untying his restraints and helping him to his feet. Judging by Ruger's pained grimace and the awkward angle of his elbow jutting out, the arm was broken.

Two figures appeared in the door and Cillian turned, narrowly ducking to avoid one man's fist. His arms flew up to block another blow, and he feinted right. The idiot fell for it, and Cillian struck him hard on the jaw, then again in the gut. He grabbed the man by the neck and tossed him to the ground with a crash. The second goon advanced, but Cillian was ready, his body pumped from the fight. "Bring it, arsehole," he growled, waving his hand in invitation.

This man was taller and wiry, but his eyes were shrewd. He paused, assessing Cillian. His hands wove together until a shower of sparks rained from the ceiling, stinging Cillian's skin. He ducked, covering his face with his hands as searing heat burned against his flesh. While he was distracted, the man hit him in the face. Blood ran from Cillian's nose. He dropped to the ground, sweeping under the man's legs to send him toppling.

Another blast of ethereal light filled Cillian's vision. He flinched away, anticipating another hit to the face, but it never came. A grunt, followed by an "oof," and another body collapsing.

The light faded, and he blinked to find Ruger standing over him, a hand outstretched.

Cillian took it and stood, stanching his bloody nose with his shirt. "Thanks, mate."

Ruger nodded. One of his eyes was completely swollen shut, but he was obviously well enough to knock out a guy, so that was something.

"Can you do magic?" Jayne asked. Shadows lined her eyes, and her face looked ashen.

Ruger stretched one hand, and gold light danced between his fingers. Relief filled his face as if he hadn't expected it to work. "Thank God." His voice was raspy and worn. He sounded a decade older. "Something in that room was dampening my powers. I'm not as strong as normal, but—"

"It doesn't matter." Jayne touched his elbow. "We'll take whatever magic we can get."

Ruger's eyes darkened with concern. Jayne didn't explain. She ushered them to the door, but when they emerged in the corridor, a dozen members of La Liberté faced them. Including that bastard Tristan Lowell.

"Don't make this any messier than it needs to be," Lowell said, hands raised as if trying to appear peaceful. But the squadron of Adepts behind him said otherwise.

"A bit late for that," Jayne spat, fists raised. Cillian knew she wasn't fit for hand-to-hand combat, not in her condition. She looked like she'd gotten a bad dose and needed a doctor and antibiotics. But she'd do anything to get Ruger to safety. Even if it got her killed. Cillian knew that much.

Several Adepts waved their hands, summoning orbs of light that illuminated the paintings on the wall. Before they could strike, Ruger closed his fingers into a tight fist, and an explosion of black smoke filled the corridor. Cillian coughed and waved the smoke from his face. A thick hand grabbed his arm, and he was about to strike out when he heard Ruger's voice.

"It's me. I'm the only one who can see through it."

Cillian let Ruger lead him through the smoke, jostling against bodies that could have been friend or foe. The smoke was too thick to tell. Even Ruger coughed, and Cillian wondered how taxing it was for him to hold a spell like this. Already, the smoke was fading, and several figures came into view.

"There!" someone shouted. Footsteps pounded nearby.

Too close. They're too close.

They reached the staircase. The smoke had dispersed now, with only a lingering haze remaining. As they hurried up the steps, the thundering footsteps behind them multiplied.

Jayne yelped beside him as someone grabbed her arm. Cillian was amazed at her speed as she fought back, kicking her attacker in the outer thigh, swinging her free fist toward the stranger's face. When the man grabbed her other hand, she bashed her forehead against his. He groaned and slumped backward, releasing her. Another figure grabbed for her, but Cillian slid between them, slamming his elbow into the new attacker's face.

"Cillian—" Jayne protested.

"Get Ruger out," Cillian ordered. Three others rushed him. He ducked and blocked, but one blow hit him in the stomach, knocking the wind from him.

"Cillian!" Jayne shrieked, more panicked this time.

"Go!" he roared, taking another hit to the face. He swung his fists with deadly precision, hoping to cause as much damage as he could. He wouldn't go down without a proper fight, that was for damn sure.

He took a hit to the temple, and black spread across his vision. He didn't see if Jayne and Ruger got out, but he didn't hear her screams or cries, so he had to believe they had. He tasted blood in his mouth, on his tongue. His arms and chest throbbed. He sank to his knees just before something cracked against his skull and everything went dark.

20

WHEN ALL IS LOST

Lights twisted and spun around Jayne, circling her like a kaleidoscope of colors. Gravity shifted, pressing in on her so tightly she couldn't breathe.

She tumbled forward, landing on something hard and wet. Shaking her head violently, she looked up and found herself atop the Pont des Arts. It had started to rain, and around her, pedestrians strolled past with umbrellas up as if nothing was amiss. A second later, Ruger emerged from the portal, landing a bit more gracefully but still on his knees. He coughed and sputtered, wiping his mouth as he looked around through his nonswollen eye.

"There's a safe house not far from here," Ruger said hoarsely. "If we can get there, we'll be in the clear."

Jayne whirled, searching for the portal, but it was cloaked again. And she'd run out of bottles to smash. "But Cillian—"

"He gave himself up so we could escape. If we stay and get caught, his sacrifice will be for nothing."

"Sacrifice?" Denial and rage burned in her. "You say that like he's dead! He's not dead, Ruger! We just need to go back in and grab him!"

"Jayne—"

The ground rippled like water, and a figure shot out of the portal. Jayne's heart leapt, but before she could rush and embrace Cillian, she faltered.

It wasn't him. It was Tristan Lowell.

"I can't let you leave just yet," he said, striding toward them.

Jayne met him halfway, her nostrils flared and her blood pulsing with fury. "Where's Cillian?"

"He's with my people. If he behaves, he won't be harmed, but we need something from you first."

"No, you can go to hell. Now open the damn portal and let us back in."

"It's sealed. My superiors sensed the breach and put us on lockdown. Even I can't get back in."

"Liar." Jayne drew closer, ready to shove him over the rail and into the river.

"Go ahead and try to get in like you did before. I hope you can swim." His eyes gleamed as if he knew she couldn't do it.

Jayne clenched her teeth so hard her head pulsed with agony. She cut a glance at Ruger, who was staring hard at the ground where the portal had been. Slowly, he shook his head.

He couldn't get in, either.

Despair and fiery anger swirled inside her, boiling so hot she couldn't breathe.

"Work with us," Lowell said, his expression strangely pleading. "We can come to an arrangement."

"I have a better idea." Jayne swung her fist. It collided with Lowell's jaw. He staggered, and she hit him again, knocking him out cold. Pain radiated from her knuckles, but it had been worth it. Shaking her hand to ward off the throbbing, she dug her hands under his arms to lift him. "You gonna help, or what?" she snapped at Ruger.

"What the hell are you doing, Jayne?" Ruger demanded, but he used his good arm to help her lift Lowell's limp form.

"They took one of ours. So, we'll take one of theirs. It's leverage, Ruger. Didn't you learn anything in CIA school?"

"This isn't how we operate."

"I don't give a shit. They have Cillian."

It was a wet job, especially with the rain and Ruger one-handed, but they managed to drag Lowell off the bridge, draping his arms around their shoulders to give him the appearance of a buddy who'd had a bit too much to drink. No one spared them a second glance. When they'd crossed the street and reached the covered area of a bus stop, Jayne used the last bits of lingering magic to encrypt a call to Amanda and fill her in.

"I'm sending someone to pick you up," she said. "Have Ruger perform a Cloaking spell, and stay put. A car will be there in five minutes."

Jayne collapsed on the bench, her gaze pinned on the Pont des Arts as if Cillian might appear at any second. He'd given himself up, and she'd just left him there…

Ruger muttered an enchantment, and the air shifted around them. The Cloaking spell, no doubt. With a heavy sigh, he sank onto the seat next to her, wincing slightly. The bench sagged from his weight. He propped Lowell's lolling head on the wall behind the bench.

"The bastards hurt you," Jayne said without breaking her gaze.

"Nothing that won't heal."

Jayne arched a doubtful eyebrow, her gaze roving over his crooked arm, which was definitely broken, and the mass of blood staining his shirt. It seemed centered around his rib cage, and she hoped he hadn't cracked a rib. Or two.

"How long were you in there?" she asked.

"It was hard to keep track. It felt like a few weeks."

Jayne flinched. "God." She covered her face with her hands.

"I'm all right, Jayne. Would you believe I've been through worse?"

"Yes. But Cillian hasn't."

"He's tough. Tougher than you think. He'll be all right."

"Ruger—"

"You heard them. They need something from you. They won't risk the only leverage they have on you."

"Why did he have to play the hero? We could've made it."

"Maybe. But he didn't want to risk you. I'm sure you can imagine that feeling."

"Yes, I can." She remembered realizing the Kingdom had abducted Sofia. The utter helplessness and desperation. The knowledge that she would do *anything* to keep Sofia alive—even raise Medb herself.

"Now." Ruger turned to face her fully. "You want to tell me what's going on with your magic?"

No good beating around the bush. Jayne dived into the story, explaining what had happened in Fontainebleau and that strange ringing sound she'd heard. By the time she'd finished, a black sedan had pulled up beside them.

Ruger scrutinized her, his dark eyes softening. Though she was keeping her emotions at bay, he still seemed to sense the frustration in her. "We'll figure this out, Jayne."

"I know we will."

Ruger opened the door to the car and carefully eased Lowell inside. Jayne would have used a bit more force, but to each his own.

Before climbing in after Ruger, Jayne cast one last look at the Pont des Arts. But as much as her desperate heart longed for it, Cillian didn't resurface from the portal. She couldn't shake the feeling that she was abandoning him as she got into the car and watched the bridge fade from view.

21

BLOOD WILL OUT

Pierce led Sofia down a hall to a set of double doors that opened to what looked like a computer lab. The sleekest, most elegant computers she'd ever seen lined the tables and desks, some with two and three massive monitors, and others smaller and more compact like laptops and tablets. In the back of the room was a huge wall of servers, no doubt to power all the technology in the room.

A man with thick-framed glasses and floppy blond hair stood and approached them. He stood almost a foot taller than Sofia. With a broad smile, he extended his hand.

"Hi! I'm Jameson. You must be Sofia?"

"Yes. Nice to meet you." Sofia took his hand, which was warm. Her gaze skated over the room, where a full team was working on computers. "What is it you do here?"

"We work in encryption and decoding. Mostly, we handle cybersecurity to protect whatever information passes from the TCO to other entities." He gestured toward the wall of servers. "It's totally secure. No one outside this room can access this information. Your secrets are safe with me."

"Good to know."

He cocked his head at her, his eyes glinting with excitement. "But I hear you have a rather unique problem, is that right?"

"Yes." Sofia's grip on the strap of her bag tightened. She felt uncomfortable just handing her father's journal over to this stranger—not just because she didn't trust him, but because this room looked like your average IT department. Everything here seemed normal. So...nonmagical. Pulling out Henry Thorne's journal seemed like it would shatter the illusion.

Get a grip, she told herself before taking out the worn leather book. Jameson took it gingerly and placed it atop his desk, frowning as he scrutinized it from the binding to the brittle pages. "Fascinating," he murmured as he flipped through it. "I've never seen such intricate coding."

"Does that mean you can't decode it?"

"Not necessarily. Whoever encrypted this knew what he was doing. I recognize the Caesar shift, which is simple enough. But he's combined several different forms of coding." To Sofia's surprise, Jameson inhaled deeply. "And magical coding as well."

The hairs on Sofia's arms rose. "Magical?"

"He sealed it with spells as well as mathematical codes." Jameson pressed his hands together and a faint green light emanated from his palms, illuminating the journal. For a moment, Sofia wondered if he was searching for invisible ink. Then, he said, "But you've already cracked one of those codes, haven't you?"

"Yes. With my blood."

Jameson raised an eyebrow. "Blood magic? That's deep stuff. This guy wasn't messing around." The air hummed as he pressed his fingertips against the pages, his eyes closed in concentration. "Unfortunately," he said, his voice distant as he maintained his focus, "it seems your blood isn't the only thing required to unlock it."

"What else is required, a severed limb?"

Jameson chuckled. "Thankfully, no. But the blood magic has a dual key. You've inserted the first prong of the key. The other prong is still necessary to unlock what's contained here."

"Can you tell what the other prong is?"

"More blood. From someone other than you."

A chill raced down Sofia's spine. Her first thought was Ruth, but no… Ruth must have tried unlocking the journal, and Sofia had no doubt her mother would have used blood already.

"A sister's blood," Sofia whispered, more to herself than to Jameson. "It has to be."

Jameson nodded absently as he pulled out a notepad and started jotting down lines of untidy script. "Ah. Familial DNA. That would make the most sense. How many sisters do you have?"

"It's just the two of us."

"Then breaking the magical code should be fairly straightforward. The nonmagical code, however, might take me a while." He glanced up, his eyes full of an eagerness Sofia often saw in Jayne when she faced a particularly delightful challenge. "Mind if I make copies of these pages?"

"Can't you just keep the journal here to study it?"

"Afraid not. It's linked to your blood. As soon as the magic within senses your absence, it will revert back to its former state. And of course, without your sister's blood, we'll never get through all the layers."

Sofia thought of the innocent book of proverbs this journal had appeared to be. How many times had Sofia and Jayne been in the same room as this book over the years? They'd been so close to unlocking it without even realizing it…and now Jayne was all the way across the world, and they weren't speaking to each other.

God, what a mess. Sofia wanted to call Jayne right this moment and scream and cry at her. She wanted to assure her she'd love her no matter what, but couldn't she see how reckless she was being, diving into missions with wild abandon?

Then again, wasn't Sofia doing the same thing? She wasn't necessarily in the field, but she was taking risks. Even using her blood to unlock the journal had been a risk. She wasn't so naïve that she didn't understand how valuable blood could be. Besides, she was actively working against Ruth. That was possibly the most dangerous risk she'd ever taken.

And despite the secrets that might be revealed from this journal, Sofia's curiosity outweighed her fear. She needed answers. And Jayne did, too. Sofia couldn't blame her sister for seeking them in her own way.

"Yes," Sofia finally said. "I'll wait while you make copies. And don't worry, I'll find a way to get my sister here."

22

A SCHEME IS AFOOT

The car brought Ruger and Jayne to a fancy safe house across the city Montmartre, where Amanda herself had portaled in to debrief them. She also brought a team of specialists to run painstaking tests on Jayne to assess the severity of whatever had happened to her magic. Though every muscle in Jayne's body ached with exhaustion and grief, she forced herself to recite the events of Ruger's rescue and Cillian's capture.

Jayne's frustration mounted when Amanda insisted she finish Ruger's debriefing in private. "Hold up," she snapped, slicing her hand through the air like a time-out. "What are we doing to get Cillian back?"

"We'll be negotiating a prisoner exchange," Amanda said. "Tristan Lowell for Cillian. It should be fairly straightforward."

"Straightforward? They could be torturing Cillian right now! Have you made contact with La Liberté yet? We need to get this in motion."

"We haven't finished questioning Lowell yet."

"To hell with Tristan Lowell! Throw him to the wolves for all I care. Our priority should be protecting our own. We need to get Cillian back, Amanda. Now."

Amanda's lips grew thin, her eyes darkening with a fury that almost made her unrecognizable. "Need I remind you that I am your superior? Don't you dare take that tone with me. Perhaps when you're director, you can call the shots. But for right now, the decision rests with me. Now get out before I suspend you from this assignment. Return to your flat. We will contact you when we need you."

Jayne looked to Ruger, but his face was stony and impassive. His silence said it all: he sided with Amanda on this.

Seething, Jayne stormed out of the safe house. The air shifted when she stepped over the threshold and through the Cloaking spell Amanda had cast on the building. The door shut behind her, and she balled her hands into tight fists, resisting the urge to scream. That would draw far too much attention.

Besides, screaming wouldn't do any good. Screaming wouldn't get Cillian back.

It's all your fault. You've dragged him into this insane world. And now you're going to get him hurt, or maybe killed. And damn him for trying to play the hero!

Maybe screaming *would* help. But not here.

First things first. She was covered in scrapes and bruises and desperately needed food. After she was clean and fed, she could deal with the more pressing problem: How was she supposed to rescue Cillian if she didn't have any magic? She'd run out of Quimby's handy glass bottles.

She needed to draw magic from some other source. She remembered the feel of the grimoire she'd touched in the TCO library.

Jayne took a moment to orient herself. Her flat was in the 15th arrondissement, and this safe house was in Montmartre, the 18th. Wondering briefly just how many safe houses the TCO had in a city as large as Paris, she glanced at the map on her phone and picked out the closest metro stop. As she strode down the sidewalk, she dialed the number of the TCO line she'd memorized in case of emergencies and pulled on the Torrent for a tiny Cloaking spell of her own. It was weak and wobbly, but at least no one on the street could hear her.

"Bill's Pizza," a voice said smoothly.

"Red herring," Jayne said immediately, reciting her identification code.

"Hold, please." After a moment, the voice said, "Officer Thorne, identity confirmed. Do you need assistance?"

"Yes. Can you connect me to Katie Bell in the TCO library?"

"Just a second." A few beeps, and a line began ringing.

Katie's warm, familiar voice was like a soothing embrace to Jayne's ears. "Katie Bell speaking."

"Katie, it's Jayne Thorne. I was wondering if you had any information on where grimoires might be located in Paris?"

A pause. "What kind of grimoires?"

"Any kind."

"One moment, dearie." Jayne heard the distinct clacking of keyboard keys as Katie no doubt searched through the database. "My records show there are two low-level grimoires located in the Mazarine Library."

Jayne remembered the dome-shaped building right next to the Pont des Arts. "That's perfect. Can you text me the information?"

"Sure thing." Katie hesitated again. "Is everything all right, Jayne?"

"Absolutely. Just a snag is all. Thanks so much, Katie." She hung up and took a deep breath, trying to push the memory of Cillian's battered and beaten face from her mind.

He'd given himself up so easily. Like it was nothing. Why the hell had he done that?

For you. He did it to save you.

Jayne shook her head, gritting her teeth against the anger and shame warring within her as she descended the steps to the metro line.

Back in the 15th, she stopped by the Franprix on the corner to grab some essentials—tea bags, a few boxes of frozen pies, a foot-long baguette, and sandwich fixings—then trudged up the steps to the building of her flat, her heart heavy as she took the lift to the second floor. But when she opened her door, she froze, a chill sweeping over her.

On the floor in front of her was a picture of Cillian. He wore the same clothes from earlier, and his button-up shirt was stained with blood. A deep gash ran across his cheek, and his nose was crooked as if someone had broken it. But his blue eyes burned with defiance as he stared directly at the camera. Directly at Jayne.

Agony swelled in Jayne's throat as she set down her bags, bent over, and picked up the picture. She tried to make out Cillian's surroundings, but it was too dark and blurry. A bright light had been shone on his face to illuminate his cuts and bruises. But he was alive.

Jayne turned the photo over in her hands and found a phone number scrawled on the back of it. Her pulse skittered. She knew exactly what this was: a ransom note.

Voices echoed down the hall, and Jayne quickly stepped into her flat before anyone noticed the picture in her hands. Her breaths were sharp and ragged as she thought through her options, distracting herself by putting her groceries away before tackling the problem at hand. She could—should—report this to Amanda and Ruger, who would likely do nothing because they were still waiting on negotiations. They'd both made it clear that extracting information from Tristan Lowell were more important than Cillian's well-being.

Option Two was to move forward with Jayne's original plan. Katie had texted her the titles of the grimoires at the Mazarine Library. She could go there, find the books, draw magic from them, and hope it was enough juice to cast a Tracking spell to locate Cillian.

Or, Option Three…she could call this number and see what they wanted.

Jayne only took a second to consider before she was dialing the number. It took her a few tries, what with the international codes and all that, but at long last, the line was ringing. She tried to drown out the thundering pulse in her ears as she waited for someone to pick up.

"Hello, Jayne Thorne," said a cool female voice she didn't recognize. Her French was impeccable, the tongue of a native.

"Hello, strange person who knows where I live," Jayne replied calmly in her own American-accented but perfect French. "Why didn't you stick around and say hi so we could have this conversation face to face?"

"Don't take us for fools. We know the TCO keeps you well protected."

"I don't know what you mean."

"Of course you do. Don't be coy. We want to offer you a deal. We have something you want."

"If by something you mean a human being, then yes, that's correct." Fury swelled inside her, but she kept it at bay. *Be cool, Jayne.*

"And you have access to something we want."

Jayne didn't like the sound of that. "I'm listening."

"Our understanding is you have an affinity for grimoires. If you locate one for us, we'll return your friend."

"Only one problem with that: it's impossible. My magic isn't working. But you guys knew that already, didn't you?"

"That won't be a problem for you. We'll take care of it."

"What the hell does that mean?"

"We've injected you with a substance that dampens your magic, but only when triggered by us. We will simply…not trigger it, so long as you agree to play by our rules."

Cold dread seeped into Jayne's body. They'd injected her with something? And they possessed the trigger? This was all kinds of bad.

"My boss is in charge of negotiations for a prisoner exchange," Jayne said, trying to keep her voice level. "You should take this up with her."

"Ms. Newport does not possess the same skills as you do. Or the same amount of desperation. She does not value this man's life as much as you do."

"So, what, you'll just circumvent her prisoner exchange and hand over Cillian once I give you the grimoire?"

"Not necessarily. We will expedite the prisoner exchange. And ensure your friend remains unharmed."

"This picture shows he's been harmed plenty," Jayne said, unable to contain the rage in her voice.

"Unharmed any *further*," the woman amended.

"You want me to find a grimoire for you *and* give you back your guy? Doesn't really seem like a fair trade to me."

"You broke into our secure Time Catch, Ms. Thorne. You injured our men. You took something of great value to us."

"Ruger didn't belong to you. He was your prisoner."

"Regardless, we are significantly wounded from your attack, and we will retaliate on this man of yours unless you comply with our demands. So, what will it be?"

Jayne's head was spinning as she considered her options. Unfortunately, she didn't have time to run this by Amanda or Ruger, but she figured that was exactly what this woman had intended. "With whom am I speaking?"

"Why does that matter?"

"I'd like to know who I'm negotiating with. It's the least you can do."

A pause. "*C'est* Gina Labelle."

Good God, the leader of La Liberté? Why was she making this call herself instead of making one of her goons do it?

"Do we have a deal?" Labelle asked.

Damn her, Labelle knew exactly how to play Jayne to get what she wanted. *It's Cillian,* her mind said quietly. *He'd do anything for you. It's your turn now.*

"Tell me about this grimoire."

"It's a necromantic text known only as the Book of Shadows. Its location often varies, as its protectors keep it heavily guarded because of the magic contained within. We only know it's currently located here in Paris, and, unfortunately, we're on a bit of a tight schedule."

"And why is that?" Jayne asked. "You got another mass murder planned somewhere?"

Another silence fell between them, this one heavy with accusation. In a clipped tone, Labelle said, "What happened in Fontainebleau was an accident. We didn't know there would be so many casualties. The loss of life was very painful to me."

Jayne didn't believe her for a second. "Right."

"We are not the only ones searching for this grimoire. We need you to find it before they do."

"They who?" Jayne asked.

"You are familiar with the organization known as the Kingdom?"

Jayne sucked in a breath. The Kingdom. Ruth. Of course, her mother and her merry band of psychos were looking for the grimoire, too.

If Ruth wanted this grimoire, then damn skippy, Jayne had to find it first.

"All right," Jayne said slowly. "Before I agree to this, I need a sign of good faith. Release whatever hold you have on my magic. Right now. Prove to me that it will work."

Labelle was silent for so long that Jayne thought she'd hung up. But then, after a moment, she said, "We've deactivated it. You can use your magic."

Jayne reached for the Torrent. Like a friendly companion, the glistening river of stars greeted her, eager and ready. She wanted to weep with relief as the power swelled inside her. She immediately searched for the layered Tracking spell, ready to find Cillian on her own. To hell with Gina Labelle and her creepy bargains.

But before she could grab the spell, the lights vanished, leaving Jayne cold and empty.

"Was that proof enough for you?" Labelle's voice sounded smug on the other line, as if she'd known what Jayne had been trying to do.

"Plenty," Jayne bit out.

"You have three days to locate the grimoire. Every day after that, we will cut off one of his fingers and send it to you."

Horror puddled in Jayne's gut, and her anger flared again. "You know, we have your guy, too. If you hurt Cillian, I might have to sever a few of Lowell's body parts as well."

Gina hissed, and the line crackled slightly. "Watch yourself, girl. Don't make idle threats with me. I can see right through them."

"You're more naïve than I am if you think I won't disembowel Lowell if it means getting Cillian back safely. You called me because you think I'm willing to bend the TCO's rules to get my friend back. That means you know I have no problem with crossing those lines."

Labelle's breathing hitched slightly. After a moment, she said in a slightly ragged voice, "Three days. Do we have a deal?"

"Yes. And if you hurt Cillian, I'll hunt you down and curse you into oblivion."

Labelle laughed coldly. "Good luck doing that without your formidable magic."

Before Jayne could respond, the woman had hung up.

Luckily, Jayne didn't need to wait long before Amanda summoned her back to Montmartre to give her the results of the tests they'd run on her magic. And to share whatever top secret information Ruger had disclosed during his super-secret debriefing that Jayne wasn't allowed to be a part of.

After taking a quick shower and grabbing a *merguez frites* from a street vendor, Jayne headed to the safe house, hoping she wasn't about to get fired for going behind the TCO's back. A light rain pattered around her, making the streets wet and miserable. It fit her mood.

She was never planning on giving over the necromantic grimoire to La Liberté. But would Amanda believe her when she said as much?

Slightly out of breath after hiking the hill to the safe house, Jayne knocked on the red door. When it opened, she passed through the shimmering Cloak barrier once more.

"Have a seat." Amanda gestured to the dining room table where she and Ruger sat. Jayne didn't like the grim looks on their faces.

"Is this where you tell me I only have one month left to live?" Jayne asked. She was met with severe, unflinching expressions.

"This is serious, Jayne," said Ruger.

Jayne wiggled impatiently in her chair. "Just spit it out. I can handle it."

Amanda nodded once. "Very well. Your link to the Torrent has been tainted by some kind of foreign agent. Your magic and the Torrent are both fine, but when you combine the two, the agent kicks in—like a poison."

Well, this lined up with what Labelle had said. Sort of. "Is there any way to remove this foreign agent?"

"We don't know. We've never seen this before, but it is some sort of dark magic. A spell we don't recognize. I've sent a sample of your blood back to Langley to be analyzed by the TCO lab. Our team will research tirelessly to find a cure."

A cure. Now it really *did* sound like she was dying.

Jayne must have looked absolutely freaked out, because Ruger said, "Your magic is fully functional. When we tested it, it was working perfectly. But when you're around La Liberté, the agent inside you is activated."

"Yeah," Jayne said glumly. She'd *really* been hoping Labelle had been lying, just trying to scare her. But it sounded like she'd been telling the truth. "That's what Gina Labelle said, too."

Her voice deadly soft and cold, Amanda asked, "I beg your pardon?"

In a rush, Jayne filled them both in on her conversation with Labelle and what La Liberté wanted her to do. Amanda's lips grew thinner and thinner with each word Jayne spoke, and when Jayne finished, the woman's mouth was practically nonexistent. Ruger rubbed the bridge of his nose like Jayne was some wayward teenager who couldn't follow the rules.

"By the Goddess, Jayne, what the hell were you thinking?" Amanda snapped. "You just blew our entire negotiation for a prisoner exchange!"

"Not to mention the ammo you've given La Liberté," Ruger added. "Now they have you under their thumb because they know you'll do anything to retrieve Cillian."

Being scolded like an errant teenager got her back up. "Look, I know it was dangerous, but I went with my gut. Something told me we wouldn't get another opportunity like this. I'm not the only one who's desperate. Now we know that *they* are willing to do whatever it takes to get this grimoire."

"And you agreed to get it for them," Amanda said, shaking her head. "You realize Cillian could die because of this?"

Jayne resisted the urge to recoil from those words. Instead, she stared Amanda down. "I have a plan. Would you care to hear it, or would you like to yell at me some more?"

Amanda huffed an angry breath and waved a hand at her. "We are all ears, Jayne."

Ignoring Amanda's sarcasm, Jayne scooted to the edge of her seat, smoothing her palms on her pants. "What if we use Deirdre

Green to create a copy of the grimoire they want? A fake to give La Liberté? I know she's a civilian, but she's still working with us, right? She's as good with ancient manuscripts as I am. I can help her. We can make a passable faux grimoire."

Amanda's lips pinched in disapproval. "As soon as they discover it's not real, they'll kill Cillian."

"Not necessarily. They'll have to bring Cillian to the drop location, right? We'll surround the place with TCO guys. We withhold the grimoire until we see Cillian—proof of life and all that. Then, once we know where he is, our guys can move in and grab him. It might get dirty, but the fight should distract La Liberté from examining the grimoire too closely. They'll be so caught off guard they won't have time to authenticate the manuscript. We can put some nasty magic in it, just in case, to throw them off and buy ourselves time to get away."

"You're talking about sacrificing our own men for this insane plan of yours. People could die, Jayne."

"They're already dying!" Jayne said, her temper finally flaring to life. "And they will continue to die once La Liberté has that grimoire. Labelle called it the Book of Shadows, which sounds particularly awful. And...Ruth is looking for it, too. I assure you, if I don't find it for them, they will get it some other way. And who knows what sort of chaos will ensue."

Amanda stared at her with steely eyes, but Jayne held her gaze, unwavering. She knew she was right about this. Their enemies were multiplying. They would have to take a risk sometime.

Amanda exchanged a glance with Ruger, whose gaze was contemplative—not angry, which Jayne saw as a good sign.

Finally, Amanda sighed, drooping as if the fight had literally left her body. "Okay. Let's iron out this plan of yours."

23

AN OLIVE BRANCH

Sofia scribbled furiously, her brow furrowed in concentration. Her pen paused, poised in the air, as she glanced back at her father's journal to make sure she wasn't missing anything.

So far, Jameson had decoded two of Henry's mathematical ciphers and sent the keys to Sofia. The TCO had extracted a sample of Jayne's blood and sent it from Paris, but the lab had to run tests on it first before Jameson could use it to unlock the magical portion of the journal. While she waited for this development, Sofia was leafing through the pages to translate various phrases here and there, using an empty office in the TCO Amanda had given her access to. Most of the decoded phrases were ingredients for magical potions and elixirs, but she was certain the TCO could use this information. And then, once they had Jayne's blood and unlocked the rest, hopefully everything would piece together and make more sense.

Silence pressed in on her, broken only by the light ticking of the clock on the wall. Sometimes, the stillness in the air grated Sofia's nerves, putting her on edge as if she were waiting for something sinister to break the silence. But today, the silence was a welcome companion, like a blanket shrouding her from the outside world, removing all distractions.

Ever since Medb's rising, there had been a presence stirring inside her, so foreign and unfamiliar that it made her skin crawl. Her gut reaction was to shove it down, but those instincts had failed her. Those instincts, coupled with a dangerous magical Suppression spell, had brought on a deadly disease that had almost killed her. Twice.

And yet...she wasn't quite ready to open herself up to that magic. That potential for darkness. Just like Ruth. If she wasn't in control 100 percent, she didn't know what might happen.

Sofia set down her pen and massaged her temples, momentarily distracted by the warring thoughts within her. Her deeply embedded fear of becoming like Ruth had been a solid barrier between herself and her magic. Always in the way, but it was for her own good. And Jayne's.

Now, she wasn't so sure. The wall was crumbling, and she didn't know if she felt relieved or terrified. Jayne used her magic to help people. To protect the world. It had kept their enemies at bay. Surely, it wasn't all bad, right?

But Ruth would have made Jayne into a weapon. And the things she wanted to do with Sofia's magic... The memories made her ill. If she embraced her powers once more, how easy would it be for her to slip into that mold Ruth had created for her? One wrong step, and she might fall, consumed by the training Ruth had ingrained in her for years.

This is different. You have new mentors now. People who can help you channel your magic the right way.

But what *was* the right way? Sofia knew firsthand there was no black and white when it came to magic. There were so many gray areas. She felt like a player on a chessboard, unable to see the squares in front of her because of the smoke and mirrors. One step forward could put her in enemy territory, endangering herself and those she loved.

Her fingers moved to her wrist, where she'd worn the Suppression bracelet for so many years. Though she'd taken it off ages ago, she still felt its effects. But, for the first time, she wondered if the effects lingered not because of the spell...but because of her. Her own willpower. Her own restraint.

She remembered the day she'd removed the bracelet. After her second diagnosis of cancer. The chemo—the wretched poison inside of her—was worse than death. Worse than the darkest magic imaginable. She didn't think anything human could be so frightful. The migraines. The nightmares. The constant body aches and fatigues. The thought that she might not live to see tomorrow. Or the day after. The frailty and fragility that made her feel like she was ninety years old.

Cancer was the worst magic...because it wasn't magic at all. It transformed her body, changing her against her will. It multiplied as if it had a mind of its own. A foreign enemy she wasn't prepared to fight.

And it almost took her away from Jayne.

Sofia straightened in her seat, resolve quivering through her and melting away her anxiety. The stark reminder pulsed in her mind: *I'm doing this for Jayne.*

Her gaze fell to the open journal on the table, and another reminder trembled within her: *I'm doing this to stop Ruth.* How many other Adepts out there, like Sofia, were being conditioned by Ruth to be puppets? Players in her sick game?

Sofia could save them.

She hunched over, returning to her decoding and her notes. Henry's scribblings were disjointed and nonsensical, but she knew there was something helpful in here. She'd already found so much. Once they pieced everything together, the TCO would use this to their advantage. She could use Jayne's help on this. Jayne was the bookish one. She might see something right away.

But Jayne was still knee-deep in her Paris assignment. Sofia had sent her a text earlier, finally breaking the silence: *I'm sorry.*

I'm ready to talk when you are. But Jayne hadn't responded. Sofia didn't know if it was because she was still angry or if she was too involved in her mission to respond.

Sofia turned the page, her fingers lingering on the worn paper. A heavy force jolted inside her, jerking her forward. She gasped, her vision going dark. In her mind, she saw Ruth, her face contorted with fury. Gone was the cruel smugness of her features Sofia was so accustomed to. This woman before her was an animal, enraged and vicious.

A sharp pain lanced through her, and Sofia groaned, hunching over. The sound of her own voice pierced through the foggy haze, and her vision cleared. The pain vanished, leaving Sofia gasping for breath, a cold sweat breaking out on her forehead.

Sucking in deep, rattling breaths, she sat up, pressing a hand to her chest. Magic crackled within her, responding to the power that had overtaken her, acknowledging the presence of something else.

Sofia stared at the words in her father's journal. Something had reached out to her from this particular page. Something important.

Heart racing, she began writing again, her handwriting untidy as she frantically jotted down everything she could. Her eyes flew from her own notepad to the journal, back and forth, back and forth, until her head was throbbing.

When she'd decoded all she could from that particular page, she sat back, exhaling and wiping sweat from her brow. Only then did she allow herself to read the words she'd translated. When she did, her heart lurched painfully.

A single phrase stood out among her notes. A phrase that turned her stomach and made her skin prickle.

A contingency—to end her, should she venture too far into dark waters. This is her secret. The vault she vows to keep locked forever. Guard it well.

24

IS THAT A SWORD IN YOUR POCKET, OR...

While Amanda stepped out to marshal their resources and get ahold of Deirdre, Ruger helped Jayne map out a plan to search for the Book of Shadows. She already planned to search the Mazarine Library, since Katie had told her of the two grimoires there. Ruger mentioned a few more Paris libraries she could check out as well.

When Jayne's brain ached after going over the plan a fifth time, she changed the subject. "What happened to you in that Time Catch?"

Ruger went still. "We really need to focus on this, Jayne."

"Yeah, I know. I've got the plan down. Reciting it a million more times isn't going to change that." She tapped her temple. "Eidetic, remember? But Amanda called me back here because you had some information to share. What was it?"

Ruger leveled a stare at her as if assessing whether she could handle this. "Gina Labelle is a Rogue."

Jayne's eyebrows shot up. "A Rogue? Huh."

Ruger cocked his head. "You don't seem particularly surprised."

"Well, I'm not. Cillian smelled another Rogue on the Pont des

Arts. I never in a million years would have thought it was her, but it makes sense now. It's also kind of scary, if you think about it. I mean, who's her Master? Who's turning her? I thought she was the Head of La Liberté. Is there someone above her? That's not cool."

"That's a good question. When she shifted in front of me, no one else was in the room. Doesn't mean there isn't a powerful ally somewhere who's helping her. But that's not all. They questioned me about the Torrent—how to access it, how to force additional entry points, and how to draw energy from it in other ways. And they also had a lot of questions about Rogue magic."

"What kind of questions?"

"Luckily, questions I couldn't answer. The origin of Rogues, the evolution of their magic, and how to...how to unleash it."

Jayne's blood ran cold. "Unleash the ancient Rogue magic?" She told him about reading the history of Rogues in the TCO library—how the magic created sentient animals, mutating them into monsters that ancient Adepts tried to control and wield for themselves. "It sounds a lot like the Kingdom's experimentation on Rogues, doesn't it? They must have found out the same things."

That made him rub his chin thoughtfully. "You're becoming quite handy, you know that?"

She curtsied. "I try. So what's the endgame? What happens if she manages to figure out how to unleash Rogue magic?"

"I'm not sure. Perhaps Labelle believes that unleashing it will make her and all other Rogues more powerful. I sensed some tension among their ranks about Rogues versus Adepts. It's a sore spot for them, it seems. Some Adepts tend to look down on Rogues, viewing them as inferior."

Jayne could totally see Ruth and every other nutty Kingdom acolyte believing the same thing. Maybe that explained why the Kingdom and La Liberté hated each other so much.

The door opened, and Amanda entered. "We've got Deirdre

on the next flight to Paris. She'll be arriving shortly. In the mean-time, Jayne, you need to get some rest before she gets here."

"Can't I start searching these libraries?" Jayne asked, gesturing to the list she and Ruger had compiled.

"You're no good to Cillian if you're too weak to carry on with the mission. Go take care of yourself. When Deirdre lands, we'll contact you, and you two can get to work."

Jayne chewed on her lower lip. She hated waiting, especially knowing Cillian was out there, imprisoned and alone. Perhaps Labelle had gone back on her word and was already torturing him. The thought sent curdles of dread rippling over her.

Not Cillian, not Cillian, please don't hurt him, please please please.

But Amanda was right. The exhaustion was dragging Jayne downward, seeping into her bones. She hadn't risen from her chair in hours, and she suddenly felt glued down as if she couldn't stand even if she wanted to.

And Cillian was a big boy. He knew the risks. He was strong. He'd make it. He had to.

"All right," Jayne said. With monumental effort, she pried herself from her chair. Her limbs felt like lead. She jabbed a finger at Ruger. "You get some rest, too, buddy. You still don't look so good." She turned to Amanda. "Has he even been checked out by a doctor yet?"

Amanda smiled tightly. "He has. And don't worry, I'll ensure he takes care of himself."

"I'm fine," Ruger said. But one eye was still swollen shut, and the cuts and bruises on his face looked rather nasty. Plus, his arm was encased and in a sling. At least he'd changed out of his bloody clothes.

As Jayne stared at him, something finally registered in her brain: Ruger was back. He was alive. He was safe.

In one swift movement, she launched herself into him, throwing her arms around him, careful to avoid his injured arm. He made an uncomfortable sound in his throat before awkwardly patting her on the shoulder. He was so tall that even with him seated, Jayne was near eye level.

When she withdrew, she offered him a smile. "Sorry. I just never got to do that. Or express my gratitude that you're alive. And, you know, not dismembered or anything."

Amanda gave her a stern look, and Jayne raised her hands in surrender. "Okay! Going now. Off to rest."

~

Jayne only expected to sleep for a few hours, but when her phone rang and she slid out of the hazy fog of a much-too-long nap, she realized it was eight in the morning. She'd slept for freaking ten hours.

Groggily, she answered the phone with a slurred "Hello?"

"Deirdre just landed," Amanda said. "We've sent a car for her, and she's headed your way."

"Got it. Thanks."

Jayne took a quick shower and donned a button-up blouse and pencil skirt, realizing how much she missed being in libraries. Even just wearing her most librarian-esque outfit made her nostalgic for the stacks at Vanderbilt and Trinity.

A light knock sounded at the door, and Jayne hurried to open it. Deirdre stepped in, her hair pulled into a messy ponytail and her dark eyes wide with a mixture of awe and excitement as she drank in the grandeur of the flat.

"Deirdre!"

Jayne surged forward and embraced her tightly. Deirdre, normally reserved, stiffened for a moment before hugging her back. Jayne let her go, remembering their shared experiences at Trinity—both as librarians and pawns in the Kingdom's game. Deirdre hadn't revealed all she'd endured at Alarik's hand, but being the wife of a psychopath who ran a terror organization couldn't have been easy.

"Has the TCO been treating you well?" Jayne asked.

"They have. All those libraries...they're endless." Her clipped Oxford accent was more posh than ever.

"I'm a bit jealous, you know. Stuck out here on assignment instead of perusing all those fabulous tomes. I've only read one book this week, can you imagine? You ready to get your librarian on?"

Deirdre laughed. "Always."

"Have they briefed you on what's happened?"

"Amanda said you're having some glitches with your magic. Is it something Alarik did?"

"No. The folks we're up against have managed to poison me, and it's affecting how I access the Torrent. We're working on it."

Deirdre blanched. "Poison?"

"I mean, it's magical. Not as serious as it sounds. I'm totally fine."

Jayne picked up her bag and withdrew her glasses—which, after Amanda's handy magical LASIK trick a few weeks earlier, were just for show—before putting them on. She checked herself in the mirror. Oh yeah, she'd totally been missing this "hot librarian" look.

"How do I look?" she asked.

Deirdre grinned. "Sophisticatedly bookish."

Perfect.

Looping her arm through Deirdre's, the two of them left the flat.

Once they emerged from the complex, Jayne led the way to the nearest metro station. For a moment, she allowed herself to gaze up at the architectural beauties surrounding her, the pillars and balconies and archways so unlike what she was used to in the States.

As they walked, a companionable silence fell between them. Deirdre wasn't much of a talker. It resonated with Jayne's introverted temperament, especially now. Damn, but she was nervous.

After a while, Jayne cast a sidelong glance at Deirdre and asked, "How are things really? With you? With the TCO? I bet you have whiplash."

Deirdre had gone from being a respected research librarian at Trinity, married to a psychotic madman who wielded magic, to working for the U.S. government and taking a vow of secrecy. Joining the very enemies her husband had been fighting against.

"I really have been mostly in the libraries all day, which, of course, I love," Deirdre said. "They've got me researching ancient texts about lore and magic that might be useful."

"You lucky duck," Jayne said. "That sounds fascinating." What she wouldn't give to just sit in the TCO library all day and study magic over the years. She already felt so behind, having only tapped into her powers recently.

"It really is." Deirdre's whole face lit up. "It helps merge the two together—my world as a librarian, and this new world with…"

"Magic," Jayne muttered.

"Yeah."

Jayne understood this, too. That was why her undercover assignment at Trinity had been so exciting. Books and manuscripts were her element. Throwing in magic, something entirely new, had added a thrill to the assignment that Jayne loved.

"Is it weird for you?" Jayne asked. "Being around it so much?"

Deirdre shrugged one shoulder. "I've been around it before. With…with Alarik." Her voice trailed off with a tremble, and Jayne couldn't quite place whether it was from ingrained fear of the man, or grief at his death. A twist in Jayne's stomach reminded her *she'd* been the one to kill him. Did Deirdre resent her for that? The guy had been a madman, but Jayne knew Deirdre had cared about him at some point.

"It is strange the way the TCO handles it, though," Deirdre said, her expression thoughtful. "It's a very different approach from how Alarik used magic."

"How so?"

"Alarik was more in touch with the spirits and the Earth. He craved that natural essence, that power. You remember, I'm sure, his ethos: he believed in bringing the world back to simpler times, when magic could be accessed through the elements."

Jayne nodded. That was the Kingdom's mantra: Shut down all technology. Plunge the world into archaic darkness.

"But the TCO uses technology alongside magic," Deirdre said, her face splitting into a wondrous smile. "It's mind-blowing."

Jayne chuckled, thinking of Quimby's inventions. "Tell me about it."

They descended the stairs amidst a throng of pedestrians. Jayne kept her arm tucked into Deirdre's to ensure they didn't get separated as they navigated toward the metro line.

While they waited on a bench for the metro to arrive, Jayne asked Deirdre, "Have you been to the Mazarine before?"

"Once, but it's been years. I've been longing to go back. Did you know it has a Gutenberg? I was here on a special assignment and they took it out for us. It was remarkable. They rarely let anyone near it. A shame. I know you'd go mad for it."

Jayne felt a twinge of envy at all this woman had seen and experienced. But that was exactly why Deirdre was here. Jayne did a few small *Wayne's World* bows with both hands, quipping "I'm not worthy!"

"Don't be silly, Jayne. I'm the one who's lucky to be working with you."

The roar of the looming metro train barreling down the tunnel had them on their feet, and as the doors slid open, they clambered inside. Deirdre tucked herself into a corner, looking like an exotic mouse as she tried to avoid jostling against other people. The vehicle lurched and groaned, and they were on their way.

Thankfully, the Bibliothèque Mazarine was only a few stops away. Deirdre seemed as uncomfortable as Jayne was, being so tightly squashed together with other people. Her face twisted into a pained grimace that relaxed slightly once they climbed the steps that took them aboveground.

"Public transit," Jayne commiserated with a shake of her head. "An introvert's nightmare, am I right?"

"Is my discomfort that obvious?" Deirdre offered a nervous smile.

"You're not alone, friend." Jayne patted her shoulder.

They strode uphill toward a bustling street of towering buildings and a crowd of pedestrians. Jayne gulped at the sight of the Pont des Arts stretching over the river Seine, trying not to remember the shock and grief of losing Cillian.

You'll get him back, she vowed as she turned away from the bridge and focused on the lovely façade of the Mazarine. They entered the small building adjacent to the library to get their visitor passes.

A smiling woman from behind a desk greeted them. In French, she asked, "Hello! How can I help you?"

"I'm Dr. Hall, and this is my associate Ms. Thomas," Deirdre said in perfect French, gesturing to Jayne. "We called ahead about accessing the letters of Pope Leon?"

"Oh yes! You're the ones from Oxford." The woman beamed as she slid a clipboard to them. "Fill these out and I'll get you your passes."

The woman shuffled away as Deirdre filled out the card on the clipboard with such detailed accuracy that Jayne had to whisper, "You've done this before, haven't you?"

Deirdre's lips twitched but she said nothing. Jayne peered over her shoulder as she filled in credentials about her research background and provided three contacts at Oxford as references. Jayne remembered how Deirdre's husband, Alarik, had posed as Professor Albon and given fake credentials. Jayne, ever diligent, had looked up his references and found them to be fake. Would the woman behind the Mazarine's desk be equally suspicious?

The woman returned and slid them badges across the desk. After glancing over the information on the clipboard, she smiled again. "Thank you! You can proceed to the library. Ask for Madame Leveque. She'll show you to the archives."

Deirdre thanked the woman while Jayne remained quiet, careful not to give away her obvious American-accented French and blow their cover. She wondered briefly if the TCO library had a spell to change her accent in addition to her fluency levels. She could get down with having a British accent. No, Australian. G'day, mate!

"Jayne?" Deirdre whispered, pulling her back to their mission.

"Sorry. Daydreaming. Lead on."

They stepped through the door, which opened to a marble passageway that looked like it belonged in a castle—with pillars and winding staircases, plus a balcony overlooking them. The floor was smooth and decorated with black and white tiles. Statues lined the walls as they passed. Jayne gazed upward and found the source of the dome-like roof she'd seen from the outside. A circular window brought a stream of sunlight from above like a heavenly glow.

They passed through a set of huge wooden double doors and found another woman, this one small and stout, who sat behind a desk.

Deirdre said, "Bonjour. We're looking for Madame Leveque." She and Jayne lifted their badges like they were cops or something.

"She is on a break. I am Louise. I will help you." The woman tucked a few unruly blond curls behind her ear and inspected their badges. Without so much as a smile, she stood from her desk and said, "Follow me."

She led them into the reading room, and Jayne stopped short, every inch of her tingling with excitement.

An enormous, cathedral-like ceiling towered over them, and from top to bottom were shelves and shelves of glorious books.

Chandeliers hung from the ceiling. Statues and busts sat adjacent to glass displays of various texts and manuscripts. A high balcony wrapped around the length of the room with decorative iron railings, behind which rested even taller shelves. Ladders were spread throughout the room, and Jayne longed to climb up and see what treasures she could find from the tallest shelf. In the center, other library visitors sat studying, reading, and working on laptops without a care in the world.

Louise led them through the reading room far too quickly. Jayne wanted to stop and gawk some more, but she hurried to keep up with Louise and Deirdre. They were taken into a room that was roped off. Louise removed the chain and waved a bored hand to the room at large. "These are the archives. The catalogues are over there. If you have any trouble locating what you're looking for, please let me know."

She turned and strode back through the reading room without waiting for a response. For once, Jayne was grateful for a librarian who didn't take her job too seriously. It offered them the freedom to explore as long as they liked.

Before diving in, Jayne reached for the Torrent to check that her magic had returned. When the green river of stars gleamed in response, she blew out a breath and got to work. Her fingers drifted over vellum and parchment, her movements slow and meticulous. She perused each text carefully. Her hand paused before moving on as she connected to the Torrent, waiting for the telltale sign of a grimoire reaching out to her.

After about an hour, a prickle of energy warmed Jayne's fingertips. She removed the book, a nineteenth-century text on Latin epigraphy. The subtle nudge of magic was so slight compared to the blast of power she'd felt in Vanderbilt that fateful day when her magic had awakened.

"This must be one of the low-level grimoires Katie told me about," Jayne muttered, running her hand gently over the leather cover.

"Oh, you've met Katie?" Deirdre said distantly, still searching through manuscripts. "Lovely woman. Quite the subversive for a CIA officer, once you get to know her."

Thinking about the adorable woman in her hand-knitted sweaters, rabble-rousing with her precious books, had Jayne giggling inside. Then again, most librarians were free-thinkers. It was part of their charm.

Jayne closed her eyes, focusing on the magic contained within the text. She knew it wasn't the Book of Shadows, but she couldn't pass up the opportunity to learn what spells it contained. A flash of images crossed her mind: a blossoming tree, the crunch of gravel underfoot, and the smell of fresh pine. Warmth seared through her forehead, and she jerked her hand back suddenly.

"Jayne?"

Jayne looked up and found Deirdre watching her with a puzzled look. "Your forehead…" She gestured to her own forehead vaguely.

"Heh. Sorry. Got carried away." Jayne swallowed and returned to the bookshelves, hiding her glowing rune from Deirdre. Medb's totem had reappeared, and with it, that same strange, icy feeling in her chest. It coiled inside her like a serpent waiting to strike, and the whispering chill of it lifted the tiny hairs on her arms. Eventually, she was going to have to explore this. But not yet. And definitely not here.

She and Deirdre spent a few hours roving over manuscripts, even inspecting those from the wrong time period in case the Book of Shadows was misplaced. Jayne had found the second low-level grimoire but had avoided touching it in case the strange foreign presence reared its ugly head once more.

Her eyes were bleary from concentrating for so long. She removed her glasses and rubbed her eyes with her forearm. "It's not here, is it?"

"Doesn't seem like it." Deirdre sounded tired, too.

"Are you sure we can't just ask someone?" Jayne remembered how easy it had been to talk about the Book of Leinster at Trinity.

But Deirdre shook her head. "The Book of Shadows moves around often. From what I've researched, its keepers are paranoid and secretive. If we go around outright asking for the book, it's sure to set off alarm bells."

Jayne nodded, unsurprised. It would've been so much easier if they could just request the damn thing and have it brought out. Just like Alarik had done when he'd been posing as Professor Albon. She could try, but who knew what sort of books would appear.

"Come on," she said with a heavy sigh. "Let's grab a bite to eat and we can hit our next stop."

Linking arms with Deidre, Jayne strode toward the exit, but something made her stop. The back of her neck tingled, and a faint ashy scent wafted in the air.

"What is it?" Deirdre whispered, no doubt alarmed by Jayne's expression.

Goose bumps rose on Jayne's skin, and the answering magic swelling within her confirmed her suspicions: someone else was here. Someone with magic.

Jayne didn't dare turn around. Not with Deirdre at her side. Her lips barely moved as she whispered, "Keep moving. Don't look around. Act natural."

Deirdre stiffened but followed Jayne's lead as they headed out. Deirdre was anything but natural, her movements jerky and that beautiful high-cheekboned face paler than usual. But Jayne couldn't blame her.

When they emerged from the library, Jayne's chest pulsed with warning, a beacon alerting her to danger. Whoever her magic had detected was still right behind them.

They stepped onto the sidewalk, surrounded by passersby, and Jayne released Deirdre. "This might get dirty, so watch out.

But don't go too far—there could be others waiting to grab you while I'm distracted."

Deirdre nodded and turned toward the crowd. Jayne kept her eyes on her curly hair, ensuring she stayed close, before she finally turned to face the threat behind her.

He was tall, dark-haired, with a long, hooked nose and cruel, empty eyes. And he looked vaguely familiar...

"I figured we'd be seeing each other again," the man said. His voice was accented. Jayne couldn't place the country, but it sent a wave of memories through her. Ruth's cruel smile. A rush of powerful magic. The searing pain in her forehead when Medb's gifted totem had bonded with her...

Jayne's eyes narrowed. This man had been there that night. He worked for the Kingdom.

She chose to feign ignorance. "Sorry, who are you again?"

Irritation flashed in the man's eyes. "The name's Blaine. But I shouldn't be surprised you don't remember me. Your kind only cares about the rich and powerful."

"*Your kind?* What the hell is that supposed to mean? You should be more precise with your insults."

Blaine cocked his head at her, clearly annoyed. "Did you find it, then?"

Again, Jayne played dumb. "Find what?" Her hands slid behind her, and she wiggled her fingers, searching for her magic. Now would not be a good time for that stupid poison to kick in.

Blaine smirked. "You're no fool, Jayne Thorne. I know we're both looking for the same thing. But, unlike you, I didn't come alone."

His eyes held hers as he turned and drew a sword that was strapped to his back.

Jayne cocked her head, frowning. "A little old-fashioned, but okay. We can Game of Thrones this."

Only then did she notice the odd gleam to the sword. The

steel seemed warped and twisted, stretching and shrinking as if it were malleable and made of clay. And it shrieked.

Oh, God...

Bile crept up Jayne's throat. "Is that...a *Rogue?*"

Blaine watched her horrified expression smugly. "I can wield it to be whatever weapon I wish."

Bewildered, Jayne glanced around, wondering why the people around them hadn't noticed this crazy man wielding a shape-shifting sword. But a ripple in the air answered their question. They were cloaked. She wasn't sure if Blaine had done it or if the Torrent was hiding them from view, protecting itself, and in turn, Jayne, but she didn't have time to think it through.

Her eyes latched onto the sword. The triumph in Blaine's expression made her blood boil.

"What makes you think I'm alone?" Jayne challenged.

"Oh, you mean Alarik's mousy little wife?" Blaine chuckled. "That's hardly backup."

Jayne's hands curled into fists. Hot rage coursed through her. She stared him down, waiting for more Kingdom operatives to show up. But perhaps his only backup was this sword-slash-Rogue.

She could totally take them.

Blaine took a step toward her. "Tell me where the book is, and I won't sic my Rogue on you."

Her eyes narrowed. He talked about the Rogue like it was some object to be wielded, when in reality, it was a human being. A brief swell of sympathy filled Jayne as she looked at the gleaming sword. She didn't even know if it was male or female. Old or young. Did it work for the Kingdom? Or had it been taken against its will?

Jayne pressed her hands together, calling the river of stars and summoning green sparks to her fingertips. Light exploded within her as she raised her hands in a challenge. A burst of power rushed through her chest, and heat prickled along her skin.

Fear flickered in Blaine's eyes, but he recovered quickly, swinging his sword. Jayne ducked just in time, but she felt the slice of air just above her head. She raised her hands, intending to melt the sword or snap it in two, but she faltered, knowing it wasn't just a sword.

I don't want to hurt you, she thought, her chest tightening. But she remembered the unstoppable Rogue she'd killed in Alarik's Time Catch. If this Rogue got too out of control, she might not have a choice. Who knew what kind of experiments the Kingdom had subjected it to?

Praying her magic would work, she summoned a Block spell and layered in a Shield just as Blaine lunged for her again. She put more force behind it than she thought—when the sword slammed into the invisible barrier, it went flying, clattering to the ground several feet away.

Jayne gathered magic in her hands and speared it toward Blaine, freezing him in place before he could grab the sword. The Rogue sword twitched slightly on the ground, inching closer toward her.

Sweat poured down Jayne's face, and her skin burned. *Easy now...* She would never shake the mental image of the Adept bursting into flames from his uncontrollable magic. Keeping one hand flexed toward Blaine to hold him, Jayne only had a second to summon another Block spell, but this one wasn't quick enough.

The sword shot forward. The Block spell deflected it, but not entirely. The blade sliced into Jayne's forearm, and she hissed in pain. Her hold on Blaine loosened, and he surged forward, wielding spirals of magic between his hands.

The sword hovered over Jayne, prepared to strike again. In a flash, Blaine was there, leering in front of her with delight etched into his unpleasant face.

Scrambling for a way out, Jayne felt for her magic but didn't know who to strike—Blaine or the sword? She crammed her eyes shut and reached for the Torrent, snatching the first spell she saw. It resembled a woven basket of light, gleaming eagerly as if it had been waiting for her this whole time.

Of course. The Carry spell!

Jayne grabbed it and threw it over the sword. In a flash, the sword vanished, and something heavy settled over her, dragging her downward. The spell would weaken her, but she'd rather take on one man while weak than have to face a Kingdom Adept *and* a sentient sword.

Blaine's face slackened, his eyes wide with shock. "What... what did you do? Where is it?"

"Your Rogue is tucked somewhere safe, envisioning all the ways he could cut you to ribbons," Jayne said brightly. Using Blaine's astonishment to her advantage, she sent a surge of magic that hit him squarely in the chest, sending him reeling. As soon as he landed, red sparks danced on his hands. He jolted upright, storming toward Jayne, his face contorted with rage, but she was ready. She hit him with wave after wave of magic, slamming all the force of her power into him. When he crumpled, blood pouring from his nose, Jayne swung her fist into his jaw for good measure, knocking him out completely.

Winded, Jayne checked the cut on her arm, but it wasn't too deep. The weight of the Rogue wore on her, making her body sag from the pull of it. Vaguely, she wondered if the sword could still stab her even through the Carry spell. But she had a feeling with Blaine knocked out, she'd be safe.

Her eyes quickly landed on Deirdre, still tucked in the crowd with terror on her face. Jayne quickly approached her, taking her arm and forcing her feet to move even as sweat poured down her brow and neck.

"Are you all right?" Deirdre breathed. "It was like you...disappeared for a moment there. I looked back and you were gone."

"You couldn't see the fight? Can you see Blaine over there?"

Deirdre shook her head. "No."

"Hmm. That's interesting. It's like the Torrent performs some sort of Cloaking spell to hide us. Maybe so the civilians don't see danger? And yes, I'm okay, just have a shape-shifting sword hidden by magic and tethered to my body. Come on, let's get out of here before that bastard wakes up."

25

A MONSTROUS BETRAYAL

Cillian didn't know if it was day or night when he woke. His head ached—hell, his whole face ached. Before he'd fallen asleep, he'd yanked on his nose to set it, and that was enough to make him howl in pain and curse up a storm. These stupid terrorists and their stupid power-hungry designs on the magical world. For a brief moment, he wished he'd never met any of them, but that would mean not having met Jayne, or discovering his own powers as a Rogue, which, admittedly, were pretty cool.

If he got out of here alive, he needed to do some research into the history of Rogues instead of just relying on Jayne to share information with him.

"I can help you there."

He yelped and jumped. A tall, thin figure materialized out of the darkness in the corner of the room.

Gina Labelle. Cillian recognized her from the pictures in the TCO file.

"You must be wondering how I can hear your thoughts. Not every Rogue has that particular power. I, though, come from a long and distinguished line, and am one of the strongest, most gifted Rogues you'll ever meet."

"Sounds like you're braggin' now."

She uttered a bark of a laugh. "Aren't you the brave one? Not bragging, dear Cillian. Sharing facts. How much have they told you about your abilities? About your history? About the powers we possess?" She waited for a response, but he didn't answer. They hadn't told him much at all, and he hardly wanted to admit that. "Nothing? Pity. Should you care to know more about your lineage, your place in the magical world, what you're capable of, all you need to do is say so, and I will share all I know."

"What's the catch?"

"You join forces with us. We could use a Rogue such as yourself. Strong. Smart. Dedicated to the cause."

He shook his head, ignoring the pain from his broken nose. "No. No way."

"We wouldn't use you for your gifts like they will. We will honor your spirit and strength. Teach you, not hold back vital information about your powers. Your magic."

He bared his teeth. "Not gonna happen. Sorry."

Labelle stalked around him slowly. He was reminded of his mother's sleek seal-point Siamese cat, who would wind around his feet when she was hungry or wanted love. He hadn't thought of Jezebelle in years, and here was Gina Labelle, slinking around in the dim light as if she were channeling the cat from his memories.

"Tsk. Isn't that sweet? Your mother was quite beautiful. As was the cat. Purebred, was she?"

"Stay out of my head." Without thinking, he envisioned a wall of ebony marble and pushed against her, hard. He sensed her taking a step back.

"Oh, well done. You're already learning. I can teach you so much, Cillian. So much more than that silly girl."

A stab of panic coursed through him. How had he done that? "Leave me alone."

"I will do no such thing," Labelle snarled. "You've cost me

someone dear, Rogue. You best hope he is returned to me undamaged, or we will have a much bigger problem."

"Tristan Lowell is dear to you? Why?"

She pressed on without answering. "You will tell me everything, from what the TCO offices look like to the depth of the girl's power, or I will send you back to her in pieces." Labelle examined her nails, which he noticed were quite long, and quite sharp. "They haven't had time to train you properly, I'm sure. Advanced interrogation techniques are quite effective. Have you ever drowned before, Cillian? Do you know what that feels like? It will break even the strongest man, the sensation of water pouring deep into your throat and nose and into your lungs. You won't last a minute."

He growled, deep and loud, the sound rumbling through him, making his bones shiver.

"There, there. Give me what I want and I'll return you to them unmolested."

"I don't know anything, and if you truly can read my mind, you know I'm telling the truth."

Gina Labelle's long, sharp eyeteeth glimmered when she smiled.

"Let's see, shall we?"

∼

It felt like hours. Days. Weeks. He had no idea who he was, what he thought, why he was fighting her. And fight he did. A wolf pup against a robust, battle-scarred lion. He held his own, for a time, but he was nothing compared to her. Finally, exhausted, ribs broken, face bleeding, he fell onto the floor and whined in submission.

She scraped her claws along his leg deeply for good measure, then transformed them back into their human states.

"How," he gasped. "How can you change me like that?"

Labelle licked a bloody finger fastidiously, her tongue again small and pink. "If I give you that knowledge, you'll share it with your Master. And I can't have that. Stay with us, Cillian. I will heal you. I will share all of my knowledge. You do not need to be subjugated to a Master who knows nothing about your true nature. You are more than them. You are better than them. You have powers you can only dream of. Magic of your own. But you must agree to fight for me, against the TCO, and help us finish our quest to find the grimoires. Relent. Agree. I will make the pain stop."

He was panting in agony, his head swimming, black dots swirling around him. It would be so easy to agree. To end this torture.

But he would be betraying the one person he actually gave a damn about. His mind felt muddled and thick. Jayne's face floated into his vision, blurry and indistinct. The brown hair morphed into blond, the brown eyes to blue. Sofia. Sofia and Jayne. The faces of the sisters flickered and shifted, both of their eyes full of pain and worry. Worry for him.

He couldn't betray them.

He wouldn't.

With a mighty roar, he dragged himself to his feet.

Gina Labelle swiped a paw across his face, and he fell.

26

BATHOS

When Jayne told Amanda she had a Rogue in her pocket, the woman took it in stride. Jayne had to give her credit for that. After calling several officers to the Montmartre safe house, Amanda set up a portal to the TCO so they could escort the sword Rogue to one of the holding cells. Jayne flinched at the term, but Amanda reassured her it was a temporary precaution until they could assess how dangerous the Rogue was.

"Will you be able to…help him?" Jayne had almost said *train him*, but she had to remind herself this wasn't an animal. It was a person who might have uncontrollable shape-shifting abilities. From what she'd seen of Blaine's methods the last time she'd run into him, his Rogue was likely to be unpredictable at best.

"We'll try," Amanda said, her brows knitting together in concern. "He's certainly in safer hands with us than he is with the Kingdom. We would never be so cruel as to turn a person into an inanimate object. It goes against nature, and our very sacred magical vows."

Jayne couldn't argue with that. She knew the Kingdom was experimenting on Rogues, trying to harness their magic. She'd seen it firsthand. The very concept made her sick to her stomach.

Even if the TCO didn't know much about Rogues yet, Amanda was right: this was still the safest place for him.

The men surrounded the portal and then gave Jayne the go-ahead to release the Carry spell. A huge weight fell from her shoulders...and then tumbled through the portal. Immediately, the officers around her surged forward to surround the sword, wielding their own Shield spells. The sword Rogue whipped into the air, still in "kill Jayne" mode. It—he?—flew toward her. She staggered backward, but the Shield spells held. Jayne would have liked to follow the officers and see that the Rogue calmed down, but her presence was obviously making things worse. She watched, her heart twisting, as the men restrained the sword before the portal door slammed shut, leaving her alone with Amanda.

This is the best thing for him, she reminded herself. *It's for the best.*

～

Deidre was waiting for her back at the flat, sitting at the breakfast nook, half hidden by a giant stack of books. She looked up, her eyes bleary and tired, but her smile seemed genuine. "Hi, Jayne."

"Hey. Want some tea?"

"I'd love a cup, thanks."

Jayne fixed them both steaming mugs of Earl Grey and plopped on the chair opposite Deirdre. "Can I help with the research?"

Deirdre stifled a yawn and reached for her tea. "Not much to go on, I'm afraid. There's all kinds of lore on the Master of Shadows and the pages within his book, but nothing concrete."

"What do you have so far?"

Deirdre handed her a few books. "These both mention the

Master's shadowed illumination, which is supposed to unlock the key to a great treasure."

"Shadowed illumination?" Jayne had seen plenty of illuminated manuscripts, many of which were elaborately decorated or illustrated texts.

"It's supposed to be an illustration made of shadow. Like, imagine a shadow in the shape of an arrow, pointing to an 'X marks the spot.'"

"That would be grand. Makes things super easy."

"Yeah, only no one can agree on where this particular shadowed illumination is."

"I'm guessing the Book of Shadows has its location?"

Deirdre gestured to the book open on her lap. "Based on my findings? Yes."

Jayne sat up straighter, putting on her imaginary librarian cap. "How can I help?"

Deirdre nodded toward a hefty stack of books on the floor beside her. "Those are the ones I haven't looked through yet." She shot Jayne an apologetic look.

But Jayne grinned like an eager puppy. "Are you kidding? This is the life, am I right?"

Deirdre chuckled as Jayne lifted a few books off the stack and got to work.

An ordinary twenty-three-year-old woman might find this task dull and tedious. But not Jayne Thorne, CIA Librarian. She dived into research as if it were a swimming pool full of pudding. She didn't know much about the Master of Shadows—certainly not as much as Deirdre did—so she drank in the information like she was dying of thirst. Within an hour, she'd taken copious notes about the elusive Master of Shadows, a powerful magician believed to be from the fifteenth century. There wasn't much about the Master himself, but plenty about the Book of Shadows, an ancient Wiccan text he was said to have written. Many believed it to be a myth, so much of what Jayne read was pure speculation. She wrote it all down anyway.

"What do you suppose the shadowed illumination leads to?" Deirdre asked thoughtfully, breaking the silence.

"You mean the *great treasure*?" Jayne asked. Their voices sounded odd after an hour of silence.

"Yeah."

Jayne looked up from her studying, her eyes bleary. She thought of La Liberté and the Kingdom and how they sought more power—and a necromantic grimoire would give them that power.

Then Jayne focused on the word *necromantic*.

"My guess is it leads to his burial site," Jayne said softly. "I think the shadowed illumination is a guide for raising the Master of Shadows. He must be a fallen Master, like Medb."

A stunned silence met her words. Deirdre's face drained of color, and her eyes nearly popped out of her face. "My God," she whispered, raising a trembling hand to cover her mouth.

"I know," Jayne said in a low voice. Horror swirled in her stomach, but she wasn't as shocked as Deirdre. If her experience with Medb was any indication, it was possible the fallen Masters each had a powerful totem to gift whoever raised them. And La Liberté and the Kingdom were after these totems.

Jayne couldn't allow that to happen.

She and Deirdre returned to their research, though Deirdre kept gnawing anxiously at her fingernails, and Jayne knew the woman was rattled by this revelation.

Another pot of tea later, Jayne came across something that gave her pause. *Many historians believed the Master of Shadows to be an artist who created illuminated manuscripts, each with a hidden meaning.* "Whoa, that's weird." She scratched her head.

"What?" Deidre asked, looking up.

Jayne stared at the passage she'd just read as several puzzle pieces clicked into place. "Deirdre, what if the Master of Shadows was an artist?"

"An artist? What do you mean?"

"All this time, we've been researching grimoires and Master magicians and Adept history, but what if we're going about this all wrong? Maybe the reason he's so elusive is because he hid his magic in his illustrations! What if he was pretending to be an average Joe, flying under the radar? Maybe he didn't want to draw too much attention to himself as an Adept, so he hid his abilities."

Deirdre tapped her chin thoughtfully. "It's worth looking into." She laughed, shaking her head. "I can't believe I didn't think of that before. Sometimes it's hard to merge my two worlds—the nonmagic and the magic."

"That is something I can totally understand." Jayne remembered all too well the shock of realizing there were necromantic grimoires right under her nose in her precious libraries. "But... does it ever bother you?"

Deirdre's nose was already in a book. "Does what bother me?"

"Merging your two worlds. Do you ever feel like...you're going to lose one of them?"

Deirdre looked up, her face sobering. "Why would you think something like that?"

Jayne sighed, sagging back in her chair. "I don't know. This whole craziness with La Liberté screwing around with my magic and stealing first Ruger and now Cillian, it makes me wonder who I was before all this happened." She gestured nonsensically with her hands. She couldn't stifle the feeling of utter helplessness when she couldn't access the Torrent. And thinking about what Cillian must have gone through to look like he did in that photo made her sick to her stomach.

"Jayne, even before I knew you had magic, I envied you."

Jayne's eyebrows lifted. "Really?"

"Really. When I first met you, you were this smart, confident, kickboxer librarian who was clearly incredibly smart. You had this air about you that told me you could handle anything. And that wasn't just your magic talking. It was you."

Jayne pressed her lips together, unconvinced.

Deirdre leaned forward, pressing her hand to Jayne's shoulder. "You are more than your magic, Jayne. Never forget that. One thing I learned from Alarik was that magic has the ability to completely consume a person. Just like it did for him." She paused and took a shaky breath, her face crumpling for a moment.

Before Jayne could stop herself, she said, "I'm sorry."

Deirdre stared at her. "For what?"

Jayne hesitated. She almost said, *For killing him,* but she wasn't sorry about that. Still rattled by the frequent memories of the act, yes, but…not sorry Alarik was dead. Instead, she said, "For everything he put you through. And…for your loss."

Deirdre offered a sad smile. "Thank you. For the record, I don't resent you for taking his life. I really don't. He'd become a monster. I'm not sorry he's gone. I just…I spent so many years desperately searching for the man I fell in love with, trying to bring him back somehow. But that version of Alarik died years ago, leaving a power-hungry tyrant in his place."

Sorrow filled Jayne's chest as she tried to imagine a less scary Alarik. But she couldn't. How twisted had he become to completely shift into a new person? Had he once been kind and gentle? Someone Deirdre could love? Jayne almost wished she could've met that version of Alarik.

Deirdre went on, "Jayne, my point is, you are different from Adepts like Alarik. Magic is just one side of your multifaceted persona. You're also a fierce fighter. A researcher. A loyal friend. And a doggedly determined TCO officer."

Jayne grinned at that. Chagrin filled her, flaming her cheeks. "Sorry, I don't know where all this came from. You must think

I'm an idiot, complaining to you about my magic when..." She trailed off, now feeling even more idiotic.

"When I don't have magic?" Deirdre smiled wryly. "Honestly, I think I'm one of the few people you can talk to about this, because I *don't* have magic." She shrugged, her expression lightening. "I think sometimes you Adepts need a reminder that a whole world exists out there without magic. Some people live long, fulfilling lives without ever knowing about the Torrent."

Jayne stared blankly at her for a minute. *Wow*, she thought. Had she really needed that reminder? She'd always thought herself to be down-to-earth. But maybe magic had gone to her head. "Well, I sure hope you don't think I'm a self-absorbed Adept with an inflated ego."

Deirdre laughed. "Not at all."

Relief filled Jayne until she felt like she was breathing fresh air for the first time in days. It seemed so silly to think she was nothing without her magic. Of course there was more to her than that. She *was* a kickass kickboxer. An enthusiastic researcher. A lover of fantasy books. A quoter of movies. And a damn good librarian.

A small smile lit her face as she happily dived back into her research.

27

TRÈS RICHE

Long after Deirdre had fallen asleep on the couch, politely declining Jayne's insistence that she take the bedroom, Jayne remained at the table, researching well into the night.

She'd already blown through several cups of tea to keep her awake. She knew she couldn't possibly get any sleep knowing Cillian was enduring all manner of horrors when she still hadn't found the Book of Shadows. Besides, they had already wasted one day. Only two left before Gina would start cutting off fingers.

Jayne shuddered, closing the book titled *Fifteenth-Century Painters* and moving on to *Illuminated Manuscripts Unlocked*.

When she reached a section about the famous fifteenth-century illuminated manuscript known as Très Riches Heures du Duc de Berry—The Very Rich Hours of the Duke of Berry—she froze, certain her muddled, exhausted brain was playing tricks on her. She slid the massive text closer and read aloud, "The intermediate painter of the Très Riches Heures is often referred to as the Master of Shadows due to his usage of shadows in his style of painting. Though there is no documented proof, the Master of Shadows is believed to have been Barthélemy van Eyck, a miniaturist also known as the Master of René of Anjou. Scholars believe he worked on the illustrations between the 1420s and the 1440s."

She looked up blankly, not seeing the room. "Oh my God. I found him." She hastily returned her gaze to the text, skimming for any other reference to the Master of Shadows. It wasn't until she turned the page that she read one other passage about the book: "The Très Riches Heures is located in the Musée Condé in Chantilly, France."

"Deirdre!" Jayne shouted.

Deirdre uttered a short yip before sitting bolt upright on the sofa. "Beg pardon?" she mumbled sleepily.

"I found him."

Deirdre shot up in mere seconds, rubbing her eyes as she hurried over. She bent over Jayne's shoulder, squinting as she read the text.

"The intermediate painter of the...Très Riches Heures..." She trailed off with a gasp. "Oh my God..."

"I know, right?" Jayne exclaimed. "We thought the Book of Shadows was a grimoire, but it's not. It's a book of hours—a collection of prayers. It's mostly illustrations, and I'm certain the shadowed illumination is found inside it."

A high-pitched, excited giggle burst from Deirdre's mouth. She shook Jayne's shoulders with enthusiasm Jayne had never seen in her before. "Jayne, you did it!"

Jayne's brain was firing off one idea after another as everything slowly came together. "We'd speculated that maybe he hid his magic in his illustrations. It makes sense that he'd hide it in something simple. Something easy to overlook because he wanted it to stay hidden."

Deirdre laughed again, practically giddy from this revelation. "Did you find out where the Très Riches Heures is located?"

Jayne turned the page and pointed to another passage.

"The Musée Condé in Chantilly, France." Deirdre clapped a hand to her forehead. "Of course! It's in a museum, not a library!"

"We need to get this information to Amanda," Jayne said, rising from her chair. "It's early enough that we can catch the first train to Chantilly. Then, we'll grab the Book of Shadows—"

Deirdre raised a hand. "Hang on. You can't just steal the book."

Jayne blinked at her. "What?"

"Think about it. It's not something you can walk out with, like at a library. It's in a museum. There's a good chance it will be on a special display, and that whatever they have out isn't the real thing anyway. The real book will be in the vaults. There will be alarms in place."

"Okay, that makes sense. But I should be able to magic us into the place, and get the alarms turned off, right? We'll need to swap it out with a forgery to buy ourselves some time. How long will it take you to put that together?"

Deirdre's head jerked back, her expression incredulous. She sputtered a few times before finding her voice. "I—Jayne, this will take time. It's nothing like the grimoire I was preparing to forge before. I need specific materials. This is a book of hours, illuminated, and it's—"

"We don't have time," Jayne said, trying not to snap at Deirdre. It wasn't her fault. "Okay. Here's what we'll do. We'll talk to Amanda. I'm sure she can work her CIA voodoo to get whatever materials you'll need. Keep in mind, this means we now need two forgeries. One for the museum, and one for La Liberté. After we nab the book and replace it with the fake, we'll give the book to you to make a more precise copy, then make the trade and get Cillian back." Jayne clapped her hands as if everything was settled.

Deirdre gnawed on her lower lip. "You make it sound a lot easier than it is."

"The plan is flawed and full of holes, but we can do this. I know we can. Cillian's life depends on it." Jayne took Deirdre's hand and squeezed. "Are you with me on this?"

Deirdre nodded solemnly. "I'm with you."

"Good. We need to get to Montmartre, now."

When Jayne explained their situation, Amanda's worried face turned thoughtful. She didn't speak, though, which made Jayne want to throttle her boss. Wouldn't be the smartest move, but it would be satisfying. She tried again.

"You see the issue, I'm sure. We have to get our hands on the book, like, now."

Ruger came into the living room, carrying a plate of croissants fresh out of the oven. He put it on the coffee table, and the delicious scent made Jayne's stomach audibly rumble. "Help yourself," he said, amused. "What's up?"

"Other than we need to stop time so Deirdre can make a forgery of the grimoire? I'm open to ideas."

As she said it, it hit her. Apparently, it hit Ruger as well, because their eyes met, and in unison, they said, "Time Catch."

Amanda was shaking her head before the syllables danced out of the air. "No, no, no. No way. We are not making a Time Catch. That is expressly forbidden by the organization's bylaws."

"Forbidden?" Jayne asked. "Why?"

Amanda cocked a brow. "Really? Both of you have been kidnapped and held in Time Catches. You know how dangerous and harmful they are. It is illegal magic, dark magic. And it's not how we operate. Should magical law enforcement organizations take to making Time Catches, we would be no better than those we seek to stop."

Amanda was shaking slightly. Jayne didn't know if it was from fear or fury. She certainly looked angry at the mere suggestion. How was Jayne to know Time Catches were illegal?

It made sense—they took an exceptional amount of magic and did seem to be the lairs of the big baddies they'd come across, but still.

"What's your idea then? Because we're running out of time." Jayne tapped the top of her wrist impatiently, then moved the hand to her chest. "'There's nothing left except to try,'" she declaimed.

"You're quoting books again," Ruger said. "What's that from?"

"*A Wrinkle in Time*. Madeline L'Engle. It seemed appropriate." She flashed him a grin, but he frowned in response.

"Wrinkles in time," he murmured, then looked at Amanda. "The Time Catch simulation. Could we put Deirdre and the tools she'd need into the simulation? Will it work for a nonmagical?"

"No. Civilians can't exist in Time Catches. It won't work."

Deirdre, who'd been silent through the whole exchange, raised a hand shyly.

Amanda huffed out a breath but called on her as if she were a star pupil. "Officer Green? You have something to say?"

"Alarik, my former husband, took me into a Time Catch once. It felt awful, but I was able to cross in and out. He was…" Deirdre wavered, looking at her feet. Jayne squeezed her friend's shoulder.

"He was testing to see if you survived it?" she asked softly, and Deirdre nodded.

"What an arse. But you were okay?"

"It felt quite odd, like I was rippling, somehow, coming loose from my skin. But yes. I survived. Obviously," she added with the ghost of a laugh.

Jayne grabbed a croissant and tore off a chunk. "We should try it. At least we know Deirdre can't be hurt by a simulation."

Amanda was leaning forward now, almost toppling off the sofa in her excitement.

"Would you be willing to try, Officer Green? We will certainly find another way if you're uncomfortable with this plan."

The coddling version of Amanda was surprising, yet again. Was she only prickly with Jayne?

Deirdre had picked up a croissant, too. She put it down carefully and squared her narrow shoulders. "Yes. I will. This—the grimoire—it's too important not to try."

"It's settled," Ruger said, clapping a big hand against his knee and standing. "You ladies eat. We'll prepare a portal and warn Katie Bell we might need some of her clerics to help. I'll have Hector bring the simulation. He's the best we have at Time Catches."

"Hector? My mentor Hector?" Jayne asked.

"Your mentor *Hector*?" Ruger asked incredulously. "What am I, chopped liver?"

"Long story," Jayne replied, waving her hand. "He helped Cillian and me work on the spells to find you." She gave him her sauciest grin. "Don't worry, Rug. You'll always be my first."

"Jayne," they all groaned.

An hour had passed before they were all assembled. Hector and three young Adepts dressed in CIA Casual—khakis and blue button-down shirt—stepped into the living room of the Montmartre safe house. Hector introduced them as Katie's clerics. They carried leather bags filled with all the tools Deirdre would need to assemble the forgeries.

Hector himself carried a small red leather rectangular box with a gold latch. There was a spell on the latch; Jayne could see the air shimmering around it.

"Hiya, Hector."

"Miss Thorne. Where is Mr. Pine?"

"Kidnapped. By the same jerks who took Ruger."

Hector looked truly disturbed. "I'm sorry to hear that. I'm fond of that Rogue. He has spirit."

"That Rogue will be happy to hear it. Thanks for coming so

fast. We need to hurry this along, folks. Can you cast the simulation now? I'll take Deirdre and the clerics inside, and we'll make the grimoires."

They all lined up on one side of the living room and watched Hector carefully set the box on the floor.

"I've adjusted this to be what we needed based on what Katie thought would be appropriate. The clerics have all the materials we could find. Ready?"

"'Ready, Santa!'" Jayne called. Everyone looked at her. "Rudolph," she said, brows furrowed. "Don't you people like holiday classics?"

Shaking his head, Hector murmured some words to release the latch, and opened the box.

A library shimmered into view.

"Ooh," Jayne breathed. "Good. Books. This I can manage. How long can we stay in here, Hector?"

"The record for the simulation is two weeks. After that, it degrades completely. You'll notice it isn't the same as a real Time Catch right away. Just…pay attention. If you hear a clock ticking, you have to get out immediately."

"And if we don't?"

"Don't test it, Jayne," Amanda snapped. "We don't need to lose anyone else."

But it was Ruger who laid a hand on her arm. "She's not joking. If you hear the clock ticking, get out. I've already told Amanda, but La Liberté knows we use the clock as a warning signal. They used it against me in their Time Catch. We haven't had time to change our simulation yet, so it's imperative that you leave the moment you hear it. Just in case they've managed other mischief. Am I clear?"

The vision of Ruger battered and hurt, and Cillian in the same boat, made Jayne drop all pretense. "Fair enough. Everyone heard that, right? If I hear the clock and call to abort, you do not hesitate." There were murmurs of assent from her team. "All right,

Deirdre. Take my arm, and we'll step right through. Let's go cook up a book."

Without another word, Jayne dragged Deirdre right through the shimmering veil.

As far as Time Catches went, this one was downright cozy. The only reason Jayne knew it wasn't real was the fact that she could see the living room of the Montmartre safe house, with Ruger, Amanda, and Hector standing there staring in at them as if they were in a fishbowl. They didn't move. It was like they'd frozen solid.

Deirdre gaped beside her. "This is kind of weird."

"It is," Jayne replied, feeling a deep chill running down her own spine. This library was as unnatural as a three-headed cat. "Are you feeling okay?"

"A little nauseated. We'd better hurry."

"Agreed. What do you need?"

"The materials."

At her words, the clerics leaped into action, opening their satchels and spilling the contents on the table. Vellum, parchment, inks, and, thankfully, pictures and models of the book of hours. Deirdre didn't waste any time; she started giving orders, and soon they were all working hard.

Jayne loved every second of this. Deirdre was spectacularly talented, and the clerics almost seemed clairvoyant, anticipating everything Deirdre needed almost before the words left her mouth. It was like watching a neurosurgeon rewire a brain.

When they grew tired, the library provided coffee, tea, and scones. One of the clerics smiled at Jayne through a crumble of dough. "Katie said you enjoyed them, so she sent some along in the box."

"Katie is my new best friend," Jayne said, dumping a pile of clotted cream on a chunk of scone and shoveling it in.

When they were sleepy, bunk beds appeared. Bathrooms, showers, even a treadmill showed up. Katie must have sent a little bit of the enchantments from the TCO library itself, and every time Jayne fell into the soft sheets, she was so incredibly grateful.

It was eerie, being in this floating, transparent world. Every few hours, Jayne would check on the safe house. It was like looking through shimmering air into a painting. She was tempted once or twice to step back through and update them on their progress, but she was too afraid to leave Deirdre alone in the Catch in case she couldn't get her back out. That would be very, very bad.

The grimoires were nearing completion when Jayne heard the first ticking.

"Stop, stop. Everyone stop."

A hush fell over their workspace.

Tick.

Tick.

Tick.

"We gotta go. Right now."

"But it's not ready, Jayne," Deirdre argued. "I still need to—"

"It's perfect. We gotta go. Pack it up, boys!"

The clerics were three steps ahead of them. All of the materials disappeared into one satchel. Their dorms disappeared—the beds and the treadmill and the table and the fridge, poof—all went back into the other two satchels.

Tick.

Tick.

Jayne grabbed the grimoires in one hand and looped her other arm through Deirdre's. They all approached the shimmering transparent wall.

"Now," Jayne said, and stepped through.

She and the grimoires and the clerics landed back in France. Deirdre was not on her arm.

She said a very bad word, shoved the grimoires at Ruger, and dove back in.

Darkness. A wall of black. A flash of white. That ominous ticking, clamorous now in the void.

Deirdre was sitting on the floor, a book next to her. It had a small booklight attached, enough to illuminate the pages but casting nothing beyond Deirdre's lap. Jayne approached quickly.

"Girl. *Gulliver's Travels*? Really?"

Deirdre looked up, her tear-streaked face pale and thin. "Oh, thank God, Jayne."

"How long was I gone?" Jayne asked, wrapping the sobbing woman in a hug.

"I don't know. I don't know. Just get me out of here."

"Hold on tight." This time, Jayne pulled Deirdre into a bear hug, even going so far as to twine her leg around Deirdre's ankle, and fell forward through the veil with Deirdre going first.

They landed in a heap on the soft rug of the living room in Montmartre to utter cacophony.

Hector rushed forward with the lid of the box and slammed it closed, shouting "Lock!" at the top of his lungs. Ruger hauled Deirdre to her feet, patted her down for wounds, and gave her a huge white handkerchief to dry her tears. Amanda, ghostly pale, was holding her necklace and weaving some sort of spell that made the room feel warm and comfortable. It was only as she warmed that Jayne realized she was freezing cold and shaking as if she'd been outside in the snow for hours without a coat.

"You're okay," Ruger was telling Deirdre. "You're okay now."

"What happened when you went back in?" Hector asked, face a mask. He offered Jayne a blanket, which she wrapped around herself gratefully. She didn't want to think ever again about the bleakness she'd felt, the clanging clock, the look of anguish on Deirdre's face. But she forced herself to speak without wavering.

"She was alone, with a single book. There was nothing there.

A void. An abyss." Jayne shuddered. "I am so, so sorry, Deirdre. I thought you were with me. I didn't realize…please, forgive me."

"It wasn't too long," Deirdre finally managed. "I only reread the book s times. The library…left it for me. It was one of my favorites as a child. I am terribly hungry, though. I went through the last of the scones a few days ago."

Jayne gaped, horror spreading through her body. To think of her sweet, gentle friend in that hole, starving in the dark, and that Jayne herself had created the situation? "You were there for, what, at least a week? It wasn't even ten seconds out here. Really, Deirdre, I don't know how to apologize."

"It's okay." Deirdre squeezed Jayne's hand. "I'm out now."

It wasn't okay. It would never be okay.

"Never again." Amanda stomped through the living room, berating Hector and Ruger. "Destroy that thing, now."

Hector laid a protective hand on the box, protesting, "We'll never learn—" but Amanda's eyes glittered with fury.

"Destroy it. I will not allow that to happen ever again. It's too dangerous for Adepts. For a nonmagical? No. End its existence. That kind of alternate universe sentience is an abomination."

Amanda was screaming now, enough that Ruger stepped to her side and walked her from the room. Hector gave Jayne and Deirdre a weak smile.

"Sorry. I did say it was unstable."

"You're officially demoted, Hector," Jayne said with a sigh. "I don't know if we'll survive any more of your mentoring."

28

THE SUBSTITUTE

Six hours later, Jayne stood on the vast grounds, gaping at the magnificent castle that was the Château de Chantilly. It was a gloriously sunny day, not a cloud in the sky, and the colors surrounding her were almost too vibrant: polished white concrete walkways snaked between vivid green lawns, and the sapphire lake sparkled in the sunlight. The sheer grandeur of the building, the epic crowds, the tourists calling and shouting and taking photos, were only part of her nerves. She had to break in and steal one of their most valued treasures and get out without anyone noticing. Just another walk in the park. Not.

She adjusted her bag on her shoulder, checking for the millionth time that Deirdre's forgery was safely tucked inside. The exterior of the grimoire was perfect, with the exact aged calfskin for the vellum, though since they'd run out of time, there were a few interior pages they'd been forced to fudge with a little help from Amanda's magic. It looked stellar to Jayne, but Deirdre kept complaining about how "sloppy" it was.

It would have to do. Besides, based on Deirdre's research, the book wasn't on display because the manuscript had degraded so much. So the good news was Jayne wouldn't have to make the swap out in the open in front of hundreds of eyewitnesses.

The bad news was she had to somehow sneak her way into the archives of the museum to where the actual book was located. They'd debated her going in as a scholar, as they had at the Mazarine, but they'd discovered the general curator of libraries she would ordinarily work with, Marie-Pierre, was on holiday, and the time it would take to create a request going through another channel was too long. They needed the Book of Shadows, and they needed it now. So smash and grab was the order of the day.

Jayne took a deep breath, hoping La Liberté had kept their word to give her access to her magic again. She reached for the Torrent. The once solid thread linking her to the magic river of stars was now as faint as a spiderweb. She clung to it like a lifeline before the green stars flowed into her mind, flooding her senses.

The Torrent seemed foggier than normal, like she had to squint to see the spells clearly. But after a moment, she found what she was looking for: the Tracking spell. She pictured a simplified form, a variation of it. A Find spell. It was shaped like a glistening white diamond. Jayne grabbed it, opening her eyes and resurfacing with the spell sparkling along her fingertips. She stared intently at the château before her and focused on her memories of the grimoires she'd come in contact with. The most poignant memory was the first time she'd first felt magic—at the Vanderbilt University archives in Nashville.

How could she forget that life-changing moment? The river of stars swirling in her mind. The cold chill that washed over her. The scent of roses and woodsmoke.

A faint light glimmered in front of her. Sucking in a breath, Jayne reached out to touch it, but her hand passed right through. It almost looked like a trick of the light, a glare from the sun. If she didn't know any better, she would've brushed it off.

But she did know better. This was the Find spell. And it had found the grimoire.

Excitement buzzed through her. Or maybe that was just the caffeine. Either way, a smile spread across Jayne's face as she stepped forward, following the sparkling light as it led the way to the Book of Shadows.

Jayne walked for what felt like hours, past exquisite floor-to-ceiling paintings that made her want to weep with awe, past breathtaking sculptures, ornate chandeliers, magnificent ball-rooms. After half an hour of weaving through tourists and strug-gling to keep her gaze on the spark of light, despite the beauty around her that called to her, Jayne's heart felt like it might burst from her chest.

I'll come back. One day, I'll take a vacation and come back here like a proper tourist. I swear it.

It didn't reduce the pure agony wrestling inside her as she passed yet another magnificent piece of art that she yearned to stop and scrutinize for hours.

When she entered the reading room, she thought she might faint. Bookshelves stretched on and on, for what looked like miles of nothing but perfect, wonderful-smelling books. The shelves reached all the way to the massive ceiling, so high Jayne would've had to climb several sets of stairs to reach the top.

She searched, but the insistent glare of light was clear: the Book of Shadows wasn't here.

Even though leaving the reading room caused her physical pain, her limbs going tense as if her body was responding to the magical call of the books, she set off again, following that gleam of light like her life depended on it. She almost wished Deirdre had come with her, just so she had someone to back her up. But that would have been too much to ask, and operationally, it would be hard enough to sneak just one person into the archives, let alone two. Deirdre was better served staying with the second grimoire while Amanda added the spells to it. Unlike this grimoire, they weren't just misleading some nonmagical museum curators who were clueless about the magic contained inside the pages. They were trying to fool La Liberté, who most likely already expected Jayne to dupe them in some way.

When the Find spell led Jayne through narrower hallways with fewer people, she paused to grab a quick Cloaking spell to mask her from passersby and errant cameras. Her skin prickled, and a shimmering curtain surrounded her body, making her feel odd, as if she were dreaming. She had the sense she was no longer in the crowd, and that made her relax a bit.

Almost there, she thought. *It has to be close now.*

When a man wearing an official-looking uniform walked toward her, Jayne instinctively pressed herself against the wall, holding her breath as he passed. She didn't know how the spell worked—if it masked her completely, or if some sounds and smells lingered—but she didn't want to take any chances.

She rounded a corner, and the Find spell froze. Jayne almost didn't notice—she passed right through it, then glanced around in confusion, only to find the light lingering behind her.

Oh, she thought, finally noticing the alcove the light was hovering in front of.

She looked around the corner, down a short hallway, and saw a vault. Like a bank vault. And it was flanked by two guards.

Great.

She couldn't fight to knock them out. Even though she could easily tackle two burly men, it would attract too much attention.

Jayne straightened as she remembered a spell she'd come across while going through training. She reached for the Torrent again, searching for the Sleep spell. She'd only seen it once, so she hoped she could identify it again...

Yes! There it was. It almost resembled three spheres stacked on top of each other. If Jayne squinted, it looked like a sparkly *Z*, as if it was saying *hey, catch some z's*. Totally easy to remember if she thought of it that way.

Jayne grabbed the spell before slowly approaching the guards. The first one stiffened at her approach but didn't look directly at her, which meant her Cloaking spell was working. Holding her breath, Jayne wiggled her fingers in front of the man's face, releasing a small portion of the Sleep spell as she did so.

The man yawned and slumped backward, his head rolling back against the wall and a snore rumbling from his throat.

Quickly, before the other guard noticed, Jayne did the same thing to him. He, too, conked out against the wall.

Not for the first time, she wondered how many cool places she could now sneak into using her magic. It would save a lot of time instead of going through official channels. But that was wrong, too. Her inner librarian shushed the thought before it could grow into anything naughty.

She accessed the Torrent again and grabbed an Unlock spell. Lights gleamed in her mind, and she pulled on the spell before unleashing it on the vault door. The wheel rattled slightly as it started to move. Energy crept up and down her arms, making the small hairs on her skin stand up. Then, the wheel spun—three times to the right, twice to the left, once more to the right—slowing...and with a soft *thunk*, the heavy door swung open. Huh. If she wanted to take up bank robbery, now she knew how. *Stop with the life-of-crime ideas, Jayne. You are a rule follower, not a rule breaker.*

At least, you were.

Jayne entered the vault and carefully closed the door behind her.

Compared to the ballrooms and libraries, the room was quite small. But even so, it was larger than Jayne's massive bedroom in the Paris flat. The space was a locker room full of safes housing the museum's most treasured artifacts.

Jayne glanced around, finding her helpful ball of light to lead the way. When she looked at it, it sprang into action as if waiting for permission. It floated forward, past the first two rows of safes, pausing midair in front of one near the middle of the room. She scrutinized the safe, which wasn't labeled, before using another Unlock spell to open it.

The safe door opened, revealing a stack of manuscripts that looked like they could be thousands of years old.

A hard lump formed in Jayne's throat. *Don't touch anything except the Book of Shadows,* she warned herself. Her heart fluttered so madly in her chest it felt like she'd trapped a hummingbird in her body.

She pulled a disinfectant wipe from her purse and cleaned her hands as carefully as she could, remembering all her training as a librarian when handling delicate manuscripts.

Jayne slowly leafed through the documents, squinting at each label. Once she realized they were sorted alphabetically, she moved faster.

Then, she found it. In elegant handwriting, the label read: *Très Riches Heures du Duc de Berry.*

All she saw was the same ancient vellum that was on all the other manuscripts. But she felt the book's power. It thrummed in the air, vibrating off her skin like the deep hum of a powerful electric charge.

Gotcha. Her throat turned dry as she took the fake manuscript from her bag. Clutching it under her arm, she used her free hand to ease the grimoire out of the safe and slide the forgery into its place. A small table sat nearby, and Jayne carefully placed the grimoire on the surface, then paused to wipe her sweaty palms on her jeans.

She sucked in a sharp breath as she got a good look at the grimoire. The manuscript was very old. The bindings barely held the worn manuscript in place, and Jayne feared the pages would fall right off. But the deep red vellum matched Deirdre's forgery perfectly. No one would know unless they pulled the item from the safe and inspected it closely. And Jayne hoped that by then, she'd be long gone.

After glancing at the door to ensure no one was approaching, she leaned closer to scrutinize the crimson cover of the Book of Shadows.

Not that she needed proof. The energy in the air was proof enough that something with powerful magic existed in this room.

But she had to be certain.

Sweat trickled down her neck as she tried to control her shaking hands. Pressing a palm to the cover, she closed her eyes and waited.

It sang to her in a language she didn't know in a voice that wasn't discernible. A flash of light seared against her eyes. Her stomach jerked, and nausea swelled inside her. A series of images hurtled through her mind. A medieval painter, writhing on the ground, his eyes overcome with black. A female sculptor with black veins stark against her pale skin, sobbing as she chiseled away at a sculpture. A man in a dark corner, scribbling lines of poetry and muttering to himself, tearing out chunks of his hair a little at a time.

With every image, Jayne sensed a darker presence lurking in each artist's mind. And in that moment, she understood.

The Master of Shadows wasn't an artist. He certainly wasn't the Duc de Berry. He was a muse. And he took over the minds of eager artists. He possessed them.

Well, *that's* not horrifying. Jayne quickly withdrew her hand.

This was definitely the Book of Shadows. And the Master was so very different from what she had originally thought. He wasn't an artist trying to hide his magic. He was a disembodied magician trying to force his way into human hosts, using them as puppets.

Was he even human? Did he have his own body?

The questions had to wait. She was running out of time.

Her breathing was ragged now as she slowly placed the book in her bag. She'd emptied her purse ahead of time to ensure nothing jangled against the manuscript as she walked. But even so, she would have to walk more carefully on the way out.

Jayne was about to turn and leave the room when a tall, red-haired woman walked in and froze, her eyes snapping to Jayne as if the Cloaking spell weren't there at all.

And Jayne was absolutely certain she'd closed that door. Yet this woman had opened and entered without a sound.

"You," the woman said sharply. "What are you doing in here?"

Shoot. How did this woman see her? Had the spell worn off? Or maybe the grimoire's magic canceled it out somehow?

Think fast, Jayne. "Uh, I got lost!" Jayne forced an embarrassed giggle, but it sounded too shrill. "I'm looking for the bathroom. Can you help me?"

The woman's dark eyes narrowed. And that's when Jayne smelled it. Burning iron and rotting violets. It took her a moment to place the scent, but when she did, her blood ran cold.

Ruth. This woman smelled like Ruth Thorne. Which could only mean one thing: she worked for the Kingdom.

Get out, get out, get out! Jayne forced her expression into nonchalance. "My friend is waiting for me out there." She gestured vaguely to the open door. "I should get back."

Before she could sidestep the woman, an icy coldness whispered against Jayne's skin. She stopped in her tracks, alarm prickling against her. The woman's lips moved.

Instinctively, Jayne dropped to the floor just as a spell burst in the air, searing the top of her head. Face against the carpet, Jayne closed her eyes, grabbed a Block spell, layered it with an Attack spell, and jumped to her feet just as the woman sent another curse toward her.

Jayne ducked, then intensified her spell and tossed it. The magic slammed into the woman's chest, knocking her back against the wall. She slumped down, knocked out. Which was all well and good, but the odds that there was only one of them were slim. Ruth could be hiding around the corner for all Jayne knew.

Pulling a fresh Cloaking spell around her, Jayne clutched her purse against her chest, and ran.

29

NOW REACH DEEP INSIDE...

All Jayne could think of as she fled was: *This is so not ideal.*

Not only did she have a terribly fragile manuscript in her purse that was no doubt taking a beating with her hurried steps, but she also didn't have a cute ball of light to follow this time. As she weaved down hallways, making quick turns in case the Kingdom operative woke and was trailing her, she feared she was only working her way deeper into the museum instead of finding a way out. Was this hallway familiar? She couldn't remember because she'd been so focused on that damn Find spell.

Cursing herself for not paying more attention to her surroundings—or at the very least leaving some magical bread crumbs—Jayne paused for half a second to get her bearings. There! She was certain she'd seen that painting of putti floating on a series of clouds before. She set off again.

Sure enough, the hallway opened up to a familiar ballroom filled with paintings and sculptures. Jayne was halfway across the room when magic sliced through the air, sharp as a blade. She dived to the ground, but not fast enough. A biting pain tore through her shoulder, cutting deep. Her Cloaking spell had slipped somehow, and she was now totally exposed. Jayne bit the inside of her cheek to keep from crying out, her free hand clutching at her upper arm and coming back wet with blood.

Oh God, she thought in horror. The woman had just cut her with magic. As if she had an invisible sword. Then again, if she smelled like Ruth, that meant she was powerful enough to be in the madwoman's presence long enough to pick up her rancid scent. Someone higher up than the usual thugs they sent after Jayne.

At the thought of her mother's cold face, Jayne ducked behind a glass display. She inhaled, slow and steady, her mind traveling back to her training. With the clarity of her thoughts came a plan of attack.

Jumping up from her hiding space, Jayne spotted the red-haired woman back on her feet, mere steps away, smirking in triumph. Red light glowed from her hands, spinning and spiraling.

But Jayne didn't give her a chance to act. One after another, she summoned spells. Attack. Block. Shield. Blind. All at once, she flung them at the woman, the magic colliding on itself like explosives detonating.

A deafening *boom* shook the ground, but Jayne didn't stop to linger. She whirled around, sprinting toward the exit, hoping her dizzying spells were enough to buy her time to get the hell out of there.

For good measure, Jayne summoned another Cloaking spell and added a Shield spell, gritting her teeth against the aching throb in her head from carrying so much magic. Her purse seemed to get heavier with each step. Sweat poured down her face, trickling down her back.

A spell seared past her, sending a spike of heat into her left ear. Her shield shrieked in response, flickering slightly like a light bulb about to die. Her defensive spells were wearing off. Damn it.

Jayne reinforced her shields as she flew through the reading room, running in zigzags that must have made her look drunk. But it also made her harder to target. Thankfully, the Cloaking spell held; no one in the château seemed to see her frantic flight. No one but the Kingdom member who was after her.

Faintly, Jayne registered that once she left the château, she was screwed. There was no portal waiting for her. No magic escape. She would be stranded, out in the open, exposed. She'd arrived by train, for God's sake. What did she expect, to lead this woman on a wild goose chase until she got to the train station? The grimoire's magic would've sucked her dry by then.

Jayne was only delaying the inevitable. She needed a new plan.

As soon as she exited the château, Jayne carefully set her purse down on the ground and pressed her back against the nearest pillar. She held her breath, waiting. Listening.

A light brush of magic in the air. The faint whiff of rotten flowers. Grabbing another Attack spell, Jayne lunged. Her fist collided with the woman's jaw and her magic burst forward. The combined power sent the woman flying back several feet. Before she could get up, Jayne was on her again, sending blow after blow. Punch to the gut, kick to the inside of her knee, an Attack spell straight in the chest. Jayne never let up, the onslaught of her magic and kickboxing skills overpowering the woman until she finally slumped over, unconscious, her nose and lip dribbling blood.

Jayne waited a moment or two to ensure the woman wasn't getting up. Then, for good measure, she draped a Cloaking spell over her, just to make sure the civilians wouldn't see a bleeding woman and be alarmed. But a glance over her shoulder told her no one had noticed. The line of tourists waiting to get into the château seemed oddly at ease. Chatter filled the air. The bystanders were none the wiser.

Making a mental note to ask someone exactly how all magic seemed to be miraculously hidden from the outside world when things got hairy, Jayne retrieved her bag. The weight settled over her again, but this time it was a comfort. As if the grimoire was saying, *Mission accomplished.*

Stay out of my head, creepy grimoire.

Jayne returned to the flat, panting and drenched in sweat. Carrying the grimoire from Chantilly had felt like dragging twenty-pound dumbbells, even sitting quietly on the upper deck of the train, praying no one spoke to her. Jayne carefully set her bag down on the couch, collapsed next to it, and took a deep, cleansing breath. The place was empty. Good. She needed to regroup.

She leaned forward, and fresh pain laced through her. She inspected the wound in her shoulder from that crazy woman's magic invisible blade. Hesitantly, she reached for the Torrent, exhaling with relief when the river of stars shimmered into view. She grabbed a Healing spell and pressed it to her arm, wincing at the blast of warmth that spread through her body. Flames licked her skin, and she tried not to imagine herself bursting into flames. What a way to die...

But soon, the warmth left her, and the injury was healed. Even the bruise from the spot where Tristan Lowell had manhandled her was gone. Well, at least she could still do Healing spells. *Thank you, La Liberté, for not yanking my magic at this particular moment.*

Jayne needed to report in, but unease froze her in place. As soon as she turned this grimoire over to Amanda, it would be gone. The TCO analysts would take it and inspect every inch of it. Who knew what they would find? Or if they would find anything? Jayne had been one of the few who could connect to the Book of Leinster because Medb had called to her. What if this was similar? What if only she could access the secrets contained inside? She remembered the way the images had appeared in her mind in the vault at Chantilly.

This might be her only chance. Jayne's eyes stayed glued to the manuscript peeking out from her bag. It hummed, an intense presence that called to her, while she wrestled with her conscience.

Don't do it. You know these things can go wrong.

It's just a book. A magical book, but a book nonetheless. If you don't know what's in it, how will you ever play this off to La Liberté?

Good argument. You win, devil on my shoulder.

She would have to be careful. She'd handled some dark grimoires before, and they could be particularly nasty. Closing her eyes, she reached for the Torrent and grabbed a Shield spell, draping it over herself like a blanket. For good measure, she layered on a Cloaking spell on top of that, hoping that together, both spells would protect her from the grimoire's influences.

After ensuring her magic was in place, shrouded over her like a sparkling transparent curtain, she pulled the manuscript from her bag. As before, a riot of sensations overwhelmed her. Icy cold fingers crept up and down her arms before clenching tightly within her chest, cutting off her breath. Goose bumps rose on her skin, and the hairs on the back of her neck stood up.

Maybe this wasn't such a good idea. But she had to try. Jayne focused on her breathing, trying to soothe her nerves. But the other presence lingered inside her, making her breaths feel sharp and shallow. Like a dark cloud smothered her lungs.

Make it quick, Jayne. Get in, get out.

Okay. Three, two, one... *Go!*

Jayne opened the grimoire. A burst of white light seared her eyes, momentarily blinding her. A series of images fired through her brain in rapid succession, like she was watching a slideshow on fast-forward. The images flew past her too quickly for her to register anything. *Wait*, she wanted to scream. *Too fast! Stop!*

But the onslaught of magic had only just begun. The brightness intensified until her head throbbed and her eyes burned. She shut them, but the relentless downpour of images persisted, pounding against her skull like a drill. The more she tried to focus on them, the more the pain intensified until her brain felt like mush. The barrage stopped as suddenly as it began.

"Ah. Hello, my spirit child." The voice was a scraping whisper in her ear, like nails on a chalkboard. It sounded like several voices layered into one. Neither male or female, or both. A fierce, overwhelming power. Like the magic within the grimoire had personified itself.

Jayne stiffened, momentarily forgetting about the images crashing through her. She realized what was happening. The images smothering her had been a distraction. Now that she could look around, she found coils of dark shadows leaking from the grimoire, stretching toward her. One had speared her right in the chest. The other wrapped around her neck, pressed up against her ear. That would explain the disembodied voice. A soothing, sleepy feeling caressed her, lulling her. She felt the strongest desire to close her eyes and take a quick nap.

But with that feeling came a memory of Ruger's panicked voice saying, *Agnes Jayne! Get out now!*

This was the same feeling from when she'd been practicing magic with Ruger the first time, and something within the Torrent had beckoned to her, eager to trap her. Whatever magic was contained in this grimoire was made of that same power.

And it frightened her.

"Who are you?" Jayne asked, trying to seem confident, but her shaky voice betrayed her. *Or rather,* what *are you?*

"I am the beginning and the end," the voice murmured. Though it was soft, it grated against Jayne's ears like concrete. "I am magic itself. I am power. I am yours."

She didn't believe for one second that this was Torrent magic speaking to her. This was just someone who thought very highly of himself. That was all. Perhaps trapped in the Torrent somehow.

"I need to find the shadowed illumination," Jayne said, trying to steer the conversation in the right direction. "Can you show it to me?"

"Oh, but I already have, spirit child. You've been anointed with the contents of my grimoire. Everything you need is in that clever mind of yours."

Wrinkling her nose at the word *anointed*, Jayne asked, "Your grimoire? Are you…the Master of Shadows?"

A deep chuckle rumbled in her ear, making her bones rattle. "No. I am the Master of all."

Whatever the hell that means… Jayne clenched her fingers into fists, trying to bat off the shadows stretching toward her like serpents. Her vision clouded, and panic raced through her. She had to get free from this crazy invisible power. *Now.*

"Um, okay," Jayne said. "Great. Many thanks. See you around."

She moved to close the grimoire, but the shadows froze her in place, locking her limbs.

"I think not," the voice said. "I've not come across this much power in eons. I'd love another taste."

Oh, God. This grimoire is going to eat me whole. Yep. That was exactly how she was going to die. Her tombstone would read: *A book ate her.* Horror swarmed inside her, and she reached for the Torrent. But nothing was there. It felt as empty as it had in Fontainebleau when she'd first lost access to her magic.

No, no, no, no…

The voice laughed again. "I told you, spirit child. I *am* magic. You cannot use it against me."

Jayne's throat constricted. Terror gripped her as tightly as the shadows did. She couldn't move. Couldn't breathe.

This can't be happening.

Of course it can. You were the dummy who decided to open the book. Good job, lame-o.

The shadows pressed on her, licking, caressing, then choking her, coiling around her like a boa constrictor. The magic was going to suffocate her right here in the apartment. The TCO would find her dead body. Sofia would hear of her death from a stranger, and no one would be able to rescue Cillian.

The thought of them sent a bolt of determination through her, melting away her terror. She was Jayne Thorne, for God's sake. A CIA Librarian. A Master magician.

This invisible power, this arrogant asshole, whoever he was, should be bowing to *her*.

Power surged inside her, and Jayne felt the presence go still. Whether from shock or fear, she didn't know. But she had startled it.

Good.

She drew on her icy power again, and it swelled. The chilled coldness that once felt so foreign and frightening now spread through her, creating snowy imprints down to her fingers and toes. The horror and panic seeped out of her, leaving courage and anger in its place.

"How dare you," she hissed. But it wasn't her voice speaking.

It was Medb's.

Warmth prickled on her forehead, and Jayne's heart lurched in recognition. The Earth totem. She was drawing magic from Medb's totem.

Power flooded through her as if a dam had burst. The marking on her forehead grew hot, and she knew without seeing that it was glowing right now. As her skin burned with power, alarm and uncertainty filled her. Hector had warned her against trusting this strange new power. What if she lost control?

But she didn't have a choice. This grimoire was more powerful than any of Jayne's foes. She needed to bring out the big guns.

For the first time, Jayne let go. She relinquished control of her magic and allowed Medb to take over.

"You cannot—" started the voice, but Jayne cut it off.

"You will not take me," she growled. "You want to taste my magic? Well, choke on this."

Her power burst forward, strangling the shadows, twisting and writhing against them until they were forced back inside the grimoire. Gritting her teeth, Jayne struggled against the thick magic still wafting in the air. It felt like treading through molasses. But she pushed on, reaching forward with great effort until her hands clasped the edge of the manuscript. A scream ripped her throat as she tugged at the massive weight, yanking until the book slammed shut, taking its creepy magic with it.

Everything fell silent. The bright lights vanished. The eerie presence disappeared. Nothing penetrated the silence but Jayne's ragged gasps. Sweat poured down her face and neck as if she'd just finished training. And in a way, it had felt like that. Brutal. Exhausting. Like the magic in the air had solidified into three hundred pounds of massive weight that Jayne had to lift in order to shut out the grimoire's influence.

She took a moment to catch her breath, to ground herself in the safety of the flat, before processing what had happened.

The grimoire had come to life and tried to devour her. Medb's totem had saved her. She had just fought off some crazy-ass magical god who had wanted to eat her whole.

Holy. Shit.

30

IT'S MY WAY OR THE HIGHWAY

After her little run-in with…whoever that had been, Jayne wasted no time depositing the grimoire with Amanda and Ruger. For safety, they portaled back to Langley. Amanda didn't want to chance opening the grimoire outside a controlled environment. In a clean room designed specifically for this purpose, and using some heavy-duty bespelled gloves, the three of them carefully flipped through the manuscript, snapping pictures of each page. Even with the protective gear, Jayne felt the dark presence oozing from the grimoire, creating a foggy haze over her mind. They had to take frequent breaks to make sure they still had their heads before continuing.

"Terrible," Amanda said when they'd finished. Her face was pale. "Insidious."

Ruger was also looking slightly nauseated. "We must keep this very safe. I can't believe it's been out in the world alone."

"Agreed," Jayne said. "Lock it in a dungeon and throw away the key. This dude is seriously creepy. The darkest of dark magic."

When Ruger left with the grimoire bundled in protective

spells, Amanda gave Jayne a nod of approval. "I'm proud of you, Jayne. A lesser Adept would have been subsumed."

"I'm sure many of them have been." Jayne shuddered at that horrible thought. "Blech. I need some fresh air."

After a ten-minute stroll around the courtyard admiring the Kryptos sculpture, Jayne felt well enough to join Deirdre, who seemed much recovered from her mishap in the Time Catch simulation and greeted her warmly, to assist in finishing the final document to give to La Liberté. The clerics were there helping, and for a moment, Jayne was in her element, her focus only on binding and vellum and parchment and that old familiar smell of ancient books. Magical only in the sense of transporting stories and important facts. Completely harmless. Safe. It was why she loved books so much. They took you on an adventure without putting you in any danger.

Hours later, arms and legs aching and neck strained from hunching over for so long, Jayne inspected the final product. It looked identical to the grimoire itself. The only difference was the complete lack of magic.

But Jayne now had a taste of that magic. She knew its imprint. Tentatively, she reached for the Torrent and pictured an exact replica of the dark sense of the grimoire. A shimmering three-dimensional book shape appeared before her, and she latched onto it before shrouding it over the fake grimoire. The air prickled with that same intensity she'd felt earlier, an echo of the overwhelming power emanating from the Book of Shadows.

It was so potent that even Deirdre went stiff, her dark eyes wary. "What did you do?"

"I replicated the magical imprint from the original Book of Shadows," Jayne said. "If La Liberté tries to sense it with their magic, they'll feel a power almost identical to the real thing. It should buy us some more time."

I hope, she added internally, not wanting to worry Deirdre. The woman had been through enough.

"You need to be careful, Jayne. This is dangerous."

For once, Jayne didn't feel like deflecting the concern and worry with a joke. "I know. I promise. I will be." She gave Deirdre a hug, then set off for Amanda's office to make the encrypted call to Gina Labelle. Ruger and Amanda hid out of view across the room, in Jayne's line of sight so they could coach her if things got off track.

"Here goes nothing," Jayne said, hitting the connect button. Seconds later, Labelle popped up onto the screen, looking disturbed and sporting a long scratch down one cheek, but she spoke smoothly enough. "Do you have what I asked for, Jayne Thorne?"

"I do. I have the grimoire. It's a nasty piece of work."

"I expected nothing less. The exchange will happen tomorrow, noon, on the Pont des Artes. Come alone."

"Not a chance in hell, Labelle. I'm bringing my people. Feel free to bring yours. We'll do this exchange, the grimoire and Lowell for Cillian, and don't you dare forget the antidote to the poison. And then I hope to never hear from you again."

There was no response. The screen went black.

"I assume that means they've agreed to our terms?"

Ruger and Amanda shared a concerned look. "Possibly. Better get some rest, Jayne," Ruger said. "This is going to be a challenging exchange."

"You get some rest. You still look terrible. What's wrong? Can I help?"

"Can you?" Amanda asked, leaning forward. "Can you access the Torrent? A Healing spell would be wonderful right now. Nothing seems to help. It's almost as if they've enchanted the wounds."

"Why didn't you tell me?"

Ruger shook his head. "You've been a little busy, Jayne."

Jayne shut her eyes and reached for the river of stars, only to find it again a faded imprint of itself. She cursed, loud and long.

"They turned off my magic again, the bastards. I'm telling you, I am going to tear Gina LaBelle limb from limb when all of this is over." She laid a hand on Ruger's arm, the one not in a sling. "I'm sorry. I hate that you're hurting and I can't help you."

"I'll be fine, Jayne," he rumbled, his deep voice a comfort to her. "And so will Cillian. We'll get him back, and find a cure for their poison, and then we'll take out Labelle together."

"Promise?"

He grinned. "Promise."

～

The next day, Jayne placed the forged grimoire in her bag and bid Deirdre farewell. The other woman looked positively terrified and gave her a tight hug.

"Reach out to me when all this is finished, will you? I'd like to get dinner. Have some normal conversation. Ancient books, warm ale, some chips and gossip."

"Absolutely. Though no horror films. You know I'm a wuss."

"Not a problem. I doubt they will be my preferred genre anymore, anyway."

Aw, damn. She hadn't meant to make her remember the awfulness of the Time Catch. "Seriously, thanks so much, Deirdre. We couldn't have done it without you. And I am so sorry about before."

"It's all right, Jayne," she said softly. "Truly. Though I won't be doing it again. I'll stick with the real world, thank you very much."

Amanda had prepared a portal, and without another word, Jayne stepped through into the Montmartre safe house.

Several officers waited there to escort her to the drop location. Jayne recognized a few from that night at Medb's tomb. The man in front was tall and slim and wore slacks and a button-up shirt as if he were strolling to work like any normal person.

Jayne smiled in greeting. "Seo-joon, my man. How goes it?"

He grinned. "Nice to see you again, Jayne. Still kicking ass with the books, I see?" He eyed her bag as if he could sense the fake grimoire inside. Good. It was giving off some magical signals. That should buy them some time with Labelle and crew.

"Always. Let's get this show on the road."

Jayne led the way to the Pont des Arts. The team of TCO officers blended in easily with the crowd of pedestrians, keeping their distance from her to make it seem like they were strangers merely walking the same route.

To Jayne's surprise, when she reached the bridge, her eyes immediately latched onto Sofia's tidy blond hair pulled up into a bun. She stood alongside Amanda and several other TCO officers as they waited at the drop location. Though they were dressed like tourists, Jayne couldn't help feeling like they stuck out. Amanda's stiff posture and the rigid expressions of the officers around her screamed *Secret Service* or something else conspicuous.

Plus, there was Tristan Lowell. He had a few fading bruises on his cheek and jaw, and his hair was a bit unkempt—nothing like the French model he resembled when Jayne first met him. He wasn't wearing handcuffs or any such visible restraint, but Jayne could tell something magical kept him bound to Amanda. He jerked oddly whenever she moved as if tethered to her by a magical rope.

The nearby civilians were absorbed in their own worlds, oblivious to the madness walking among them.

"Sofia?" Jayne asked hesitantly, stepping onto the bridge alongside her sister.

Sofia offered a thin smile. "Hey. Nice to see you."

The greeting was so distant. As if they were second cousins who didn't particularly like each other and only got together once every five years. Sofia's text had seemed like a peace offering, but maybe because Jayne had never responded, Sofia was giving her the cold shoulder again. She swallowed around the knot of emotion in her throat.

"What are you doing here?" Jayne glanced from Sofia to Amanda, waiting for an explanation. But Amanda remained still, and Jayne assumed the spell linking her to Tristan was requiring all of her energy at the moment.

"Amanda thought this was a good opportunity," Sofia said. She sounded strong and capable, as though she knew more about the situation than Jayne herself.

Jayne chewed on her lip, biting back a retort. She heartily disagreed. Things were going to get nasty during this exchange, and she didn't want Sofia anywhere near it.

Sofia read the anxiety on her face. "We're surrounded by officers who know what they're doing, and I've been training, too. I'll be fine, Jayne. Besides, Amanda pointed out if La Liberté tries to strike at us with the same thing they did to you, at least I know how to fight."

"Yeah, at the dojo! Not against a bunch of magic-wielding terrorists."

Sofia gave her a flat look that Jayne read all too well. It said, *Taste your own medicine, Jayne.*

Right. That was exactly Sofia's point during their big argument.

"This is different," Jayne hissed. "I'm field trained. You're not."

Defiance gleamed in Sofia's eyes. "I'm already here, Jayne. Deal with it."

Jayne opened her mouth to argue, but Sofia turned away, facing the opposite end of the bridge.

Jayne stifled a groan as she adjusted the bag holding Deirdre's forgery. It felt like this mission was already going sideways.

The TCO officers arranged themselves up and down the bridge. Jayne was sure they were trying their best to keep a low profile, but between their sunglasses and the way their hands were hanging loose at their sides, ready for their fighting stances, they looked as subtle as a stray elephant.

Amanda kept Lowell on one side of the bridge, and Jayne stood next to her with her bag. She felt his eyes on her but studiously ignored him. She was counting down the seconds to when she'd never have to lay eyes on the man again.

At long last, a figure appeared on the opposite end of the bridge. Jayne recognized her immediately: Gina Labelle. A crowd of people assembled behind her. Her La Liberté cronies, no doubt. When Labelle's eyes fixed on Lowell, her expression hardened slightly.

Beside Amanda, Jayne felt Lowell tense.

For a moment, the opposing sides stood there, glaring at each other. Though passersby drifted between them, the hostility in the air was so intense it felt like a battlefield.

Jayne sucked in a breath. "Here we go."

Together, she and Amanda strode forward, along with Lowell, yanked by his puppet strings. Jayne kept her gaze forward, even as she felt her sister's eyes on her from behind.

Labelle strode forward as well, flanked by the beefiest men Jayne had ever seen. When the two sides met at the halfway point, Jayne got a good look at Labelle's face. The woman's lips were tight with fury, her eyes ablaze. That scratch looked even nastier in person. Her stare was still pinned on Lowell, though, and for a moment, Jayne wondered if she despised him. Then, Labelle's cold fury shifted to Amanda, and Jayne understood.

Labelle was pissed that Lowell was hurt. *Ha! Suck it up, lady,* Jayne thought. *You already beat up Ruger and Cillian. You're lucky we didn't tear Lowell's arms off. I certainly was tempted.*

There she went, getting bloodthirsty again. But this was for a good cause. She wanted her wolf back.

"Do you have it?" Labelle asked in a low voice.

Jayne didn't move. "Where's Cillian?"

Labelle's eyes flashed. "We'll bring him out once you show us the grimoire."

Jayne had expected this. Slowly, she pulled on the protective gloves she and Amanda had worn earlier—only for show, of course—before withdrawing the grimoire from her bag.

One beefy man came forward, but Jayne backed up a step. "Not until I see Cillian."

The man halted and arched an eyebrow at Labelle, who nodded. From the other side of the bridge, a short, squat woman pressed her hand to the shoulder of the man next to her, a scrawny fellow with bright red hair. As the woman touched him, his appearance shifted. He grew in size, shoulders filling out, his hair lightening to a golden blond. Jayne gasped. Cillian had been bespelled to look like someone else. He still wasn't himself. His normally vibrant blue eyes were haunted and rimmed with shadows. A large bruise on his nose was faded and yellow. A scruffy layer of stubble coated his chin and jaw, and he looked like he hadn't slept in days.

Rage filled Jayne. What had they been doing to him? Had they kept him in a Time Catch, like they had with Ruger? It could have felt like weeks...

A hand gripped Jayne's arm, and only then did she realize she'd taken a step forward with her arms up, ready to fight them all herself. Amanda held on to her, keeping her in place.

"Hand them over," Labelle ordered.

Jayne glanced at Amanda, who nodded once. Together, they headed toward Labelle with Lowell in tow. Behind them, the TCO agents shifted, ready to move as soon as Amanda gave the signal.

Gingerly, as if the dark magic might burn, Jayne handed the grimoire into Labelle's waiting arms. As soon as she did, a crackle of magic split the air, pricking Jayne's ears and howling against her bones.

"Now!" Jayne yelled.

The TCO agents sprang into action. In a flash, four of them were at Cillian's side, hurrying him away from the bridge. A few bewildered members of La Liberté chased after them, but Amanda unleashed a jet of white light toward them, knocking them over. Lowell staggered, falling to his knees. Labelle rushed to his side, whispering an incantation. Something cracked, and Amanda cried out, clutching her side.

"Amanda!" Jayne rushed over to her, catching her before she fell.

Labelle sneered and grabbed Lowell's arm, yanking him toward her like he was nothing more than a doll. His steps were clumsy, but he was no longer tethered to Amanda. Together, they darted away, fleeing the scene of chaos.

Gritting her teeth, Jayne straightened, prepared to unleash a can of whoop-ass on them, but something stopped her. Where was Cillian?

Bright lights flashed up and down the bridge as the TCO battled La Liberté. Screams and shouts echoed. And somehow, the ignorant passersby magically dodged the fight, sidestepping the fray as if it were merely a spot of mud to dodge during their clueless Parisian stroll.

Jayne squinted, looking past the brawl. In the distance, she caught sight of the burly prisoner—Cillian—still being escorted by TCO agents, but just behind them were a pair of La Liberté goons, closing in fast.

"Oh, no you don't," Jayne muttered, sprinting toward them. She ducked to avoid a spell in the face, then leapt over a man who had fallen, bleeding profusely from his leg.

When she was close enough to intercept Cillian's pursuers, Jayne's instincts tingled, itching to reach for the Torrent.

But if there was any moment for La Liberté to incapacitate her, it was right now. She couldn't use magic.

Instead, she quickened her pace until she was close enough to tackle the nearest pursuer. She brought him down hard, pinning him with her legs before pounding her fist into his jaw. He wrestled with her, but her grip was unyielding. They rolled, and pain split through her arms as concrete scraped against her skin. She slammed the man's head into the ground once, twice, three times, until he finally went limp.

Hissing at her throbbing injuries, Jayne jumped to her feet. Cillian and the officers had halted, engaging with the enemies who had caught up to them. Cillian swung his fists with violent fury. From the bridge, the rest of La Liberté rushed toward them, no doubt eager to overpower them and imprison Cillian once more, as well as any TCO officer they could lay their hands on.

Like hell.

When Jayne caught up to Cillian and the others, she eagerly joined the fray, sweeping her legs under the nearest assailant and bringing him crashing to the ground. She kicked him in the head, rendering him unconscious.

"Jayne!" Cillian was at her side in an instant. She touched his shoulders, resisting the urge to throw her arms around him and never let go. There would be time for a passionate reunion later.

"We need to split up," she said to the other TCO officers, led by Seo-joon, eyes bright with the excitement of the fight. "There's too many of them. Cillian and I will draw some away, split their forces."

"We will?" Cillian asked.

But the other officers were nodding. "Copy that," Seo-Joon said. They took off toward the bridge to intercept the horde of La Liberté operatives racing toward them.

Jayne grabbed Cillian's arm, pulling him in the opposite direction. She wasn't sure where they were going, but they couldn't go back to the bridge or La Liberté would intercept them. And there were too many for Jayne to fight without magic.

Had their distraction worked? Had Amanda and Sofia gotten away? Jayne couldn't see them from here, and she couldn't waste time fretting. She had to believe they were safe.

"Come on!" she urged Cillian. Her arms still ached from the tussle earlier, but she pushed on.

They rounded a corner and ducked under a pavilion outside the Louvre. She peered around the corner, then smiled. It had worked. A crowd of La Liberté pursuers sprinted toward her. The pair of men in front were clutching a small pendant dangling from their necks. Tiny tendrils of magic were coiling from their fingers.

Something pulsed within her in recognition. Whatever was hanging around their necks was linked to the poison inside her. It must be the trigger!

"Can you shift?" Jayne whispered to Cillian. "I can't help you."

His eyes met hers. "No. I can fight, though."

"Good. Try to take their necklaces. They're dampening my magic somehow."

Comprehension glinted in his eyes. "Got it."

Jayne turned away, then doubled back and pressed a firm kiss to Cillian's delicious lips. When she withdrew, he offered that charming half smile that made her insides squirm.

"What was that for?" he asked, though he didn't seem displeased.

"For being alive." She grinned at him before leaping forward, charging the closest men head-on.

A bubble of magic surrounded her almost instantly, reminding Jayne of that otherworldly veil separating Adepts from non-Adepts. She hit the first man twice, left, right, and he staggered backward, eyes wide and cheeks red as if he hadn't expected the physical attack instead of a magical attempt.

Jayne cocked an eyebrow and grinned, issuing a challenge. This was going to be fun.

Growling, the man surged forward, hands up, throwing some sort of spell at her, but Jayne was ready for him. She ducked, pivoting to the side, and snatched the chain from the back of his neck. The chain snapped, and something metal clattered to the ground.

The man froze, his face draining of color. He stared from Jayne to the trinket on the ground. A whisper of magic crept along Jayne's skin like a gentle breath. If she hadn't been waiting for it, she might not have noticed.

She threw a weak but well-placed Stunning spell, right into his crotch. The man gaped at her, face draining of color, but didn't lunge toward them. She winked at him in triumph.

From behind her, Cillian grunted as he assaulted two others. Jayne quickly engaged the goons behind him before they surrounded him completely. Knocking them all out would be impossible—they were too greatly outnumbered. But she didn't need to beat them. Just destroy all their necklaces.

Cillian, however, didn't get the memo. He was spinning, kicking, a absolute tornado of fury. He slammed his meaty fist into the guy's head, then kicked him for good measure. The poor fellow slumped over, unconscious, as a trickle of blood oozed from his mouth.

"A bit overkill, you think?" Jayne asked, ducking to avoid another man's spell. *Come on, Torrent. Gimme some more magic!*

"They deserved it." Cillian's gaze darkened with vengeful rage, and Jayne didn't want to know what those monsters had done to him to earn a look like that. He yanked off the unconscious man's necklace, and she stamped on it, breaking the pendant.

After Jayne and Cillian destroyed two more amulets, the rest of La Liberté figured out what they were doing. Each of them clutched their pendants tighter, whispering enchantments that made Jayne's skin prickle, before tucking the chains under their shirts.

As if that would help.

Icy anger swelled within her. These assholes were messing with her magic. Like she was some damned puppet they could jerk around at will.

She'd make them pay. All of them.

A roar of fury split through her as she roundhouse-kicked a wiry man who bent over like a snapped twig. Beside her, Cillian was in Beast Mode, grabbing at throats and slamming his fist against their faces again and again until nothing but a bloody pulp remained.

Gentle Jayne might have fretted over the amount of blood spilling on the ground or the shrill screams and limp bodies surrounding them. But Ice Angry Jayne didn't give a rat's ass. They'd poisoned her. Incapacitated her. Taken control of a part of her. They'd tortured and imprisoned Cillian and Ruger. Hurt her people.

Fury burned inside her, creating a volcanic void that made her see red. When silver sparks ignited along her hands, she realized it was more than just her rage.

Her magic was back.

"Yippee-kai-yay, mofo!" she whooped before aiming a high kick into a man's chest.

"Did it work?" Cillian asked breathlessly.

"What do you think, wolf?"

At the huge spill of magic, Cillian had shifted without a thought.

"Go get 'em." Jayne jerked her knee between a man's legs. As he crumpled, she reached for the Torrent, and a glittering stream of stars appeared in her mind.

"Hulk, smash," Jayne whispered, a gleeful smile spreading across her face. The glorious river of stars welcomed her as if they were old friends, parted by only distance and time. Jayne found herself laughing as she grabbed an Attack spell and slammed it against the man closest to her.

He flew back several yards before flipping backward over the edge of the railing, falling with a scream into the water below.

Guess I put a little too much force in that one.

She wasn't the only one to notice. The remaining goons stumbled away from her, retreating before she magicked them into oblivion.

Jayne's hands were still in tight fists, sparks flying, her breath sharp and shallow as she watched the cowards flee. Beside her, Cillian was growling, lips pulled back in a frightful sneer showing all of his sharp teeth. The remaining La Liberté thugs took one look at him and bolted.

"I'm going after them." What surely sounded like a growl to the world were clear words in her head.

"No, don't," Jayne panted. "You saw how many were on the bridge. And if they all have those necklaces, then it's definitely not over. Live to fight another day, right, Pine?" She put a hand on his furry shoulder, grateful for the warm, comforting pull of magic thrumming inside of her. She concentrated, and he came back to his human form.

"Now *that's* how it's supposed to work."

He rubbed his chin, and she saw his knuckles were bleeding.

"Let's go see if the others are okay, and get you bandaged up."

He looked down at her, face awash with something like joy. "Thank you, Jayne. For saving me."

She squeezed his hand. "Always."

31

HERE WE GO AGAIN

Sofia was officially in over her head.

Jayne had run off, chasing after La Liberté with Cillian by her side. It wasn't the smartest choice. If Cillian got recaptured, this whole charade would have been for nothing.

Their departure, along with the rest of the team duking it out with La Liberté, left Sofia huddled next to Amanda, who still hadn't recovered from whatever Gina Labelle had done to her. Jets of magic blasted around them, and Sofia ducked her head, clutching Amanda's arms to keep her pressed down, away from the fight.

"We should be helping them," Amanda growled, jerking her chin toward the center of the bridge where a dozen men and women grappled, exchanging spells and blows.

"You want to join in and get yourself killed?" Sofia yelled, waving an arm toward the fray. "Be my guest. But you'll be down in seconds." She gestured to Amanda's side. The older woman had a hand pressed against a wound, but her fingers didn't hide the stain of blood. "What did that woman do to you?"

Amanda's nostrils flared. "She severed the Binding spell."

Sofia flinched as another spell exploded nearby. "That's it?"

"The spell I cast bound Lowell's magic to mine. It could only be unlocked with my own enchantment. What Labelle did broke the spell by force, taking a piece of me with it. It's like the spell was a chain, and instead of unlocking it, Labelle broke the links, and yanked. She meant to inflict harm by severing it." Amanda winced, tightening her arm around herself.

"We need to get you safe, then. You're too much of a target just lying here." Sofia wrapped an arm around Amanda's waist and tried to haul her up.

"I can't leave my team." Amanda remained stiff, refusing to let Sofia move her.

The fear in Sofia's chest exploded into something volatile, and she snapped. "Don't be an idiot, Amanda! You sit behind a desk all day and delegate. That's your job. To know when to do things yourself or let your people take care of it. Now get your act together and look at this strategically. You're wounded. You can't fight. If you go in there, your team will be obligated to shield you from harm. You're a liability. So take my help and get out while you still can."

Amanda's mouth fell open as if Sofia had morphed into a lizard right before her eyes. Sofia couldn't blame her. She didn't know where that outburst had come from. But something hot and dangerous was inside her, waiting to be unleashed. As if yelling at Amanda had only been the beginning.

It made her wary, but it felt good, too.

Amanda's lips tightened as she composed herself, nodding once. "You're right."

Damn right I am, Sofia thought grumpily.

Amanda cast a Cloaking spell and didn't protest again, too focused now on her injury. Sofia helped her off the bridge, glancing constantly over her shoulder, afraid someone might be pursuing them. But everyone was too engaged in their own duels to notice.

Sofia draped Amanda's arm around her shoulders and helped

the woman hobble faster. They made their way down the sandy path under the linden trees. At the first bench, Amanda groaned, "Stop. Please."

Sofia carefully lowered her onto the bench. She gasped when she noticed the blooming stain of blood on Amanda's shirt. The wound was getting worse. A lot worse.

Amanda's eyes closed, her face turning gray. "You—you need to…seal the wound. Stop the bleeding."

Sofia's stomach dropped. "What? Adepts can't heal, Amanda, it's—"

"Not heal. Cauterize."

Bile crept up Sofia's throat, and she shook her head, afraid she'd be sick. "No. I can't. I've never done that before."

A brief flash of clarity broke through Amanda's gaze as she stared intently at Sofia. "You were Ruth Thorne's protégé, and she never taught you a simple Fire spell?"

Sofia's mouth clamped shut. Ruth *had* taught her a Fire spell… but this was different. Sofia might kill Amanda if the spell got out of control. Or it wouldn't ignite at all.

With her free hand, Amanda snatched Sofia's arm, her fingernails digging into flesh. "Are you the powerful witch who swore her allegiance to the TCO…or not? The choice is yours, Sofia. You can leave me, go find another Adept to help, and risk me bleeding out on this bench. Or you can suck it up, embrace your power, and put away your fear for good." She raised her eyebrows. "What will it be?"

Sofia stared at her, stunned. But hadn't Amanda just echoed the same sternness Sofia had emulated earlier? They'd both needed a good verbal slap in the face. That same thrumming energy took hold inside her, roaring to life. Resolve filled her, and she nodded.

Amanda sighed with relief, her expression sagging as if the pep talk had taken all of her effort. She leaned against the bench and slowly rolled up her shirt.

Sofia bit back a cry as she inspected the crimson gash still pouring blood. It looked like Labelle had gutted Amanda with a jagged piece of glass.

"Whenever you're ready," Amanda hissed, her body taut with pain. Her face looked paler by the minute.

Sofia licked her lips and scooted closer, sucking in deep breaths. *You can do this,* she told herself. She closed her eyes, shoved aside her fear, and embraced the power coursing through her.

The Torrent appeared, a glistening river of stars that flowed freely through her veins. Her eyes pricked with tears from the sheer intensity of it, the volume of liquid energy filling her ounce by ounce. Myriad spells whooshed toward her, almost too quickly for Sofia to grasp them. But then she found it: the Fire spell, a flickering flame beckoning to her.

Sofia grabbed it, then jerked back to reality, her head spinning as if she'd just gotten off a violent roller coaster. Flames danced in the palm of her hand, heating her face and stinging her eyes.

You can do this.

Holding her breath, she brought the fire to Amanda's wound and pressed down hard. Amanda bucked and jerked, her head thrown back and the veins standing out in her neck as she choked on a scream. To her credit, she remained quiet, her fingers digging deeper into Sofia's arm.

Sofia didn't feel any pain. She let the spell consume her, focused only on her task. She kept her palm flat and firm against Amanda's abdomen, despite the woman's squirming, even knowing the fiery touch inflicted so much pain.

Scorched flesh sizzled. Steam rose from the wound. Though Sofia couldn't see it, she felt it: the raw, gaping edges of the gash coming together, sealed with heat. When the puckered flesh had closed itself, Sofia withdrew, and the fire in her hand vanished.

She blinked as if coming out of a stupor. The blaze inside her diminished, receding back into...wherever it had come from. Her soul? The Torrent? Now that she was herself again, she gaped at the sight of so much blood in front of her, and her hands started to shake.

It was like there were two pieces of her—Scared Sofia and Powerful Sofia. The latter had taken over her mind and body, acting when she couldn't.

She should have been afraid of this other side of her, this lethal, unstoppable presence. What if it turned on her? What if it turned on Jayne? But as Amanda relaxed against the bench, exhaling in relief, Sofia felt nothing but gratitude.

Thank you, she told her other self, *for saving Amanda's life.*

She swore she felt something inside her rumble as if to say, *You're welcome.*

32

A NEW PLAN

Jayne paced outside the door to a second-floor bedroom in the Montmartre safe house, waiting impatiently for the TCO physician to finish running tests on Cillian.

She was surprised when Sofia appeared at the top of the stairs, two cups in her hands.

"Peace tea?"

Jayne took the cup. "Thank you." She took a sip. Moroccan Mint, one of her favorites. Sofia really *was* ready to make up.

"Are you okay?" Sofia asked, eyes clouded with worry. "That was a pretty intense fight. I've never seen anything like it."

"I am just fine. How about you? I hear you healed Amanda, all by yourself."

"Cauterized her wound. Not healed." Sofia shuddered. "That was awful. Anyway, I have to go back to Langley. The cryptanalyst who's working on Dad's journal called; he needs me for something. I just wanted to bring you some tea. Make sure you're okay."

The worry in Sofia's eyes made Jayne feel terrible. "I am. But we need to talk soon," she said.

"Yes," Sofia answered softly. "We do."

The door opened then, and Sofia, seeing Jayne's eager look, waved her off. "Later. Go check on him."

"Thanks, sis." She gave Sofia a quick hug, then raced into the room.

Cillian was propped up on one of the double beds, his face haggard, but his eyes brightened when he saw her. "Jayne." He tried sitting up, then winced.

"Lie back down," Amanda barked from the sofa, not even looking up from the paperwork she was reading.

Cillian sighed and gestured to the chair next to him. Jayne sank into it, her knees bouncing with pent-up energy.

"Are you okay?" she asked.

Cillian smiled, stretching the large bruise on his face. "I've been through worse."

"Did they...*do* anything to you? Anything...not visible?" Jayne wasn't sure how to word her question.

Cillian frowned. "My teeth are all still intact, if that's what you mean."

Jayne shook her head and coughed out a tiny laugh. "I mean your Rogue magic, your mind, did they tamper with anything inside you?"

"Oh." His eyes shuttered. "No, they didn't. I've got a few cuts and bruises, but they'll heal. It really wasn't that bad, Jayne. La Liberté asked me a few questions about you and your magic, but once they realized I didn't know much, they mostly left me alone." He offered a hoarse chuckle. "I think they were disappointed I wasn't as useful to them as Ruger."

Tears pricked Jayne's eyes. She knew he was sugarcoating it. The hollow look in his eyes told her he was leaving out the awful bits. "God, Cillian, I—" She broke off, the words dying in her throat as she choked on a sob. Instead of bursting into tears, she smacked Cillian in the shoulder.

"Ow!" he protested.

"Jayne," Amanda scolded, still not looking up from her papers.

"Don't you dare do that again," Jayne hissed through her tears. "Don't you ever try to play the hero for me, Cillian. I am not a damsel in need of saving."

"I'd never dream of calling you that." Cillian massaged his shoulder.

"What the hell were you thinking, giving yourself up? Did you *want* to be killed?"

"Of course not. But they were going to take you, and I couldn't—I couldn't let that happen." His eyes were so lost and broken that Jayne's ire abated almost instantly.

She knew the fears in his head because she'd experienced them firsthand. Watching him getting captured was exactly what he'd feared for her.

Jayne stared into the ice-blue depths of his eyes, seeing the panic and desperation within them. This was going to be a problem. "Listen. You can't let your feelings for me get in the way of the mission."

Cillian shook his head. "What? My feelings for you—"

"They made you sacrifice yourself without thinking. Tell me honestly, if we weren't dating, would you have done the same thing?"

"Yes."

"Really?"

Cillian opened his mouth, then shut it, his brow furrowing as he considered this. "I—I don't know."

Jayne leaned forward, pressing her hand against his knee. "You are sexy as hell when you play the knight in shining armor. But I don't need that from you, Cillian."

He cracked a smile, but his eyes were still tormented. "I know you can handle yourself. I do. But without your magic…"

Jayne winced. He didn't need to say more. Hadn't she been struggling with this since La Liberté had infected her with that poison? *Without my magic, I'm worthless.*

Cillian had seen her weak and helpless. That was what this

was really about. He viewed himself as her protector. Someone to step in when Jayne was too weak to defend herself. Was that what being "her" Rogue meant?

The thought put a sick taste in her mouth. Jayne, the fainting damsel who needed a big, strong man to step in and defend her honor.

Ick.

"I felt something in me awaken during the fight when we rescued Ruger," Cillian went on. "Like I was...called. Chosen to protect you or something. It felt like my duty. Like I am—"

"I swear to the goddess if you say you are burdened with glorious purpose, I will be forced to murder you."

Cillian snorted. "I wasn't going to say that."

"Right."

"Truly."

Jayne sighed. "What happened to my magic was unfortunate and unexpected. But I'm smarter now. I'm being more careful. So, yes, if some otherworldly force takes out my magic, you have my permission to wield the sword of destruction and step in to save me. But please give me the chance to save myself first. Okay?"

Guilt flooded his face, and he nodded, looking like a scolded child. Jayne scooted closer so she could touch his face, her fingertips running along the scraggly stubble along his jaw. She brushed a kiss against his lips before leaning her forehead against his. She sighed, just breathing in his musky, manly scent and feeling his warmth against her. He was here. He was safe. He was alive. And that was what really mattered.

After a moment, Cillian asked, "You really think I'd be sexy as a knight?"

She grinned and winked at him. "We'll play with that idea later."

Heat flooded his eyes, and a powerful yearning coiled in Jayne's stomach.

As if sensing the sexual tension in the room, Amanda said, "That's enough, Jayne. He needs to rest now."

Jayne groaned and withdrew from Cillian, already missing his warmth. "Will he be staying here?"

"While he recovers and is fully debriefed, yes," Amanda said, finally looking up from her paperwork. "I'll be here, and there are plenty of officers stationed nearby. He'll be protected."

Jayne nodded. Though she knew it was better for Cillian to be surrounded by allies, she still hated the idea of returning to the flat without him.

She turned to leave, but something snagged her thoughts. "Hey, whatever happened to that sword Rogue I brought in?"

"Our team was able to coax him to shift back into his human form," Amanda said. "He's in pretty bad shape, though. He endured a lot at the Kingdom's hands, suffered quite a trauma, but we're confident he'll pull through with the proper therapy. And perhaps speaking to another Rogue might help." She looked at Cillian, who smiled grimly.

"Another Rogue?"

Jayne explained about the fight with Blaine and the sword Rogue. Cillian winced.

"Aye, I'll talk to him," he said softly. "Poor bugger must be a wreck."

A fresh wave of hatred for Ruth and the Kingdom bloomed in Jayne's chest. God, what was with all the inhumane lunatics running around wielding magic and controlling people? She was sick of it. Monsters, all of them.

At least the Rogue was no longer stuck as a sword. And he'd be okay.

Jayne shook the dark thoughts from her mind and focused on Cillian again. "I'll come back tomorrow, okay?"

Cillian nodded, his blue eyes never leaving hers as she left the room.

To her surprise, Ruger stood in the hall, leaning against the wall. His injuries seemed to be healing nicely, but one eye was still swollen and bruised, and the broken arm was still in a sling. He was playing the role of *casual* a bit too intently, which only raised Jayne's suspicions.

"What's up?" Jayne asked.

Ruger straightened. "Just giving you two a minute is all."

Jayne scrutinized him. "You sure that's all?"

"I may have been a little bitter at being benched for the mission," Ruger admitted in a grumble.

"I hear you, brother. Trying to go up against the magical baddies with no magic feels the same." Jayne sobered, eyeing the injuries that still looked so fresh against his dark skin. "Why don't you let me heal you?"

Ruger stiffened. "Not a good idea, Jayne."

"Why not? I did it with Cillian at Medb's tomb. We know it doesn't burn me up. At least let me try."

"Jayne—"

"If you don't let me do it now, I'll just creep into your room while you sleep and do it then."

Ruger sighed heavily. "All right. Go ahead."

Jayne inched closer, drawing on power from the Torrent. Thank God it responded, but she had no idea how much time she would have before La Liberté would freak out and take away her magic again. She found the Heal spell at once and gently cast it over Ruger's broken arm like a transparent blanket.

His arm twitched, but nothing happened.

Gritting her teeth, Jayne tried again, focusing on the image of two pieces of ripped fabric being sewn back together. Channeling all her magic, she thrust the spell onto Ruger again.

Still nothing.

"The hell?" Jayne dropped her arms with a frustrated huff.

"It's all right, Jayne. It's a magical break, not a regular one. We need a magical solution. Amanda is working on it."

"It's not all right. These jerks are messing with my magic,

hurting you and Cillian, and Amanda, and it's starting to really piss me off."

"Understandable. But I'm sure we'll figure out a solution. You've been pushing yourself a lot lately. Rescuing two fellow officers in the span of a week, plus what La Liberté has put you through? No one expects you to be at 100 percent."

"*I* expect myself to be at 100 percent. This"—she whirled her hand around her body—"is unacceptable."

Ruger smiled. "Whatever they've done to you, it can't be permanent," he said. "Nothing can impede your link to the Torrent. Not forever. The bond is too strong."

At that heartening news, she relaxed a bit. "I hope you're right. At the very least, we've discovered how they're controlling their access to my magic." She quickly filled him in on the amulets La Liberté wore around their necks.

Ruger nodded slowly, his gaze distant. "I noticed a few of my guards wearing those. I could feel the magic emanating from it, even when I was chained. I've never felt anything like it."

Jayne winced at the vision of Ruger in chains. "It seems to be some kind of trigger."

"If that's the case, then breaking the necklaces won't be enough. You'd have to eliminate the source of the spell, wherever that is."

She sighed. Yep, back to square one.

Ruger eyed her. "It can't be easy, being cut off from your magic like that. Especially since you've had a taste of the power of the Earth totem and of the Master of Shadows."

Jayne raised her eyebrows. "You think?"

"I mean, you seem quite agitated. Talk to me, Jayne. Let me help."

She sagged back against the wall opposite him, deflating. Ruger knew her too well. "Yeah, I'm agitated. I have all this new power, but it's all corrupted. It keeps flickering out like a candle in a breeze. Medb comes and goes, popping into my head when things get dire, but only then. We have a whole new enemy, who is talented and has control over me, and another creepy Master in that damn grimoire. You're hurt, Cillian's hurt, Amanda's hurt, Sofia is still pissed at me. I've not had any proper pie or time to read. I'm all sorts of peopled out."

"And?" he asked gently.

"And..." She swallowed her monstrous pride and admitted the truth. "What good am I to you now, especially when I can't protect everyone?"

Ruger scowled, his eyes darkening. "You know better than that, Jayne."

"Do I? You told me I had unparalleled power, power you'd never seen before. That's why you approached me at Vanderbilt."

"And that's true. But don't pretend like magic is the only thing we focus on here. You went through training just like everyone else. You know we teach skills beyond magic. You're still learning."

"Yeah, sure, but I'm supposed to be a Master magician, Ruger. If we were fighting some James Bond villain, then I bet I could kick his ass in a heartbeat. But we're not. We're fighting real people. Ruth Thorne and Gina Labelle. Two women who clearly don't care who they hurt in their quests for power, with two highly trained terror groups at their beck and call. We need as much magic on our side as we can get, and your star quarterback is out of the game with a pulled hamstring. I'm useless to you without my magic."

Ruger was silent for a long moment. Then, he said, "By your logic, I'm worthless now, too."

Jayne blinked. She hadn't expected that. "That's ridiculous. What are you talking about?"

"I was hired for my fighting skills. Did you know that? I started as a field agent in the CIA before the TCO recruited me. The doctor still wants me off missions until I'm fully healed. I can't fight until this arm heals, so what good am I?"

She gritted her teeth. "That's not the same thing, and you know it."

His dark eyes bore into hers. "Humor me. Answer my question. What good am I?"

"You—you're a wealth of knowledge," Jayne sputtered. "And you're my mentor. You can still teach me."

"Okay. What else?"

Jayne felt like she was being quizzed, and she huffed in exasperation. "You've got good instincts. You know the enemy better than any of us, since you've been on the inside. You were able to withstand the torture they inflicted on you, which shows resilience and strength. Even if you can't fight, you can still cast spells, strategize, analyze information and data, piece clues together..." She trailed off, glaring at Ruger's smug expression. "It's still not the same thing."

"No, it's not. But you're being too hard on yourself. From what I hear, you kicked ass today."

A tendril of satisfaction bloomed inside her at his praise. "Yeah, I suppose there was a bit of ass-kickery in there."

"You can't give in to helplessness, Jayne. If you do, it means they've won. You are learning one of the hardest truths imaginable. No matter what criminal is thwarted by our actions, another will rise to take their place. There are always people in the world who want to take a shortcut, who want power. This is true in the real world as well as the magical world. We will never, ever be fully safe. This war doesn't ever truly end."

A lump formed in her throat at that. She hadn't been thinking long-term. It made sense. Terrible sense. "You're right." Her gaze snapped back to his. "Wait...the grimoire. The forgery. Did they...?"

"Seo-joon saw them leave with the forgery. But I have no doubt they've noticed by now it's not real."

"I admit, I would have paid good money to see the look on

Labelle's face when she realized she'd been duped. You know they'll retaliate."

"Yes, they will."

"We should track them down before they do."

"Yes, we should." Ruger's eyes glinted.

Jayne stared at him, suddenly suspicious. "You have a plan, don't you?"

"Maybe," he said. "But first, I need you to tell me what you saw in the Book of Shadows."

Jayne stilled, her heart hammering madly in her chest. "How do you know about that?"

"Grimoires are sentient, and sometimes, they speak," Ruger said. "Our analysts heard it calling for you."

Jayne's blood chilled at those words, and a hiss of trepidation crept over her skin. Whatever strange, powerful force lived in the grimoire, it still sought her. Not great. She could go three lifetimes without wrestling with the Master of Shadows again.

"Did it hurt anyone?" she asked.

Ruger shook his head. "Our invocationists are professionals. They know how to handle even the most violent of grimoires."

Jayne shivered at the thought of even more violent grimoires.

Ruger nudged her elbow. "Go on, Jayne. You can tell me."

Almost grateful for how easily he read her, Jayne took a deep breath and described the horrifying experience of being smothered by shadows as the disembodied voice whispered in her ear. She recalled the relentless flow of images in her mind, and the immense power emanating from the book. When she told Ruger that she overpowered the grimoire with her Earth totem, he raised a dark brow.

"You used the totem? To fuel your magic?" His voice was full of surprise.

"I know, I know, it's dangerous. But the grimoire had my normal magic trapped. Something inside me knew I needed another power source." Jayne wasn't sure where her words came from, but they felt right.

Ruger was silent for several long moments, his jaw working back and forth, his eyes glazing over. Jayne fidgeted, shifting her weight as she waited for him to respond.

At long last, he asked, "Have you tried accessing those images again?"

"Of course. But there's some mental block in my way. I can't remember anything the book showed me specifically, just the general sense of things."

Ruger nodded as if he expected this.

When he still said nothing, Jayne asked, "What are you thinking?"

He blinked as if just realizing she was there. He rubbed his jaw, tapping a finger against his cheek. "I think the grimoire branded your magic somehow. Even though you vanquished the presence within, it still marked you."

"Whoa, creepy. How do I get rid of the mark?"

"You can't. A mark from a grimoire that powerful is permanent."

"Okayyyy. So what can I do?"

"I think you should try accessing your memories again…using the Earth totem instead."

"If I could do it again, I would. I've tried. But nothing. It's an unreliable source of power right now. It seems like it's only available when I'm in dire straits."

His smile was almost contagious. "Then we'll create a situation that triggers it."

33
DRAGON'S BREATH

Ruger's idea was easier said than done. While the magic of the Earth totem came to Jayne's aid during the grimoire's attack, it did not come so easily when she wished it to. They tried for an hour at the flat in the 15th, and nothing worked.

It certainly seemed to realize that the magical threats Ruger was presenting her with wouldn't actually hurt her. Even the giant roaring dragon that spewed fire all over the flat and singed the curtains caused absolutely nothing else to happen.

Jayne wondered if this totem magic was also somehow sentient. If it had an ounce of Medb's stubbornness, then she was doomed.

Finally, exhausted, she flopped on the sofa. Ruger sat across from her gingerly, babying the arm still in a sling.

"Try again," he urged. Though it was her nineteenth attempt, his tone was nothing but patient.

Classic Ruger. The epitome of ease when Jayne was failing spectacularly.

"I really don't think it's going to work," she protested, rubbing at her temples to ward off a throbbing headache. She was about over all of this.

"Try. Again." The words weren't forceful or stern, but the fire in his voice made Jayne reconsider arguing with him. "Remember, this isn't like tapping into the Torrent. The rules are different. The power source is different. Surrender yourself to it just like you do for the Torrent. Allow it to take you in freely."

Jayne suppressed a shudder. It sounded like giving herself over to some dark force. She'd done it before, but that was when the grimoire had almost eaten her. It was hard to replicate that same sense of desperation. She didn't like the blatant unknown of it all. What if the power took over her mind and spirit like the grimoire had almost done? What if the poison from La Liberté affected the totem and it went haywire and electrocuted her?

"You know, Hector told me it was a bad idea to give in to the totem's magic," Jayne pointed out, knowing full well she was just stalling.

"Hector doesn't know you or your track record with magic. I trust your instincts, Jayne. This power saved you twice now—once at Medb's tomb, and again with that necromantic grimoire. You're holding back. Stop second-guessing yourself and trust your instincts."

"My instincts say *not* to put my arsenal of magic into some unknown entity's hands."

Ruger sighed. "That's the problem. It senses your reluctance. It won't open up to you if you don't open up to it."

"This is magic we're talking about, not a golden retriever," Jayne snapped.

"You know as well as I do that magic is a living, breathing entity." Ruger was completely unfazed by her frustration.

Jayne grumbled something incoherent and crammed her eyes shut.

"Relax," he coaxed. "Don't force it."

Jayne took a deep breath and relaxed her muscles. The tension left her arms and legs as she sank back into the soft cushions. She focused on the sounds of traffic echoing from the open door of the balcony. The breeze whispering against her face. Ruger's steady breathing in front of her.

Something thrummed in her chest, and she flinched instinctively, then relaxed again. Her magic was eager, waiting to be utilized. It just needed a conduit. A power source.

Mentally, she itched to reach for the Torrent like she always did. Instead, she shifted her attention slightly. She reached closer to that power that dwelled within her, strong and yet dormant. She focused on the prickle of heat in the center of her forehead where Medb's totem had bonded with her. She thought about the icy anger that took over her mind on the bridge.

And then, she pulled. An unrestrained tug. Energy cracked open inside her chest, bursting like a dam had exploded. Icy coldness filled her as if she'd unleashed a lifetime's supply of wintergreen chewing gum in her bloodstream. Jayne sucked in a breath, suddenly finding it hard to breathe. Warmth stung her eyes, but she had no idea why. Was it sorrow? Shock? Awe? Pain? She felt nothing at all but openness. Raw, unleashed power. Brutal and unstoppable.

It frightened her and excited her all at once.

"Whoa," Ruger murmured.

A bolt of clarity slid into Jayne's mind, and she blinked rapidly, surprised to find tears on her cheeks. But that wasn't what had startled Ruger.

She was glowing. A pearly white light emanated from her hands as if she were a ghost. She lifted her fingers in front of her eyes and wiggled them, expecting them to be semitransparent. But she was still solid. Just...more luminescent. Like a human glow stick.

Ruger's dark eyes moved to her forehead, no doubt where the totem glowed more starkly. "Okay," he said slowly as if trying to calm down a raging bull. "Now carefully...try to access the images from the grimoire."

"You say that like it's easy." Jayne's voice was ethereal, like several versions of herself layered into one.

"You can do this. The power isn't dangerous."

But it certainly felt dangerous. Jayne searched within the bright light, trying to locate the images just like she would access the Torrent for a spell. But it was all a jumbled mass of blinding stars and incoherent flashes. Like she lived inside a disco ball. Blurred shapes whizzed past her, so quickly she couldn't make out details enough to grab them.

"I—I can't," she said in a strained voice. "It's...too much. Too much."

The images twisted into a sickening kaleidoscope of sight and sound until nausea roiled in Jayne's stomach. She hunched over with a groan, shutting her eyes against the sheer intensity of it all. *Too much. Too much.*

As if the power could hear her, the light receded, crawling back inside her like a mama bear returning to her hibernating cave. Her skin stopped glowing, and the images and ice vanished, leaving her panting and winded like she'd sprinted a mile.

"Are you all right?" Ruger asked quietly.

Jayne nodded, though she wasn't. Her skin felt clammy, and her hands wouldn't stop shaking. "It overwhelmed me. I... couldn't see anything. Couldn't..." She trailed off, unable to find the words. Waves of hot and cold racked through her body like fever chills.

Ruger sat forward and took her hand. His massive palm was calloused but comforting. "It was the first time you've willingly tapped into this power. I think this was a good start. You need to practice, almost like stretching a muscle. A little bit more each time until your body adapts."

"You sound like Hector."

"That's because Hector and I know that exploring new magic takes time."

"But we don't *have* time," Jayne argued. "I need to figure out the shadowed illumination before La Liberté figures out it's a fake and comes for my head. You need to let me examine the grimoire again."

"I know you're worried," Ruger said. "But we're still three steps ahead of them."

Jayne ground her teeth together. Instead of this relentless training, they should be making their way to the burial site of the Master of Shadows. The sooner they got there, the sooner they could prevent the inevitable destruction La Liberté would cause. Or the Kingdom. Jayne hated to think of what dark plans Ruth had in store if she got the totem, especially one from a magician as dark and twisted as the Master of Shadows. Jayne would never forget that vision of the Master possessing the minds of desperate artists. In Ruth's vile hands? Terrifying.

Ruger's cell phone beeped, and his thick brows furrowed when he glanced at the screen. "Amanda needs us. Says it's urgent."

Jayne struggled to her feet, amazed at how exhausted she felt. A slight pulse in her head made her dizzy for a moment, but it passed quickly.

Ruger noticed. His eyes were guarded as he slowly rose, extending a hand to her for a lift.

"You all right?"

"Just peachy. Let's go."

∼

Sofia and Cillian were waiting when Ruger and Jayne arrived. Sofia's mouth was pinched with worry, and Cillian's eyes blazed with intensity. He looked loads better—his eyes weren't as shadowed, and he'd showered and shaved. Aside from the cuts and bruises, he looked almost completely normal.

"Good, you're here," Amanda said, standing with her hands clasped in the center of the room. "We've received intel that La

Liberté *and* the Kingdom are on the move, both on the outskirts of Paris."

"Both?" Jayne asked. "Are they working together? That would be all kinds of bad."

"We don't think so. They're on opposite ends of the city. But it complicates things. We can't send you to both places at once." Amanda hesitated.

"What is it?"

"There have been sightings of an uncontrollable Rogue in Fontainebleau. We believe La Liberté is responsible."

Jayne sucked in a breath. She remembered the violent, distorted Rogue from Alarik's Time Catch. The one she'd killed. It had nearly torn her apart.

A Rogue that volatile would destroy what was left of that poor city.

"Not La Liberté. The Kingdom must have let out one of their experiments. You have to send me," Jayne said. "I have experience taming Rogues, after all." She nudged Cillian's shoulder jokingly, but inside she felt a wee bit sick at the idea of going up against another one of Alarik and Ruth's creations until she had better control of her magic.

Cillian had gone still next to her. "I'll go with Jayne."

"No," Amanda said, surprising everyone. "From Jayne's reports, you haven't been able to bond successfully with her as often as I'd like. This wild Rogue could interfere with your connection to Jayne, possibly affecting the magic that tethers you. We can't risk it."

Cillian tensed at the implication that *he* would become dangerous and volatile enough to level a city. Jayne squeezed his shoulder while Amanda continued.

"Instead, Cillian, I want you to back up Sofia and track down the lead on the Kingdom." Amanda turned to Sofia and softened slightly. "If you're up for it, that is."

Jayne raised an eyebrow at the gentleness in Amanda's

expression. Generally, Amanda was a no-nonsense type of woman, not to be contradicted or questioned. Her orders were orders. But when she spoke to Sofia, she seemed more like a mother about to offer ice cream to a toddler. Had something changed between them since Sofia signed on with the TCO?

Sofia lifted her chin, eyes alight with energy Jayne had never seen before. "I can do it."

Not even an ounce of hesitation.

Jayne was surprised. Gone was the paranoid, frightened sister she was accustomed to. Jayne had changed, but Sofia had changed, too. Right now, she seemed like a hardened warrior ready for battle. A surge of pride swelled in Jayne's chest. She made a mental note to ask what had happened to change her attitude…and to smooth over the rough patch between them for good. But for now, there wasn't time.

"I'll go with Jayne," Ruger said, his voice deep and commanding.

Amanda's eyes turned to steel, sharpening as they fixed on Ruger. "Absolutely not. Cillian is cleared for missions, but you're not. You suffered greater injuries than he did. I can't have you out in the field right now. Seo-joon will go with her."

A muscle ticked in Ruger's jaw. "I'm going. End of discussion."

After a moment glaring at one another, Amanda sighed. "Fine. But be prepared. The reports of the Rogue are probably a distraction while La Liberté tries to work spells to open the grimoire." Amanda met Jayne's gaze. "Get to Fontainebleau. Subdue this supposed Rogue before it wreaks havoc on the area. Then get back here so we can work on the shadowed illumination."

Jayne nodded once.

Amanda glanced between Cillian and Sofia. "You two, get to the Château de Chantilly. Tamara has been watching the area and spotted several Kingdom operatives massing nearby. We assume they're still searching for the grimoire and don't realize Jayne liberated it from the vault. Knowing their tactics, they'll simply force their way inside, civilians be damned. Stop them, and make sure no one gets hurt in the process. We can't have any more casualties in the name of this war, do you understand me?"

"Yes, ma'am," Cillian said.

Sofia gave him a smile. "We've got this."

"Any questions?" Amanda asked the room, the question more of a demand, as if she were daring someone to speak up. Her eyes gleamed with a challenge.

Ruger was still a mass of stone next to Jayne, unmoving. But he made no objection. Sofia and Cillian rose from their seats, exchanging a glance. Jayne knew why they were worried—hell, she was worried. They had never been on a mission with each other before. Never trained together. They hardly knew each other. Would they be okay? Would they figure out how to trust each other?

They'd better.

"Good. Dismissed," Amanda said. And they all filed out of the room.

34

A FORGIVING SHADE OF BLUE

Jayne hesitated in the hallway alongside Sofia and Cillian, feeling the pressure of unsaid things coming between them.

Cillian, bless him, caught the look between the sisters and said quickly, "I'll wait for you two downstairs."

Jayne smiled gratefully at him as he retreated down the hall.

"Jayne," Sofia said at once, drawing closer.

In an instant, they were embracing, arms clutching each other tightly. She felt Sofia's shoulders shaking with silent sobs.

"I'm so sorry," Sofia whispered against her shoulder. "I never should have doubted you."

"I said terrible things," Jayne said. "I didn't mean them, Sofia." She drew away and sniffled, willing herself not to break down and cry. "I know what you did was to protect me. I understand it now, but I'm sorry I didn't before."

Sofia shook her head. "You're doing what you feel is right. And after working with the TCO these past few days, I can see it clearly. They are making a difference, Jayne. And I'm proud of you for fighting alongside them."

"Does this mean you're fighting, too?"

Sofia raised her chin. "Yes. It's time to stop hiding."

Jayne grinned and squeezed her hands. "You're a lioness, Sofia. I knew you had it in you."

Sofia touched her chin. "Just be careful, okay? If you want, I can braid your hair like I used to."

Jayne frowned. "Why?"

"There's this spell I used to do..."

Jayne frowned. "What kind of spell?"

"A spell called the Three Winds. A Binding spell is put on a ribbon, and when the ribbon is knotted and you blow on it three times, it locks in whatever magic you put there."

Jayne's brain struggled to function, like the gears had locked in place, rusted from disuse. "So...so all those times you braided my hair..." Her voice sounded numb.

"Well, not every time, but yes. And I'd add a Shield spell to protect you."

"Oh." A hard lump formed in Jayne's throat. Though the rational side of her knew this was Sofia's way of showing love, of trying to keep Jayne safe, she also felt...betrayed. She'd thought those moments had been Sofia comforting her. But really, her older sister was just summoning magic and not telling Jayne about it.

It felt like a lie. All of it.

She did it to protect you, not hurt you, Jayne reminded herself. She couldn't forgive Sofia overnight for all the lies and betrayal. It was a process. But she could start here and now by not getting angry at this revelation.

She forced her attention on something else. "What are the Three Winds?"

"An ancient magic. It helps solidify the Binding spell."

"That's why you blew on my neck? I always thought that was so weird."

Sofia laughed. "Yes."

"Interesting. I'll have to remember that one." Jayne forced a smile that Sofia probably saw right through.

Leaning forward, Sofia said, "I want to come clean with you. About everything."

Jayne froze, every inch of her body stiff with anticipation. This was it. This was what she'd spent her whole life waiting for. The truth about her parents. The truth about the magic that had been hidden from her for so long.

And yet...they both had an assignment. A mission. As much as she wanted to plop down on a couch with a huge slice of pie, a bottle of wine, and talk to Sofia for hours about everything, now was not the time.

Sofia must have noticed her face fall, because she quickly said, "I'm sorry. I shouldn't have offered right now."

"No," Jayne said quickly. "It's not that." *Did* Jayne want Sofia to come clean about everything? Would it make things easier...or harder? Well, things were already hard enough. Their explosive fight had proven that.

Maybe it was time they hashed all this out. Even if it got ugly. No matter how painful it would be, at least they'd get through it together.

Jayne swallowed hard. "Let's talk when we get back. Okay?"

Sofia straightened, her eyes alight. "Yeah. Let's do that."

They embraced again for a long moment. Jayne memorized her sister's raspberry scent, the softness of her, the warmth and comfort she always felt in her arms. She didn't want to lose this feeling. This sensation of home. Of rightness.

Because this might be the last time she felt that way.

Blinking tears from her eyes, Jayne kissed Sofia's cheek and drew away before she turned into a blubbering mess.

In the living room, Cillian waited with his arms crossed, looking like a model straight from a *GQ* magazine. The healing scars on his face only made him look more rugged and manly.

Jayne approached him and threw her arms around his neck. "No getting captured this time, 'k?"

Cillian snorted. "Wasn't planning on it, love." He leaned in, his lips capturing hers with a delicious heat that sank all the way down to Jayne's toes.

She pulled apart a fraction, her lips still brushing against his. "Take care of her, will you?" she whispered against his mouth.

"I will." His promise was a low rumble in his throat that only made it harder for Jayne to part with him.

She kissed him again, long and lingering, all tongue and no mercy. Cillian groaned with agony when she pulled away, and she grinned in response.

"Stay alive, and we'll continue this conversation later," she said with a wink.

"Such a tease." He offered a lopsided grin as Sofia appeared at his side, ready to go.

Ruger had a car, which made Jayne roll her eyes at Amanda's public transit dictate—next time she sent them into a foreign country with no portal access, a rental was going to be the first request—and he was relatively quiet on the drive to Fontainebleau. Jayne felt restless with pent-up energy. She was eager to put this mission behind her and get back to Sofia and Cillian.

"What do you think, Rug? Rogue trapping can't possibly take that long, right? In and out."

"Ha ha. I have no idea what we're about to face. You need to be prepared for anything, from a wild Rogue to Gina Labelle in the flesh."

"There's a lot of ground to cover, and I doubt they've made much progress with the cleanup from the earthquake. Where do we even start?"

"At the edge of the disaster, and work our way in. I'm going to park on the other side of the forest. We'll go in on foot."

An hour later, slightly winded, they came upon the charred remains of Fontainebleau.

"My God," Ruger said. "It's even worse in person."

"It's hideously bad. And something is wrong," Jayne replied. Hunks of rubble and debris surrounded her, just as she remembered. But the air was silent. Void of any living thing. Empty.

An eerie suspicion crept over her skin. Each footstep reverberated against her ears, jarring against the stony silence around her. No investigators. No civilians. No officials.

Just Jayne and Ruger, amidst a ghost town. And no sign of a violent Rogue anywhere. Jayne knew she would have seen one immediately. The huge, bumbling giant of a Rogue from Alarik's Time Catch had been impossible to miss.

There was no Rogue here.

"Trap?" she whispered.

"Definitely," he grumbled back. "Split up. Stay alert. Do a perimeter search. Send up sparks if you get into trouble, and I'll do the same."

"I don't know that we should split up," Jayne said, but he was already moving west. The hairs on her arms stood on end, and wariness swelled in her chest until she couldn't breathe.

Wrong, wrong, wrong.

Jayne stopped in her tracks. A shiver rippled down her spine. No, this wasn't right. She shouldn't be here.

Get out. Now!

"Oh, shit," Jayne whispered. Dread pooled in her stomach. La Liberté had sent false intel to lure Jayne here. To what? Kill her? Imprison her? By now they must know the grimoire she'd handed over was fake. It would make sense that they sought retribution for the trick.

All right, bastards, Jayne thought, gritting her teeth. *Let's get this over with.* She wiggled her fingers, searching for...resolve? Courage? Power? Something to get her through this. She closed her eyes and looked for the Torrent. Nothing.

But she was so much more than just her magic. She knew that now.

Her hands curled into fists. Ice spread through her chest, igniting into a violent flame that burned and charred everything in its wake. The powerful fury coursed through Jayne, merciless and all-consuming. Her eyes flitted around the area, passing over rubble and remains and dirt, searching for the enemy she knew lurked nearby.

Her wild anger made her impatient. She spread her arms and shouted, "Well? Here I am! Come at me, bro!"

Silence met her words, but she wasn't fooled.

"Marco!" she shouted.

Nothing.

Well, fine. If they were going to take forever to make their move, Jayne would make herself useful. Do the perimeter search as Ruger directed.

Jayne moved east, and as she did, the faintest whisper of magic tickled her left ear, brushing against her like a slight breeze. If she hadn't been attentive, she might have missed it. She looked to the sky for Ruger's sparks, thinking maybe it was him calling for help. Nothing.

Another gentle tickle, and her instincts roared into overdrive. She ducked, dropping to the dirt. Something hot whizzed just over her head, searing her scalp. She hissed in pain, hoping whatever spell that was hadn't burned her hair right off. She happened to like her hair.

Another more intense burst of magic split the air, cracking like thunder. Jayne rolled away from the sound, limbs and joints bumping over sharp rocks and jagged concrete. Bright light burned against her vision, momentarily blinding her. She raised her arms to shield herself and tried to send up the sparks. Nothing. Damn it. Why couldn't the damn TCO use wands like the rest of the fantasy world?

The searing light faded, and she hesitantly lifted her head. There was a huge, smoking hole where she'd stood moments ago.

Either La Liberté had terrible aim, or they were toying with her.

Jayne needed a new plan. Where the heck was Ruger, to start? He was supposed to be her backup. Her imagination kicked into overdrive—Ruger had been captured again, or worse, he'd been turned when La Liberté held him so long and was leading her into the trap instead of helping her get out of it...

Slow your roll, Jayne. That is impossible. Ruger would never switch sides.

After glancing over the area once more, Jayne decided that even hidden behind a chunk of rubble, she was too exposed. Less than two hundred yards away were the destroyed remains of the Château de Fontainebleau—heaps of massive concrete and marble, smashed pillars and staircases; myriad spots for her to hide behind.

Screw the perimeter, she decided. She was going for the heart.

Jayne sprang into action, her legs pumping furiously as she sprinted toward the château. Remembering her training, she bobbed and weaved as if a gunman chased after her. Duck, zigzag, left, right. *Make it hard for them to take aim*, she reminded herself.

Energy sizzled in the air, and Jayne dived to the right, not knowing why, just knowing she had to. A second later, green light engulfed the spot next to her, igniting an ethereal emerald flame that nearly melted her skin off. Jayne tumbled and rolled, then rose to pat herself down in case she'd caught fire. Sweat broke out, pouring down her face and neck as she kept running. She impatiently wiped her brow and continued to race back and forth, this way and that, to throw off her attacker.

She wasn't dead yet. It meant her strategy was working.

She hoped.

The remains of the château loomed closer. Almost there...

Magic exploded behind her, but she wasn't fast enough this time. Something sharp sliced into her left leg, and she went down, arms scraping against rock, her face throbbing and one leg completely numb with pain.

Nope. Not numb anymore. A white-hot fire erupted along her shin, and for a second, she thought the green flames had gotten her. When she glanced down, she found a bloody gash the size of her fist. Like the spell had taken a chunk of her leg with it.

Damn, she thought. *There goes my bob-and-weave strategy.*

Jayne tried in vain to reach the Torrent to heal herself, but still nothing happened. She tried to send up sparks. Nothing. She couldn't scream for Ruger; that would draw the attacker's attention to both her position and the fact that she had backup. Wherever he was.

Swearing, she ripped off a part of her sleeve and tied it around her shin to stop the bleeding, then dragged herself to her feet. She couldn't run on it, instead hobbled frantically, feeling ridiculous and foolish, knowing her assailant could easily outrun her and take her out.

But for some reason, they didn't.

Yep. They were totally toying with her.

A spell shot past her head. Then another slammed into her shoulder, but she caught herself before falling. A stinging burn spread across her upper body, but it wasn't bleeding, and the pain was bearable. She soldiered on until she finally made it to the first massive chunk of rubble and ducked behind it, gasping for breath. A stitch formed in her side, and her leg pulsed in agony. Her face felt so hot she thought she might faint.

Use your skills, said a voice in her head that sounded a lot like Ruger. *You can't use magic, but you know how to fight, even with an injured leg. You aren't helpless. Fight, Jayne!*

Where the heck are you, dude?

Ruger was down, no question about it. She couldn't escape in her condition, and she couldn't leave him behind anyway. She had to beat whoever was after her. That was the only way out.

"Let's do this the old-fashioned way," she muttered, dropping to the ground to smear dirt on her face and arms like a bona fide badass. Her stark white skin stood out too much among the gray dust and brown dirt. Luckily, she was wearing dark colors, so her clothing wouldn't be too noticeable. She tied her hair back and crept around her hiding spot before darting to the boulder a few yards away. She pressed her back against the rock and waited, trying not to breathe too loudly.

Nothing happened.

Okay. Good. Keep going.

Jayne ducked between three more hunks of concrete before she found an enormous, hulking shape that looked like part of a roof with half a pillar attached to it. Jayne took a step back to survey it, searching for notches she could use as footholds.

Yes, this could work.

Hoisting herself up, she avoided using her bad leg as she climbed atop the rubble, shimmying up the broken pillar until she perched above like a crow surveying the wreckage. She was at least ten feet high, so unless her assailant could fly—and she wouldn't put it past them—then they wouldn't be able to see her.

With the bird's-eye view, she searched the rubble field for Ruger. Had he made it to the other side? She didn't see sparks, or the big man's hulking form.

Jayne pressed back down against the concrete, sliding onto her belly and keeping her face low. She waited, remaining perfectly still. Not even a speck of dust floated in front of her. After a while, her limbs started to ache, and her arm fell asleep. But still she waited, a predator ready to pounce.

Just when she thought her attacker had vanished, a lone figure stepped into view. Jayne held her breath, searching behind him, waiting for more to appear.

But no. It was just one man.

And she recognized him: Tristan Lowell.

A seething anger boiled underneath Jayne's skin as she watched him approach, his face still battered and bruised from the fight they'd had. She wanted to spit on him, but that would give away her hiding spot.

So, she watched him, eyes narrowed in concentration. His long hair fell to his shoulders, now neat and clean, as opposed to lank and greasy like when she'd last seen him. His dark, shrewd eyes cast around the debris, cold and calculating. He was clever. Alert. Too smart. Jayne marveled that she hadn't seen it before. She should've realized the moment she'd met him.

He was a cold-hearted bastard.

Come closer, little French boy, Jayne coaxed. *Just a little closer.*

When he was directly underneath her, Jayne lunged. She threw herself on top of him, using his body as a cushion for her landing. She still scraped her elbows when they hit the ground. He collapsed with an "oof," and she scrambled atop him, slamming her fist against his jaw again and again.

He squirmed beneath her, snatched her wrists, holding them away from his face. His body jerked as he tried to throw her off, but her legs pinned him down, despite her shin screaming in pain.

"Cast a spell at me now, asshole," Jayne growled, slamming her forehead against his.

A weak moan poured from his lips, his eyes rolling back in his head. Satisfaction spread through Jayne as she staggered to her feet.

But her triumph was short-lived. He wasn't knocked out. He snatched her ankle and tugged until she crashed to the ground in a heap. He pinned her arms down, but she jerked her knee up between his legs. He howled, and she spun out from under him.

They both rose, fists raised, and faced each other. Jayne advanced, but Lowell raised both hands in surrender.

"Wait," he rasped. Blood oozed from his nose. "I need to say something first."

"Sure you do," Jayne spat before lunging again.

Lowell caught her fist and twisted her wrist. She cried out as pain shot up her arm.

Suddenly, he released her, palms out again. "Jayne. You need to hear this."

"What?" she growled. "What do I need to hear?"

"Tiriosis."

Jayne scowled at him. "I beg your pardon?"

"The poison inside you is called Tiriosis. And there is no antidote."

Jayne shifted her weight, easing off her bad leg. The heck was he doing? "If there's no antidote…," she said slowly.

Lowell stepped closer, and for some reason, she let him. "The Torrent isn't the only magic inside you, Jayne. You can heal yourself without it."

Jayne blinked at him. How did he know that? Was word out about the Earth totem?

"Why are you telling me this?" she finally asked.

"Because I'm not your enemy."

Jayne snorted at that. "Sure."

Lowell offered a wry smile. "Think what you like. But we're on the same side." He straightened, his expression sobering and his jaw going tight. "Ruger is on the western edge of this field, about five hundred feet from where you inserted. He's alive, just a little Knockout spell, and safe for now. I wanted to talk to you alone."

"You're insane, Lowell."

"The name is Tristan. Say it."

"Why?"

"Would you rather I fight you in earnest? I have my magic, as you might have noticed." He pressed a hand to her leg and she saw stars. Not the ones she wanted, either. "It's a simple request."

"Okay, weirdo. Tris-tan," she enunciated, and he gave her that infuriatingly French lopsided smile. Honestly, kicking his ass would give her an immense amount of satisfaction, though Jayne suspected they didn't have much time. She needed to find Ruger and get them out of here.

"Jayne," Tristan said softly. "They're coming. You have ten minutes to get yourself situated. Access your true magic and expel the poison. It's vital. Now say my name again. Just my name." The urgency in his tone got her attention.

"Tristan."

She felt the spell shimmer around her, as if she'd walked through a thick fogbank, misty tendrils shooting around her body, and a vast sense of relief filled her as the Torrent appeared. Still sluggish, but there. He'd given her some sort of access. As if his name...

"Oh!"

"Yes, oh. It was Gina's idea to tie the Binding spell to my name." At the look on her face, he continued. "We've been tampering with your magic since you arrived in France, when I touched you that first day, with this spell. It was extra protection for us in case you knew how to use the totem's magic. But you will only have the barest protection, at least until you've rid yourself of the Tiriosis for good. You need to get yourself someplace safe and fix things."

"Wait. You bespelled me? With a Binding spell?" She remembered the nasty bruise on her arm from where he'd grabbed her. "Was it you who poisoned me, too?

He ducked his head. "Yes. My apologies. I didn't know you then."

"You don't know me now."

"Don't I?" His mouth quirked into a smile. "Seriously, Jayne. You must go. And you'll need to knock me out, too."

Jayne raised an eyebrow, gazing at him with incredulity. "What?"

"If I'm conscious when my comrades find me, they'll be suspicious. You have to knock me out. The spell is simple; it looks like a boxing glove."

"Don't you *want* your comrades to find me?" Jayne asked. This felt like another trap.

"No, I don't."

"Why not?"

"I have my reasons."

Jayne's nostrils flared as she drew closer to him. "If you really want me to trust you—and if, as you say, you're not my enemy—then you'll tell me your damn reasons."

Tristan sighed and wiped a trickle of blood from his face. "My goals no longer align with my...superiors. I don't like their motives, and I don't like the lines they are willing to cross to get what they want." He gestured to the ruins around them. "It wasn't just civilians. We lost people here, too. I lost a dear friend that day. I can't sanction these actions any longer."

Jayne thought of the explosive earthquake that had killed a thousand people in this very spot. Her eyes raked over the devastation around her, and something hardened in her chest. "You should've thought of that a while ago, buddy."

"I know." For a moment, grief and disgust twisted his features so much that Jayne's nasty retort died on her lips.

Silence fell between them. She crossed her arms, wincing as the wound in her leg throbbed painfully.

"Jayne. Now."

Jayne felt like she should say something else first. *Sorry* or *good luck*, or something...less hostile. Even if this guy was a douchebag, he was still helping her.

She cleared her throat. "Um, thank you. I think."

She didn't bother with magic. Her fist collided with his jaw, and he went down.

35

A GIRL TRANSFORMED

Jayne felt slightly guilty leaving Tristan's unconscious form just lying there in the rubble while she fled.

Only slightly. Just because he'd been nice and released the spell against her, and was apparently also a turncoat, didn't mean she hated him any less.

She hobbled as far as she could before the pain in her leg made her vision blur and her head spin. She stopped, wheezing and clutching her leg while leaning on a hunk of concrete for support. She needed to get to Ruger. But she couldn't make it far like this, especially if Tristan's comrades were on the prowl.

She used the meager power Tristan had restored to her to reach into the Torrent and snatch a Cloaking spell, then, comfortably hidden from plain view, got to work.

Okay. Tap into the totem's power. I can do that, right? Easy peasy. Just like I did at the flat with Ruger.

Her mood soured at the thought of those mostly fruitless attempts in her living room, but she shoved the bitterness away. Her life literally depended on this. It had to be now.

While she caught her breath, she thought back to when she'd used the totem's power to fight off the influence of the grimoire. In a panic, her thoughts had turned to Cillian and Sofia. Thinking of them brought a wave of determination that empowered her, opening the floodgates for Medb's power.

She focused on that power. That sense of strength and unstoppable energy. With that in mind, she gently pulled, just like she had with Ruger coaching her.

Her mind opened up to the magic within her, and it swelled, a light inside brightening until it filled her completely. The familiar icy coldness seemed to freeze and burn her all at once.

Easy, easy, easy. Part of her feared she might frighten it away. Another part of her worried the power would overwhelm her completely, shutting her true self out like the grimoire had.

She bit down on her lip to keep from fighting this presence that still felt so foreign to her. Instead, she reminded herself of Medb. Her power and regal authority. Her commanding tone. The gifts she'd bestowed on Jayne.

She was a warrior. A goddess. And Jayne had a portion of that power.

Light exploded in her chest, and she embraced it, welcoming it as it warmed every inch of her. Gone was the chilly sensation that made her feel clammy. All she felt now was pleasant heat and immense power. Her skin tingled and her insides thrummed. Instinctively, she crouched down and put glowing hands to the wound in her leg. The Healing spell appeared instantly, and she grabbed it before pressing it to the bloodied cloth wrapped around her shin.

The intensity of the light grew hot, burning Jayne from the inside. She knew she should feel afraid of spontaneously bursting into flames like so many other Adepts had done...but she felt nothing but calm.

She'd healed before. And this was Medb's power. Jayne knew she could handle it.

The wound sealed itself, and the pain in her shin vanished.

She could put weight on her leg again. She did the same thing to the injury in her shoulder, too.

Relief filled her, and a small smile spread across her face.

Now for the poison…

Jayne directed Medb's magic to the Tiriosis, as Tristan called it. This time, it took nothing but a thought to send the magic to the right place. Light flooded her mind, momentarily blinding her. Something jerked near her navel, and she practically fell on her face. Her blood felt like it was on fire. The power within boiled her insides. She gritted her teeth, choking on a scream as energy pulsed with nauseating speed, coursing through her like a violent waterfall.

The poison is a part of your body, Medb's voice whispered in her ear. *It has been inside you for too long. You need the Earth to heal you.*

"Okay," Jayne said aloud, still blinded by the light. "I have to get to Ruger, and then you can tell me how."

He is safe. I have seen to it. I must show you now.

A flash of blue light, and magic erupted from Jayne's fingertips. When the light vanished, a simple door materialized in front of her, casting a shadow on the rubble.

A portal.

Jayne blinked. She'd never created a portal before. But this didn't feel like her magic. This was Medb's doing.

For a moment, she hesitated. This could be a trap. She had no idea where this portal would lead.

Shouts echoed behind her. La Liberté had found Tristan. She was out of time.

Praying she wasn't making a fatal mistake, Jayne swung open the door and stepped through the portal.

Jayne found herself on a sidewalk lined by trees, their branches almost completely bare. Green hedges surrounded her, trapping her like a maze. And in the distance, she recognized a building she'd only seen once: the Luxembourg Palace.

She straightened, her mouth falling open in shock. She was in the Luxembourg Gardens! This was only a five-minute walk from her flat in Paris.

Why did Medb take her here? Jayne had assumed that stepping through the portal would take her to Medb's tomb.

"Why are we here?" she asked, glancing around as if expecting Medb herself to materialize in front of her.

No one answered. Shocker.

Jayne frowned, looking around. No one was here. It was the middle of the day, and not a soul lurked nearby.

She was completely alone. No tourists or civilians. No joggers weaving through the gardens. Just her and the trees.

She swallowed down her unease and raised her arms. "Uh, hello? What am I supposed to do?"

Greet the earth, said Medb's voice in her head.

Jayne glanced down toward the gravelly sidewalk underneath her. "Hello, earth."

She could almost feel Medb rolling her eyes.

"Okay, okay." Jayne bent a knee and pressed her fingers against the rocky ground. The surface felt cool to the touch. Jayne closed her eyes and focused on the earth beneath the sidewalk, the strong roots living underneath that linked to the trees.

An aching, hollow emptiness settled in Jayne's chest, and it took her a moment to realize why.

It was currently autumn. The plants weren't in bloom. The few leaves lingering on the trees were brown and dying, the trees going dormant for their long winter's rest.

"How am I supposed to do this?" she muttered under her breath.

Bring life to the garden, Medb commanded. *You have the power within you to restore this place.*

Jayne's first thought was that people would see…but then she understood. That was why no one was here. So she could perform any magic she wished.

"Am I really here right now?" she wondered aloud. "Or is this some kind of vision?"

Medb didn't answer. Jayne sighed, remembering all those times in Dublin when she'd tried to summon Medb's presence to no avail. The woman could be so stubborn.

Call the earth, Jayne. It is yours to command.

Jayne shifted so she sat cross-legged on the ground, then rested her hands on her knees as if she were about to meditate. She inhaled deeply, then exhaled, trying to ignore the eerie silence that pressed around her.

Feel the earth. It has a magic of its own.

Jayne closed her eyes again, calling to life the power of the totem inside her. It flashed brilliantly, eagerly, as if waiting for her. And there were no barriers this time. It appeared effortlessly, causing Jayne to grin broadly at her success.

She sent the power of the totem down, down, down, deep within the earth. To the winding roots growing beneath her. The rich soil layers deep. The worms and insects and other wriggling things that depended on this garden. She focused on the decaying leaves, the dormant flowers, the withering plants, the dry soil.

And she pushed her light into them.

Luminescence bled through her closed eyelids, and that familiar scorching sensation burned in her chest. Her eyes flew open, and an explosion of color greeted her. The trees were now in full bloom, their brilliant green leaves shining in the sun. Pink and lavender and violet flowers gleamed in rows that lined the lush grass of the gardens. The colors were almost too real. Very Wizard of Oz.

Jayne stood, laughing, and unexpected tears pricked at her eyes. The sight was a vision, like a dream come true. She'd never seen such beauty in all her life. Well, except for when she'd been in libraries.

The joy in Jayne's chest swelled until she almost couldn't breathe. Okay, now she definitely couldn't breathe. She collapsed on all fours, choking and gagging, struggling to get oxygen, but her airways were closed. Blood rushed to her head, and her mouth opened and closed like a fish, which was ironic because she needed air, not water, to breathe...

Something slithered inside her, crawling up and up until she coughed once, and suddenly she could breathe. She inhaled deeply once, twice, three times until her heart rate returned to normal. She rubbed her chest and sat back on her heels, stunned and confused.

A strand of glowing green magic crept along the sidewalk in front of her like a worm. She knew exactly what that was: Tiriosis.

Acting on instinct, Jayne summoned a small jar and draped it over the Tiriosis, afraid if she touched it with her bare hands it would infect her again. She screwed on the lid and cloaked it with the Carry spell. The TCO would definitely want to study this thing. It was dangerous.

And it was no longer inside her.

In her mind, Medb rumbled with approval. *Well done, my child. Well done.*

36

THE POWER WITHIN

Sofia didn't like this assignment. She'd joined the TCO to stop Ruth, and she was doing just that. But somehow, going off with her sister's boyfriend on a mission she hadn't trained for didn't seem like the best idea.

"Stop your fidgeting," Cillian said, his tone gentle. "It's making me anxious."

She hadn't realized her leg was bouncing up and down until Cillian pointed it out. She stilled, but her insides quivered with unease.

When the driver dropped them at the grounds of the Château de Chantilly, Sofia all but leapt out of the vehicle, eager to put this mission behind her and get back to that conversation with Jayne. They were so close to finally putting all this behind them.

Cillian fell into step beside her and shot her an infectious grin. "Eager to kick some Kingdom ass, are we?"

Sofia almost flinched. *Dear God, I hope I don't run into Ruth...*

"Something like that," she said vaguely, her attention wandering as she tried to sense something out of the ordinary. Civilians surrounded the château, ogling and taking pictures. A line formed outside for people purchasing admission tickets.

No screams. No magic. No suspicious characters. Everything seemed normal.

Which only made Sofia more tense.

"Do you smell anything weird?" she asked Cillian, remembering what Jayne had said about his keen sense of smell.

He inhaled deeply, frowned, and shook his head. "Nothing but sweat and cigarette smoke."

"We'd best get inside and see what they're up to."

Amanda had given them museum passes so they were able to bypass the line. They crossed the medieval moat and entered the castle's marble-walled keep. A sharp portcullis guarded the entry, pulled up high to allow visitors access. She wanted to stop and admire the grounds, the glorious fountain, and the lake surrounding them, but she had a terrible feeling they needed to hurry.

The attendants welcomed them, breaking people into tour groups based on their tickets. Sofia and Cillian were set to go straight into the Musée Condé.

"Through here," a heavily accented voice directed. She listened with half an ear as the guide started in with the various architectural features of the château and how they'd changed as the building was added to over the years, trying not to be too obvious as she searched the crowds for trouble.

"Looks like we're all good," Cillian said as they entered the first ornately decorated room.

"So far—" Sofia's voice cut off when a huge *boom* shook the ground. The château trembled, and cracks formed in the ceiling. Something crashed deeper within the château, and screams filled the air.

"No!" Cillian roared, his arm pointing up.

The cracks were widening. The roof was collapsing.

Without thinking, Sofia flung out her hands and drew power from the Torrent. Green light spilled from her fingers and surrounded the château, forming a glowing orb around it. The cracked roof above them froze, suspended by Sofia's magic.

She exhaled in relief, but it was short-lived. The force behind the explosion tugged at her magic, weighing her arms down. She wouldn't be able to hold it for very long.

"Cillian, get as many people out of there as you can!" she cried in a strained voice, her arms shaking as she struggled to hold the spell.

Cillian darted forward, disappearing into the frantic crowd. People dashed past Sofia in their haste to get away from the destruction.

Heaviness settled in her arms, and she groaned, falling to her knees. But her hands remained up, keeping the roof intact. Beads of sweat formed on her brow, and she itched to wipe them away. Her breath came in sharp gulps, and her head spun. She tugged on more power from the Torrent, and her vision cleared, her fatigue fading ever so slightly.

She had bought herself more time, but she was still weakening.

Maybe I can seal the roof back together. Just like I sealed Amanda's wound.

She inhaled deeply, trying to remain calm, and slowly fetched the Fire spell. A single flame ignited along her pointer finger, small and insignificant, but she sent it toward the damage in the roof. The flame grew in intensity as it found the massive cracks. She weaved her hands, threading the magic and shaping it into wet cement. Closing her eyes, she envisioned the damage room to room as if she were floating through the château.

Seal it, she ordered. *Repair the damage.*

The cement seeped into the cracks, a dark gray liquid filling each fissure. Sofia's brows scrunched in concentration as she sought out all the structural damage.

When it was finished, her arms dropped of their own accord. Momentary alarm filled her; she feared the roof would collapse.

But it held.

The glowing orb vanished, and the château, and all its many treasures, remained intact.

Still on her knees, Sofia sank backward on her rear and let out a half sob, half laugh. She wiped sweat from her forehead and neck and closed her eyes, allowing exhaustion to claim her.

"Sofia!"

Her eyes opened, and she found Cillian hurrying toward her, his face drawn with worry. Behind him, the crowd had thinned significantly, leaving only a few stragglers to gawk at the miraculously fixed concrete.

Cillian helped her to her feet and touched her shoulders. "You all right?" He looked her over, his blue eyes concerned.

"Yeah," she said breathlessly, chuckling in disbelief. "I'm great."

"I found a Kingdom operative by the vault," he said, and that sobered Sofia up real quick. "It was Blaine. He threw some spells my way but hustled out the back."

Sofia frowned. "They must have thought they could break into the vault and grab the Book of Shadows by blowing it up. Idiots."

"He certainly was more than happy to kill all the people inside. Jerk. I really don't like that bloke."

She bit her lip. The château was too big for them to ensure everyone had gotten out safely. There were likely still civilians in the rooms, and the Kingdom might attack again.

"Let's see what we can do," Sofia said, striding forward. Cillian joined her, and they herded more people out into the keep, where the staff were moving people away from the building. She started back in for more when a cold shiver of magic tickled along her back. She whirled, hands up in defense, to see a figure standing on the far side of the keep, staring intently at her.

Ruth Thorne. Her cold eyes drilled into Sofia, and her cruel mouth curved in a smile. It was the same smile she'd given Sofia when she was a child and succeeded with a difficult spell.

Pride. And hunger.

Ruth had seen what Sofia had done. And it made her gleeful.

Her mother's lips formed a word, and Sofia struggled to understand. Then the word whispered in her ear as if Ruth had sent it across the expanse between them.

"Oops."

Enraged, Sofia raised her hands, intent on flinging as much magic as she could at the woman...

But Ruth had vanished into the crowd, leaving Sofia with a cold sense of foreboding rippling down her spine.

37

LEVELING UP

J ayne only spent a moment sifting through her new powers—
and relishing the feeling of untethered access to the Torrent
—before she rose from the ground and hurried back
through the portal.

She wasn't sure how much time had passed, but the ruins of
Fontainebleau were empty. She kept her magic close, savoring
the way it swelled within her, unrestrained and free.

When she reached the place where she'd knocked out Tristan,
she stopped short. He was gone.

The rest of La Liberté had definitely been here.

The question was, were they gone? Or were they lying in
wait?

And where in the heck was Ruger?

She pulled the Tracking spell from the Torrent. As quickly as
she imagined his face, the spell clanged inside her like a bell.
There. By the western wall.

Jayne kept her steps quiet and careful as she proceeded
through the wreckage. Warmth tickled her fingertips, a sign of
her magic ready and waiting to strike. She almost wished those
French bastards would show up just so she could fight with her

magic again. She missed the feeling, and La Liberté was long overdue for an ass whooping. They'd held the puppet strings over her magic for far too long.

Jayne pressed on, her pace quickening the farther she went. With not a soul in sight, it seemed La Liberté had, in fact, left already.

Just when Jayne caught sight of Ruger motionless on the ground, she stopped instead of rushing forward, her newly restored senses prickling with awareness. Agitated energy filled her, a clear warning sign.

Someone was watching them.

Jayne reached for the Torrent—ah, that glorious river of stars was back in full force!—and grabbed a Block spell. She whirled just as a blast of magic ricocheted off her shield and evaporated in the air.

Jayne threw a Cloaking spell over Ruger, just in case, then grabbed an Attack spell and held it at the ready, waiting for her assailant to show himself. But when the air cleared, there was nothing there. Nothing but silence and stillness and wrongness.

"Are we really playing this game again?" Jayne shouted, anger rising inside her. She was sick of their games.

"Don't shoot!" cried an unfamiliar voice with a thick French accent.

"You shot first, Han."

"Please. I will come out if you swear it."

Jayne rolled her eyes. "I swear it." *But that won't stop me from carting your ass to the TCO.*

Slowly, a figure stepped out from behind a pile of rubble, arms raised and trembling. She squinted, recognizing the burly man from that day on the bridge when they'd gotten Cillian back. He'd been one of the ones chasing them.

Jayne intensified the spell, her hands growing green and sparks flying, and the man shrieked, "Please! Don't hurt me."

"You're my enemy," she growled. "And clearly you mean me

harm. Why else are you lurking here? Why else did you just try to kill me?"

"Not kill, I swear. I was under orders to distract you."

Jayne's blood ran cold. "Distract me? From what?"

The man shook his head slowly. "It doesn't matter. It's too late."

Jayne was getting really sick of this pathetic man's vague answers. She took a step toward him. "You'd better start explaining yourself, or I'll—"

"Look." The man gestured over her shoulder.

Frowning, Jayne turned, following his gaze. At first, she saw nothing. Then, a blinding flash, and a plume of lime-green smoke rose in the air, like a semitransparent mushroom cloud.

The magic inside her started to churn uncontrollably and alarm coursed through her, swift and violent, unlike any sensation she'd ever experienced.

The ground began to quake.

She needed to move.

As the rubble around them shifted and groaned, the man from La Liberté panicked like a horse faced with a fire. He screamed, nearly falling between two large chunks of rock. Before he could hurt himself, she'd tossed a Binding spell on him, then the Carry spell, and he disappeared into her bag, squirming like a toad.

Without stopping, she yanked the Cloaking spell off Ruger, and pushed a Wake spell toward him. It worked, and he sat up, blinking.

"Jayne?"

"Gotta go, right now. This place is falling apart again. I might have pissed them off. Up, up, up!"

She got to him just as he hit his feet, and grabbed his hand. "We need to get to the car, and get back to Paris."

"What happened?"

"Long story short—Tristan gave me back my powers. Now come on, we need—"

"A portal. We need a portal."

She didn't stop to think, or argue, or explain the myriad reasons she couldn't create a portal on her own. She simply shut her eyes, ignoring the moving earth beneath her feet, and envisioned the living room of the safe house in Montmartre.

"Well done," Ruger said, and she opened her eyes to see the portal floating in the air in front of them. They scrambled through and it closed behind them with an audible *pop*.

38

WHEN EVERYTHING GOES AWRY

On the drive back to Paris, Cillian was having trouble keeping Sofia calm. Ruth Thorne's malicious grin before she disappeared from the château's keep was damn eerie and had clearly rattled her daughter to the core.

He slid her closer to him in the back seat and edged his arm around her shoulders. "It's going to be all right, lass."

"No, it's not. She's absolutely mad, and she doesn't care who she hurts. And that's my fault. If I'd just fought her from the beginning—"

"From what Jayne's told me, you did. You saved Jayne from that monster, and now the entire might of the TCO is on her tail. We're going to stop her. You watch."

"I'm not strong enough to do it myself. I need Jayne's magic. I think together, we have a chance. But things are so weird between us, I don't know that she'll work with me."

"She will. Jayne's not mad at you. She's mad at herself. Stupid girl thinks she can control everything when she's only starting out. We can't even get in sync on her calling me to shift."

"She'll figure it out. She always was the smartest person in the room," Sofia said, a bit of lightness in her tone. "She'll be insufferable if we can't heal her magic, though, so we need to figure out what's happening so we can help her."

"The lass can handle herself, even without her magic."

"She can fight like a tiger, yes. But she's more vulnerable than you know right now. Even when she was a baby, Ruth had a terrible effect on her. We must keep her safe so she doesn't try to take on Ruth head-to-head again. Promise me, Cillian. Promise me you'll help me protect her, no matter what."

"I can't promise that, lass. She got mighty pissed at me when I tried to save her on the bridge and got myself captured. Lectured me like I was a schoolboy and everything." He withdrew his arm and patted her on the knee. "But I'll try. Fair?"

"Fair."

When they reached the Montmartre safe house, Sofia all but fell out of the car in her haste. Cillian thanked their driver, who nodded sagely, and followed suit. Together, they sprinted into the house. A pair of TCO officials stood sentry inside the door. Cillian and Sofia exchanged a look. This was new.

Thankfully, the officers nodded as if expecting them. Inside, they found Amanda pacing the room like an agitated lioness, her red hair a frizzy mane around her face. Seo-joon was on the phone, speaking frantically, and several other officials were in the room as well. Cillian recognized Pierce, Amanda's assistant.

"Thank the Goddess," Amanda said, her face sagging in visible relief that startled Cillian. This woman usually kept her emotions locked tight. If she was showing this much, then something must be very, very wrong. "Are you hurt?"

"No," Cillian said, answering for both of them. "We're fine. What happened?"

"The grimoire's been stolen. We had it in a secure vault in Langley, waiting to be examined, and there was an attack."

"At Langley? Someone came into your CIA and stole the damn thing?"

"The Book of Shadows?" Sofia asked at the same time.

"Yes, to both your questions," Amanda said grimly.

"How?" Cillian demanded. "How'd they manage it?" Anger had taken the place of his surprise, and he felt the sudden urge to pummel something with his fists.

"By distracting us." Her eyes flashed with the same fury Cillian felt. "A spell was cast, a powerful spell, that froze everyone in place. The grimoire was taken, and the thief portaled out. We can track the portal, but it will take time, especially since it's been closed. The problem is, we fear whoever cast the spell, whoever opened the portal, was one of ours. It's the only logical scenario."

"You have a mole, then?"

"It would seem so." Amanda was incandescent with rage, and Cillian didn't blame her. An inside job. Traitors everywhere. The magical world was getting more and more complicated by the day.

"Were they working with the Kingdom or La Liberté?" he asked.

"That's the problem. We don't know. But we now need to take stock of everyone—and everything—before we make another move. There could be more traitors in our midst."

"We can't!" Sofia blurted. "We have to act now. Whoever stole that grimoire could be moments away from finding the Master of Shadows' burial site. If they raise him—"

"I know," Amanda snapped, her familiar curt tone returning. "But we need to assemble a team first, and I can't do that if I don't trust my people. The only ones who are not under suspicion are those in this room, plus Jayne and Ruger. It happened while all of you were here with me. I found out only after you'd left for your missions."

"You have to send us after it," Cillian said. His blood pulsed with eagerness. He really wanted to beat someone up right now.

"I plan to," Amanda promised. "But this is bigger than just you two. We need all hands on deck. We need Jayne back."

Sofia tensed next to him. "She's not back yet?"

"No. And word just came that another earthquake shook Fontainebleau minutes ago. Seo-joon is trying to get answers as to what might have happened."

"Oh God," Sofia said, small sparks trailing from her fingers. She buried her face in her hands.

Cillian couldn't blame her for being upset. In the few weeks he'd known her, he had quickly understood Jayne was her entire life. Sofia's greatest fear was losing her sister. And now, she was imagining it as a real possibility.

"She's strong," Cillian said, rubbing Sofia's back. "She can take care of herself."

"She *is* strong," Amanda said, her eyes softening as she gazed at Sofia. "It's not a matter of whether she'll survive. It's only a matter of how long she'll be delayed."

"This was all a test," Sofia whispered.

Cillian and Amanda gaped at her.

"The château. It was a test. For me. Split up Jayne and me, keep her distracted long enough to see what sort of magic I possess. How strong I've become."

"What are you talking about?" Cillian asked.

"Ruth was there. Why was she there? She always makes her goons take care of things. She doesn't like getting her hands dirty." Sofia looked up, her eyes alight with a mixture of terror and rage. "I know how her mind works. This is just like when I was a kid. She loved springing tests on me, hoping to catch me off guard. That smile she gave me—it was the same one she used when I passed a test."

"What was your test?" Amanda asked quietly.

"Keeping the château from collapsing. They set off an explosive, and the roof cracked."

"Dear God...and you succeeded?"

"Yes."

"I'm impressed, Sofia. But not at all surprised." Amanda gave her a wide smile. "I bet Ruth Thorne is quaking in her boots knowing both her daughters have surpassed her."

"Why would she test you?" Cillian asked.

Sofia grimaced. "She always tested me before introducing a more complicated magic. She had to be sure I was ready."

The room was quiet for a moment. Then, Amanda said, "She believes you'll return to her."

Sofia nodded, looking ill.

"And she has powerful magic waiting for you," Cillian continued. "The question is, what is it?" He almost didn't want to know.

The door burst open, and Jayne strode inside, dragging a huge, unconscious man behind her. One leg of her pants was soaked in blood, and she had scratches along her face and neck. Ruger was right behind her, looking downright happy.

"We've got a present for you," Jayne grunted before dumping the man on the floor in front of her. Heaving a deep breath, she straightened and took in everyone's grim expressions. "Okay... who died?"

39

THE STUDENT BECOMES THE MASTER

Everyone spoke at once, detailing the circumstances that led them back to Montmartre, but it was Amanda whose face shined brightest.

"*Jayne* created the portal here from Fontainebleau?"

Ruger nodded. "She did. Conjured it up in a heartbeat. This new power will certainly be handy."

Seo-joon hung up the phone. "No new fatalities, thank goodness. The BMC has everything roped off and cloaked so no one can get into the area. There wasn't anyone around except Jayne and Ruger."

"And a few La Liberté members. Like this fellow." Jayne kicked the man at her feet. "Might want to get him out of here. I have an update, and he doesn't need to hear it."

Seo-joon pulled the man to his feet and shot her a grin. "Great work, Jayne. I'll take it from here. Come on, buddy. Let's get you tied to a chair and tortured—I mean debriefed."

At the horrified expression on the terrorist's face, Seo-joon laughed. "We aren't like your people. We have ethics. Stop freaking out."

When the door closed behind them, Jayne waved her hand

and created a shimmering clear barrier on the door so they wouldn't be interrupted. The whole team looked at her in wonder, Cillian especially.

"You were right, it was a trap, but not like we expected. No Rogue, but Tristan Lowell was there. He lifted the spell that's been on me and told me about the Tiriosis."

"Tiriosis?" Cillian repeated, his brows knitting together.

But Jayne was already pulling the jar from her pocket. Her hands moved, and the jar opened. A wriggling green worm ejected itself onto the floor.

Sofia yelped and jumped back as if it were a poisonous spider. Cillian unleashed a string of expletives.

Amanda snapped her fingers, and Pierce hurried forward, taking the jar from Jayne's hand. Within seconds, the Tiriosis was safely bottled up again.

Jayne watched Amanda turn the jar over in her hands ruminatively, the little green thing inside swirling like some sort of ectoplasm.

"You know what this is, don't you?" Jayne asked.

"I do. How did you get it out—" Amanda broke off, stunned.

"Totem magic," Jayne said shortly. She took a step closer to Amanda. "What is Tiriosis? How do you know about it?"

"It's the force that caused the Torrent to deteriorate all those years ago. You said Tristan Lowell gave you this information?"

"Yes. Amanda, what's going on?" Jayne asked, trying to keep the frustration from her voice. Amanda was looking at the poison as if it held the answers to the beginnings of the universe.

But it was Ruger who answered. "Tiriosis is the most powerful magical poison in the world. If Gina Labelle has acquired Tiriosis, La Liberté has access to monumental amounts of power. Power big enough to shut down the Torrent entirely. To put us all back in darkness again."

Oh God... Jayne remembered the people in Fontainebleau

who were combing over that crater. She'd thought they were looking for survivors.

"The spell La Liberté did at Fontainebleau was to break open the Torrent and get their hands on this Tiriosis crap? They weren't going after the grimoire?"

Ruger shook his head, his voice grave. "No, they were seeking the grimoire, I know that for a fact. I think they were also seeking to involve us. To involve *you*, Jayne. They wanted to test the Tiriosis on a Master."

The thought made her feel sick all over again. That this had been a huge setup all along, some sort of experiment? No wonder Tristan had said he wasn't aligned with his superiors. Their methods were barbaric. What if she'd died? What if she'd been incapacitated permanently? Jayne fought back the icy anger that sparked inside her. She, unlike Gina Labelle, didn't want to hurt those around her, and blowing up now wouldn't help things.

"How can we even believe what that little Frenchie says anyway?" Cillian asked.

"We can trust him," Amanda said at once. "He is not our enemy."

Jayne frowned. That had been Tristan's exact phrasing. She stared hard at Amanda, knowing there was more to this story.

"Except...Tristan is the person who injected me."

But Amanda didn't seem to notice the accusation in her gaze. "He would have been under orders to do so. Trust me, if he'd given you a full dose, you wouldn't have just lost your magic. You would have lost your life."

Amanda touched the triangular pendant on her necklace. She and Ruger shared a long, knowing look.

"So you're saying he did me a favor by poisoning me? You have a very strange way of thinking, Amanda. There's more going on here, isn't there?"

"Jayne, you simply must trust me right now. There's no time

for us to continue speculating. The grimoire was taken from our vault."

"Excuse me?"

Ruger roared to life. "How in the hell could that happen?"

Amanda closed her eyes briefly. "Inside job. Someone tricked us; we don't know exactly who, or what, has transpired. That doesn't matter right now. We must find the shadowed illumination before Ruth gets her hands on it. That is our most pressing concern. She now knows how powerful Sofia is, and she probably already knows you have your magic back, Jayne. She isn't going to wait any longer to make her move. Whatever that is, we must stop her, now."

"How does she know about Sofia's powers?"

Sofia briefly explained what happened in Chantilly. Jayne whistled, long and low.

"You know, Mom's kind of a bitch."

Sofia sputtered out a laugh. "Yes, she is."

Amanda clapped her hands together. "We'll deal with all this later, but for now…" Her eyes met Jayne's and flickered with momentary concern. "If you can create portals, I assume you're back at full power. Can you access the totem—your Earth magic—and use it to retrieve your memories of the Book of Shadows? If you can, we can use them to discover the location of the illuminated manuscript, and end this."

"No problem," Jayne said without hesitation.

Ruger smiled at her, proud as a newborn's papa. "Good. Do it. Let's beat them at their own game."

Though Jayne's mind still snagged at the mind-blowing revelations: *The TCO had a mole? The Torrent had been poisoned? How? By whom? And why was Tristan suddenly one of the good guys?* She knew Amanda was right. Those questions could wait. If what Sofia speculated was true, then Ruth could be about to come into power. A lot of it.

She was after a totem. Gina Labelle was too. And Jayne had to stop them both.

Assuming one of them hadn't gotten to it already. Jayne remembered the plume of green smoke she'd seen in the distance from Fontainebleau, and the way the man had said, *It's too late.*

The ground had rumbled then, too, similar to the moment in Fontainebleau when La Liberté had blown the city apart and infected her with Tiriosis.

Dread gnawed at her gut, but she shoved it away. It couldn't be too late. It couldn't.

Amanda put her hands on her hips, the no-nonsense leader back again. "What do you need, Jayne?"

"Just…a moment of silence, please."

A hushed whisper fell over them. Jayne's eyes closed, and the room vanished from view. She pictured herself alone in the Luxembourg Gardens again, the leafless branches surrounding her, the leaves on the ground rustling with the wind. In her mind, she crouched to the earth, pressing her hands into the soft soil and feeling the energy coursing within. The power emanating from the Earth's core. The pure, untainted magic at her fingertips…

When she felt Medb's power shine to life, a voice echoed in her mind. *Hello, Master. What do you require of me?*

Jayne took a moment to register the bafflement of having a queen like Medb at her beck and call. After a moment, she said quietly, "I need to unlock my memories of the Book of Shadows. I need to find the shadowed illumination."

Though Jayne couldn't see her, she almost felt the queen smile.

Open your mind to the magic. Allow it to heal your memories as it did your body.

Jayne nodded, pressing her fingers more firmly in the earth. She breathed deeply, and with that inhale, swarms of powerful energy surged through her as if she were drawing in the magic itself through her lungs. It grew inside her, a balloon growing bigger and bigger and bigger...

A flash of images rushed through her brain, and Jayne's hands clenched in the soil as she struggled to keep up. *Too fast,* she thought.

Miraculously, they slowed. As they did, Jayne made out various paintings flitting across her mind. She passed by each one as if swiping through social media on her phone. She wasn't sure how she knew these weren't the right ones, but she did.

She paused when she came across something she recognized. A symbol of a triangle with a swirl in the middle. Where had she seen that before?

It represents the Water spirit, Medb told her. *Just as I possess the Earth spirit.*

Then, Jayne remembered: the same symbol had been on the necklaces La Liberté had worn. The same amulets that had weakened Jayne's magic.

Water? La Liberté revered...water? It was possible, since their portal had been in the Seine...

Almost there, Medb murmured, and Jayne snapped back into action, flicking through the images once more. They all had some sort of water representation in them, lakes and rivers and waterfalls.

The Master of Shadows possessed the Water totem. That was why La Liberté was after it. They were obsessed with water and wanted the Water totem for their own.

Good, Medb whispered. *Now, this one.* The earth rumbled in response, called by some mystical force hidden in the painting.

Jayne slowed the images, freezing on the one Medb had indicated. It was from the Très Riche Heures, the panel for October. A simple painting of a farmer in front of a castle wall. Wheat stalks grew next to him. A cart rested beside him. And across from the crops was a winding, narrow river.

At first glance, the painting seemed rather ordinary. Nothing exceptional. But as Jayne scrutinized it, she made out a faint shimmer of light glistening along the edge of the river. And across from it, masked by the stalks of wheat alongside the farmer, was a rippling shadow.

Jayne sucked in a breath. The shadowed illumination. She'd found it. But...where was this scene? There was a palace, and she recognized the Seine. But that river was miles long with many, many castle châteaus along it. How was she to find this one small place where this particular illumination was?

Trust the earth, Medb urged. *Use it to guide you.*

Jayne envisioned the ground in front of the river, letting it call to her. It wasn't long before another image shimmered into view. A modern image, of a bustling city, the Seine sparkling at the base of the footpath, and across the river, the ornate walls of the Louvre Palace.

Not a small place after all.

Jayne's eyes flew open, and she found Cillian, Sofia, Ruger, and Amanda staring at her. She didn't have time to dwell on what they'd seen or ask if she'd appeared to be talking to herself. She wiped her sweaty palms on her jeans and straightened.

"I know where it is." She gave Cillian a high five. "Let's do this."

40

ALONG CAME AN OSSUARY

Everyone munched on jambon-beurres while Ruger and Amanda set up their command in the Montmartre safe house, locking out anyone not on the mission for "operational security reasons," as Amanda told her boss. Once everyone had eaten and suited up, Jayne led the team, including Cillian, Sofia, and Seo-joon, down the streets of Paris. She had cloaked them so they could move without drawing attention, but some people stared their way as if they sensed something passing. It was the only way; they were too peculiar not to stand out. A dozen men and women dressed in black and packing magical heat, led by a woman trying to reach out to the spirits of the Earth?

Yeah. Not weird at all.

To be fair, the TCO's weapons were concealed. And at least they weren't wearing bulletproof vests or helmets or anything too obnoxious.

They passed the Louvre and crossed the river on the Pont Royal, then walked the footpaths along the Seine. Jayne paused every few minutes, crouching down and touching the ground to feel Medb's energy, almost like a magical compass ensuring she was headed in the right direction. The earth thrummed as if a powerful force lived in its depths. Jayne was able to interpret this vibration and use it to guide her like an inner Earth Radar. She had no idea how this magic worked but surrendered herself to it. Medb wouldn't screw with her, of this she was certain.

Oddly enough, the magical humming led her past the Musée d'Orsay, up the Boulevard de Saint-Germain, and to the entrance for the Assemblée Nationale metro station.

"The Master of Shadows' burial site is on the subway?" Cillian asked doubtfully, arching an eyebrow at Jayne.

"Shush. Don't question the magic or it will devour you."

Brief uncertainty flickered in his face, and Jayne stifled a laugh. To be honest, she was just as bewildered as he was. She'd hoped the shadowed illumination was somewhere off-grid, not in a hub in the middle of a huge city, surrounded by so many civilians. They'd already lost too many people to this mad quest. Jayne couldn't bear to lose more.

They descended the stairs, weaving through passersby, and descending another flight of stairs—stopping, of course, to purchase metro tickets, because Jayne would be damned if she was going to steal a ride on the subway—before they finally reached the metro platform.

"So...now we just wait for the metro to get here?" Sofia asked, gnawing on her lower lip in worry.

"No," Jayne murmured as the thrumming pulsed in her chest. "No, we don't. Follow me."

Without preamble, she jumped down onto the subway tracks.

Someone inhaled a sharp breath behind her—probably Sofia —but the TCO officers were obedient to a tee and easily hopped on the tracks alongside her. Even Seo-joon shot her a grin as if eager for an adventure. After a moment, Cillian and Sofia followed suit, though both of them looked uncertain at the prospect of standing in the path of a deadly metal machine on wheels.

"Uh, Jayne?" Cillian asked, clearly questioning her sanity.

But she ignored him, focusing instead on the solid rightness pounding inside her. *This way,* Medb's voice called.

Jayne, done with questioning the queen, followed it.

They marched down the tracks, into the black abyss of the subway tunnel. When they were completely hidden from the platform, Jayne summoned a ball of green magic to light their way. For a moment, she reveled in how easy it was to access her magic. For the umpteenth time, she sent a silent prayer of gratitude to Medb, the Torrent, the Earth totem, and whatever other magical spirits watched over her. She was shocked at how incomplete she'd felt without magic. Incredible, really, considering a month ago, she didn't know magic existed outside of her favorite books.

The ground rattled, and somewhere a distant subway car ground against its tracks. It was too far away to pose any real threat, but Sofia still hurried to Jayne's side.

"Any chance we'll be squashed by the Paris Métro?" she whispered. "That would be a fun way to go."

Jayne snorted. "Don't be ridiculous. If any form of transportation is going to snuff me out, it will most definitely be a Segway."

Sofia laughed, the sound echoing and bouncing off the tunnel walls and making Jayne feel extra light inside. As long as she could keep Sofia smiling, it meant she wasn't afraid.

They kept walking until the energy in Jayne's chest throbbed almost painfully. She stopped, bent over to touch the ground, and frowned.

Here, the voice seemed to say. *Here.*

But...where? There was nothing but this dank subway tunnel. *Wait a minute.*

Something seemed to move to her left.

Jayne lifted the ball of magic higher to illuminate the wall beside them. It looked like the rest of the tunnel, but...she waved a hand, and a thin veneer of wood and rock crumbled to the ground. Another tunnel! But definitely not a subway tunnel. This was misshapen and decayed, like some forgotten cave that had deteriorated over time. The air within smelled musty and damp and...slightly rotten.

But Jayne wasn't afraid. If there was ever a good spot for a hidden burial site, this was it.

She flexed her fingers, and the glow of her magic burned brighter. Squinting, she leaned forward, trying to inspect the tunnel more closely. Looking inside, she barely made out rectangular pillars that supported the rocky ceiling. And painted on the pillars was a spread of the most colorful graffiti Jayne had ever seen.

Her breath caught. She remembered seeing similar pictures online when she researched the libraries of Paris. An illegal entrance to the catacombs near the Sorbonne University Library. She'd gone down that—ahem—rathole for a few hours. "I know what this place is. A secret entrance to the catacombs under Paris."

"The catacombs?" Sofia hissed. "As in, a place full of skeletons?"

"Yep!" Jayne said merrily as if she'd just announced they would be riding the Ferris wheel instead of about to step into an underground graveyard. "We're looking for a Master who's been dead for hundreds of years. What did you expect, a fae summer palace?"

Behind her, Seo-joon laughed. "That would be sweet."

"Fun fact," Jayne said. "Most of the unofficial catacomb entrances are illegal. But there are so many of them that the authorities can't possibly monitor them all, so explorers are rarely caught. They have parties down here, tag with graffiti, lead ghost tours. There is a thriving, completely illegal community."

"Comforting," muttered Sofia.

"Think we'll find Indiana Jones down here?" Cillian asked, sounding almost hopeful.

"I wish," said Seo-joon. "I have a question or two for him. There's no way those artifacts he found didn't possess magic."

"You know Indiana Jones isn't a real person, right?" said Tamara, who'd appeared by Seo-joon's side.

"Blasphemy," Seo-joon said.

Boots rustled and pebbles shifted as the TCO officers clambered into the ancient passageway behind them. A few of them lit up their fingers with magic like Jayne did, though theirs was a bit more subdued, like an old flashlight that needed a new bulb. Even so, the added light did help Jayne make out more details. The graffiti wasn't just painted on the pillars—it was painted on the entire wall. Some were cartoony, others were blocky letters spelling out a message, and some were elaborate paintings of breathtaking scenery. The place seemed like a haven, a monument to art and injustice and everything the Paris vigilantes couldn't speak out against in public.

"How many people do you think know about this place?" Sofia whispered, her eyes wide with awe.

"Enough to come in and tag the place. I imagine the entries are only known to an exclusive group of people. Like a fancy club, only it's underground in a musty ancient passageway full of bones," Jayne said, running a hand along the wall and frowning when her fingers came back damp. "Like I said, hundreds of miles of uncharted catacombs here."

"Which means if we die down here, no one will ever know." Sofia shuddered.

"Is that a better way to go than being squashed by a subway?" Jayne asked, her lips quirking in a wry smile.

"Hardly. But I doubt you'll find a Segway down here."

The sisters chuckled, their laughter echoing in the vast tunnel.

They walked for what felt like hours, climbing over heaps of rubble and squeezing through narrow passages. Some chasms were covered in graffiti, like the entrance. Others were emptier, filled with nothing but dirt and rocks. Upon closer inspection,

Jayne made out piles of bones and skulls lining the walls and suppressed a shudder. The labyrinth of catacombs had been built in the old quarries under the city to entomb Paris's dead. The ossuary housed millions of bodies. She had to admit, being underground with this many dead Parisians was a bit disconcerting. She couldn't help but wonder what sort of power the dead gave to the Earth.

They walked on, deeper and deeper. Jayne didn't need to pause as frequently; surrounded by earth, she could feel its magic quivering around her, an eager energy coaxing her onward.

The farther they went, the more damp the walls became. Soon enough, their boots were sloshing along the muddy floor.

"We must be nearing the Seine again," Jayne muttered, remembering in her research that some of the catacomb passages were flooded. Perhaps this was one of them.

"Oh. It makes total sense," Sofia said. When Jayne shot her an odd look, she added, "Water totem. It makes sense that the burial site is near the river."

Jayne frowned. How had she not pieced that together?

At the bewilderment on her face, Sofia laughed. "That's why I'm here, sis. To shed light on the obvious."

Jayne shoved her shoulder.

A few steps later, an aching wrongness sliced through Jayne's body, and she stopped, her hand pressed against the wall of wet dirt next to her. It felt like someone had twisted a knife inside her, and she groaned, falling to her knees.

"Jayne?" Cillian was there in an instant, his hand on her shoulder. "What is it?"

"Something's wrong," Jayne wheezed. "Something's really, really wrong."

Abomination, Medb's voice hissed in her mind. *A violation against the laws of nature and magic. They will perish, all of them.* Her seething fury took up Jayne's entire head, searing with a bright light that nearly blinded her.

Distant voices surrounded her, but she couldn't tell if it was the group in the tunnels or the voices of restless spirits. One voice in particular stood out to the others, a cold, cruel voice that Jayne knew all too well.

"You are mine."

Her eyes flew open, and the bright light faded. "No," she gasped, before jumping to her feet and bursting into a run.

Ignoring the others' protests, Jayne followed the gut-wrenching twist inside her, dodging sharp rocks and tripping over jagged rises in the ground.

The narrow passageway opened to a wide chasm. Piled up alongside the walls were heaps of bones and skulls and other remains. Water dripped from the ceiling, the sound creepy and echoing. Whispers filled her, making the hairs stand up on her arms.

And on the opposite side of the chasm was Ruth Thorne. Her eyes glowed an ethereal green, and energy rippled off her in sickening waves. Jayne shook as it tried to touch her, caressing the shield she pulled around her. It clashed horribly against Medb's power.

Thief, Medb snarled in her head. *The witch is a thief. She will be destroyed for this crime.*

Jayne stared at her mother in disbelief and horror. "What have you done?"

Ruth grinned widely, and something in the center of her forehead glowed a pearly white, just like Jayne's own totem.

Only then did Jayne notice the massive crater in the wall next to Ruth. A blast of red light flooded the chasm, making the walls and ceiling quake.

The Master of Shadows had risen.

41

SURRENDER...OR DIE!

Sofia had just caught up to Jayne when an almighty roar shook the entire tunnel. Rocks and pebbles rained from above, and Sofia flinched, covering her head with her arms.

"What—" She froze when she noticed what Jayne stared at.

Ruth Thorne, in all her powerful glory, surrounded by an ethereal glow. Her eyes shone green, and a white light highlighted the totem insignia on her forehead.

Oh my God... Ruth had the totem. They were too late. Sofia's blood ran cold, and her skin prickled with the presence of something otherworldly and powerful in their midst.

The Master of Shadows.

Jayne backed up slowly until she was close enough for Sofia to touch. The sisters joined hands and exchanged dumbstruck, horrified looks.

"What do we do?" Sofia asked. "She already has the totem."

"We can still stop her." That familiar determined edge hardened Jayne's voice. "The Master isn't fully corporeal yet. He's still just a shadow."

"Do we *want* to stop it?" Cillian asked, panting next to Sofia. "I mean, when Medb rose, she helped us, right?"

"Not before the Kingdom tried to wield her power," Jayne said sharply. "Ruth will do the same with the Master of Shadows."

The air shivered around them as the TCO officers sprang into action. A few of them summoned transparent orbs that surrounded them like shields. Others wielded glowing fire in their hands.

Jayne turned to Cillian. "I need the wolf."

Cillian nodded, no sign of uncertainty in his face. Jayne closed her eyes, a prickle of energy telling Sofia she was accessing the Torrent. In seconds, Cillian had shifted to his huge, silver-brown wolf form. Energy tickled Sofia's chest, whispering inside her, and she had the sudden urge to summon a ball of fire just like the TCO officials had.

Instead of shoving aside the feeling like she always had, Sofia embraced it. She extended her arms, reaching for the Torrent and gathering the first spell she found: the Block spell. She grabbed it and flung it outward just as several figures materialized beside Ruth. They intercepted Sofia's spell with a Block of their own.

And the battle began.

Amidst the earthquakes and humming red light emanating from the burial site, the Kingdom operatives and the TCO officials clashed in a burst of sparks and blinding light.

All fear left Sofia as she joined Jayne and Cillian to face the fight head-on. Silver sparks danced from Jayne's fingertips as she slashed through the air, knocking down one after another. Cillian pounced, claws ripping and teeth tearing.

And Sofia, who usually fled from a fight, who had always embraced her fear and paranoia, finally let it all go. A mighty cry split from her throat as she summoned the Fire spell and shot a ball of flames toward Ruth.

Ruth dodged, that strange glow encompassing her. Protecting her.

They could take down the rest of the Kingdom...but not her. Ruth had the power of the Water Master on her side now.

"You're powerful, Sofia," Ruth said. "I can sense the awakening of your magic. I always knew you had potential."

"Potential to be your puppet," Sofia spat, inching closer.

"Not anymore. Join me, and you'll be my lieutenant. You'll have power, Sofia. Power to live as you wish. No more hiding. No more fighting. I know that's what you want."

"You don't know anything about me."

"I know you want to keep Jayne safe. With the power I possess, you can do that. You two can live in peace."

Sofia shook her head. "It's far too late for that, Ruth."

Rage and defiance pulsed through Sofia, and she lunged for her mother. Light burst from her hands, spearing toward Ruth, who deflected it. The green glow of her eyes brightened, and a searing heat split through Sofia's chest. She groaned, sinking to her knees.

Another figure joined the fight, slamming into Ruth with a powerful roundhouse kick that caught her in the ribs and knocked her sideways. Brown hair swinging wildly, Jayne aimed another kick that Ruth dodged. Ruth's hands lifted, but Jayne's were already up, and she blocked her mother's spell so swiftly it made Sofia proud.

The three of them fought, but it felt more like a dance. Light glided through the air, striking again and again. Sofia ducked and parried, the magic flowing through her freely. She felt Jayne's power simmering alongside her, and she blended together with it, complementing her sister's energy and power.

Ruth was no match for them. And she knew it. Sofia could tell by the slight narrowing of those glowing green eyes, the way the light on her forehead flickered as if about to go out. Ruth was powerful, but she couldn't face Jayne's Master abilities and Sofia's reawakened powers combined.

A deafening blast shook the ground. Then another. And another.

The three of them froze, momentarily stunned by this sudden

onslaught of explosions. As it continued, rattling Sofia's eardrums, she realized they weren't explosions.

They were massive, giant footsteps.

Sofia staggered backward, pulling Jayne with her.

From within the depths of the burial site, a glowing red figure emerged, enormous and horrifying. It was humanoid, but Sofia couldn't make out any features except for burning pits where the eyes should be. The figure raised an arm, and his rumbling voice echoed in the chasm. As he spoke, faces flickered in and out of sight: those subsumed by his powers over the years.

"You all are mine. Bow before the god of Water and serve she who wields my power."

The force behind the voice made Sofia's bones hurt. She shivered, resisting the urge to fall to her knees. This Master emanated authority, reminding Sofia how feeble and puny she was in comparison.

She couldn't fight this. Not even Jayne could.

But Jayne didn't seem to register that. She threw herself forward, arms raised, and cried out, "Master of Shadows, you are more powerful than she is." She glared in Ruth's direction. "You are no one's slave. Relinquish her hold on you and be free!"

Silence met Jayne's words, and Sofia held her breath, her wide eyes pinned on the Master of Shadows.

Please, please, please, she pleaded. *Please listen to her.*

The red figure cocked his head at Jayne as if considering her appeal. The faces shifted and blurred as if each taken soul was coming to take a look at the scene. "You are of the Earth goddess," he said, his voice magnified so much it made Sofia's ears throb.

"Yes," Jayne said, her eyes alight with relief. "I am of the Earth goddess. Now bow before me, you jerk."

Another moment passed. No one moved. Even the TCO officials and the Kingdom operatives seemed to pause their battle and watch with bated breath.

"Then you pose a threat to my vessel, and you will be ousted," the Master roared before a jet of flame shot from his hand and landed squarely in Jayne's chest.

"Jayne!" Sofia screamed, her entire mind exploding with panic and fury and utter shock.

Jayne flew backward, slamming against the cave wall before crumpling to the ground.

"Jayne!" Sofia cried again, rushing forward, but she wasn't the only one.

Cillian was by Sofia's side, shouting Jayne's name along with her.

"Cillian, you have to get her out of here," Sofia yelled.

But the sound of Cillian's cries echoing along with hers jolted something awake within her. He looked her way, and a hot spark coursed between them. Her gaze snapped to his, pulse thundering in her ears. She hadn't even registered he was back in his human form. All she felt was that connection between them, that thriving bond that suddenly slid into place.

Something inside her *cracked*, like setting bones in place. As if she'd been disjointed before, but now her body was properly aligned. Cillian stretched his arms and released a roar that was half human, half animal. But Sofia wasn't afraid. A strange sense of rightness filled her. Power flared to life, buzzing so intensely her entire skeleton rattled. Torrent magic flowed freely through her body, burning every inch of her with a powerful inferno. She cried out as white flames poured from her fingertips. White sparks exploded in her vision, momentarily blinding her. There was no pain. Only power.

"Cillian," she whispered. "Now."

He shifted. But it wasn't to his wolf form. His body elongated. Wings sprouted from his sides. A long tail extended from his rear. Paws formed along his limbs, with sharp talons. A sharp beak protruded from his face, and an ear-splitting roar filled the air, making the ceiling shake.

It wasn't the Master who roared. It was Cillian—who had just shifted into a goddamn griffin. Part lion. Part eagle.

If not for the magic egging her on, Sofia would've stopped to stare at him, to drink it all in, to register her dumbfounded surprise.

But she wasn't herself right now. She was one with the magic inside her, and she was tied directly to the magic inside Cillian.

A strange new scent filled the air, both foreign and familiar all at once. It smelled like pine and strawberries, a thrilling combination that made Sofia feel at home. She knew down to her bones that this scent was her magic and Cillian's coming together as one.

Identical beams of white light surrounded her and the griffin. Even the Master of Shadows paused to watch, though it was impossible to tell where his empty eyes were focused.

"Now," she said again, and together, Sofia and Cillian pounced. A deft, lithe grace took over, moving Sofia's body in ways she never thought possible. She twisted and arced, dodging blows as the Kingdom fighters finally responded with an onslaught of spells.

They were powerless against her. She cut them down one by one, and when another enemy popped up, Cillian swiped with his talons or batted them away with his wings or nipped at them with his beak.

They were a deadly duo.

Sofia faltered when she caught sight of her mother, whose eyes were wide with shock. But even Ruth Thorne was small potatoes compared to Sofia's real target.

The Master of Shadows.

Sofia faced him, though he towered over her by more than a foot. She screamed, and magic poured from her mouth, assaulting him with a transparent white fog.

Cillian was by her side, glowing with that same strange mist that thickened as it filled the chasm. A dense, heavy magic penetrated the air, piercing through the Master's red glow.

"Another Master," the red figure murmured, his booming voice almost contemplative. The faces within him flickered and shifted in excitement.

Sofia didn't allow herself to stop and consider these words. She brought her hands together, and a streak of white light shot into the Master's chest. He stumbled backward—he actually stumbled.

"Relinquish her hold on you," Sofia bellowed, and her voice sounded like multiple voices layered together as one, "or I will destroy you."

"Sofia—" Ruth said, and Sofia was happy to sense an edge of panic in the woman's voice.

"Silence, witch!" Sofia snarled at her mother. "This doesn't concern you."

"What say you?" came Cillian's fierce voice echoing in the cave. Though he was still in griffin form, Sofia knew the Master could understand him. "Will you accept the challenge of this Master, or allow yourself to be enslaved by another?"

The mist thickened, swirling in the air beside them. The huge red figure's head tilted this way and that as if watching the magical fog's progress as it surrounded him. Behind Sofia, the TCO officers and the Kingdom operatives inched backward, pausing their battle momentarily as they waited for another explosive strike from the Master.

"I am bonded," the Master said at last. "I cannot relinquish that power."

"No," Sofia called. "But you can rest. Return to your grave and be at peace again. Do not be a weapon for this tyrant." She gestured in Ruth's direction.

"Choose your battle," Cillian roared. "Fight us or fight your bond."

The Master threw back his head and released a colossal

shriek. The ground shook so fiercely that boulders rained on them. But Sofia didn't even flinch. She remained alongside Cillian, watching the Master, preparing to fight him if they had to.

To her surprise, he turned on Ruth instead.

"No!" Ruth screamed.

Something cracked, echoing in the vast tunnels. A gust of wind burst in the air, tousling Sofia's hair and stinging her eyes. Cillian's warm fur pressed up next to her as he drew close, whether for his protection or hers, she couldn't tell.

When the wind finally died, Sofia blinked, her eyes stinging.

The Master of Shadows was gone.

42

AN UNEASY ALLIANCE

"Jayne. Wake up, Jayne."

Ugh. "No. Let me sleep."

"Now, Jayne." The urgency in the voice made her eyes snap open.

A blinding slice of pain cut through her head, and she winced, raising a hand to the back of her head. It came back wet with blood.

A haze formed around her eyes, and she blinked rapidly to clear her vision. A shadowy man hovered over her, his eyes wide with concern.

"R-Ruger?" she whispered. She looked around, gaping. Dozens of figures stood in the chasm. A strange mist coated the ground.

In a flash, her memories came back. Ruth with the totem. The Master of Shadows risen. Those creepy faces inside him. A burst of fiery pain as he shot Jayne backward.

"Oh my God." Jayne rose to her feet, then swayed as her vision went black.

Ruger caught her arm to steady her. "I've got you."

"Hang on. I can do this." Jayne pressed a hand to the bloody injury on her head and focused on the totem's magic, hoping to heal herself like she had with the Tiriosis.

Nothing happened. Medb's presence flickered within her before dying out completely.

"You were attacked by a Master raised from the dead, Jayne. You can't heal it like you can an ordinary wound. Give your body a moment to recover."

She shot an accusing look at Ruger. "You shouldn't even be here! How the hell did you find us?"

He shrugged like it was no big deal. "Your comms went out just as the battle began, and I knew you needed help. The trackers we had on you flashed out a mile back in the tunnels. Besides, the amount of magical energy this battle is emitting is kind of hard to ignore. I'm surprised other Adepts haven't shown up just out of curiosity."

This battle. Jayne's mouth grew dry as she surveyed the crowd. Her eyes snagged on Sofia, who stood next to...

"Holy. Shit." Jayne raised a trembling hand to cover her mouth. "Is—is that Cillian?"

"Yes." Something tinged Ruger's voice that made her look at him sharply. Regret mingled with uncertainty in his face.

"Ruger..." Jayne said slowly, her brain unable to comprehend the sight of Cillian the griffin.

Before she could demand answers from Ruger, a piercing scream filled the air. Jayne tensed, searching for the source.

It was Ruth. She scrambled toward the empty hole in the wall where the Master of Shadows had been, only to turn back to them with a sneer.

It was only then that Jayne realized the Master was gone. But Ruth's forehead still glowed, which meant she still had the totem.

"What happened?" Jayne whispered.

"I'll fill you in later. But your mother is about to snap, and we need to be ready."

Though he still wore a sling, Ruger sauntered forward,

guiding Jayne by the arm. Around them, the TCO officials got into formation, waiting for round two of the battle to begin.

"Get them!" Ruth shrieked, flinging her hands toward Sofia and Cillian. "Kill them! We take no prisoners today. Make them pay!"

The remaining Kingdom operatives sprang into action, launching themselves at the TCO with full force.

Jayne's fingers curled into fists. Her head pulsed with agony, but she wasn't just going to stand around and do nothing.

"Wait." Ruger's hold on her arm tightened. "You can't fight like before, Jayne. But that doesn't mean you can't help."

Jayne frowned at him, confused, but found him watching the fray, his dark eyes glittering. Then, so quick Jayne almost missed it, he flung a Block spell in the path of one of the Kingdom goons just before he struck down Seo-joon. Bewildered, the goon staggered sideways as Seo-joon cut him down, finishing him off.

"Wow," Jayne breathed. "Nice one." Her eyes found Ruth, who battled Sofia and Cillian. The griffin and Sofia fought as one, a burning white light passing between them with such intensity that Jayne stared, awestruck.

What the hell had happened between them?

Ruth's forehead glowed brighter and brighter with each strike. She cut through the air again and again, slashing with all the force of her fury. When Ruth raised her arms, Jayne reached for the Torrent, grateful she still had access to it despite her ailments. She interceded before Ruth struck, and sent a Block spell her way. It ricocheted off Ruth's spell, volleyed toward her, and exploded in her mother's face. Ruth stumbled, eyes wide and the tips of her hair slightly charred from the blast. Slowly, her glowing green eyes scanned the crowd until they locked with Jayne's.

Jayne offered her mother a satisfied smirk.

Ruth's eyes flashed with renewed intensity as she stormed toward Jayne. Before she took another step, a fierce growl echoed in the chasm. For one wild moment, Jayne thought the Master had returned.

But no...this was different.

At the mouth of the tunnel emerged a creature, its fur midnight black and its pale eyes hungry for blood. More figures appeared behind it, and one of them Jayne recognized: Tristan.

La Liberté had arrived. At their head was Gina Labelle in Rogue form: a huge, shiny black panther.

Ruger went taut next to Jayne, who shared his concern. Whose side were they on?

In answer, Tristan's powerful voice cut through the silence. "They've defiled the power of the Water god. We shall exact vengeance on his behalf. Attack!"

Men and women flooded the chasm, rushing toward Ruth and the Kingdom. Myriad sparks filled the air like fireworks as Adepts cast spell after spell. Gina's roar mingled with Cillian's as both leapt forward to slash at their targets. A luminescent green glow surrounded Ruth as she struck down her assailants. She was powerful, but she was severely outnumbered, thanks to La Liberté.

"You!" Ruth screamed, flinging a spell toward Gina. The panther pounced, but Ruth's magic cut into her, bringing her down at Ruth's feet with a whimper.

"Maman!" Tristan cried, rushing forward, helping the panther to her feet.

Maman? Jayne's head reared back as she shot a baffled look at Ruger. "Gina Labelle is Tristan's mother?"

Ruger remained stony-faced.

Jayne's mouth fell open in accusation. "You knew?"

Before she could shout her indignation at her mentor—who was keeping secrets from her, again—a figure dove toward her. Jayne dodged, crouching low just in time as a flash of red light seared past her left ear. Her brain pounded a fierce throb in her head as she rose to her feet to face her new opponent.

She recognized him. Blaine, the one with the sword Rogue who'd intercepted her at the Saint-Genevieve Library.

"Oh, it's you," Jayne said in a bored voice, wiping dust from her pants. "Here for another smackdown?"

Blaine sneered as he drew closer. "You're in no shape to best me, witch."

Jayne's eyebrows lifted. "Oh, I see. You waited until I was injured before facing off with me. Very brave of you." She brought her hands together in a mocking slow clap.

Seething, Blaine lunged, but Jayne was ready for him. She ducked to avoid his punch, whirled, and stomped on his instep. He bent over, grunting, and Jayne grabbed his shoulders with both hands, her knee connecting with his groin. He howled before collapsing to his knees.

"You good?" Jayne asked. "Or you wanna go again?"

Blaine stared up at her, his face bloody and his jaw taut with fury. He murmured a spell and slashed at her with a blinding green light.

Jayne grabbed a Block spell to deflect it, but she wasn't quick enough. A boiling heat burned into her chest, reigniting the pain of the Master of Shadows' attack. Jayne groaned, stumbling backward. Fire crept up her throat like a heartburn on steroids.

"Jayne!" Ruger shouted from next to her as he dueled one-handed with another Kingdom operative.

"I've got it," Jayne reassured him. He was injured, too. She didn't need him distracted. She could handle this weasel all on her own.

"Not so tough now, are you?" Blaine taunted, looking far too pleased with himself.

Lord, this guy is a class A douchebag, Jayne thought. She decided to play his smugness to her advantage. Clutching at her chest, she moaned loudly, her face crumpling in mock agony. "Ow!" she cried. "Oh God, it hurts so bad!"

She could almost feel Ruger rolling his eyes in her direction. He saw right through her ruse.

But Blaine didn't. His chin lifted in arrogant pride.

Jayne hunched over, stumbling forward as if in pain. Just as Blaine chuckled, she swung her head upward, colliding with his nose. A satisfying *crack* followed. Blood flowed down his face. Jayne elbowed him in the gut, stomped on his foot again, delivered a perfect back kick, and sent a burst of magic straight into his chest for good measure. He soared backward a solid six feet before landing in an unconscious heap on the cave floor.

"Good riddance," she muttered. She turned and found Ruger, his face covered in sweat as he held his own against his assailant. Even one-armed, Ruger's moves were impressive and powerful. But he couldn't carry on for long.

Jayne strode forward to intervene, but Tristan beat her to it. He spun his fingers together in a complicated twist and sent a tight spiral of magic toward the Kingdom operative. The lights danced around the man's head before smothering him completely, assaulting him with bright stars as if Tinkerbell and her friends had gone evil.

While the man screamed, Ruger landed a fierce blow that hit him in the jaw, knocking him out cold. The lights receded back to Tristan's waiting fingertips, and Jayne raised her eyebrows. She couldn't deny she was impressed. She'd never seen such a complicated spell before.

Tristan extended his hand, and Ruger took it, nodding his gratitude. A significant look passed between them, reminding Jayne of what Amanda had said about trusting Tristan. Her eyes narrowed as he turned to her and raised a single eyebrow.

"Jayne." He nodded as if they were passing by each other at the water cooler.

Her mouth pressed together in a thin line. She really just wanted to kick his ass right now. But that would be rude, considering he might've just saved Ruger's life.

Finally, Jayne said the first thing that came to mind. "So, you're a bit of a momma's boy, huh?"

Tristan's lips twitched as he glanced at his mother, who remained in panther form. Bleeding and raw, she still barreled through her enemies like bowling pins. "You could say that."

Before Jayne could respond, he dashed forward, taking on two Kingdom goons at once.

She scoffed. What a show-off. She glanced around the room, finding Cillian in a heartbeat, his talons slashing through two men. Behind him was Sofia, who fought Ruth. Light glided between them as they exchanged spell after spell.

Jayne couldn't believe it. Was this truly her sister, facing Ruth head-on? Sofia wielded magic as expertly as a Master magician. And she held her own against Ruth, who possessed the Water totem.

Jayne surged forward, intent on lending a hand to Sofia. Ruger followed her, adjusting his sling. Tristan bought up the rear, keeping their backs safe from attack.

Ruth's eyes shifted to Jayne, and fear flickered across her expression. She took in the space around her, the fallen Kingdom operatives whose bodies were strewn across the ground, and La Liberté, who still fought alongside the TCO.

Devastation filled her eyes. She knew she was losing.

"Kingdom!" Ruth shouted. "To me!"

Sofia struck, but Ruth was faster this time. Green light exploded, sending Sofia flying backward. Jayne rushed to her sister's side. Sofia's hair was a tangled mess around her face, and cuts lined her cheek and arms.

Jayne glanced up in time to see Ruth and four others surround themselves with a transparent green orb. Another blast of light, this time so blinding Jayne had to shield her eyes, and the five of them vanished into thin air.

43

A COUP D'ÉTAT

All Jayne wanted to do was sleep. But even with Ruth gone, there was still work to do.

Within minutes, Amanda and dozens of other TCO officials arrived. Amanda took in the destruction around her, clearly astounded. Honestly, Jayne considered it a miracle the whole tunnel hadn't caved in. But then she wondered if there was some kind of special, sacred burial magic surrounding the area that kept it protected and preserved. She was surprised to realize she was okay with not knowing right away. She'd do some research back at the TCO library. Manifest herself some books on the subject.

While Seo-joon filled Amanda in on what had happened, Jayne inched closer to Ruger, who was chatting with a now-human Gina Labelle. Jayne couldn't believe how civil he was being to his former captor. If anything, Gina looked more put-out than he did to be conversing.

"We're indebted to you," Ruger was saying. "We couldn't have won this battle without you and your army."

Gina's chin lifted. "We did not intercede for your benefit. The

Kingdom made us their enemy long ago, and they sealed their fate when they defiled the Water god's power."

"How did they do that, exactly?" Jayne asked.

Gina's eyes flashed as she glared at Jayne. "Ruth Thorne wielded his power as her own, enslaving him. La Liberté sought to raise him for a different purpose. To serve him, as you serve Queen Medb. Because of her, he has returned to his grave and likely will not emerge again."

Jayne opened her mouth to respond that servitude wasn't exactly her kind of thing, thanks anyway, but Ruger interjected. "We could use your help stopping the Kingdom. Ruth isn't finished. She'll be seeking other totems after this."

Gina's nostrils flared. "The TCO is our enemy as well, Stern. We are not allies."

"Speak for yourself," said a voice behind her.

Gina whirled, and Jayne sucked in a breath to find Tristan nursing a bloody gash on his shoulder. He emitted a wry chuckle at the look on his mother's face. "Don't act so surprised, Maman. You know I've been trying to leave for years. You've given me the perfect opportunity."

Gina's face turned bone white. "You would dare to forsake me in favor of these ignorant magicians?"

"Hey!" Jayne protested, crossing her arms.

"I care more about stopping a crazed magical terrorist than abiding by your sacred laws, Mother," Tristan said in a bored voice. "And I'm not the only one." He jerked his head behind him to half a dozen men and women, who shot nervous glances toward Gina as if expecting her to shift to her panther form and tear out their throats.

Gina's eyes burned with a rage that made Jayne wonder if she wanted to do just that.

"They're under our protection," Ruger said, no doubt also reading the fury emanating from the woman.

"Once Ruth is defeated, we'll return to you," Tristan promised.

"Once she's defeated, you won't have anything to return to," Gina spat, her mouth quivering. "You're traitors, all of you. And you're rescinding the sacred oath you pledged when you joined our cause." Sneering, she turned to Ruger. "They don't need your protection. They aren't even worth the effort of hunting down." She spun on her heel and shouted something at the La Liberté operatives hovering behind her. They straightened into formation behind her, trotting out of the cave like the obedient soldiers they were.

"Wow," Jayne said, eyebrows raised as she glanced at Tristan. "That was ballsy."

"Indeed." Something conflicted crossed Ruger's face as he assessed the Frenchman. "Are you sure that was...wise?"

Tristan sighed. "Drop the pretense, Ruger. It's over. She can know." His gaze shifted to Jayne. "I'm a double agent. I've been working with the TCO for months now."

Jayne's eyebrows lifted, though she registered very little shock. Honestly, she'd been suspecting this for a while. It was just too convenient, all his little hints and helpful antics along the way. After a moment, she said, "Well, you obviously suck at your job. Double Agent 101 clearly states not to tell people about your mission."

He snorted, his dark eyes dancing with amusement. "Right. I'll have to remember that one."

"Tristan, we can bring you in," Ruger said in a soft voice, "if you're worried about retaliation."

Tristan shook his head. "Our organization has been on the brink of a civil war for years now. This is the moment we've been waiting for. Happily, it was a somewhat peaceful schism. It could have been much worse." He glanced over his shoulder at the crowd behind him, his eyes filling with affection and determination. In that heartfelt look, Jayne knew he trusted these men and women with his lives. Perhaps they'd been planning this coup d'état for a while.

His gaze shifted to Jayne, that same taunting humor returning to his expression as if he were laughing at her. She stared at him, conjuring all her fury into that single, soul-shattering glare. This man was with the TCO—technically her colleague, though the thought made her want to gag. Now, she no longer had an excuse to kick his ass. Such a shame.

"This doesn't mean I stop hating you," Jayne told him.

Tristan pressed a hand to his heart. "I'd be devastated if you did. We'll be in touch, Ruger. I'll see if I can sniff out who created that portal to steal the grimoire."

With that, he sauntered out of the cave with his followers behind him. Jayne noticed they left side by side like a group of friends, very unlike Gina and her obedient acolytes.

Once they were out of sight, Jayne jabbed a hand in Ruger's chest. He didn't even flinch.

"You bastard," she growled. "How many other life-altering secrets are you keeping from me?"

He merely raised his eyebrows. "Life-altering? It seemed to me you weren't all that shocked, Jayne. I assumed you'd figured it out on your own when he saved you from the poison."

She opened her mouth, then shut it. Now that she thought about it, Amanda and Ruger hadn't been completely tight-lipped about it. They'd been pretty transparent about the whole he's-on-our-side thing. But the idea that Tristan damn Lowell had *saved* her? No. No way.

"Besides, I think you have more important things to worry about." Ruger waved a hand at something behind her.

Jayne turned and found Sofia and Cillian, now in his human form again. They both stood awkwardly, avoiding eye contact with each other but not straying too far apart, as if they were linked by some magnetic force.

A hard lump formed in Jayne's throat as she finally put the pieces together. They were bonded together by something. No one wanted to admit it—not Sofia, not Cillian, and certainly not Jayne. But there was no avoiding it now.

Jayne strode toward them. As soon as Sofia caught sight of her, she flew into Jayne's arms, the two embracing tightly as if nothing had changed. Jayne inhaled the familiar fruity scent that made her think of summer rainfall and lemonade on the back porch, now overlaid with forests and mountains. Cillian's scent was all over her.

Still. Jayne and Sofia. Sofia and Jayne. No matter what happened, they always had each other. And Jayne clung to that now, when she needed the reminder the most.

"Thank God you're okay," Sofia whispered, drawing away with tears in her eyes. "When he hit you, I—I—"

"I know." Jayne's eyes closed as she imagined the agony Sofia had been in when she'd seen Jayne go down. She hated that she'd caused that misery. She'd been so stupid to try to reason with the Master of Shadows by herself. "I'm so sorry, Sofia. But you—you were a total badass tonight! I can't believe you fought Ruth!"

Sofia offered a sheepish and bewildered smile, as if she couldn't believe it, either. "I know. Something in me just...snapped."

And there it was again, their mingled scent floating in the air, the evidence of her bond with Cillian. There was no denying it. Jayne had never been able to call Cillian to shift to any other form besides the wolf. And something in the Torrent had always blocked them from bonding completely.

Because the bond wasn't solid. Just like the text Jayne had read in the TCO Library. Their bond wasn't a proper fit, which meant eventually, whatever connection they shared would have deteriorated over time.

It was supposed to be Sofia. It was always her. It explained how Jayne and Cillian's magic had been a close fit. Almost...but not quite.

Jayne inhaled deeply and said, "So...Cillian is actually your Rogue, not mine."

A tense, awkward silence fell between them. Cillian's gorgeous blue eyes were full of guilt and regret. Sofia's cheeks turned pink as she glanced from Jayne to Cillian.

Sofia spoke first. "Jayne, I—I swear to God, I didn't plan this. It just happened, and we—"

Jayne raised a hand. "Stop. I don't blame you, Sofia. Not at all. That bond probably saved both your lives. And mine." She paused, biting back frustration and confusion and hurt that swirled together in her chest. "But...how?"

"I don't know. Maybe because my magic wasn't awakened until recently," Sofia said quietly. "We never had the chance to bond properly until now."

"I've felt it before, though," Cillian said, gazing at Sofia. "In Amanda's office, when you two were fighting. I felt the call to shift. I didn't know where it came from, but it must've been from your magic, Sofia. Remember those white sparks? And again, at Chantilly. I very nearly went all-out wolf in the middle of the panicking crowd."

"That makes sense," Sofia said quietly. "I felt something shift, too, but I didn't know what it was."

Jayne couldn't deny that she'd had her own doubts about Cillian being bonded to her. But even so, this was too much for her. Sofia and Cillian were talking about this like it was a sure thing. Jayne had been knocked out of their world when the bond snapped into place. They'd only had moments to process this, and it sounded as if they'd accepted it. As if it was inevitable for them both.

But Jayne hadn't. This was new for her, and it overwhelmed every part of her senses.

Suddenly, she couldn't breathe. The air was too thin. She swallowed, but her throat was too dry.

Forcing a wobbly smile, she said, "Okay. Okay. I'm not mad. I swear I'm not. But I can't be here right now."

Without looking at either of them, she turned and walked away. She expected Ruger or Amanda to stop her, but perhaps the broken expression on her face stopped them, because they let her pass. Tears streamed down her face as she exited the cave, leaving behind everything she thought she knew.

44

STARTING OVER

After a long nap, a generous helping of pie, and a few hours of reflection with her hands against the soil of the Luxembourg Gardens, Jayne knew what she needed to do.

She'd been avoiding the flat—and the Montmartre safe house —because she figured that was where Sofia and Cillian would be. And if something urgent came up, Amanda would call her. So far, her phone had been quiet.

Jayne took that as a good sign. No brutal retaliation from Ruth or Gina. Though, if she was being honest with herself, she would've loved a mission to distract her.

But no. This needed to be dealt with. And she knew what she had to do.

She texted Cillian to meet her in the gardens. She was a coward, she knew. Summoning her boyfriend instead of showing up at the flat to face her problems head-on was pretty cowardly. But Jayne didn't care.

She'd found a solution, and this was how she was handling it. It twisted through her heart like a jagged knife, a pain so intense she couldn't bother with courage right now. At the moment, she was barely keeping it together.

Besides, being in the gardens rejuvenated her magic after being so damaged by the Master of Shadows. She could feel Medb's presence stirring to life inside her once more, which was comforting. She'd already managed to heal herself from a few lingering injuries from the Master of Shadows.

Cillian took only a few minutes to arrive, leading Jayne to believe he'd been waiting around for her to reach out. His eyes were guarded and full of anguish, his hair mussed as if he hadn't cared to tame it before rushing over.

Jayne forced a smile and patted the bench seat next to her. Cillian hesitated for only a second before joining her. For a long moment, they stared at the naked trees, the hedges in front of them, the joggers and civilians strolling past, oblivious to the inner turmoil of the two seated on the bench.

Finally, Jayne decided to just rip off the Band-Aid. "I think we should break up."

"Damn it, Jayne," Cillian growled, running a hand down his face as if he'd expected this from her. "Just because my magic is bonded with Sofia doesn't change how I feel about you!"

Jayne closed her eyes to block out the pure agony on his face, but it still shone in her mind, tormenting her. Making her wish she didn't have to do this.

But she did.

She took a breath and continued, "But it will, Cillian."

"That doesn't mean we just end things. We can work through it."

"What you have to do to bond with Sofia properly? You have to be completely focused on her." She touched his arm. "You won't be able to leave her side, and you won't want to. And I would never ask that of you."

"Jayne—"

"You know something has been off between us for a while. This has been a lot of fun, and I'm grateful to have you in my life.

But it's best for us to stay good friends. We are bonded in our own way, Cillian. But not as lovers. Not anymore."

"Do I get a say here?"

Jayne sighed. "You're a protector, Cillian. And a damn good one. But I don't need a protector. I need an equal. Someone to challenge me."

His head reared back, his eyes flashing with hurt. "Are you saying I don't challenge you?"

A denial rose to her lips, but she shoved it down. In a broken voice, she said, "Not in the way I need you to."

Cillian fell silent, the hurt on his face twisting into raw, brokenhearted anguish. Jayne hated herself with a fiery passion for doing this to him. She would rather gut herself right here than break his heart.

"God, Jayne." Cillian ran his fingers through his hair, mussing it up even more. Jayne wished he wouldn't do that. He looked devastatingly sexy when he did that. Lord, she would miss those muscles. The quirk of his lips when she joked with him. The way he held her close after they made love.

She would miss everything about him.

"You can't—you can't leave me," Cillian pleaded. This big, beautiful, warrior of a man was actually pleading with her. "I love you, Jayne."

She couldn't hold it back anymore. A sob broke through her, splintering her defenses and causing an onslaught of emotion swelling inside her. A gaping hole opened up in her chest, threatening to swallow her. Tears streamed down her face. She wiped them away, but they wouldn't stop. It was like a faucet behind her eyes had turned on and she had no way to shut it off.

"Jayne." Cillian touched her shoulder—as if he should be comforting her right now.

"Don't," she moaned, covering her eyes to stifle the flow. "Please don't."

He dropped his hand. "Why not?"

"Because I don't love you. Not like that." The words were strangled, but they had to be said. She couldn't allow him to hold on to the hope that they could be together.

It wasn't just the bond with Sofia. It was the realization that they didn't fit together—in more ways than one. Their bond only solidified what Jayne had already suspected. And it made the breakup easier because now they could make a clean getaway. They didn't have to train together anymore.

Jayne cared about him. Deeply. She loved being with him, kissing him, teasing him… But she didn't *love* him. Their relationship still felt casual to her. Not the aching, all-consuming love she read about in books. The pure kind of love she yearned for.

Jayne hiccupped as another sob broke through her. She couldn't look at Cillian. She just couldn't. "I'm so sorry," she whispered before rising to her feet. He didn't follow. "Please take care of Sofia. And don't blame her. This isn't her fault."

Cillian said nothing. And Jayne still couldn't look at him.

Weeping freely, Jayne turned from him and left the gardens.

Instead of going straight to the flat, Jayne circled around to the opposite side of the gardens to cry her heart out. She didn't care that people stared at her. She didn't care that she looked like an insane mess, a crazy American who wore her heart on her sleeve.

When she was all dried up, she pulled out a pack of tissues from her bag to mop herself up before heading back to the flat and texting Sofia. No need to disguise her anguish from her—she would know the minute she saw Jayne.

Jayne had washed her face and made a cup of chamomile tea when Sofia knocked softly on the door. Jayne opened it and found her sister standing there, holding a massive, towering confection of conciliatory pie, her eyes puffy as if she, too, had been crying. It made the already festering guilt inside Jayne swell even more as she realized she'd unintentionally been punishing Sofia.

Sofia entered, and Jayne took the pie and closed the door. When Sofia opened her mouth, Jayne raised a hand to stop the apology on her lips.

"I swear to God, Sofia, I'm not mad at you, and if you try to apologize for something that's not your fault, I'm going to make you turn around and walk out."

Sofia's mouth clamped shut, and she nodded vigorously. The desperation in her eyes told Jayne she would agree to anything to keep her from leaving.

"I don't want to talk about Cillian," Jayne said. "But, so you know, we just broke up."

Sorrow filled Sofia's face, but she looked unsurprised. As Jayne had suspected, it was probably written all over her face.

Before Sofia could offer sympathy, Jayne soldiered on.

"I want to talk about magic. I'm ready for you to come clean. About all of it."

Surprise lit Sofia's eyes, followed by a mixture of relief and trepidation. "Okay. Cut me a piece of this ridiculous pie, and let's have some wine, too, and I'll tell you. It's a long story."

Their treat assembled, they sat side by side on the sofa, slices of pie and glasses of wine at the ready. For a long moment, neither of them said a word, and Jayne let her sister collect her thoughts.

"I'll start at the beginning," Sofia said in a soft voice, her hands together on her lap. "When Ruth first started teaching me magic."

For hours, Sofia poured out her life story, the side without secrets, the side that included magic. Ruth had trained her from a young age, sensing her potential right off the bat. But Ruth was a brutal teacher. And she would stop at nothing for more power. Jayne was horrified—but not entirely surprised—when she heard Ruth had wanted to sacrifice Jayne to gain more power. That was when Sofia put her foot down, refusing to continue with Ruth's magic lessons.

So, Ruth had kidnapped Jayne and taken her to Yosemite, along with their father, Henry. Sofia had followed and fought Ruth to get Jayne back. She couldn't save Henry. After learning about the fire, Sofia had thought for years that she had caused their parents' deaths.

When Sofia admitted this, she started crying again, and Jayne closed her eyes, suddenly understanding so much. Why her sister had taken such desperate responsibility for her. Why Sofia had needed company every anniversary of their death. Why she had sworn off magic forever—not just because of Ruth, but because she thought her magic had killed people. And that was frightening. Certainly deserving a lifetime of paranoia.

When Sofia told Jayne about their trip to Miami, Jayne raised a hand to stop her, her brain working furiously to recall the events of that trip. Realization slammed into her with all the force of a sledgehammer. "I knew something was fishy about that trip! Calle Ocho, right? And that...that fight?" She couldn't form a coherent sentence, so instead, she covered her mouth, horrified that she'd been so blind. She and Sofia had taken a spring break trip to Miami. While visiting Calle Ocho, the weirdest brawl had broken out on the street. Jayne had suffered one of her more brutal ocular migraines, and in the haze of all of it, she could've sworn she'd seen a wolf running wild.

Her wide, stunned gaze settled on Sofia, who had the gall to look guilty. "There was a Rogue there, wasn't there?"

Sofia winced and nodded. "I fought him."

"You—you *fought* him? Damn, Sofia!" Jayne let out an impressed whoop.

"Don't be impressed. We barely survived. I had no magic, only my kickboxing skills. Anyway, I was there to track down a witch to give me a Suppression spell. Remember that bracelet I always wore? That was dampening my powers all those years."

"Wild." Jayne sat back against the sofa, dazed from this revelation. "But what was a Rogue doing there?"

"He was there with Aaró."

Jayne wrinkled her nose, struggling to put a face to the name. Then, her eyes widened. "Oh! The redheaded dude from the Kingdom? The one Cillian worked for."

"Yep. The same guy. He was looking for the same witch I was. They duked it out after we left. I...I still don't know if she survived. She was a badass, so she probably did. But Aaró survived, too, so I can't be sure..."

Regret welled in Sofia's eyes, and for a moment, Jayne wished she'd met this witch Sofia admired so much. She sounded incredible.

"At any rate, it was a mistake to get that bracelet. It caused so many problems—the cancer, for one thing."

"Did you try to find the witch after your cancer came back?" Jayne asked. "See if she survived, and get her to remove the spell?"

"I did," Sofia admitted. "She wasn't anywhere to be found. I'd taken the bracelet off by then. But the effects still lingered." She shook her head. "I was a fool, Jayne. I should have let you in from the beginning. I should have given you more credit."

"Yeah, you should have." Jayne paused. "But I understand why you didn't. And...being without my magic, even for a short amount of time, showed me just how much you sacrificed by giving yours up. It was awful, Sofia. I can't believe you did that... for me. I forgive you. For all of it."

Sofia stared at her with moist eyes. "Do you? Truly? Because I wouldn't."

Jayne laughed. "You're the most forgiving person on the planet. You'd forgive anyone."

"Not anyone." Sofia's eyes darkened.

Jayne couldn't help it—her thoughts turned to Ruth. Their mother had gotten away. Again. And this time with a totem.

God, this was bad.

Jayne changed the subject. "What about Dad?"

Sofia's eyes turned guarded. "What about him?"

"Does he have magic, too?"

Sofia hesitated. "As a kid, I thought he didn't. Ruth never included him in our lessons, and I assumed he just didn't want to be a part of it. But…now that I know more, and after studying his journal for so long, I think Ruth shut him out, just like she shut you out. She didn't find him worthy, or some bullshit like that."

Jayne flinched, aching for her father. Though she'd been so young when he died, they'd had a great relationship. Lightning Brain, he'd called her. She hated how Ruth's poison had tainted their little family.

"I'd love to see what you've found in his journal," Jayne said, her heart thrumming with eagerness. She knew if Sofia had found anything important, she would've mentioned it. And yet, Jayne couldn't help but feel like if she knew what Sofia had found, she might be able to piece it together. Two heads were better than one, after all.

"I was actually hoping you'd help me." Sofia's eyes brightened as she withdrew the worn leather journal from her bag. "I need your blood."

Jayne's eyebrows shot up. "Shouldn't you buy me dinner first?"

"Oh, hush. The journal is sealed and can only be unlocked if it has blood from both of us. I've already given it mine. The TCO is still analyzing yours at the lab, so there hasn't been time to use it for this. Besides, I think we need to do it together, in person." She cocked her head at Jayne, an unspoken question in her eyes.

"Okay." Jayne stifled the discomfort wriggling in her at the thought of using blood for magic. Even she knew that was a bad idea.

But she trusted Sofia with her life.

Using a safety pin from the desk, Jayne pricked her finger. A bead of blood welled on her skin. Sofia held out her hand, and Jayne stuck the pin in the tip of her sister's forefinger. They turned to the open journal, and each let a drop of blood spill onto the parchment.

To her surprise, instead of staining the journal and making Jayne's neat-freak brain go crazy, their blood vanished, seeping into the journal like it was Tom Riddle's diary or something.

Magic crackled in the air. A shimmering curtain whispered against Jayne's skin, causing the hairs on her arms to stand up.

Whatever had cloaked the journal had just been unlocked.

The sisters waited, hovering over the book with bated breath as they waited for something to happen. Anything.

At long last, the words on the pages began to shift slightly. Mathematical equations melted into legible words and phrases.

"My God," Jayne whispered in awe, her eyes flying across the page as she read her father's notes about magical herbs and potions.

"I think Dad was some kind of scientist, a botanist or herbologist or something like that on the side," Sofia said, flipping through the pages. "He wrote down so many formulas and equations that it was hard to decipher anything at all. But I was able to identify some plants he often referenced for magical potions, like aids for casting spells."

Jayne's eyes widened. "That's amazing."

Sofia bit her lip, her eyes flashing with uncertainty before she continued. "And then I found this." She flipped open Henry's journal and pointed to a note she had decoded.

Jayne stared at the note, her heart lurching painfully in her chest.

A contingency—to end her, should she venture too far into dark waters. This is her secret. The vault she vows to keep locked forever. Guard it well.

"Oh—oh my God, Sofia," Jayne breathed, her pulse roaring in her ears.

Sofia sucked in a sharp breath. "That's new." She pointed to the string of numbers underneath the note. Squinting, she muttered, "Another code perhaps?"

Jayne leaned closer, staring at the numbers. "I—I don't think it's in code. I think it's a set of coordinates."

Stunned silence met her words. Then—

"Holy shit, you're right," Sofia whispered, covering her mouth in shock.

Jayne laughed with excitement. "So...should we look it up?"

Sofia drew in a shaky breath. "Hell yes."

45

X MARKS THE SPOT

"Absolutely not."

"But Amanda—" Jayne argued.

"I am not allowing you and your sister to go off on some dangerous mission on your own when Ruth is still at large—and thoroughly pissed off."

Jayne's eyebrows lifted at Amanda's usage of such a crass term.

"This is our father," Sofia said hotly. "These coordinates might lead us straight to him!"

"Or it could lead to yet another trap," Ruger's voice rumbled from behind them. "We still have no idea if Henry is in league with Ruth or not."

"He's not," Sofia said through clenched teeth.

A doubtful silence met her words. A swell of anger filled Jayne at the thought of Amanda and Ruger disbelieving her sister. A string of protestations formed on her lips, but Ruger interrupted her.

"I agree with Amanda. While you are the most powerful magicians we know, you're both still new to this. Let us send a team there. If there's anything that relates to your father, you can portal there immediately."

Jayne's mouth closed.

Amanda sighed, her jaw ticking back and forth. After a moment, she nodded. "Send the Beta team, with Seo-joon leading. They'll know what to do."

"If our dad is there, a SWAT team is going to frighten him away," Jayne protested.

"I don't care," Amanda said, clearly tired of arguing. "It's all you're getting."

"We'll hook up a camera to one of their helmets," Ruger offered, his smooth timbre a contrast to Amanda's clipped tone. "You'll see whatever they see."

Jayne exhaled grumpily. She had a mental image of Henry catching sight of the TCO team and vanishing forever, leaving no trace of his location. Could she risk that?

But Ruger was right. Ruth could be lying in wait for them. She could be monitoring every place that was connected to Henry. And without some more rest, neither one of them could face their mother again.

Jayne met Sofia's gaze. She looked just as unhappy. But they both nodded their assent.

∾

Two hours later, Jayne and Sofia sat in Amanda's office, her wall of screens feeding them footage of a bumpy car ride along the side streets of Havana, Cuba. How Seo-joon had assembled the team and gotten there so quickly was a marvel.

"You made popcorn?" Ruger asked, arms crossed as he leaned against the wall. He arched an eyebrow in Jayne's direction as she munched.

"Of course I did," Jayne said, tossing more of the buttery goodness into her mouth. "This is probably the most exciting thing I'll ever watch." She didn't mention the fact that chewing on popcorn prevented her from chewing off her fingernails in apprehension of what the team might—or might not—find.

"We're here," said a muffled voice from the screen. The car lurched to a stop, and several dark figures exited the vehicle.

Jayne squinted, but she couldn't make out anything except blocky concrete shapes that were probably buildings. Next to her, Sofia held her breath.

Several minutes passed as the men canvassed the area. One of them held a device that lit up with a green glow.

"Found something." Seo-joon's competent voice filled the room.

Jayne's heart skittered, and she leaned forward in her seat. Whoever had the camera bent over to inspect something on the ground that Jayne couldn't make out.

"Portal residue."

Jayne blinked. Portal residue? So, someone magical had been there...but now they were gone.

Just before a crushing disappointment swept over her, one of the men said something else.

"Not just any portal. A Time Catch."

Jayne stiffened, eyes wide as she exchanged a glance with Sofia.

Amanda spoke into the radio. "Are you saying there was a Time Catch at the location?"

The camera moved up and down. Seo-joon was nodding. "Affirmative."

"Oh my God," Jayne whispered, covering her mouth. If Henry had been in a Time Catch, he could have been there for years— decades, even—without them knowing. He could have grown old and died in the Time Catch. Time passed differently in there. Jayne knew that from terrible experience.

"Hang on," said one of the men. "We found more residue."

Everyone waited with bated breath. Even Jayne abstained

from munching on popcorn for a whole minute, which exhibited monumental restraint on her part.

Seo-joon swore under his breath. "Whoever was here knew what they were doing. They left us a message using portal residue."

Jayne frowned, and Amanda looked bewildered. "Do you have the proper equipment to read it? That is elaborate magic…" She trailed off, a finger resting thoughtfully on her lips.

Ruger agreed. "It sounds like whoever was there was very powerful." The darkness in his eyes told Jayne that wasn't a good sign. It meant whoever was out there was possibly as advanced as the TCO. Or even more so.

They could be a dangerous threat, depending on whose side they were on.

"Happens we thought of that. I stopped off to see Quimby before we left. We've tagged the message so you can see for yourself," Seo-joon said. "Take a look."

The camera zoomed out, and Jayne's eyes narrowed as she scrutinized the screen. Along the dusty ground were myriad glowing green shapes, almost like glow worms. The night-vision filters coupled with the portal reader made the resolution a bit grainy, and it took Jayne several moments to finally piece together the words.

To end again—X.

Jayne read it over and over again, certain she misread a letter or something. When she was sure that was what it said, she glanced up at Amanda and Ruger. "What the hell does that mean?"

But they looked just as perplexed as she did.

To her surprise, Sofia spoke up, her gaze distant.

"I know what it means. And I know who wrote it, too. She is a very powerful witch, and her name is Xiomara."

To Be Continued…

COMING SOON...

THE KEEPER OF FLAMES

Book 3 in the Jayne Thorne, CIA Librarian series

Summer 2023

ACKNOWLEDGMENTS

It takes a village, especially when one is building a brand new world with a brand new pen name with a brand new cowriter. We are deeply indebted to the following fabulous people for their help bringing this second book in the Jayne series to life:

Laura Blake Peterson; Kim Killion; Phyllis DeBlanche; James T. Farrell; Erin Moon and the whole Tantor Audio team; Marie-Pierre Dion, Conservateur Général des Bibliothèques at Château de Chantilly, France; Salt and Sage Books; Jennifer Jakes; Kelly Stepp; Alisha Klapheke; John McDougal of Murder by the Book; Barbara Peters of Poisoned Pen Bookstore; Jayne Ann Krentz; our Facebook groups—Joss Walker's Readers and Rogues and R.L. Perez's Coven of Readers; our Instagram families; our IRL families: Randy, Jameson, Jordan, and the parentals; Alex, Colin, Ellie, and the whole Perez clan; our favorite librarians, who inspired these tales; and our readers, without whom these stories would not need to be told.

Thank you, all, from the bottom of our hearts!

And from Joss, to R.L.—thank you for stepping in and becoming the greatest partner a writer could ever hope for. Here's to many more adventures!

ABOUT JOSS WALKER

photo credit: Suzanne DuBose

Joss Walker is the fantasy pen name for *New York Times* bestselling thriller author J.T. Ellison, where she explores her love of the fantasy genre and extraordinary women discovering their power in the world. With Jayne Thorne, CIA Librarian, Joss has created a lighthearted urban fantasy series perfect for lovers of books, libraries, romance, and of course, magic.

Join Joss Walker's newsletter
https://josswalker.com/subscribe

ABOUT R.L. PEREZ

R.L. Perez is a YA fantasy romance author, perfectionist, anxious Type A worrier, and proud Hufflepuff. She's published three series set in the same world, featuring witches, romance, and time travel. When she's not working on her books, she's either napping, diving into a good book, obsessively watching Netflix, or playing with her two kids. She loves chocolate, loud laughter, and alternative rock music.

Join R.L. Perez's Newsletter
https://subscribe.rlperez.com

ABOUT TWO TALES PRESS

Two Tales Press is an independent publishing house featuring novels, novellas, and anthologies written and edited by *New York Times* bestselling author J.T. Ellison, including the Jayne Thorne, CIA Librarian series under J.T.'s pen name, Joss Walker.

To view all of our titles, please visit

www.twotalespress.com

∼

From the Lt. Taylor Jackson Series
The Wolves Come at Night (#9) (Fall 2022)

Whiteout (Taylor Jackson 7.5)

Where All The Dead Lie (#7)

So Close the Hand of Death (#6)

The Immortals (#5)

From Our Thriller and Dark Suspense Collections
A Thousand Doors

Dead Ends

Mad Love

Three Tales from the Dark Side

From Joss Walker
The Eighth Road (Joss Walker & R.L. Perez)

Tomb of the Queen (Joss Walker & Alisha Klapheke)

Master of Shadows (Joss Walker & R.L. Perez)

The Keeper of Flames (Joss Walker & R.L. Perez)

From Willow Haven Press,

our imprint supporting R.L. Perez

Twisted by Time

Devoured by Darkness

Bound by Blood

The Cursed Witch

The Fallen Demon

The Lost Phoenix

The Demon's Kiss

The Angel's Vow

The Reaper's Call

Ivy & Bone

CPSIA information can be obtained
at www.ICGtesting.com
Printed in the USA
LVHW110547240522
719553LV00001B/2

9 781948 967389